LISA ARMSTRONG

Déjà View

HODDER

First published in Great Britain in 2004 by Hodder and Stoughton
First published in paperback in Great Britain in 2005 by
Hodder and Stoughton
A division of Hodder Headline

A CIP catalogue record for this title is available from the British Library

ISBN 0 340 83730 6

Typeset in Plantin Light by
Phoenix Typesetting, Auldgirth, Dumfriesshire

Printed and bound in Great Britain by
Mackays of Chatham Ltd, Chatham, Kent

Hodder Headline's policy is to use papers that are natural, renewable and
recyclable products and made from wood grown in sustainable forests. The
logging and manufacturing processes are expected to conform to the
environmental regulations of the country of origin.

Hodder and Stoughton
A division of Hodder Headline
338 Euston Road
London NW1 3BH

To Ros and Clem, my parents

Huge thanks to my family for regularly coming to check up on me at the bottom of the garden and take my pulse while *Déjà View* took shape. As ever your visits were unbelievably distracting and more welcome than I can say.

Large amounts of gratitude go to Carolyn Mays and Alex Bonham at Hodder and my agent Jonathan Lloyd at Curtis Brown for remaining cheerful, encouraging and patient even in the face of missing manuscripts. Your comments were invaluable, as was your stoicism when I drove over my computer.

Thanks to Pippa, Emily, Carolyn, Melanie, Yaron, Ali, Kitty and Flora for input on the cover, all of it conflicting. And Cazza, my life wouldn't be the same without your calming influence.

Finally thanks to all my married friends, especially all the women for their insights into how other people's marriages do and don't malfunction. The amount of voyeurism I've been able to indulge in under the pretext of research has been fantastic.

Sydney and Charlie Murray had the perfect marriage. They knew this because everyone kept telling them so. Charlie was happy to go along with the consensus – any consensus really – provided it didn't prevent him from getting to work by 8.27 a.m. And Sydney was so busy having affairs she could only assume that perfection was a relative term.

Granted, these affairs were in her head and mostly with her marriage guidance counsellor. Not that she divulged this to anyone. He wasn't really her type, but he looked soulful and seemed to listen. And some days that was enough to make her want to throw herself at his two-tone trainers. She didn't tell Charlie about the marriage guidance at all actually. He hadn't wanted to accompany her to these sessions; had looked incredulous when she had first suggested them and then refused to discuss the matter with her ever again, so that she sometimes wondered whether she had ever broached the subject with him. The simple truth was that the counsellor spoke the occasional nugget of wisdom, smiled, and he'd seen *Whatever Happened to Baby Jane?*, one of Sydney's all-time favourite films, which was more than could be said for Charlie, who hadn't had time to go to the cinema since 1993 and even in those heady days, had preferred films with subtitles and harrowing subject matter. And now that she was thirty-six, a wife, a mother, with a rather exotic name that she still hadn't found a way of living up to, and an annual subscription – courtesy of her mother-in-law – to *Good Housekeeping*, she knew better than to underestimate talents such as a ready smile and a penchant for old black and white films.

Personally Sydney felt she was a little young for *Good Housekeeping*. She had after all been known to wear the occasional Top Shop T-shirt, though more to impress herself than anyone else. Besides, while she might technically fit *Good Housekeeping*'s demographic, her mind-set was more . . . well, she didn't know what it was. She liked reading *Heat* when she was waiting for marriage guidance. And *Private Eye*, and *Vogue*, *Allure* . . . anything she could get her hands on really. Still, *Good Housekeeping* was better than a subscription to *Horse and Hound*, which is what Francine had bought her one year.

She was a little young for Charlie too. Not that their fifteen-year age gap had ever been much of an issue. Or it hadn't been until Charlie had got cross. She couldn't quite pin-point when his mid-to-late life crisis had first kicked in – two months ago possibly – because it had settled in slowly, a prolonged grumble here, a pained silence there, the whole ill-tempered package rumbling into an ambient background of soggy anger. All she knew was that while other husbands occasionally found religion, or more often mistresses, golf or the pub, Charlie had found Cantankerousness.

Sometimes the imaginary affairs were with the marriage guidance counsellor. Sometimes with Charlie himself. Or rather, with Charlie as he had been BC. Before Cantankerousness, Charlie had given every impression of being a reasonably normal human being. Cleverer than most perhaps – which, with hindsight, Sydney could see was always going to be slightly problematic – and with an unhealthy interest in the Chancellor of the Exchequer's every move. He also, even though it was apparent to everyone that he had fallen head over heels with Sydney almost the first time he clapped eyes on her, sent her notes so dense with legalese and sub-sections that they could only very loosely be described as love letters. But Sydney had consoled herself with the knowledge that they had taught her to think rationally. To this day her shopping lists remained models of logic and clarity. And in essence, he was sound, decent and roadworthy, unlikely to have affairs with other women.

That said, Sydney sometimes felt it would be simpler to compete with a mistress, golf or the pub than with Charlie's particular canker, although it wasn't that easy dealing with Canningtons, the legal chambers to which he set off – at an increasingly hurtful speed – every morning. A mistress might get lardy thighs or run off. Canningtons, though some of its barristers were flabby in the extreme, showed no signs of going anywhere without Charlie. What was it John Mortimer said about barristers breakfasting with murderers, lunching with a judge and dining with an actress? Charlie was more likely to breakfast with his laptop, lunch with a White Paper about national insurance scams and forget to have dinner. He never forgot to be grumpy though. He could harrumph for Britain. But he loved her and the girls, even though he quite often forgot about them along with everything else.

She did suffer the odd guilty twinge about the affairs. But then the marriage guidance counsellor had relocated up north – which on bad days Sydney couldn't help seeing as another rejection. Mostly, though, there were good days. Two adorable children (even more adorable since they'd both been safely delivered to full-time school and the adoration was now tinged with a bittersweet poignancy),

3

one clever, if silent (at least he didn't argue) husband, a lovely house and Hamish, a West Highland terrier with only faintly disconcerting digestive problems whom Charlie had bought as a companion for Sydney when Molly had started school.

With the girls both at St Margaret's, Sydney had found her soul at a loose end, even if her time was quite amply filled with errands for her family. It wasn't as if she hadn't had other offers to mop up any ennui – should she be foolish enough to feel any. The Clifton Crescent Book Club, which was always inviting her to make up numbers. The request to run the Clifton Crescent residents' association.

There was also the offer to become a class rep, a task she was informed was only mildly onerous once you'd drawn up the nit rota, organized the traffic patrol, the summer fayre, the Christmas party, and attended half a dozen meetings with the school head. After that came the repeated invitations to become a life member of The Rolling Scones, because 'We stay-at-home mothers must fly the flag for our cause'. Sydney never discovered quite what the cause was, other than a desperate need to look busy in the face of the showy, rush-rush-rushiness of the school's working mothers. So far she had politely fended off all invitations to join The Scones, which as far as she could gather were a virulent strain of local mafia who cooked communally over a giant Aga while assassinating everyone not in the group.

Going back to work four days a week had clearly been a positive step towards becoming one of those glamorous rush-rush-rush mothers herself – or at any rate escaping a life measured out by the number of times she called London Transport's Lost Property on Charlie's behalf or rushed down to chambers in the middle of the morning with something he'd left at home. Linda certainly thought so.

4

Although being in dire straits in the *IQ* magazine offices, acutely understaffed and in the process of threatening to kill herself if Sydney didn't come and help her out, Linda could be said to have had a vested interest. The important thing was that Sydney was convinced she was doing the right thing in the long term and that Charlie was bound to come round. Eventually.

Sydney was an optimist. But this morning, as he peered over the parapet of *The Times* in that myopic way of his which could sometimes seem curmudgeonly to strangers – or perhaps it *was* curmudgeonly, increasingly Sydney couldn't tell – even she thought it might take slightly longer than eventually to win him over.

'Is there any bacon?'

'You're eating it,' said Sydney patiently.

Charlie studied the cinderized but organic flotsam – Sydney *always* bought organic, particularly since she'd gone back to work, which she knew was a guilt reflex – scattered over the sub-Saharan dried-up pool of egg yolk on his plate and nodded philosophically. 'So I am.'

Sydney cast a wary eye towards the hob where their elder daughter Harriet, who had been cooking for the family since she was six, though she had yet to master fried breakfasts, was juggling pans. Luckily Harriet was too engrossed with the egg poacher to hear.

Given that Charlie normally wouldn't notice whether he was eating cornflakes or the packet, the bacon request was a ruse, Sydney knew. A delaying tactic designed:

i]   to make her late for work.

ii]   to remind her of the futility of her work.

ii]   (sub-section b) clarify any misunderstanding that might arise between them pertaining to Sydney's

5

mistaken belief that he had come round to the idea of her going back to work.

He tried again. He was making a big effort. 'Is that a new dress?' Which was ominous. Behind his new glasses his eyes narrowed as he contemplated an ancient velvet skirt that still just about did up over her stomach. 'Going out?'

Sydney silently counted to five. The Murrays never rowed. It was their USP as a couple, according to Linda. It was one of the reasons she'd asked Sydney to come back to the magazine as an agony aunt. So now, even if she'd wanted to row, Sydney couldn't because it would break the Trades Descriptions Act.

'Wednesday today.' She tried to sound breezily impervious to any intended criticism that might be lurking in her husband's seemingly innocuous enquiries. For the past two months, she had been going into work every Monday, Tuesday, Wednesday and Thursday.

Charlie glanced at the date at the top of *The Times*.

'So it is.'

Hamish let out a companionable little whine. A small but deadly rustle of air escaped from beneath the kitchen table. He wagged his tail sheepishly.

'Uggh, that's gross!' Molly wrinkled her nose and pushed away her bowl of Puffa Wheat, which she had no intention of finishing anyway, and buried her head in *Young Scientist*.

'Where's your brace, Harriet?' mouthed Sydney. She didn't want Charlie weighing in on this one.

Harriet looked close to hysteria at the prospect of having to tell her parents she hadn't been able to find it for two days.

'Sydney, will you please do something about Hamish's diet?' said Charlie reasonably and not for the first time.

'He's very emotional since Nellie died,' said Molly.

6

'I see Dad hates his bacon.' Over by the hob, Harriet's lower lip quivered ominously. Sydney felt her shoulders rise protectively, like a street hawker defending his patch from police predators. In Harriet's case the predator was her own rampant sensitivity.

'I do not hate it,' said Charlie wearily.

'He loves it,' said Sydney simultaneously. She wished she'd taken the chance to sprinkle some sunflower seeds on the bacon while he'd been buried in *The Times*. He wouldn't have noticed a little extra crunch this morning and he could do with the roughage. It might leaven his mood.

Charlie and Sydney exchanged glances, antagonism momentarily forgotten in this mutual display of unconditional love for their daughter.

'Even my own parents think I'm hopeless at everything!' Harriet hurled the metal spatula into the pan. It bounced on to the floor quite spectacularly, inspiring Harriet to stamp on it. Then she tripped over it and burst into tears. Sydney's heart concertinaed. She must have stubbed her toe as well as her pride. How could sensitivity be so bloody, violently insensitive?

'You need it on a lower heat.' Molly's nose finally emerged from her copy of *Young Scientist*. 'Meat vaporizes at 250 degrees Centigrade.'

'I hate you,' Harriet announced to no one in particular.

Charlie hurriedly crammed the charred remains on his plate into his mouth. 'Mmm, mmm, mmm.' He licked his fingers. 'Delicious.'

Sydney instantly forgave him the comment about her dress.

'It looks burnt to me,' said Molly. 'Carbon is carcinogenic,' she added helpfully.

Harriet let out a wail of bloodcurdling poignancy and

slammed out of the room. Sydney heard her stumble on the stairs and had to stop herself checking on her. Harriet kept falling over lately. Instead, she bent down to pick up a fleck of paint that had been dislodged from the wall. Charlie grabbed his briefcase and his coat, which was draped over the piano where he'd left it the night before.

'Must go.' He folded up *The Times*. Was there a note of reproach in the way he flattened its corners, Sydney wondered, momentarily forgetting that Harriet's volcanic moods had been fully evolved way before she'd started working again.

She tried another tack. 'Fancy anything special for supper tonight? I could pick up something on the way home.'

He put his coat down momentarily and contemplated her with the slightly embarrassed, confused look of a pensioner who has just been apprehended wandering around the grounds of Buckingham Palace at midnight in his pyjamas. Then he retaliated with his master thrust. 'That would be lovely. But I don't want to wear you out. I know how exhausting that office is.'

'No problem,' she said breezily, ignoring his reference to the location of Clifton Crescent, which while one of Primrose Hill's premier streets, was a hell of a hike from the Tube. 'It really isn't that tiring. Steak Béarnaise all right?' Harriet would probably have the recipe for Béarnaise. Before she worked Sydney used to buy it ready-made.

'I probably have to work late tonight,' he began, tantalized by the Béarnaise, which as Sydney knew, was his favourite. 'Just leave something cold for me. Or I could pick up a pizza.'

Being an exceptionally reasonable couple, that was about as close to rowing as the Murrays ever got.

But oh, how the weasel words of marriage wounded, thought Sydney, watching Charlie make his way down the hall. In the normal scheme of things, offering to cook someone supper – and having the offer refused on the grounds that it would be an onerous burden – would be tokens of caring, considerate love. But in this instance the caring, considerate love was freighted with seething, resentful agendae.

i]   Charlie saw himself as the provider.

i.b]   He was the provider. Before she went back to work Sydney used to feel she ought to go around with a Sponsored By Charlie sign hung round her neck. But Linda had pointed out that people might assume she was a crack dealer. Even now, her salary from *IQ* didn't make her entirely self-sufficient. But it was a gesture. And she was the one who'd found the house and convinced Charlie the wet rot-raddled wreck would make a perfect home for them. According to Gavin, the estate agent, 64 Clifton Crescent was the finest of all the stuccoed terraced houses in their street. Though how he could tell the difference Sydney didn't know, since they were a job lot built by a speculator who'd gone bankrupt in 1864.

ii]   Just because you were handsomely provided for with two adorable-ish children, one workaholic husband and an open invitation to take over as secretary of the local residents' association (primary aim: removal of stone cladding on number 21; secondary aim: obstruction of planned Sainsbury Local on the grounds that it did not fit with community spirit of small independent, criminally over-priced local shops) didn't mean you were immune from feeling that something was missing from your life.

The Murrays' warfare may have been subtle in the extreme, but their children believed in all-out guerrilla tactics. From three floors down, Sydney heard Harriet slam the door to her bedroom. Molly looked up from her book stoically. 'I expect she's sobbing now.'

Sydney eyed her younger daughter wearily. Why had she felt short-changed until she'd gone back to work? How come The Rolling Scones were content to spend hours talking about new recipes they were sampling to tickle their husbands' taste-buds? It wasn't as if Sydney hadn't been busy before she'd gone back to work. Acting as Charlie's unofficial chauffeur – he'd never got round to getting his driving licence – wheeling Harriet off to all the specialists who were meant to be helping her dyslexia, and organizing four people's lives had been quite full on, but she'd still felt a void. A void that hadn't even gone away when Charlie's mother, Francine, had given her the hardback of *How to Be a Domestic Goddess* the previous Christmas.

Even so, why the urge to take on more? It wasn't – as Charlie had pointed out on more than one occasion – as if their house ran like clockwork. Sydney spied Charlie's coat lying on the piano. He'd be ringing soon to ask her if he needed it. In addition to being one of the untidiest people Sydney had ever lived with, Charlie was incapable of functioning on a practical level. When they'd met, this forgetfulness had been one of his endearing USPs. That a man could clearly be so brilliant in his chosen field and yet in danger of concussing himself with a kitchen cupboard door on the rare occasions he felt the need to open one, had struck Sydney as profoundly endearing once upon a time. Sometimes she dreamed that he'd mislaid one of the girls somewhere. It was fair to say that after twelve years of marriage the charm of this had evaporated marginally. Actually it struck her now as being less of a selling-point and more like a rare form of Passive–Aggressive Acute Bloody Mindedness.

8.35. Sydney called up the stairs with what she hoped was an air of unflustered authority.

Her voice wavered slightly when she glanced at her watch and realized she had ten minutes to complete a school run that took fifteen under optimum conditions – i.e. between 1 and 3 a.m. Molly appeared on the top landing. White, baby-blonde pigtails. Tiny grey tunic. Three Puffa Wheats clinging to it like thistledown, adding a surreal glow to her appearance. She was so beautiful Sydney caught herself mooning over her daughter like a love-struck Romeo.

'Harriet's locked herself in the bathroom,' Molly announced with her father's incendiary calm.

8.36. Sydney lay on the floor outside the bathroom, pushing a note under the door. She didn't need x-ray vision to know that her daughter was also crouched on the floor, sobbing. She could hear her. Thinking how hot it must be in there, she worried Harriet might pass out.

'Go away.'

'Come on, I miss you.'

'I doubt that when you think I'm so useless at everything.'

'Harriet, you know that's not true.' Sydney kept her voice even and then spoilt it by telling Harriet to stop feeling sorry for herself in a jokey voice. Harriet didn't have a sense of humour. It was one of the issues Sydney wanted to raise at the next PTE.

'There, I told you. You all think I'm stupid.' There was more muffled sobbing and the sound of taps being turned on full. Drowning? Surely Harriet was too young to be attempting suicide?

'Harriet, open this door.' Voice sounding less jokey by the second.

'Go away.'

Stalemate.

Why was it, Sydney wondered, that like all imperial forces, Charlie always withdrew whenever trouble was brewing?

Molly loomed above Sydney's head and pressed her mouth against the bathroom door. 'You're making us late, you cow.'

'Molly!' Sydney tried to fix her with a disapproving glare. It wasn't easy from the floor. Her younger daughter stared back at her belligerently, tears coursing down her cheeks, making her look like a small Gwyneth Paltrow.

'What's the matter with *you*?' said Sydney harshly.

'It's the class play dress rehearsal. We're performing next week. I need to take in my curate's costume today.'

'What curate's costume? What curate?' Why were they having a play at the start of November? What were they celebrating? Divali? Hanukkah? Sydney's knowledge of religious festivals was sketchy.

'I told you last week,' Molly sobbed. The bath sounded as though it was getting quite deep. What exactly was a curate? And what in God's name did they wear? She ran to the little drawer she kept locked in her bedside table and pulled out an antique crucifix that had belonged to her great-grandmother, who according to family legend had converted from Judaism to escape persecution in Russia. She handed it to Molly and returned to the landing.

'Harriet, will you come out now please!' Would her daughter recognize the difference between a rhetorical question and a craven plea?

'You never listen. I'm neglected because Harriet gets all the attention.' Sydney looked down at her small daughter who was shaking with distress now. She took a deep breath. 'Molly, you said nothing about this costume and you know it. I'm perfectly happy to help you as much as I can, but you must stop pretending everything is somebody else's fault.'

'But it's eight-thirty-nine.' Molly wiped her arm across her face, creating a lake of snot and tears on her cheeks. Sydney reached into her pocket for a Kleenex.

'I'll just have to write a late note for you. We'll say the car broke down.'

'But that's a lie.'

'Sometimes lies are necessary.'

'When?'

Sydney was stumped. Now didn't seem the moment to dismantle one of the fundamental shibboleths of civilized society. 'I suppose curates wear black and white, like vicars.' That at least shouldn't present too much of a problem. Sydney had created an entire sub-section of her wardrobe devoted to black – a doomed attempt to look as though she hadn't forgotten to lose a stone after her pregnancies.

'Harriet.' She aimed for cheerful authority this time. 'We really need your help with a costume. You're the only one in this family with the style to get us through this.'

There was an agonized delay while Harriet considered her options, which were, roughly, waiting to asphyxiate slowly in a bathroom where the window had never opened since the cleaning lady Juanita's brother had painted it to the frame, or demonstrating her flair in the costume department. After a few moments' deliberation, the taps were turned off, the plug was freed and the door unlocked. Shrouded in steam and framed in the doorway, Harriet

13

looked strangely apocryphal, like a contestant on *Stars in Their Eyes*. 'I don't think Molly looks very nice in black,' she said with a glimmer of satisfaction.

9.22. In an ideal world Sydney would now be proceeding with implacable efficiency along the Docklands Light Railway to her office and Harriet would be at school with her brace in her mouth. Instead, she was back outside number 64 because Charlie had called her mobile and asked her if she would mind nipping back home to read him some vital information contained in a letter he had left next to the plate of burnt bacon. And there was no sign of the brace.

She did mind, very much, but somehow she felt churlish saying so.

Her neighbour Mrs Protheroe's reflection loomed ominously in her wing mirror, a skeletal figure in pink satin with a crown of purple-tinged hair, heckling from the pavement as Sydney struggled to park between the beaten-up wreck belonging to Daniel, the distressingly handsome student from number 62, and a skip.

As Sydney stepped out of the car, Mrs Protheroe brandished a copy of the *Daily Sport* under her nose. 'Look at this!' She thumped the paper with a gnarled fist. Sydney looked at the headline. *Ten ways to tell if your neighbour is a werewolf.*

'That's helpful,' said Sydney neutrally. She wondered if she ought to ring the office to say she'd be late or whether that might merely draw attention to the situation. She backed up the steps to her front door. There appeared to be a removal van outside number 69, which suggested that the developer who had, in the view of the entire Crescent, committed a gross act of vandalism by ripping out all its cornicing, had finally sold it. Strange, there had been no signs.

'Maybe we could have a chat tonight, Mrs P.' If she didn't take a firm stand now it would be after lunch before she got to work.

'I'm a bit delayed.'

'Nanny problems?' asked Linda sympathetically. Being single and childless, she assumed that all problems in later life boiled down to nannies, orgasms and a lack thereof. They were the only excuses that elicited any of her sympathy.

'I'll explain when I get there.'

'That's okay. The girl I wanted you to see just called to cancel.'

For once Sydney was thankful that Linda's never-ending search for a PA to replace the saintly Helen, who after eight years' devotion was shortly leaving to work for VSO in Africa, had once again been thwarted. 'I'll be in by ten,' she offered as compensation.

'No panic. I'm popping out for an hour to Accounts.'

Sydney was always amused by her friend's lies. Why, when Linda was perfectly happy to discuss her abortions (two); her phone sex disasters (six); her boyfriends who had turned out to have serious fetish issues (three); her years in therapy (five) with anyone who expressed a passing interest, she couldn't simply come clean about her twice-weekly trips to the hairdresser was beyond Sydney. But they clearly ran against the ethical grain of the *IQ* office.

'I'll see you later then.'

'Cometh the hour cometh the woman. But don't fail me. I need you. It's a viper's nest here and you're the only one I can trust.'

Marginally gratified, Sydney called a taxi to take her to the Tube station.

Vipers was putting it a bit strongly, Sydney thought, hurriedly searching for Charlie's missing letter. But things at *IQ* had become a bit tumultuous lately. The doorbell rang. Sydney opened it to say she'd be out in two minutes. A small upturned face with vivid eyes and a dark bob gazed up at her.

'I'm really sorry to disturb you,' a considered, upper-class American accent floated up to her. 'But I'm supposed to be moving in across the street today. Only it transpires the builders haven't finished some vital work. The removal men have disappeared and the electricity isn't working . . .' She trailed off. She was clearly distressed. Sydney paused uncertainly.

'I wondered whether you were having a power cut too, or whether it had been uniquely bestowed on my house. I'm Eloise Fairweather,' she added.

'I'm afraid it's unique,' said Sydney, taking in the woman's tiny, fluttery hands and small, pointy, white teeth, which were so perfect and dazzling she must have got them in Harry Winston's. She suddenly felt like a huge velvet blob.

The woman's shoulders sagged visibly and to Sydney's horror she began to sob.

'Listen, I didn't mean to sound flippant. Moving's a nightmare.' The woman's shoulders heaved like crashing surf. 'Do you want to come in and use the phone or something?'

The heaving subsided momentarily. The head nodded and Sydney led her into the kitchen, relieved she'd removed the worst of the debris.

Sydney left her guest to make her phone calls and returned

five minutes later to find her scrutinizing the kitchen pinboard, with its haystack of invitations from the past twelve months, telephone numbers and the Council's litter hotline. Visibly startled, she seemed to have made an encouraging recovery, which made Sydney feel slightly better about turfing her out.

'I was just admiring the art.' She blushed. 'It's very interesting. Is this a farm?'

'An abattoir. Harriet – my elder daughter – is very active when it comes to animal rights.'

'I see.' She clearly didn't.

'It's sweet of you to call it art,' continued Sydney. 'My husband thinks it's Harriet's passport to life-long therapy.'

The visitor gazed at her blankly and tiptoed over towards Molly's Impressionistic take on My Little Pony. 'These flowers are adorable.' She craned her neck. She was tiny. But perfectly – exquisitely – packaged, right down to her pony-skin pumps. Clearly she liked horses too.

'That picture is of My Little Pony, surrounded by, let's see, all seventeen of Molly's Sylvanians. I'm afraid Molly's mad on them. And My Little Pony. She's got at least ten, each more garish than the last. She combs them obsessively. Still, perhaps it means she's gearing up for a career as a horse whisperer. Or Vidal Sassoon.'

The stranger's eyes had drifted back towards the sunshine-yellow walls of Sydney's hallway and the lovely landscape oils painted by Sydney's mother. Then she turned to a coffin-shaped box, embellished with fake silk flowers and a silver plaque, that had pride of place on the piano. 'Don't tell me. My Little Pony's boudoir.'

Sydney shook her head. 'Nellie's coffin.' She noticed Charlie's coat again. She picked it up. He would, she decided, be needing it. Maybe she should call him.

Eloise looked at the box gingerly. 'Who's Nellie?'

'Our ex-tabby.'

'You're kidding.'

'Don't worry. She was ancient. She died this past summer. We've had a bad run recently. Homer, our hamster, went AWOL three months ago. Under the floorboards we think. Hasn't been seen since.'

The stranger looked aghast. 'Can't you get cholera from living with dead things?'

'She's been cremated. She's not just rotting away. Harriet can't bear to think of Nellie confined to the earth.' Their cleaner, Juanita, on the other hand had said that if they left it there much longer a curse would descend on the back of the house and she would be unable to clean there. She didn't clean Charlie's office either – since the time she'd thrown away some vital briefs and nearly set fire to the spaghetti wiring in there. Soon the whole house would be out of bounds to her noxious detergents for one reason or another.

Sydney glanced at her kitchen clock. She needed to go. The woman turned weepy again.

'I'd better leave. I really shouldn't take up any more of your time.'

Sydney capitulated. 'Would you like a quick coffee? I'm expecting a cab any second to take me to work but I'm sure it can wait a few minutes. You look as though you need fortifying.'

'Only if you're positive it's no bother?' She sat down before Sydney could answer, and a wave of Shalimar engulfed Sydney, taking her back to another life. She flashed Sydney a grateful, dewy smile. 'I give you my word I won't doorstep you every morning.'

Sydney wondered where Linda was in the blow-dry chain. 'I love the way you've decorated,' said Eloise, gazing at

Molly's cactuses next to the sink. 'It's so . . . organic. How many children do you have?'

'It feels like twenty-two sometimes, but it's just two,' said Sydney, frothing some milk. 'And they both loathe washing. You've probably smelled them?' She placed her last clean mugs on the table, whipping away Harriet's brace that grinned up at her from the bottom of one. 'Although lately the little one, Molly, has found God. It's a phase quite a lot of them seem to go through. I'm hoping it will encourage her to try and walk on water.' Eloise looked on nonplussed. 'Or at least take a bath.'

Sydney willed the kettle to boil. Eloise seemed to have no idea what she was talking about.

'How lovely having girls – and such different personalities.'

'How did you know they were different?'

'I saw you all leaving for school.' She gazed round the room dolefully. 'What a beautiful platter.' Eloise put down her bouncing bunnies mug and pointed to a chipped, mint-coloured plate garlanded with pale pink roses that had pride of place on Sydney's old blue dresser.

'It was my mother's,' said Sydney. 'Nellie used to lie on it and one day she broke it,' she added quickly. 'I ought to throw it away, but . . .'

'. . . you can't,' finished Eloise gently.

Sydney nodded. Sometimes she missed her mother more badly than she thought she ought to. She changed the subject. 'Is your husband American too?'

Eloise pushed her Bovril-coloured bob behind her ears so that it framed her heart-shaped face like two commas, and laughed. 'No, Dylan's as English as they come. Or rather as Welsh. I still haven't got my head round the subtleties of your nation state. I'm from San Francisco originally, you see.'

Sydney was conscious of the ticking clock but she was fascinated by Eloise. She had never met anyone who would even consider wearing a Chanel mini-skirt to supervise moving house. 'Have you been married long?'

'Six months.' She turned her eyes rapturously on Sydney. They were, Sydney could see now, a mixture of green and violet. 'And we've known each other for seven and a half. It was quite a whirlwind. More of a hurricane actually.' Eloise giggled. 'We met in the middle of one of the worst storms to hit New York in twenty years. It was practically a monsoon. The rain was bouncing off the sidewalks right up to my thighs and since I was wearing my brand-new Marc Jacobs' dress and matching coat I naturally thought I deserved the last remaining cab in New York more than Dylan.'

'He had different ideas?'

Eloise shrugged. 'He was wearing Brooks Brothers. That was before I got him into Missoni. I had to explain the laws of outfit priority in Manhattan. Jacobs before Brooks Brothers. It's Darwinian. You can't blame him entirely. He was already in the cab at the time. The stupid driver had forgotten to turn his light off.'

'So you hijacked his taxi anyway?'

'I prefer to think of it as car pooling. It's very environmental. Dylan seemed a little taken aback to begin with, especially as I lived downtown and he was up in the Eighties somewhere.' She paused, pursing her lips again to blow on her coffee. She was like an extraordinarily pretty doll. Molly would adore her, Sydney thought, though Harriet might be a bit more sceptical. 'But I have to say he rose to the occasion. By the time he dropped me off he'd asked me to go to St Barts with him on holiday. Six weeks later we were married.'

Sydney thought of Charlie's thoughtful and prolonged courtship of her. 'Wasn't that a bit risky?'

'I love risks. And as you'll discover, he's pretty gorgeous, clever, charming. I thought he was bound to be psycho or gay. And look at the great ring.'

Eloise thrust a tiny, delicate hand at Sydney so that she could get a better view of her diamond engagement ring, though it could probably have been seen from space. No wonder Eloise had such good muscle tone. It must weigh a ton.

'It is very beautiful,' said Sydney admiring the rose-cut facets. 'It looks antique.'

'It is. It was Dylan's mother's, or grandmother's or something.'

'That's romantic.'

Eloise grimaced. 'Hideous setting. So I got Asprey's to design a new one.' She wiggled her fingers ecstatically.

A rattling of keys at the front door heralded the arrival of Juanita. She swept into the kitchen, barely registering Eloise, and sank on to a chair. 'My God!' She reached for the coffee pot and realizing it was empty, looked desolate. 'I'm going to keel this woman.'

Sydney looked sympathetic. 'What's she thrown now?'

'Thees!' Juanita held up an ancient Mason and Pearson hairbrush, matted with an incriminating tangle of pale mauve hair. 'And called me sperm of a beetch.'

Eloise looked at them both with mounting alarm.

'Our neighbour, Mrs Protheroe,' explained Sydney.

'The one with the bad armchairs in the front yard?'

'Wait till you see her mattresses,' said Sydney. 'I don't know where she keeps getting them from. Sometimes the area outside her house looks like Tate Modern.'

Eloise was not amused. 'Clearly our estate agent chose his viewing times carefully. There was never any sign of discarded junk whenever we came to look.' She drummed her fingers on the side of her cup. 'We'll have to see what we can do about that. It's hardly adding to the beauty of the road.'

'Mrs Protheroe's all right,' said Sydney, magnanimously overlooking her neighbour's suggestion the previous evening that Sydney join Weightwatchers. Juanita scowled at her in disbelief.

'She's just gone a bit strange since her daughter stopped speaking to her,' Sydney continued. She didn't want this new neighbour coming in and thinking she could throw her illiberal views around without encountering any objections. 'She used to be a pillar of the community. She's lived in Clifton Crescent longer than anyone – since just after the war I think.'

'The Falklands?' said Eloise.

'Malvinas,' snapped Juanita.

Eloise beamed and held out her hand again. 'Delighted to meet you, Malvinas, I'm Eloise Fairweather.'

'Delighted too,' said Juanita, flattered by Eloise's good manners. The phone began ringing. 'And I help you kick thees old bag out,' she whispered conspiratorially when Sydney got up to answer it. It was Happy Cabs to say their driver had had a puncture but would be there shortly.

'How shortly?' Sydney asked guiltily. At this rate she wouldn't get to the office before Linda disappeared for a mammoth lunch with one or other of her contributors. Juanita got up reluctantly to find a broom and shift some mountains of post around.

'Why don't I drive you there?' said Eloise. 'I might as well. My car's outside and let's face it, I don't have anything else to do.'

'Oh, I couldn't let you. It takes ages in the traffic.' Sydney really didn't think she wanted to be beholden to this person. 'And the removal men might turn up any minute.'

Eloise reflected for a moment. 'Okay. But at least let me take you to the Tube. And you can tell me about your cleaner. I'm looking for a good one. I have certain bacteria issues and frankly I'm a little worried about cleanliness in Europe.'

Eloise's black Mercedes sports car, almost as shiny as her bob, pounced into the traffic. Sydney did up her safety belt and gripped the sides of her seat.

'Are you happy, Sydney?' asked Eloise, pressing her foot on the accelerator.

Sydney was so taken aback she didn't answer for a moment. Surely the misgivings of the past few months weren't that visibly etched on her face?

'Haven't really thought about it,' she mumbled. She ought to be happy, with the job and everything. People always said she ought to have been happy *without* the job. 'Yes, I suppose so. English people don't ask themselves those kinds of question very often. We just sort of chunter on. Not sure I can recommend Juanita unreservedly though.' Sydney thought of the little piles of unopened letters – one in particular – that disappeared for days, sometimes weeks, to reappear in some illogical new location, and decided life wouldn't be worth living for any of them if Juanita went to work for Eloise. 'She's more into displacement than actual cleaning and tidying.'

'Why doesn't that surprise me?' Eloise sighed. 'Honestly, domestic staff . . . speaking of whom, my God, who's that?' she asked as a hunched figure in a voluminous, shabby black coat with a face like a haunted camel's waved violently at Sydney.

'That's Miranda Plympton,' said Sydney. What was Miranda doing in the area? Probably heading out on a recruitment drive for The Rolling Scones. Even though she knew Sydney would be at work. Any minute now she'd be dropping one of her concerned notes through the letterbox about how stressful Sydney must be finding it all. She sank further into the passenger seat.

'I thought those velvet hair bands went out with the wimple.'

'She's the wife of one of my husband's colleagues.'

'She looks about a hundred.'

'Not quite. But she is a founding member of the local cooking group. They bake cakes together. I expect they'll ask you to join.'

'Oh, please. Are you and I the only women who have careers around here? What exactly is it that you do by the way, Sydney?'

'Just helping out a friend on a magazine,' Sydney said vaguely. She didn't want to discuss her job. That way subterfuge and deception lay, since Charlie had very little idea what she actually did there, and she intended to keep it that way. 'And you?'

'Sotheby's – when I was in New York. Impressionists mainly. Obviously I won't be doing that here.' She sounded wistful. 'I'm going to be working with Dylan.' She honked her horn at the car in front. 'My husband's keen for me to go into the family business. And I'm always up for a challenge. So when he said he wanted to move closer to his family—'

'His family live in Primrose Hill?'

'Wales. But nothing's very far in England, is it? They've lived there about a thousand years so I figure it must be okay. Something to do with the Plantagenets, I believe.'

Sydney wondered whether Eloise realized that the Plantagenets had died out six hundred years ago, but it seemed petty to disabuse her of what was clearly a very satisfactory family connection.

Eloise turned up the air-conditioning. 'Dylan's the first one not to go straight into the family business. He got the bug for kicking against family tradition early on when he went away to Bristol. The men in his family had always gone to Cambridge.'

'Did you say Bristol?' Sydney felt her mouth go dry.

'I certainly did. That's West Country, right?'

'Perfectly right.' Sydney's heart was beating so loudly now she was amazed anyone could hear Eloise's horn over the top of it.

'Do you know it then?'

'I went there too,' said Sydney as calmly as she could. Fairweather must be Eloise's maiden name. 'Your husband's last name isn't Glendower by any chance, is it?'

Eloise threw back her head and laughed. 'Jesus, I knew England was small, but this is ridiculous. Don't tell me you know Dylan?'

You could say so, thought Sydney. But the pertinent question was, what the hell was he doing back in England, and back in her life?

2

'I don't really see what the problem is.' Linda winced slightly at her screen before deleting a column of urgent emails, most of them from Brian Widlake, the terrifying editor-in-chief of the *Tribune*, whose weekend supplement *IQ* was. 'It's not as if you still have a soft spot for Dylan.'

Sydney peered into the dregs of a double latte and regretted the profligate consumption of calories. But not as much as she regretted telling Linda about Eloise and Dylan moving into Clifton Crescent. She had a torrent of work to sort through. Most of it emotionally draining and harrowingly torrid. And she might have known Linda wouldn't understand.

'You don't still have a soft spot for Mills and Boon man, do you?'

Sydney tried and failed to find a space for her coffee cup in Linda's overflowing waste-paper basket. She wondered why it was that having summoned her into her glass box ostensibly to deliver a gentle lecture on Sydney's work ethic, which Linda didn't feel had eased back into top gear yet, they were now discussing boyfriends from the pre-Jurassic period. She also wondered why Linda had always had such antipathy for Dylan, when they'd only met a couple of times.

'God, Syd. After the way he treated you.'

'It wasn't so bad.'

'Sydney, you caught him in bed with another woman. When is that good?'

Sydney shrugged. 'Everyone was at it in those days. That's university for you.'

Linda narrowed her eyes to turret-like slits. It was the look Sydney dreaded: it was Linda pretending to pull her defences when all the time she was getting ready to shoot a flock of piercing arrows. 'Charlie's worth ten of Dylan,' she said eventually.

'The issue of whether or not I have a soft spot for Dylan Glendower is a non-issue, since you ask,' said Sydney stiffly. 'And he didn't treat me badly. The decision to split up was mutual and amicable.' She knew her marriage guidance counsellor didn't entirely agree with this interpretation of events. But he was no longer around so his views didn't count.

Linda gave her one of her looks. 'What is the issue then?'

That was an excellent question. And one Sydney couldn't begin to answer honestly, not even to Linda.

'I nearly asked Eloise and Dylan for dinner this morning,' she said instead.

'Bit unnecessary, isn't it? Even on the Elysian Primrose Hills.' Linda was definitely distracted, Sydney decided. Otherwise she'd have been a lot more emphatic on the in-advisability of dinner with Dylan.

'Look at this.' Linda waved a fax littered with exclamation marks in front of Sydney. 'It's a letter from Hotsees.' Sydney grimaced sympathetically. Hotsees were something of a regrettable fixture in the advertising pages of *IQ*, to the chagrin of all who worked on it, since the self-heating nylon draught excluders that it manufactured, decorated with very bad prints of people's children and pets, weren't exactly visually pleasing, and *IQ* had always prided itself on the integrity of its airy layouts as much as on the integrity of its long, high-brow features. 'They're threatening to withdraw their advertising if we don't support them editorially. They're lucky we allow them to advertise their hideous crap in the first place.'

'They did fork out a hundred and twenty-five thousand to advertise their hideous crap last year, so it's quite likely they don't see it quite like that. We've never so much as mentioned their products,' said Sydney, who secretly saw the logic of a device that produced lots of hot air being given prime position on the inside cover of *IQ*.

Linda looked affronted. 'That's what journalistic integrity is all about.'

'But you've agreed to introduce a motoring column to try and tempt some car companies in . . .'

'That's different. The journalist I commissioned is our answer to Jeremy Clarkson. He gets the readers going.'

He certainly did, thought Sydney. Out to buy other newspapers.

'So how's that different from the Hotsees situation?'

Linda fished around in a duty-free plastic carrier bag and pulled out a sheaf of dog-eared papers. 'What were you saying about dinner?'

'It's all right,' said Sydney. 'I came to my senses just in time.'

'That's okay then.' Linda's brow furrowed like a rumpled bed. 'Look, Sydney, if you don't mind, I need to edit this piece on Bratislava's second poetry festival down to two thousand words by twelve o'clock. I can't understand why, but there appear to be two thousand words on the Slavic iambic pentameter alone.'

With mounting misgivings, Sydney eyed the chaotic handwriting and occasional coffee-cup ring embellishing Linda's latest unreadable commission. *IQ*'s contributors must be the only journalists allowed to submit work in long-hand. Not to mention the only journalists in London who could get away with writing on obscure subjects that no one apart from their editor wanted to read. Once upon a time, Linda's magic editorial touch had meant that even the most erudite subjects in *IQ* had turned out to be gripping reads. But recently, Sydney had noticed with regret, her judgement seemed to be less sure and she'd made a few questionable – and expensive – wrong decisions.

Perhaps Linda should have been a don after all, which is what she'd originally wanted, thought Sydney sadly. At least she wouldn't have been under the same pressure to deliver on Hotsees. But in those days brainy girls weren't supposed to be interested in Manolos, so she'd gone into journalism. She'd been exceptionally good as well, progressing from a lowly assistant at *The Times Literary Supplement* to features editor at the *Independent on Sunday* and, eventually, her current job as editor on *IQ*.

With each successive move Linda's tastes had become increasingly high-brow and her readership steadily smaller. In fact it would be fair to say that latterly she had been editing *IQ* with three of her favourite university tutors in mind, and only the scantest regard to what the public at large might want to read on a Saturday morning. Eight-page treatises on Kierkegaard, gardening features on recycling your toilet waste, and regular features such as Haiku of the Week had not made it a ratings smash, even if a few snobbish critics claimed to love it. Its readership figures were now under the radar, along with its budgets, although it had begun making regular appearances in *Private Eye*'s Pseuds' Corner.

Yet for several years *IQ* had been so highly regarded by other journalists that Linda had successfully convinced the old owners that the magazine's readership, though small, was highly influential. But Schmucklesons, the huge Swedish conglomerate that had recently bought Icon Publishing, the owners of the *Tribune*, didn't want small and influential. Schmucklesons, whose closest link to the creative printed word had previously been the E-numbers disguised as something wholesome and edible on the sides of their meatball and pickled herring tins, wanted huge and gullible. It made the business of selling advertising slogans about Hotsees to them so much easier. A paper as illustrious as the *Tribune* should never have fallen into the hands of barbarians like Schmucklesons, which also owned a raft of top-shelf magazines, including *Girls on Top, Three's Company, Swingers* and *Bombay Babes*, as well as numerous indispensable trade titles such as *Paper Clip and Stapler, Sileage Monthly* and the *Rodent Poisoner*. There had even been a furious debate in the House of Commons about it, with the opposition calling for an enquiry from the Monopolies Commission. But after Icon Publishing had donated £50,000 to the government and planted a few stories in the international press about British xenophobia, particularly with regard to Scandinavian whale hunters, the matter had been quietly dropped.

Sydney picked her cup up off the floor and saw Linda's pasty PA Helen gesticulating helplessly outside the grimy windows to Linda's office with a phone in her hand, another slung over her shoulder and one pressed against her ear. Brian Widlake's secretaries were on all three and each of them urgently wanted to talk to Linda.

'Shouldn't you take those?' asked Sydney nervously.

'In a sec,' said Linda breezily.

Sydney picked anxiously at the hem of her skirt.

Linda shrugged in an insouciant fashion, though the end result resembled a nervous tic. 'I hate it when you start wrecking your expensive clothes. Honestly, Syd, it's not worth it. It'll only be Brian Widlake wanting to know what SLT we've got on the cover this week.'

'SLT?'

'Widlake terminology. Silly Little Tart.' Linda kicked her waste-paper basket defiantly. It toppled over, scattering half a ton of papers, a mound of old coffee grounds and one half-eaten Prêt à Manger sushi on the floor. 'This office is a disgrace,' she thundered.

Sydney couldn't disagree with that. Nor could she argue that the squalid state of *IQ*'s offices wasn't a pointed reminder from Schmucklesons to pull their socks up. For while the rest of their empire luxuriated on the other thirteen floors of Icon Towers in considerable post-modern splendour, *IQ*'s corner on the sixth appeared to have been deliberately allowed to go to rack and ruin.

'It's amazing we haven't all contracted sick building disorder,' continued Linda. 'But then, this magazine is led by a woman. What do you expect from the sexist bastards that run this place?'

Sydney knew from experience that this was heading towards a long diatribe from Linda. Sexism was not only not dead at the *Tribune*, it was alive and blowing and stamping on the French manicures of the women who worked there. But right now she didn't have time to listen. She tried bringing Linda back to the number one pressing subject.

'Isn't there a way of working with Widlake?'

Linda turned on Sydney with raised eyebrows, narrowed eyes and a mouth pursed like a folded umbrella. It was the look she reserved for moments of utter contempt.

'There isn't any way of working on any brief with a man who used to call his team of female investigators on the women's pages at his last paper the Tampax Trio.'

'He is your boss,' Sydney heard herself saying. 'It's probably not wise to turn every encounter with him into a row. I mean, maybe, just maybe, and we're speaking very hypothetically here, there's room for a bit more levity on *IQ*. Look at the way *Vanity Fair* mixes Hollywood with more serious pieces. It's—'

'Yes, thank you for that homily on American publishing. But for your info they're not rows. They're lively discussions.'

New as she was to the workings of the *Tribune*, Linda's airy tone didn't fool her for a moment. It was an open secret that things hadn't been going exactly brilliantly with the magazine for some time. It was widely rumoured that Brian Widlake, a Schmucklesons' appointment, loathed everything *IQ* stood for and that it was only a matter of time before he got round to culling it. None of which helped Linda's already neurotic team behave any more normally. Especially when they saw Linda adopting a brace position similar to Custer's last stand. The more belligerent Brian Widlake became about making the paper less highbrow and more fucking eyebrow, as he put it, the more terminally obscure *IQ* got – and with it, the higher Linda's chances of becoming terminally unemployed.

'Please speak to Brian,' Sydney pleaded as Helen pressed against the glass door of Linda's office miming strangulation by telephone wire.

'I'll call him back in a minute,' said Linda, with a glint in her eye that reminded Sydney of Harriet when she hadn't even attempted to learn her spellings. 'Now, look me in the eye and tell me you're not secretly hoping that Dylan's stalking you.'

Sydney frowned. Even if Linda was on to something – and her track record for correctly diagnosing Sydney's emotions

32

before Sydney herself acknowledged their existence was unsettlingly accurate – she was not going to let her get away with not addressing her own problems.

'Linda,' she fixed her sternly over the piles of books that toppled across the desk, 'why did you pick me for this job?'

Linda looked up from the scrawl in front of her. Her features registered magisterial surprise that Sydney was still there. Her eyes darted furtively towards the rest of the office. 'Sorry, just checking. I swear to God Helen's learned to lip-read this year.'

'Answer the question. You can't even remember what it was, can you?'

'Why I begged you to come back and work with me? Let's see. Oh, that's easy. Because you're kind, intuitively wise and the most sorted person I know. Because you have an infallible sixth sense about people. And because from where I stand your life's a bed of roses and you need a few pricks in it to make you count your blessings.'

This was more or less the same response Linda had given Sydney three months earlier when she'd first broached the subject of the job with her. Sydney's initial response had been to tell her to sober up. Her life was hardly a bed of roses, more a sack of manure, and her sixth sense seemed to have been on an industrial go-slow for months.

But she couldn't pretend she wasn't tempted. The six months' maternity leave Sydney had taken when Harriet had been born had turned into a ten-year sabbatical that had eventually left her feeling dull, hopelessly out of touch with water-cooler issues, whatever they might be – they hadn't even had water-coolers in offices last time she'd worked in one – and incapable of ever functioning in a work environment again.

Charlie had naturally cloaked his horror at the prospect of

her going back to work in concern for her energy levels and commitments to The Rolling Scones, even though Sydney had repeatedly told him she'd never had any intention of joining their cooking club in the first place.

Ultimately, Sydney had turned Linda down of course. But for a few days contemplating going back to work had been fun. Even if she knew it wouldn't be worth dealing with Charlie's dismay in the end.

Except that Linda had refused to take no for an answer. And something had stirred deep within Sydney – an ambition she'd long thought buried or perhaps simply a survival instinct. After seven phone calls and three dinners at The Wolseley, she'd taken the job . . .

. . . and miracle of miracles, she seemed to be okay at it. In the six weeks since her first problem page had appeared, her postbag had quadrupled, and from the eclectic spelling and supermarket stationery, she knew she was attracting a different kind of reader from the normal *IQ* one, which presumably was a good thing. She found herself increasingly drawn into her readers' lives; exhilarated to find that perhaps Linda was right and she might be quite good at helping them, and happy to find herself pulled back into the maelstrom of office politics.

She even liked the *nom de plume* they'd come up with. As Patience Truelove – which Linda had chosen because she thought it was the kind of thing Brian Widlake would love but which was really deeply ironic and subversive – she could say things she wouldn't say as Sydney Murray; think things Sydney Murray wouldn't think. And it was so much easier being an agony aunt on paper than in real life because you didn't have to get properly involved or confront people personally.

So now, when Linda told her she was the most sorted

person she knew, she didn't immediately demur. She waited a few moments before saying that if that were the case, Linda should bloody well listen to what she had to say about Brian Widlake.

'I don't know how much more I can take,' Linda finally conceded later that morning. 'Everything I built up with this magazine is being shot to pieces. First he wants a problem page,' she raked her hands through her hair, leaving a trace of biro across her forehead, 'which is fine,' she added hurriedly. 'A bloody good idea in fact. And you're doing it brilliantly. But then he wants me to hire that sodding airhead—'

'I thought you were coming round to Poppy.'

'I said she had a certain freak-show appeal.' Linda craned her head to see if Poppy De Cadent, *IQ*'s new star columnist, beauty director and, not entirely coincidentally, daughter of Mick De Cadent, had deigned to put in an appearance yet. She hadn't, but it was only 12.30. 'I thought I might be able to draw something out of her. If you think about it, her vacuousness is very zeitgeisty. But she's causing ructions among the others. The receptionists can't understand why I hired her and I'm finding it hard to justify it myself. Helen resents the hell out of her—'

Helen resented anyone who didn't put in a twelve-hour day like she did, thought Sydney. Poppy, who barely put in a twelve-hour week, didn't stand a chance. Still, it was Poppy who had advised Sydney to try giving up alcohol to see if it had any effect on her cellulite. And Sydney thought it might have. She changed the subject. 'See how tired Helen's looking . . .'

Linda waved her hand dismissively as if she were attempting to swat a fly. As well she might, thought Sydney,

35

seeing that she had signally failed to mention that they all regularly stayed in the office until 9 p.m. when she'd courted Sydney for the agony aunt post.

'That tired look, as you put it, is just her wool rash,' said Linda blithely. 'She will insist on wearing bloody mohair every day in the winter. I think it's to make a point about not being able to afford cashmere. Jesus, as if any of us could at Helen's age.' She rolled her eyes, conveniently forgetting that Helen was only four years younger than she was. 'Anyway,' she continued, 'journalism's all about multi-tasking these days.' It certainly was on *IQ* where even Helen had another job commissioning the new food, gardening and health pages that Brian Widlake had ordained.

'To tell the truth, Helen's really not coping with the new regime as well as I'd expected,' Linda continued. She stood up to close the dusty Venetian blinds that lined her box. 'She keeps saying she needs to get a life.'

'She has been with you a long time.'

'Yes, but frankly it's probably the most exciting life Helen's going to lead. She's not exactly Miss Personality.'

The blinds came crashing to the floor in an asymmetric sweep, like a buckled accordion. Sydney kept quiet. She knew how much pride it had cost Linda to hire Poppy. When Brian Widlake had first suggested replacing *IQ*'s departing literary editor with Poppy, Linda's initial reaction had been scornful laughter. But a withering rant from Brian Widlake on just how close *IQ* was to being shut down and relaunched as a weekly celebrity handbook unless it pulled in some beauty and perfume advertising had made her realize it hadn't been a joke.

'At least I never make Helen fetch my drycleaning. Or make me a coffee unless she's making one for herself. Or do my photocopying.' This was true. Linda had always made a point of never asking her secretaries to do anything demeaning. On the other hand, she had a formidable track record for choosing secretaries who were quite happy to demean themselves. She sighed. 'Dave loathes Poppy . . .'

'You'd think Mick De Cadent being a hoary old rock legend, who once famously roasted a squirrel for breakfast while both were out of their respective trees, would have worked in Poppy's favour,' mused Sydney. 'But Dave is very hard to please.'

'It doesn't help that her mother was a deb. Annabelle isn't exactly bowled over by her either.'

'Poppy's work ethic is a bit unorthodox . . .' said Sydney, anxious now to defend Annabelle Parker from accusations of curmudgeonliness. The last thing Annabelle needed was trouble at work on top of the painful d.i.v.o.r.c.e (that no one was allowed to mention) which she was going through from her utterly irresponsible bastard of a husband who was refusing to pay any alimony to Annabelle and her nine-year-old twin boys. It wasn't easy though, because at present trouble in the office was the only reliable constant in Annabelle's painful existence. Some of the trouble, admittedly, was compounded by the fact that Annabelle was so broke, harassed and permanently red-eyed with worry about her twins that she had taken her eye completely off the ball at work. Not that anyone blamed her. It was so obvious that the husband she was d.i.v.o.r.c.i.n.g was a total shit that Sydney would have quite liked it if no one in the office discovered that he also happened to be her brother.

'It's all right,' said Linda, tugging on the blind cord, which came away in her hand. 'You don't need to defend Annabelle. You know I'd never get rid of her, even if her face is as long as the M1. We all go back too far.'

That was true at least. Annabelle had been managing

editor of *The Times Literary Supplement* and had loyally accompanied Linda to every new place of employment ever since. It was Sydney who had introduced her to Miles, when they'd all been working at the *Independent*. In those days Miles had been a thrusting young advertising executive with bags of promise, whereas now he was a middle-aged executive with a thrusting stomach and baggage. All in all, a stupendously successful piece of match-making that Sydney was still trying to live down.

'Miles still playing up then? I haven't dared ask.'

Now it was Sydney who glanced at the open door to check if anyone outside could hear. Linda followed her gaze.

'You don't honestly think the others don't realize you two are related?'

'Technically we're about to be unrelated any day,' said Sydney lamely. 'Just as soon as Miles has got round to signing the decree absolute.'

'Which he won't if it makes nailing him for money any easier.'

'I just thought it was better if we kept the whiff of nepotism out of all of this,' said Sydney, despising her own cowardliness. It was Dave's fault. He was so aggressive he made her jettison all her moral fibre every time she walked into the office.

'Right,' Linda grinned. 'As well as keeping your bank account out of it. I'm quite sure Dave has twigged that you're married to one of the country's most brilliant tax lawyers. If not, it doesn't say much for the powers of investigative journalism.'

Sydney glanced through the office window at Dave, *IQ*'s belligerent features editor, who came complete with formidable intelligence and a side serving of anger mismanagement. Most of the time his investigative talents were deployed on the computer, illegally downloading yet more hip-hop from ripandburn.com. She cringed to think of the lies she had told by omission – because the Miles thing wasn't the only occasion she'd been economical with the truth. She hadn't explicitly said she was teetering on the bread-line. But with the debatable exception of Linda, whose economic status reflected that of a journalist who'd won Best Magazine Editor, 1998, the staff of *IQ*, Newspaper Supplement of the Year, 1999, were all in various states of financial and emotional melt-down. So when they all moaned about their damp, grotty flats, disastrous love affairs, drug bills, clapped-out cars and mounting debts, it had seemed ostentatious not to roll her eyes conspiratorially and join in. And now it turned out that Dave had known she was a phoney all along.

Averting her gaze from Dave's Class War T-shirt, which seemed to be winking malevolently at her and her alone, Sydney walked back to her desk and adjusted the pile of magazines propping up one of its legs. She wondered if Dave wore a Savile Row suit on Fridays when she didn't come in. She knew he didn't understand why Linda had employed her any more than he could fathom Linda's reasons for putting up with Poppy. But the next time he made one of his snide comments about dilettante middle-class fuckwits, she would point out a few home truths. Or then again she might not.

She mulled over the reply she was still working on and stiffened the tone of it. Cruelty really could be kinder in the end. Or at least frankness could. Janie had to learn to live with her seven-year-old's untidiness and not waste money on a cognitive therapist, though she might like to invest in a cleaner. And Sarah had to stop rummaging through her husband's rubbish bins at work. She might also like to find herself a nice, sympathetic divorce lawyer while she still had some fight left in her . . . and Linda should get a grip on the Widlake situation. And Dave should be made aware that Sydney hadn't always been a dilettante middle-class fuckwit and that before Primrose Hill, when she was a child, she'd been brought up on less money than he spent on his Class War T-shirts.

Annabelle had promised not to say anything about Miles, the house in Primrose Hill or any of it. Which was sweet of her in the circumstances. Sydney checked over her finished response to Sarah and underlined the part about confronting her husband and demanding he come clean. Then she deleted the whole letter. It was hopeless. She was hopeless. She should never have taken the job as guardian of other people's souls in the first place. But Linda had told her no one else could do it as well. And when that didn't wash she'd told Sydney that the last batch of circulation figures had been slightly soft and that they were trying to freshen the magazine up a bit. That would be slightly soft as in freefall, as Sydney later discovered. But she could never refuse a friend in need, especially when she knew how much it cost Linda to admit that everything in her hitherto charmed existence wasn't going quite to plan.

Helen passed by with a plate of Snowy Doughy dough-nuts and offered one to Sydney. 'Go on. They've just sent in another crateload. In fact, have a packet for your desk. You look knackered,' she said, sympathy oozing from her mottled face. 'Would you like me to fetch you a proper cup of tea from the canteen? That machine's crap.'

Sydney shook her head. If she stopped for a break, she'd start thinking about herself and about Dylan and his motives. And she didn't want to think about Dylan at all, even though she knew that if she thought about him rationally she'd see that it was highly unlikely he had deliberately tracked her down. How could he have when they'd completely lost touch? The last time she'd read about him – eight years ago – he'd been preparing for his second expedition down the Andes and Sydney had been living in Maida Vale. His arrival in Clifton Crescent was just one of those amazing coincidences that didn't mean anything. She wasn't going to waste another second thinking about it, especially as Helen was waving at them all to come into Linda's box for a features meeting.

Had Dylan ever truly loved her?

It was impossible to decide. Especially during *IQ*'s weekly features meetings which were definitely a game of three halves. All of them bloody. The first half, where the previous week's issue was post-mortemed page by deathly page, felt a bit like being stoned to death while buried up to your neck in sewage. The second half, where everyone had to justify the pieces they were running in the next edition, was like being interviewed to get into Oxbridge by a panel of sadistic tutors, each intent on exposing everyone else's intellectual Achilles' heels while eyeing up female candidates' legs. The third half, where each member of the team outlined their big ideas for the magazine's future, was an exercise in insane optimism that ought to have been wildly entertaining but was increasingly desperate and depressing. Or, as Poppy put it, like having colonic irrigation, in that a lot of crap emerged, with only the very occasional illuminating nugget to keep the soul from despair.

Sydney went in armed with neat lists of ideas. And, like the others, she never wanted to be the first to speak.

She took her usual place in the back row of swivel chairs that were dragged into Linda's office. She'd grabbed another large cup of coffee – black this time. For once she was so grateful to have a distraction from her thoughts she didn't even feel sick with nerves about the features meeting. She felt sick with nerves about the Dylan meeting, which was destined to happen sooner or later.

'No you don't,' whispered Poppy, making a lunge for Sydney's coffee. 'You'll look like Sylvester Stallone's mother by Tuesday if you have all that. Are you still doing that non-alcohol plan?'

Sydney nodded obediently.

'Well, you must make sure you drink two litres of water a day as well.' Poppy handed Sydney a clear bottle of Japanese mountain snow with simulated dust particles on it. 'Try this. I'm testing it for my new Been There, Had That! slot.'

'Will you be including all the members of The Rolling Stones in that one?' asked Dave.

Poppy pretended not to hear. It was a talent upper-class girls were very good at, Sydney decided. Along with sleeping with The Rolling Stones.

'By the way, if you find Mick Jagger's teeth in your knickers, do let him know. I hear he's been having to live on mashed potato.'

'It's meant to be the purest water on the planet,' Poppy continued, addressing herself exclusively to Sydney. 'Jennifer Lopez is a huge fan.'

'Yet it comes from one of the most industrialized, polluted islands on the planet,' said Dave. 'Isn't that a fascinating paradox? You will be saying that in your copy, I daresay, Poppy. Rather than allowing the nice PR who whisked you off to Mount Fuji to dictate what you write.'

Poppy put on an enormous pair of Fendi sunglasses. 'Can

someone translate? Honestly, Dave, I don't have a clue what you're on about half the time.'

Now Sydney came to look at it closely, the snow did seem curiously grey for something so pure. She put the bottle down on the floor.

'Why is it that men are allowed to drone on endlessly about torque and wheel traction and it's considered a legitimate deployment of their brains, but if a woman dares to have an opinion about a mascara she's an airhead?' said Linda, who was damned if she was going to allow Dave to criticize her – even tacitly – for giving way to Brian Widlake on Poppy's appointment.

'While we're on that subject of masculine tripe,' said Annabelle, drawing heavily on her sixteenth cigarette of the day, 'what did anyone else think about the Ferrari piece last week?'

'Complete crap,' said Dave, who had been angling for the motoring column for himself, ever since Brian Widlake had first suggested it. He felt he would have been able to do a nice line in sardonic car deconstruction. But Linda hadn't even suggested him and he was damned if he was going to do anything as crass as put himself forward. So he'd done the next best thing and roundly denounced the whole idea.

'Only our esteemed motoring correspondent has just written off a Porsche and the PR's saying they'll never lend to us again.'

'Good,' said Linda. 'Let's run a piece on corporate black-mail.'

'Oh, for God's sake, Linda,' snapped Annabelle. 'You know why we can't do that.' There was an embarrassed silence while she and Linda exchanged sheepish glances. Sydney couldn't remember Annabelle ever criticizing Linda publicly before. Annabelle lit another cigarette. Sydney wished she wouldn't smoke quite so much. It couldn't be good for the twins. It was amazing she didn't get RSI from repeatedly striking all those matches.

Annabelle cleared her throat. 'What about the feature on American cultural imperialism?'

'Was that the one with the picture of Puff Daddy?' said Poppy.

'Martin Luther King, to his friends,' said Dave.

'Don't tell me he's changed his name again. I'm afraid I didn't get beyond the captions.' Poppy yawned, unfurling a pink-tipped tongue the colour of rosebuds. 'If you don't mind my saying so, Linda, aren't those the kind of features Brian wants less of?'

'First names, is it now?' Dave and Annabelle demanded simultaneously. Poppy rotated her ankles and admired her long, brown, bare legs.

'Moving swiftly on—' began Linda.

This was Dave's big moment. Sydney often thought that 2.45 p.m. on a Monday in Linda's office was where he came closest to experiencing true happiness. When he was in full flight, his shoulders hunched like an eagle's, his huge, bulgy forehead furrowed and dimpled like a relief map of the Orkney Islands, Sydney couldn't help but be impressed by his bullying intellectualism. He might be rough around the edges but he was passionate about the founding principles of *IQ*. Understandably so since he'd helped write them.

'Would you care to enlighten us as to whom you would like to read about then, Poppy?' he asked acidly.

'Someone more modern,' began Poppy, allowing Dave's venomous sarcasm to sail high above her angelic blonde head.

Dave stared round the room looking for backup. 'Normandie Keith?'

'God no. She's so over.' Poppy still hadn't forgiven her last boyfriend for lavishing praise on Normandie's legs. 'Anyway, she's not very us, is she? I know we're trying to go a bit more populist but that's no reason to sell all our beliefs down the river.'

'If we could continue,' said Linda. 'Poppy, what would you like to read?' she enquired in a bright, interested voice. She didn't want Poppy running off and complaining to Brian Widlake, with whom her relationship was clearly cosier than Linda had suspected, that the meetings were a closed shop.

'Lord, now you're asking,' sighed Poppy, seemingly amazed that anyone expected her to come to a features meeting with ideas. 'I just know what I don't want to read—'

'– words,' muttered Dave.

'The Haiku of the Week,' said Poppy. 'Talk about irrelevant.'

'The thing is—' Annabelle began in a wobbly voice, determined to make up for her earlier outburst.

'Your loss. I think you'd have found what last week's sixteenth-century haiku had to say about spin is very relevant to our times.'

'You need to get out more, Dave. Spin is last century. Issues have moved on since then,' said Poppy.

'Perhaps Poppy has a point. Brian Widlake is very keen for us to get more celebrities into the mix,' Annabelle reminded them.

There was a massed curling of lips around the room, apart from Poppy who was busy applying another coat of gloss to hers and pouting.

'Well, that's fine because next Saturday we've got a brilliant exclusive on a previously unpublished essay by William Hazlitt.'

45

Sydney's jaw hovered above the floor. Was Linda on a suicide mission?

'In that case, what about an article on SCUM?' Annabelle suggested mordantly. The others looked on encouragingly. Recently Annabelle hadn't been big on ideas. 'It stands for the Society for Cutting Up Men.'

'Where's the celebrity angle on that?' demanded Dave.

'I've thought of that,' said Annabelle. 'Vivienne Westwood used to borrow their slogans for her T-shirts.'

'Is William Hazlitt one of those National Theatre directors?' asked Poppy.

'A writer. Seventeen forty to eighteen twenty,' said Sydney. 'Linda, is that wise?'

Linda's brown eyes flashed defiantly. 'I am not going to be the editor who betrays everything this magazine stands for.'

'Gosh,' said Poppy, sounding awed. 'Seventeen forty. God, that's so—'

'Eighteenth century?' said Helen, her wool rash blotching spectacularly.

'Well, yes. Or should that be seventeenth century? I always get confused. But Dave, back on the spin front, it's bad news. No one cares about politicians any more. None of my friends bothered to vote in the last election. If you had a poem about Johnny Depp or Tobey Maguire you'd be much more on the money. You might actually pull some women readers in.'

'Right-oh. I'll just make a note of that.' Dave made an elaborate show of scribbling something down on a scrap of paper and an equally elaborate show of turning it into an aeroplane and gliding it towards Linda's bin. It landed next to Sydney's upended coffee cup. 'Actually,' he looked up triumphantly, 'I've had some encouraging emails this morning from Charlotte Rampling's people.'

The office looked at him expectantly. Dave's painstaking negotiations with some of the most difficult French PRs in the world – all done with a means to him interviewing and ultimately seducing the woman who for him embodied total perfection – had been going on for so long they were legendary throughout the thirteen floors of Icon Towers.

'They've said yes,' he crowed.

'That's fantastic,' said Poppy, generously in the circumstances.

'Fabulous,' exclaimed Annabelle, who revered any actresses who smoked.

'There might just have to be a tiny bit about euthanasia,' said Dave.

'How tiny a bit?' asked Sydney.

'She wants to dictate the piece herself and she wants it to be mainly on that subject and no other. It's very close to her heart and she's passionate about it. But I'm sure I'll be able to get a bit more out of her if I go to see her in person.'

'Oh, for God's sake,' expostulated Annabelle, who even in her befuddled state could see that fifteen hundred words on self-imposed exits hardly fitted Brian Widlake's definition of life-enhancing articles.

'Actually I quite like the idea,' said Linda.

'That's settled then,' beamed Dave.

'The editor-in-chief is also very keen for us to modify the gardening section.' Annabelle's voice quivered dangerously this time. She lit another cigarette from the ash of the one dangling from her lower lip. 'He's not convinced the article on recycling your toilet waste was glamorous enough.'

'Stella McCartney does it,' said Helen defensively.

Dave sniggered.

'Who do *you* suggest then?' Linda asked him coldly.

'Germaine Greer.' As someone who had regularly gone

out and bought his ex-girlfriend's Lillets on numerous occasions – and gone back to change them when she'd decided to go organic – Dave felt his feminist credentials were unimpeachable. It wasn't the feminization of *IQ* that he resented – he knew the pressure Linda was under lately to get more advertising in, and as far as the advertising department went, that meant pulling in more women readers to attract the advertisers. And even though he despised the fact that *IQ* had to sell ads at all, he revered Linda, secretly at least, and always had done, ever since she'd hired him right at the beginning of her reign at *IQ*. No, what really got him was the suspicion that she was increasingly confiding her problems to Sydney instead of him.

'Not that feminist who refuses to dye her hair?' said Poppy. 'Feminism is so passé. What we need, Linda, is articles on how to keep a man with underwear.'

'And how would that be?' Dave sounded outraged. 'By tying him down with your suspenders?'

'By not pretending that pleasing your man is a sin. As for the gardening column, what about Kim Wilde?'

'Tell you what,' said Dave acidly, 'why don't I see if Keira Knightley's taken up composting? In the meantime, how about you writing a ten thousand-word piece on why mascara is the new lipstick?'

A flicker of irritation rumpled Poppy's normally beatific features. 'That,' she said pityingly, 'would be plain silly.'

Linda was livid at being publicly contradicted by Dave, whom she relied on to back her up at all times. She made a note to get him to commission some more articles on why men were becoming increasingly impotent, bald, fat, lonely and depressed. Then, to cheer them all up, Annabelle asked if any nice freebies had arrived in the office recently.

'Two tickets for the opening night of the Kurdistan

Women's Film Festival,' offered Dave, who'd already pocketed every decent CD that had come into the office during the last week.

'Off the top of my head, five pairs of marabou-trimmed handcuffs and matching manicure sets – good for all those ladies wanting to pep up their marriages.' Poppy threw a meaningful look in Sydney's direction. 'Three pots of Crème de la Mer worth two thousand four hundred and something pounds – I know a great shop where you can unload them by the way; a weekend in Kyoto to see how they researched a new Kanebo triple ozone and cellular molecular facial – or something like that – and a trip to Venice to test out the new depilatory cream from Smoothie,' said Poppy. 'Oh, and a diamond nail file.'

'I'd love those,' gushed Sydney. 'The tickets to the Kurdistan Women's film festival, I mean.' She was still stinging from the week before when Dave had accused her of being the kind of person who only ever went to the cinema when there was a Richard Curtis film on. He'd made liking Richard Curtis sound almost as morally questionable as blowing up baby seals.

Dave made an exaggerated show of being shocked. 'Are you sure, Sydney? There's nothing in the festival about Notting Hill,' he said. 'Or hats. Or weddings.'

Sydney smiled graciously. It would be a good excuse for her and Charlie to go out alone together, and something profound and potentially soporific sounded right up his alley. 'That will be just perfect,' she said. 'So long as they're not dubbed. I do like to be able to hear the original dialogue.'

Trying as the features meeting had been, at least it had distracted Sydney from the whole Dylan Situation. And she

49

couldn't pretend to herself that there wasn't a Dylan Situation.

It was absolutely typical of his behaviour that just as she'd got her life more or less worked out, Dylan Glendower had parachuted in. Literally, she wouldn't be surprised, knowing his penchant for making an entrance. Sydney discouraged paranoia in herself – Mrs Protheroe had enough for the whole of Primrose Hill – but Dylan Glendower was an explorer of some repute who, it was to be assumed, knew how to work a compass and read a map. Whatever other factors might have determined his arrival in Clifton Crescent, coincidence wasn't among them.

She should never have gone back to work. This was some kind of retribution, in the same way that Dave was. She should have known it had all gone too smoothly. Charlie had taken the job more or less on the chin, especially when Sydney had explained that it really was quite a junior job – nowhere near as demanding as her responsibilities on the *Indie* had been. At first he'd been amazingly cooperative. Especially when Sydney had pulled her masterstroke by persuading Charlie that Maisie Egghorn, a jury manager he had known for years and who, at fifty-five, was looking for a new direction after twenty-eight years of working with the stroppy and the criminal, would be perfect to look after the girls when Sydney was at work.

It had all been too good to be true. That's why Dylan appeared out of the blue. To teach her not to be so greedy. It would all end in tears. Just as it had last time.

3

When Dylan Glendower had dived on top of Sydney nineteen years earlier, she had been immensely flattered. Not that she was falsely modest. In those days she had confidence in her looks, in her long, saffron-coloured hair and even longer legs. That had been pre-pregnancy, pre-learning to cook, pre-comfy nights on the sofa. But she still didn't have the confidence of the upper-class boys who swept into the city as if they owned it – which some of them probably did. Dylan swaggered, as if he could barely wait to see what life was going to offer him next. Sydney, on the other hand, felt hunched, and permanently braced for assault.

Going to university so young – she was barely seventeen – had probably been a mistake in retrospect. But she'd needed to get away from the pain of seeing her beautiful, vibrant mother slowly fade away. And there had been so many like-minded people that she had been almost shamefully distracted from her mother's illness.

Stevie, whom Sydney met during Freshers' Week by the vegetarian stall, was not one of them. But she had taken one look at Sydney, in her secondhand floral Fifties skirt (borrowed from her mother), and made a beeline for her. 'Anyone wearing one of those things must be neo-something,' she'd remarked.

In retrospect Sydney and Stalinist Stevie, as she became

known, didn't have much in common. By the second week of term, when they found themselves alone in a rowing boat, conversation had become so stilted that having a bronzed, ridiculously irresponsible third-year geography student leap off the bridge and narrowly miss their boat had constituted light relief, for Sydney at least.

'Piss off, wanker,' Stevie snarled at the blond stranger splashing around in the freezing water.

Dylan had grinned, his blue eyes sparkling in the October sunshine. To Stevie's chagrin he'd front-crawled towards them faster than Stevie had managed to row away into the bank. He leant his elbows on the side of the boat and gazed up at them both earnestly. 'I am a wanker, it's true. Take pity on a poor, humble male and lead him from self-abuse into healthy heterosexual copulation.'

Stevie was not impressed. 'Fucking public-school dickhead!' She grabbed the oars and began stabbing at the pondweed which seemed on the point of devouring their boat.

Dylan raised his arm, the water glistening on its fine hairs like liquid mercury. 'Correct again, *mademoiselle*. But you could save me from myself.'

'Are you all right?' called Sydney, leaning over the boat and watching his blond curls shine in the dappled light.

'Never better.' He grinned. 'Are you though?' He squinted in the sun at Stevie. 'Looks like Ophelia's got her oars in a twist.'

'We can manage quite well by ourselves, thanks for absofuckinglutely nothing,' said Stevie.

Dylan threw back his head and laughed. He disappeared under the water and emerged the other side of the boat. He stood up. He looked enormously tall to Sydney – at least six foot four. The water barely came up to his chest. 'I should think you can. But I'll give you a helping hand.' He pulled back some weeds that had become entangled in the oar rests and pushed them towards the current. 'There you go, me hearties.' He tugged his forelock, grinning.

'Arsehole,' hissed Stevie.

'Actually, the name's Dylan. It means god of the sea.' He grinned again, revealing two rows of remarkably even, white teeth.

'Are you sure you're okay?' Sydney watched him recede. 'You'd better get out or you'll get hypothermia.'

'I'm fine,' he beamed, waving back at her. 'Although I think I may have fatally wounded my bottom lip. You couldn't give me some mouth-to-mouth later? Around eight, say? Ninety-three Royal York Crescent?'

Sydney hadn't given him mouth-to-mouth. Not immediately. But she had taken him some carrot cake and a packet of frozen peas for his swollen lip. Which had culminated in some quite stupendous sex that had rolled seamlessly from night into day and back into night again.

Even now, nineteen years later, her stomach filled with butterflies when she thought of it and she felt the familiar tingling between her thighs.

He'd been very sweet, but persistent. And he'd made her laugh, especially when he'd pressed the bag of peas against his bottom lip which, now Sydney came to look, did seem a bit swollen.

He lay propped up on a whitish chaise longue that was pushed up against an enormous sash window. If you ignored the entrails of horsehair dangling out of the bottom of the chaise longue, and the torn clingfilm stretched across the windows, it was an exceptionally elegant setting for a student flat.

'Come and sit here and read some of your Austen to me.'
He patted the end of the chaise invitingly and swept an arm theatrically across his brow, his white cuffs dangling over his cheeks. He began to moan softly. Sydney pulled a cuff to one side in alarm.

He sat up and grinned. 'Do I look like Shelley?'

Sydney seized the chance to survey the curved mouth, fierce blue eyes and the bushy eyebrows that unexpectedly swept up towards the east. 'As in Percy Bysshe Shelley, or Shelley Winters?'

'*Touché!*'

Sydney perched daintily on the end of the chaise longue again and began reading from the copy of *Sense and Sensibility* she had in her basket. '"The family of Dashwood had been long settled in Sussex,"' she began, trying not to blush as she felt Dylan's eyes slither up and down her like serpents. He smelled of sherbet and pine. She saw a bag of sweets under the chaise longue.

'That's a divine skirt you have on, Miss Parker. How many thousands of layers does it have?'

She ignored him. '"By a former marriage Mr Henry Dashwood had one son; by his present lady, three daughters. The son, a steady, respectable young man—"'

Dylan winced.

'What's the matter? Are you in pain?' asked Sydney. He pulled his knees up to his chest and groaned.

'Where?' she asked, panicking.

He grunted incoherently. Sydney stood up and began searching for a phone. 'Should I get a doctor?'

'No,' he panted. 'I'll be all right in a minute. Please, continue. Really.'

Nervously she sat down and picked up the book. '"No

sooner was his father's funeral over than Mrs John Dashwood, without sending any notice of her intention—"'

'God, you're pretty.' He leant back on his elbow and ran his eyes over her again.

'And you're injured, supposedly. Kindly keep quiet and let me read. Where was I? Oh yes. "Mrs John Dashwood had never been a favourite with any of her husband's family . . ."'

'Christ.' His face twisted. 'On reflection it really is agony.'

'What is it?' She placed the book down on her knees and folded her arms, aware that he was teasing her now.

'That prose. It's interminable. *Sense and Sensibility* by Jane Bloody Austen. They ought to call it *Senseless and Insensible*.'

'Shut up and let me at least get to Chapter Two.'

'Chapter Two? You mean we're not at the end yet? Jesus, it's even more bloody boring than Thomas I'm-dying-of-tedium Hardy. You know, I thought Hardy was way out in the premier league of dullsville, pointless, girly narratives, but this woman wins hands down. She's even more boring than Emily Brontë and Shakespeare.' He paused. 'I know this is hard to believe, but she's even worse than Milton.'

'Right.' Sydney stood up, placed her book in her basket and strode towards the door. 'No point in me torturing you any more.' She began to bounce down the stairs but he was at the bottom before her.

'I thought you were on your deathbed.'

'I was, but you cured me. It's a miracle.' As he raised his arms theatrically, his sleeves flapped about his face. Momentarily he really did look like a tortured Romantic poet. 'Please come back and read to me so I can ogle your beautiful lips again.'

'I really don't think you're my type.'
He bent down on one knee on the pavement in front of her.

'And wilt thou leave me thus?
Say nay, say nay, for shame,
To save me from the blame
Of all my grief and game.
And wilt thou leave me thus?
Say nay, say nay.'

She was lost – and willingly – from that moment. The man could recite poetry. All his literary philistinism was a front. 'Only if you promise not to interrupt again,' she said sternly. 'Cross my heart.'

She followed him back upstairs, knowing she probably wouldn't be leaving until the morning. He cooked her boiled eggs and soldiers which seemed to test his culinary skills to the limit, toasted her skirt with a quite good burgundy – not that she knew anything about wine in those days – and wanted to know everything about her. He even seemed to listen to most of it. Then he told her a bit about his elderly parents, their lovely old house in Wales, and the publishing company which he hoped to take over one day – after a stint as a world-famous explorer. 'Really I should be applying to the City like everyone else and making a killing,' he said ruefully. 'But the smell of books, the roar of the printworks – ah yes, a little learning is a dangerous thing. "Drink deep, or taste not the Pierian spring."'

'You bloody fraud,' she said, hitting him with her Bristol Cathedral bookmark. He grabbed it from her. She was so relieved that this man she found physically irresistible seemed to like the same things she did. 'You love literature.'

'Doesn't go down well with females weirdly. Honestly,

until I began pretending to be a thug I almost never got laid.' He handed her a sprig of parsley. 'For my lady. *In loco floris*.' Their hands touched and she felt her stomach lurch. 'Now you know my secret, come and read to me some more.'

She didn't even finish Chapter One before he pulled her towards him, ostensibly so that she could extract a lash that had become embedded in his eye. And when she got that close to him it had seemed pointless not to take his cue and plant a kiss on his lips, just to show she was in control. Before she knew it she had unbuttoned the rest of his shirt. She felt him wrap his legs around her. He pulled off her lemon sweater, expertly undid her bra and told her that it wasn't just her lips that were beautiful. And then his hands seemed to be in four places at once. She could feel an enormous bulge through the layers of her skirts and decided it was only courteous to address its needs. She slipped her hands down his smooth, taut stomach, stroking the hairs that sprang over the top of his trousers and working her way lower until she felt something warm and slippery. It was the packet of rapidly defrosting peas.

'Now take off that bloody skirt,' he whispered, tugging at the zip. 'My beautiful Seren.' She raised an appalled eyebrow.

'Don't worry, I haven't forgotten your name,' he said softly. 'It's Welsh for star.'

There were no blinds but Sydney couldn't have cared less as he rolled the peas over her body, pale as the moon, and she kissed his small pink nipples and pulled off his trousers. She kissed him again. He pulled her towards him again and began kissing her now, licking her breasts and pushing into her stomach. With one hand he stroked her hair and with the other he gently prised open her legs. The sardonic smile had vanished. He was inside her and moaning – this time genuinely, she knew that. She also knew that she was hooked. They were inseparable for one delirious, heady year. Stevie stopped talking to her, but Dylan's extended circle of friends, admirers and hangers-on meant Sydney was hardly deprived of company. She loved the dichotomy of Dylan: his love of literature and his lusty adoration of the physical. And then, as lightly as it had begun, it ended. Catching Dylan in bed with the tall blonde girl from the Architecture Faculty was no big deal. It merely confirmed what she already knew: Dylan was lovable and lethal. Sydney had willed herself to fall out of love with him. They broke up more or less amicably, Sydney's heart more or less intact. At least, that was how Sydney chose to remember it now.

Then, to everyone's astonishment, she'd dropped out, gone to teach English in Milan, sometimes taking time out at weekends to traipse the art galleries of Florence or Venice on her own. When she returned to Bristol two years later to resume her studies, Dylan was a distant memory. Her old friends had left. Her only tangible connection with him was a bottle of Shalimar he'd given her on the six-month anniversary of their meeting.

Sydney threw herself into her course work, emerged with a good degree and, just when she was wondering what to do with a 2.1 in English and Italian, Linda, her oldest friend from school, had called to say that *The Times Literary Supplement* needed someone to review a new biography of F.R. Leavis. It was just a small piece; the cheque was barely worth cashing.

'I've never written anything for publication before,' said Sydney nervously. The idea of working with Linda on anything seemed intoxicating.

'You've got great tits and you wear fab secondhand clothes. The editor will love you.'

Linda had exaggerated only slightly. The editor of *The TLS* was barely aware of her existence. But Annabelle and Linda loved Sydney and she loved them, especially when they gave her more and more books to review and, eventually, a job. And it helped to be with Linda – irreverent and sharp, but the one person who had known Sydney and her family for years and could comfort Sydney through her mother's cancer.

Sydney never told Charlie about the relationship with Dylan. No point, even though she had a little fun living vicariously through Dylan's geographical conquests, which were haphazardly documented in the press. She'd heard about his endless romances, near-marital escapades and full-on affairs with married women through mutual friends, and then friends of friends, until gradually she'd put him out of her mind altogether.

Which was exactly where she liked him.

4

A couple of days later Linda summoned her into her office again. 'Guess what?' she said, her eyes shining with an ominous fire. 'I've finally found a site that looks as though it really could come up with the goods.'

Sydney's heart sank. At the age of thirty-seven Linda had achieved everything she ever wanted. But at thirty-eight she'd woken up one morning to find that the priorities she'd drawn up at eighteen had shifted.

'How do you know this one's any different from the others?' Sydney asked in a sombre voice.

'Because it's got a stack of testimonials, and I've checked up on at least six of them,' said Linda. 'And it's in Romania so they won't have all those chippy preconceptions about me being middle-class and white.'

'And single. And a workaholic,' Sydney reminded her. It ill behove her to be cynical about anyone's longings for a baby, even Linda's, but someone had to be. 'How much?' she added.

'Twelve thousand up front. The other twelve on delivery.'

'Are you sure this is a good idea?'

'They're very reputable,' said Linda. 'You should see all the paperwork you have to fill out.'

'That's not really the point,' said Sydney. The point was whether Linda was in any position to look after a child – which Sydney doubted.

Sensing dissent, Linda changed the subject to one close to Sydney's heart. 'How about a late lunch?'

Against her better judgement and mainly to distract Linda from her woes, Sydney told her about feeling ignored by Charlie, and about Mrs Protheroe telling her to join Weightwatchers.

Linda listened intently. Or at least she appeared to. Then she told Sydney what she always told her, which was that Charlie was perfect. 'And now, with Dylan, that's two blokes you've got round your finger.'

'I don't want Dylan round my finger,' said Sydney, eyeing a criminally insubstantial salad, which arrived with a very fattening smothering of Roquefort dressing.

'I see. The love of your life suddenly appears back in your life after God knows how long and you're telling me it's of no interest. Sydney, this is me you're talking to. Look, if you want my advice, the main thing is that under no circumstances – none at all, do you understand? – do you give Dylan any excuse to zoom you again. That means no dinners, no suppers, no socializing whatsoever. I take it you never got round to telling Charlie what happened with him?'

Sydney shook her head. She hadn't really got round to telling Linda either.

'Right. So are you receiving me loud and clear?'

Sydney gave her a salute. 'Loud and very clear.'

It was almost six when Charlie called. He'd never called her at *IQ* before – as if that would somehow nullify the existence of her job. At first, as he went into laborious details about how he'd popped home at lunchtime to pick up his coat, which he'd forgotten again, she couldn't think why he was calling now. She remembered about the Kurdistan

61

Women's Film Festival and, as she'd hoped, he was sufficiently intrigued to want to see it. Which was just as well, because she'd already booked Maisie to babysit. Then, in a voice that suggested he too was capable of enhancing their rich social life, he told her about meeting their new neighbour. 'The poor thing had just been told the electricity has short-circuited. Apparently it happened last week, too.' He chuckled.

Sydney's heart did a triple flip. Then she reminded herself that Charlie never invited people round if he could possibly avoid it. In the background she could hear Dave arguing over the phone with his bank manager. On the other end of the line, Charlie was telling her that he'd asked Dylan and Eloise over for dinner on Thursday.

Having been unable to stop brooding over the forthcoming dinner, Sydney was still undecided on Thursday afternoon about whether to do a kitchen supper or dinner in the dining room. The question was rhetorical since there was no one in the office to answer with any authority whatsoever. She couldn't possibly go back to Linda after what she'd said and admit that Dylan was coming round to dinner after less than two weeks in the neighbourhood. In any case, the dining room had been turned into a playroom ages ago. Even with a staple gun, she wasn't sure a month was long enough to turn it back and get rid of the Wendy house, Homer's bleak and empty hamster cage, Nellie's old cat basket, a pile of board games with half the counters missing, and piles of law books that Charlie didn't have room for in his study.

Not that it was an entirely irrelevant query. Kitchen suppers were chic, metropolitan and involved less washing-up. On the other hand, they might foster a relaxed intimacy Sydney felt it would be foolhardy to encourage. She didn't want Eloise and Dylan thinking they could pop round anytime.

She looked up guiltily to find Linda hovering by her desk with a pile of CVs. 'These candidates are all hopeless.'

'That's because they're not Helen.' Sydney buried her head back in the reply she was working on to a Richard in Sidcup who had become something of a regular correspondent. He hated his job. He hated his girlfriend. He hated his life. And just recently he'd been experiencing a recurrent fantasy about handing his keys back to the mortgage company and becoming a surfer in Belize. Where did Patience suggest he start?

'I know that,' snapped Linda. Sydney buried herself in Richard's plight. She knew Linda was angling for her to stay late and discuss Helen's replacement, but with two and a half hours until she saw Dylan Glendower for the first time in nearly eighteen years, she couldn't afford to get distracted.

'She probably won't go anyway.' Linda held up a battered CV between her thumb and finger and looked disparagingly at the nail-varnish stains spattered across one corner of it. 'Not when the crunch comes. She doesn't really want a life.'

Sydney wished Linda would occasionally take someone else's problems seriously. It was true that in comparison with Juanita or Mrs Protheroe, Sydney and Helen didn't know they were born. But sometimes – not often enough for it to be a habit, she'd make sure of that – she would have liked to have someone she could complain to. Sydney finished off her response to Richard by reminding him that being a beach bum wasn't all it was cracked up to be. Especially when you were forty-five. Fearing that might sound ageist, she added that he could always try one of the surf courses in Cornwall to see if he actually had an aptitude for beach bumdom before taking the drastic measure of emigrating to Belize. She read it through one last time and emailed the finished reply to the subs.

Then, ignoring Dave's curled lip and Linda's outraged eyebrows, she cleared her desk and made her way to the lift. She'd barely got past the mezzanine floor when her mobile went. It was Linda, begging her to hang on for a drink so that they could talk some more about the adoption website and the Helen applicants.

'Next week,' said Sydney firmly.

'What's the hurry?' asked Linda, sounding suspicious. Sydney didn't know whether to weep, or learn from Linda's self-absorption. She joined the throng of secretaries leaving the building.

'Don't tell me you invited him to dinner?'

Sydney didn't reply.

'For God's sake, Sydney. Are you completely insane?'

'Charlie invited them,' snapped Sydney. 'And it's no big deal.'

'Well, why are you making such a big deal out of it then?'

'Because that's the only way to look as though you're not making a huge deal,' said Sydney, wondering why everyone was being so irritating. Chic simple was always a bloody huge effort, especially when it came to food. But of course Linda couldn't be expected to know that. The last time she'd been in her kitchen was to put some nail varnish into the fridge.

'Are you worried that you might have aged a bit?' asked Linda sympathetically. 'He's bound to have put on weight by the way. Those athletic types always do. I read somewhere he hasn't been on an expedition for at least five years.'

Sydney dodged a puddle. 'Don't be so superficial.'

'Because you look great, you know. For an old hippy.'

'My hair needs a trim.'

'Well, see if that hairdresser of Poppy's can slip you in.'

'At six-fifteen?'

'Since you're so obviously not at all bothered about appearances, I offer the next piece of counsel with some trepidation.' Linda paused tantalizingly. 'In my view you'd be a fool not to wear that mauve velvet empire-line dress. It's a knockout and your tits look incredible in it.'

'I haven't got time to change,' said Sydney, wondering which dress Linda meant.

'Look, I know you're petrified that you might still fancy Dylan. And even more petrified he won't still fancy you. But you have an indestructible marriage. Because one, you're congenitally incapable of being unfaithful. Two, you've got loyal wife embedded in your DNA.'

'That's the same reason expressed differently.'

'Anyway, if it's any consolation, I'm sure Dylan will still secretly fancy you.'

'Oh, grow up. Jesus, I can't do this, Linda. I haven't had a drink for three weeks.'

A taxi sped past, adding an interesting mud-and-rotting-leaves patina to Sydney's tights. She switched off her mobile. Linda was right. She could never be unfaithful. The very idea of undressing in front of another man appalled her. Besides, it was morally unimaginable. She simply wanted to make sure that the four of them got on well enough for there not to be any embarrassing silences, that was all. She certainly wouldn't be wearing that velvet dress.

She finally flagged down a cab and began compiling a shopping list.

The beaming Adonis standing behind several miles of gleaming stainless steel in Selfridges' Food Hall told her the monkfish stuffed with ginger, masses of out of season asparagus, some rustic-looking salads, half a dozen cheeses, a delicious pear and apple Tarte Tatin, and several bottles of New Zealand Chablis were the perfect idiot-proof dinner party. Authentic peasant fare, he called it. Then he asked her for £280. Sydney blinked in the blinding glare of his starched white overall which, until this moment, she had found strangely comforting, and considered telling him that it was more of a kitchen supper than dinner. Hypnotized, she handed over the money and went upstairs to the fashion department.

Perhaps she should have invited Ian and Miranda Plympton over as well. Then she and Charlie might have stood a chance of looking fascinating by comparison. A beautiful embroidered Dries van Noten dress winked seductively at her as the escalator whisked her towards the first floor. 'Come on over,' it seemed to be saying. 'You never know, I might fit you.'

Back on the down escalator twenty minutes later, Sydney mused that you always did know, in your heart of hearts. Itching to spend her way out of the looming nightmare, her gaze alighted on three huge white serving bowls placed becomingly in an alcove. A discreet sign next to them informed her that they were part of the Nicole Farhi Homeware collection on the fourth floor. She duly got off the down escalator and turned round to mount the up one.

The twinkly Dries van Noten might well have fitted her, she thought, as she handed over her credit card for three of the white bowls. But she had run out of time trying to work out how to get it on.

'How are we doing in there?' the sales manager had asked brightly after Sydney had been in the changing room for ten minutes.

66

'It's not really what I imagined,' said Sydney, surveying her puce reflection and skew-whiff bra. The Dries hung in festoons, from her waist down to her knees. She couldn't tell what were meant to be sleeves, what were yet more layers, and what was quite possibly some plastic wrapping. There was no way she was going to get the top part of the dress on. Or the bottom quarter off.

'I've never had to resort to scissors yet,' said the sales executive quarter of an hour later. Her opalescent lipstick had taken on a lurid glow in the sweaty light of the confined changing room. 'Funny how deceptive women's bodies can be. You honestly didn't look as though you needed the bigger size.' They worked on in silence. 'Oh look, you've still got the tissue paper in one sleeve.' The sales manager's tinkly laugh froze as the security tag which had become wedged in Sydney's tights went off.

Sydney signed the credit slip for the bowls, as if the act of spending more money could expunge her mortification on the fashion floor. She'd just spent £360 on three bowls that would have cost £8 in IKEA. Seeing her pallor, the manager asked if she'd like them gift-wrapped and told her they would transform her dining table into a modern shrine to authentic peasant simplicity.

She wouldn't have had to make the Selfridges detour if internet supermarket shopping wasn't so bloody unreliable. Yesterday, instead of three loaves of organic sourdough, they'd brought her six small loaves of Mother's Pride. Instead of eight Aberdeen Angus fillet steaks they'd left four cook-in-the-bag lo-cal curries. Charlie had smiled in a saintly fashion and then spoiled it by saying she wouldn't be shopping on the internet if she didn't have a job.

In the taxi home, she looked at the receipts in disbelief.

What with the miserly salary *IQ* paid her, and tax, and Maisie's wages, and the Nicole Farhi dishes, she was actually in a £400 negative equity situation. She peeped into the largest carrier bag. The dishes were very nice, and they probably weren't quite like the ones in IKEA. She stuffed the receipts into an ashtray. Charlie must never know.

Fortunately, not being overly acquainted with the more banal activities of everyday life, he still thought you could feed a family of four on £12 a week, which is what he and his three flatmates had spent on food at university. Sydney was sorely tempted to offer Charlie up for anthropological study, because it sometimes seemed as though he'd never been shopping in his life. On the – very – rare occasion Sydney ever asked him to bring back a pint of milk on the way home, he'd profess amazement that it had cost more than 9 pence. He was constantly ambushed by the price of everything, which for a tax lawyer was something of an achievement. But it did mean he never, ever looked at their bank statements.

She sank back in the taxi seat as it crawled through the so-called rush hour back to Primrose Hill. Lists. She needed to make a list of topics, just in case the conversation span off in any awkward directions. Which it might very well do. They couldn't discuss work because then she'd have to tell yet more lies about what she did. They couldn't discuss the past because that would alienate Eloise and Charlie. Politics were off the agenda because judging from Eloise's performance earlier on, she probably thought Disraeli was still in power. And they couldn't discuss Primrose Hill because Eloise had made it perfectly clear what she thought should be done with people like Mrs Protheroe and Juanita, and if she vented her to-the-right-of-Hitler views in front of Charlie he might blow a gasket.

It was ominously quiet when Sydney walked into the house. Juanita had been, so the impending tidal wave of chaos caused by Molly's, Harriet's – and, most catastrophically, Charlie's – chronic untidiness had been temporarily stemmed, albeit superficially. Sunny colours glowed softly in the lamplight which threw shadows on the bookcases, making nooks and interesting-looking crannies, even if half the books were Charlie's law tomes and guaranteed to send the average reader into a coma.

Sydney dropped her bags in the hall and breathed in the scent from the lilies she'd bought in Selfridges, waiting for that inevitable middle note of Glade to kick in. Sure enough, three empty cans of the stuff – enough for Juanita to leave her mark in the sitting room – were lined up on the sparkling kitchen table, a 3D semaphore from Juanita who, though she used to pen Sydney what she called POLITE REQUESTS, now seemed to feel that writing notes was beneath her. Sydney crept into the kitchen, anxious to get the dinner organized before she sought out her daughters.

There was no doubt about it, she decided as she arranged the monkfish in the largest of the new Nicole Farhi bowls where, as promised by Selfridges, it did look extremely professional, Juanita had won the day over Glade, as she had with most household issues. When she had started her job, Sydney had tried to explain the family policy – hers and Harriet's at least – on aerosols. Juanita had elected not to hear, and then, when Sydney had repeated herself several times and given her some leaflets to read on the ozone layer, not to understand. Even when Sydney had shown her where she kept the beeswax.

Not even the posters Harriet had stuck up in the broom cupboard depicting various environmental doomsday scenarios had made any impact. To an extent, Sydney sympathized. She could see that when you had six brothers and sisters to feed back home, the ozone could piss off. But she wished Juanita could sometimes meet them at least halfway by using vinegar instead of Mr Muscle to wipe down the taps.

She put the fish into the fridge. She still hadn't heard a peep, which could only mean that Maisie had decided to let Harriet off her homework again.

She went up to Charlie's study, strictly out of bounds to the rest of the family and particularly Hamish, partly because of its hazardous wiring – Charlie was like a freak force-field of nature, guaranteed to stall all watches, clocks and satellite dishes – to find all of them, Maisie, Harriet, Molly and Hamish, curled up on Charlie's sofa watching *EastEnders* with three empty tubs of Kentucky Fried Chicken and a pile of Charlie's broken laptops. Molly was wearing her curate's costume again – which was probably taking her religious kick too far, but Sydney let it pass. Maisie stroked Hamish's head and flicked her eyes away from the screen momentarily. 'Look, here's Mum, girls.' The girls waved without averting their eyes. Maisie bustled out of the room.

The advantage of having Maisie as their part-time nanny, Sydney thought as she returned to the kitchen to arrange the salads in the other two Nicole Farhi bowls and rinse the asparagus – though at that price it should have come with its own well of purified Japanese spring water – was that she was available. The disadvantage – for argument's sake – was that she didn't appear to be familiar with any of the conventional milestones in a nanny's working day, including bedtimes, homework, home cooking, and what the small ads in *The Lady* mysteriously referred to as nursery duties. Sometimes Sydney wondered whether Charlie's ready agreement to her prominent role in their family wasn't his revenge on her job situation. He must have known what Maisie was really like when Sydney had proposed hiring her. Not that Charlie would ever deliberately sabotage his own children's welfare. But subliminally – you never knew. Still, she was not going to let him know that Maisie was getting to her. It would only encourage him.

'I'll be off then, if that's okay,' Maisie called from the front door. Her coat, which had more buttons than the dashboard of a 747, was done up to the top, suggesting that she was off even if it wasn't okay. Sydney switched the oven on. It must be 8.30 if *EastEnders* was already over. And naturally the girls wouldn't be ready for bed in any sense of the phrase.

'You're still okay to babysit tomorrow?' Sydney poked her head round the door and attempted a smile. With all the anxiety of tonight's supper she'd almost forgotten that she and Charlie would be going to the first night of the Kurdistan Women's Film Festival.

Maisie picked up her two Tesco bags as if girding herself for battle. 'Oh Sydney, love, I forgot to say tomorrow's my night at the hospital. I can't let them down. I've left a Post-It with some ideas for after-school snacks. We're clean out of cheesy twisters.'

'I thought you didn't do Fridays.' Maisie's contractual obligations to the local hospital radio station, where an adoring if admittedly captive audience waited with bated breath for two hours of *Maisie's Mellow Moments* twice a week – but not Friday – had been spelt out very clearly to Sydney from the beginning.

'Nancy called in sick,' said Maisie in a voice that suggested Nancy should never have been given her own slot in the first place. 'Hungover, more like. I warned them about her benders.' She rattled her keys ominously. 'I've told the girls to get ready for bed,' she added, in the virtuous tones of

Ingrid Bergman serenading seventy Chinese orphans out of the wilderness.

'She did enjoy the little play today,' Maisie continued fondly. 'Oh, and Harriet's been cast in the Nativity.'

The curate. A few months ago it would have been the focus of Sydney's day. A few months ago she'd have been frantically busy keeping herself occupied, running errands for Charlie, waiting for the dishwasher repair man or the electrician or the delivery from the Law Society to turn up, all incapable of giving any more precise clues as to their estimated times of arrival than 'sometime in the morning', and cooking elaborate, Fair Trade meals for the children when they clearly much preferred KFC. Tiring herself out trying to maintain an atmosphere of calm and comfort when all the time, inside, she was stoking a furnace of frustration and disappointment. But she would have remembered the curate.

Upstairs Harriet and Molly showed no signs of going to bed. Harriet was busy reading what looked like a letter and Molly was still in the curate's outfit.

'Harriet's been forging letters,' Molly said indignantly. 'She typed it on Dad's computer.'

'What's it about this time?' Sydney looked at Harriet sternly. Harriet returned the stare and turned away from her mother with a rustle. A letter fluttered out from under her tunic. It was to Miss Cavendish, Harriet's teacher, excusing her, in implausible spelling, from the following day's trip to the zoo. Sydney suppressed a smile. She pretty much endorsed Harriet's views on zoos. 'I'd have written you a letter if you asked. There's no need to forge Daddy's or my signature.'

'You weren't here.' Harriet obviously felt she had gone too far because when she spoke again, her voice had acquired a less reproachful tone. 'Anyway, even if you hadn't started a new job there's no getting out of it. We've got to go. Miss Cavendish says it's educational.' Tears against an unjust world and unseeing adults welled up in the corner of her big blue eyes and spilled over Harriet's red cheeks.

From the bottom of a memory well, long since barricaded and inaccessible to her consciousness, Sydney suddenly remembered the time she and Dylan had joined a sit-in at Bristol Zoo in protest against two Bengali tigers the zoo was trying to breed from, organized by students on Sydney's course – the self-styled Linguists Against Animal Debasement (Stevie's suggestion). Strictly speaking, it was more of a combined sit-in and lie-in; the aim was to block the entrance for as many days as it took the zoo to come to its senses and return their noble prisoners back whence they came (which disappointingly had turned out to be Chessington). It had been Dylan's first sit-in and he was only there, he told Sydney, because it meant he got to share a sleeping bag with her since, naturally, he'd forgotten to bring his.

It was absolutely typical that despite his lack of commitment, he'd won everyone round by teaching them all to play strip bridge for money. It had certainly passed the time. And got them loads of publicity.

'I tell you what,' she said, unbuttoning Harriet's tunic and pulling some errant strands of Molly's flaxen hair out of her mouth, 'in the morning, I will write a letter telling the school a few facts about zoos and why you feel so strongly about them. I'll copy some of those statistics we found on the internet. In the meantime, I've got some neighbours coming to dinner.'

The girls' eyes grew round with anticipation. 'Mrs Protheroe?'

Sydney glanced at her watch. 8.40. Eloise and Dylan would be here any moment. The evening had already taken on a nightmarish dimension, with everything acquiring a slow-motion quality. 'No. Some people who've moved in opposite. Do you think you can get yourselves ready for bed? Only I've got to finish heating up dinner and they'll be here any minute.'

'No time for a story then?' asked Harriet, climbing out of her school pinafore and leaving it on the floor where it lay like a large grey damp patch.

Sydney nodded guiltily. 'Of course I've got time.'

'How many chapters?' asked Molly suspiciously.

'One. Then Harriet can take over.'

'But she hates reading,' Molly reminded them all. 'And I'm really good at it. And I hate listening to her,' she added with the certainty of one for whom not wanting to do something had so far been adequate insurance against having to do it.

'That's why you should,' said Sydney.

She cantered through Chapter Six of *Black Beauty*, taking three pages at a time when she thought they'd dozed off enough for her to get away with it, especially as this was the fourth reading. She got to the end and Harriet told her she'd already read that chapter to them.

'Why didn't you say earlier?' said Sydney wearily.

'It sounds different when you skip pages,' said Harriet.

Sydney turned their landing light on and went downstairs to salvage something from the wastelands of her wardrobe.

She pulled out the mauve velvet dress and heard Harriet agreeing to be read to. She'd let it go tonight. But Harriet's reading, or lack of it, was becoming a serious issue. She went downstairs and began hurriedly setting the table when the phone rang. It was Miles, her brother.

'Oh, it's you,' she said abruptly. Miles had perfected the art of ringing at the wrong time years ago. Still, since it was the only thing he'd ever perfected, Sydney felt mean crushing him.

'That's nice, Sydney, I must say. What's up? Waitrose out of caviar? Marks and Sparks shares down the crapper?'

In the general scheme of things, Sydney viewed her brother's constant allusions to her charmed life as an inescapable form of VAT. The life tax she had to pay in return for not having to worry about money. But tonight she wasn't in the mood.

'Could we skip the stand-up routine for once, Miles?' She could hear footsteps outside and she hadn't brushed her hair or put on any makeup. And where was Charlie?

'You can be very arch sometimes, Sydney, you know. Not to mention bitter. It doesn't suit you, in case you were wondering.' He sounded as though he'd been drinking, which meant he was settling down for a nice long chat. 'Oh, Syd,' he groaned. 'It's Jacquie. She's having doubts.'

Privately Sydney doubted whether Miles's twenty-four-year-old girlfriend was capable of experiencing any sensation deeper than muscle fatigue, so perhaps doubts were a good sign.

'About us,' Miles continued shakily. 'She says she wants to concentrate on her career.'

The footsteps receded past the window up the street. Thank God. But that didn't mean Dylan and Eloise wouldn't be at the door any minute.

'What with her pilates, massage and yoga classes taking off big time, the gym wants her to do more hours,' Miles went on. 'That's half the trouble.'

'Miles, much as I'd love to help, I'm a bit tied up. I'm expecting some people for supper any minute.'

'Charlie's legal drones?' asked Miles sympathetically.

'That kind of thing.'

He began to sound chirpier. 'Tell you what. Why don't I call back about ten? That way, if it's really chronic, you can pretend someone in the family's been taken desperately ill and chuck them out.' Sydney put down the phone and darted upstairs.

Miles's casual relationship with truth, responsibility and the way he could breezily invoke family illness and not worry that at some point fate would pay him back by striking his own sons down with meningitis or leukaemia – Sydney's Big Fears – were a constant source of wonderment, and occasional convenience. Linda had always said she was fascinated that Sydney and Miles had sprung from the same loins. Sydney would smile enigmatically whenever Linda asked if there hadn't been some clumsy cradle-switching in the maternity ward when one or other of them was born because the idea of not being related to Miles was very appealing.

She gazed at her bedroom floor. Once again the contents of her wardrobe lay around her in a heap and had been found wanting. There was no way she was wearing the mauve dress – it would be like trying to dam a tidal wave of blubber with a page from *Vogue*. She tried it on to prove the point. Amazingly, it still just about fitted. But Linda was right about one thing, it was far too sexually provocative. She glanced at her profile and saw that she looked like a fibreglass cast of the Alps. Beneath the smooth velvet, her cleavage gleamed like pale, uncharted moon craters. It was an utterly irresponsible outfit to meet a married ex in. She padded into the bathroom and dabbed on some blusher, twisting her thick, copperish hair up into a chignon before letting it fall about her shoulders again.

Suddenly she heard voices outside. Her heart began to pound as she recognized Dylan's deep, lilting vowels and Eloise's hard little rs, like cracking nuts. The years rolled away and she had a flashback to when she and Dylan had stood on Clifton Suspension Bridge in the early hours of a summer morning, almost eighteen years earlier, a bottle of wine between them that they'd smuggled from a party. The memory was so strong that she could feel the heat of the sun on her cheeks and his curly hair tickling her collarbone as he leant over to kiss her. By then they'd known each other for eight or nine months. It seemed a lifetime back then.

He'd told her the legend of Cardigan Bay.

'I'd love to see it one day,' she said, nuzzling against his chest.

The depth of her feelings for Dylan had taken her completely by surprise, but by the time they stood on that bridge and he'd pulled a pair of walking boots out of a paper bag he'd hidden inside his coat and told her he wanted to spend the rest of his life with her, this had stopped dismaying her. She had also stopped worrying that her studies had been ambushed by a love affair she'd had no intention of starting, and apparently had no control over. She even enjoyed the sensation of falling into the unknown. Feeling his sinewy arms round her, she'd pulled him towards the edge of the bridge and they'd peered into the gorge and at the rocks beneath. She watched the water crashing against the cliffs as they shared the last drops of wine and Dylan asked her to come with him round the world. He'd made it sound such an adventure. Everyone else was so serious back then about getting a job that following your heart into the unknown seemed the most radical, grown-up thing you could do.

Sydney pulled herself back to the present. The chatter outside had stopped. She sprayed herself all over with Diorissimo and fastened a dark green Tahitian pearl Charlie had given her when Harriet was born round her neck, feeling it nestle between her breasts like a cool marble. She shoved her feet into an old pair of silver satin stilettos. The main thing was that she shouldn't drink anything tonight. The other main thing was that she was madly in love with Charlie.

The buzzer ricocheted round the house for a second time, making her nerves jangle. She was surprised by the ferocity of her panic. By the time she reached the foot of the stairs, her legs were buckling and her palms were clammier than the monkfish marinating gently in its new home. What did you say to someone you hadn't seen for half a lifetime? Obviously not 'Do you come here often?' She threw one last despairing, half-hearted glance at the mirror in the hall and almost went flying on the rug by the stairs. What if he was as flustered as she was?

What if he didn't seem flustered at all?

What if he didn't recognize her at all?

And where the bloody hell was Charlie?

By the time she lifted the first latch her heart was crashing so violently against her ribcage that she thought it would shatter. She fumbled with the second latch, trying to regulate her breathing. She could hear low voices outside again, and laughter. Perhaps she should speak first, for self-identification purposes. She must not succumb to drink. She wished that she'd taken the list idea seriously. She wished the evening was over. She wished she knew how much Eloise knew. Everything? Or had Dylan omitted a few details – as she had with Charlie? She definitely wasn't going to drink. She wished that Dylan had been eaten by wolves in the tundra. She wished she could open the damned door. She wished it would jam. It opened, and she wished the ground in front of her would too.

'Sydney!!' Before she could agonize any more she was swept up in a bear hug and whisked around the hall until she was breathless, one stiletto dangling from her foot. She closed her eyes and wished she'd had a pedicure. She wished she wasn't so shallow. He was still spinning her around. She thought about opening her eyes and letting her feet touch the ground again. And then gave up. Out of the corner of her eyes, through a curtain of her hair, she saw Eloise looking at them, a half-smile playing on her papaya-coloured lips and a strange, enigmatic gleam in her eyes.

5

'Chilli peanut, anyone?' asked Sydney.

Or rather, that's what she wanted to ask. But all she could think of was the time Dylan had tied her to a four-poster bed at some friend's country seat and poured melted Nutella all over her breasts, before licking them spotlessly clean.

Which was odd, because these days she hardly ever thought about sex and she never ate Nutella.

Dylan didn't seem to require social foreplay. He'd gone from hello to squeezing her so tightly her breasts were in danger of popping through her shoulder-blades. He seemed a bit more cushioned round his midriff than she remembered. Eventually he stopped spinning her around the room. She felt him push her gently away and place his big square hands on her shoulders, so that he could appraise her with those penetrating, mocking eyes that sparkled in the crevices of his suntanned skin like little shards of cobalt glass on the beach. She had never got over the way he was so candidly curious about people. He was so close she could see the mole on his throat. But she couldn't look at him properly.

'I can't believe it's you.' His voice burbled with the same boyish enthusiasm that had been the soundtrack to an earlier life. Sydney tried to match his gaze. But she couldn't hold it as long as he could, so she was unable to ascertain yet how much, if at all, he'd changed. She flexed her hands nervously by her sides.

'And there was I thinking you'd deliberately stalked me.' There was a slight edge to her voice, which she didn't seem able to control. Perhaps Miles was right and she did sound bitter and arch.

'Let me take your coats,' she said hurriedly. Eloise, pressed against the wall, held out the most enormous bouquet of long-stemmed lilac roses and white lilies. 'For you,' she said in her staccato rap. She pecked Sydney on her left cheek. Sydney leant forward with her right, but Eloise had already withdrawn, leaving Sydney hovering like a doodlebug amidst an aureole of Shalimar that was shockingly overpowering. She was wearing jeans. Expensive-looking jeans. But jeans. Sydney felt hopelessly overdressed. Eloise draped the flowers over Sydney's arms where their heads dangled like overgrown babies. With a start, Sydney realized they matched the flowers on the cracked dish perfectly. 'They're beautiful,' she said awkwardly. 'I'll just go and put them into some water. The sitting room's through there.'

By the time she returned, having rummaged in her cupboards for a vase big enough, they were tucked into a corner of the sofa like two hormonally supercharged teenagers.

'Drinks?' enquired Sydney in a voice that came out horribly schoolteacherly. Dylan bounced up to help her. She'd forgotten how energetic he was, as if the molecules that made up his body were constantly reacting against one another and causing minor electrical disturbances that meant he couldn't sit still. And how tall he was, and the way his blond hair crested over the top of his head . . . It had receded a little; there were more eddies and creases round his eyes than she remembered, and he was definitely more weathered. Nut-coloured like an old thatched cottage, and

81

it suited him. His eyes met hers and bubbled over with amusement. She drew back as if she'd been electrocuted.

'Great house,' said Dylan appreciatively. 'Ours is a bit more . . . Spartan. Eloise is a big fan of Penitential Chic.' He leant over and kissed his wife's miniature hand. 'And so am I now.'

Sydney poured out three huge goblets of champagne and handed them round. The rooms seemed colder than usual. Or perhaps it was the atmosphere.

'Not for me,' said Eloise. 'Do you have any fresh, organic cantaloupe juice? With ice?'

Sydney disappeared towards the kitchen to see if there was anything remotely cantaloupeish in the fridge, checking her reflection in the oven door on the way. Her face was the same colour as Eloise's lips.

Dylan appeared to be massaging Eloise's breasts when she returned with some pineapple and mango juice. 'Neck problems.' He looked up at Sydney. 'It's peering at all those Old Masters.'

'I thought you specialized in the Impressionists,' Sydney said politely.

'He's talking about all the wrinkly old squillionaires I had to grease up to,' Eloise purred. Her nose wrinkled in amusement. She looked like a small kitten. Sydney was tempted to put her outside.

They sipped their drinks in unison, grateful for the distraction.

'Of all the mid-Victorian crescents in all the world—' began Sydney.

'Incredible, isn't it?' Dylan stretched out his legs and slid his hand down Eloise's legs. 'Aren't they beautiful big old houses? We're getting a meditation room.'

'Really?' Sydney's brow creased in amazement. She

82

couldn't imagine Dylan sitting still, let alone meditating.

'Eloise wants one.' They both looked at Eloise, willing her to join in. 'Which branch do you follow?' Sydney enquired politely.

'None.' Eloise looked shocked at the suggestion that anyone might actually use a meditation room. 'But those Christy Turlington yoga clothes are heaven.'

There was another pause. 'Oh, bugger this,' exploded Dylan. 'I can't pretend. Much as I'd like to say it was fate, Sydney, our moving here wasn't a total coincidence.'

'It wasn't?' Eloise's eyes narrowed thoughtfully.

'Darling, you know it wasn't.' He pulled her closer to him and nibbled her ear. Sydney sipped her drink nervously. Reading about Dylan's conquests in the newspapers occasionally wasn't quite the same as having to watch them.

With vast self-control, Dylan stopped devouring Eloise. 'Remember Stalinist Stevie?' he asked Sydney.

'Stevie O'Connor who hated you?'

'The same.' Dylan grinned.

'Was she the lesbian?' asked Eloise, her eyes, bottle-green in the dim light, suddenly expanding like spools of un-ravelling film.

'As a matter of fact I think she probably was,' said Dylan. 'How perceptive of you, my little forensic pathologist.'

'Not really, baby.' Eloise nuzzled into his shirt. A waft of lemon and pine floated over to Sydney and made her almost giddy with nostalgia.

'Most women who don't like Dylan turn out to have sexual hang-ups, don't you think, Sydney?'

Sydney pretended not to hear. Where, in the name of all that was supposedly sacrosanct about bloody marriage, was Charlie? 'I think I'd better pop upstairs and check the children haven't murdered each other,' she murmured.

She wandered into the hall. Infuriatingly, all appeared calm upstairs. She returned to the frozen wastes of the sitting room.

'Wasn't Stevie the very ugly one?' Eloise was saying. She ran a perfect shell-pink nail around the rim of her glass.

'More to the point, in this context, she was the one I almost drowned once.'

'Sounds like a mercy killing. Being ugly must be such a burden. Do you think it's a burden, Sydney?'

'Which is how I met Sydney,' said Dylan smoothly. 'She nearly garrotted me with her oar.'

Eloise arched an eyebrow expectantly. Sydney wondered how much she knew about her and Dylan.

'How do you feel about coming to live in Britain?' she said quickly. She spied a packet of felt-tips beneath an armchair. Juanita's clearing up was especially superficial when it came to the children, whom she regarded as Maisie's territory.

'Eloise adores England,' said Dylan. 'Don't you, darling? We wouldn't have come to live here if she didn't feel confident about being able to feel completely at home.'

'So you've visited London a lot, then?'

Eloise looked slightly pained. 'I always feel it's not frequency but depth of perception that counts when you travel. I think you can tell a lot from airports, don't you? It's very big, isn't it?'

Sydney wasn't sure whether she was referring to Terminal 4 or the country. Not that it mattered. Eloise clearly didn't expect a response. 'The second time I was in London for two days. When Princess Di died. Did you ever see her in the flesh? I heard those *Vanity Fair* portraits were computer-enhanced.'

'I think you'll find Sydney is a bit of a closet republican.' Dylan grinned. 'D'you remember the time we stormed the gates of Buck House? It was a Coal not Dole march, wasn't it, Sydney? Support the miners. And Oliver Makepeace chained himself to the railings and lost the key.'

'And you went to call 999—'

'. . . and came back with a prostitute—'

'. . . who unpicked the lock—'

'. . . because she specialized in penal reform!'

They both dissolved into hoots of laughter, the ice in the room finally evaporating along with their drinks.

'More champagne?' asked Sydney, splashing half a bottle into Dylan's glass and hers and suddenly feeling fraudulent. She was hardly a bastion of counter-culture now; the most radical thing that had happened in Clifton Crescent in the last ten years had been the residents' association forcing the Council to replace the standard-issue street-lamps with Victorian-style ones.

Eloise smiled thinly. 'Who's Dole?'

'Welfare.'

Eloise pursed her lips. 'So you were a leftie, Sydney?'

Dylan chucked a peanut up in the air and caught it between his neat white teeth. 'Isn't she adorable?' He gazed admiringly at his wife. There was a small but perceptible silence.

'I love it when people assert their right to demonstrate.' Eloise peered dubiously into her fruit juice.

'Really?' Dylan looked pleased.

'Yes. It makes it so much easier to park right outside Bergdorf's when they barricade off downtown.'

'Isn't she a scream?' Fortunately all Dylan's and Eloise's questions appeared to be rhetorical. 'Anyway,' he continued, 'it turns out Stalinist Stevie's living in New York and working for the UN and she's very friendly with one of Eloise's colleagues at Sotheby's—'

85

'Who, come to think of it, *is* a lesbian,' said Eloise. 'She has *terrible* taste. The only good call she ever made was when she threw up over some godawful Hockney – and even that was a mistake.'

'And one thing led to another, especially when Eloise mentioned we might be moving to London—'

'But how did Stevie know where I lived? We haven't seen each other for eighteen years.'

'Apparently her niece works on that magazine of yours. Poppy someone.'

'Poppy De Cadent?' Sydney asked in amazement. 'She's our new columnist-at-large.'

'Stevie hardly sounds like the sort of person to have a columnist-at-large for a niece,' said Eloise. 'Isn't that a job that requires a lot of social connections?'

'You haven't seen Sydney's magazine. Eloise told me you're at *IQ*.' He turned to his wife. 'It's frightfully high-brow and left-wing. I expect the columnist-at-large has a lot of social welfare connections.'

'It's not actually *my* magazine,' began Sydney. 'I'm just a sort of glorified secretary.' So Stalinist Stevie was the Honourable Natasha De Cadent's sister. She passed round the chilli peanuts. She must remember to tell Linda that Poppy was related to a lesbian member of the Socialist Workers' Party. It might make her feel a bit better about hiring her.

Eloise brushed the bowl away as if it were a particularly nasty dose of beri-beri and pulled a solitary carrot stick out of her handbag. Her demeanour, which had shown promising signs of thawing, had iced over again.

'Frankly, I was very happy in New York,' she began apropos of their earlier conversation. 'Dylan had an extremely promising career on the lecture circuit.'

Sydney tossed back some more champagne. 'You didn't finish telling me about why you came to live here.'

Dylan grimaced. 'I felt like a monkey in a dinner jacket in New York.'

'He's terribly motivational,' continued Eloise. 'Have you ever heard him talk about the time they got stranded in the Antarctic for five days without any food or water?'

Sydney hadn't. But she knew Dylan's gift for making every person in a room feel as though they were his new best friend. 'But why here?' she persisted.

'I could have got him lots of other gigs,' Eloise continued wistfully. 'With my contacts in the squillionaire department he could have made a fortune.'

'Eloise knows everyone,' said Dylan cheerfully. 'From Kevin Spacey to Clinton. It's the job, you know. And her fabulously old moneyed family. And her innate irresistibility of course.'

'He could have made gazillions,' reiterated Eloise. 'Especially if we'd moved to Florida. One of my old room-mates does Color Me Beautiful seminars down there. Made five million last year. She's kind of a pin-up for the executive generation – and I'm not just talking about her facelifts. If you can make five mil with a bunch of swatches, think what you could do with snow and starvation.' She swatted away the bowl of peanuts Sydney was proffering. 'Don't get me started on the missed advertising opportunities, Sydney,' she said wistfully. 'One of my clients is at Frickter and Schimble . . .'

'. . . The biggest manufacturers of deodorant in the world . . .' Dylan explained.

'. . . They were desperate for Dylan. But no, he wants to come back and save the family empire. Still, I've got lots of ideas for modernizing that too . . .'

87

'. . . It's great you ended up on a magazine.' Dylan scooped up a handful of nuts. His appetite was as expansive as ever, Sydney noted. 'Though not what we expected.' He turned to Eloise. 'Sydney was a brilliant linguist.'

Eloise appeared not to consider the last comment worth responding to. 'Is she glamorous?'

'Poppy? I very much doubt it, my precious,' said Dylan. 'British women never are. Present company excepted, obviously.'

Sydney considered telling him that Poppy De Cadent had recently been voted the seventh Sexiest Woman in London by *Tatler* but decided against it. Let him think *IQ* was still the unsullied bastion of intellectual debate it used to be before Brian Widlake began to leave his grimy pawprints on it.

Dylan leant back expansively on the sofa, his eyes sweeping over Sydney again. 'You haven't changed one bit, you know.'

'I guess it's all the rain,' Eloise said thoughtfully. 'How old did you say you were?'

For a futile second, Sydney considered lying. 'Thirty-six,' she said, knocking back more champagne.

'Wow.' Eloise sounded genuinely awed. She chewed on this enormously sad age for a moment or two. 'You don't really look it.'

'Seconded,' said Dylan, who didn't look thirty-eight. How old was Eloise, Sydney wondered. But not for long.

'Of course when you're still only twenty-five everyone over thirty looks the same.' She paused to sip some juice. Sydney glanced at her watch. It wasn't even ten.

'Diana Vreeland said that at a certain age you have to choose between having a pretty face or a neat bottom,' continued Eloise. 'I think you were very wise to go for the face option, Sydney. You can always sit down.'

There was another silence. Quite nasty this time. It was Dylan who tackled it first.

'Did you decorate the house yourself?' he asked.

Sydney tried to look objectively at the room, with its pale antique furniture collected in auction rooms over the years, far too many photographs of the children, and its mint walls crowded with water-colours that Sydney's mother had painted, and wondered who else Dylan imagined might have decorated it. She disappeared again to check on the idiot-proof monkfish. Unfortunately it was doing beautifully, which was more than could be said for her. She damped her throbbing cheeks down with some kitchen towel and returned to find Harriet and Molly standing in front of Dylan and Eloise in their nighties. Eloise was offering them each a chillied peanut. Harriet eyed the bilious red coating suspiciously. 'We're not allowed additives,' she said.

'Or sweets,' said Molly.

'Are you religious?' asked Eloise.

'Are you?' asked Molly.

Dylan grinned. 'Only about Chanel and Starbucks.'

'We don't go to Starbucks,' said Molly.

'We don't eat anything that isn't free-range either,' offered Harriet.

Dylan smiled wryly over their heads. 'Radical Sydney. You'll be telling me you've stormed Gap and banned refined carbohydrates next.'

'Our cleaning lady has,' said Harriet. 'She's on a diet.'

'Cleaning lady?' Dylan smirked. 'Employing another woman to do your menial tasks? What happened to class solidarity, Sydney?'

Sydney looked at Harriet and Molly, both of whom were now crouching round Eloise with adoring looks on their faces. The bonding between them was instant and shocking. Any moment they'd be locking arms and singing 'Kumbayah'.

'Come on, you two, bed.' The alarm on Harriet's Baby G watch went off – one of the twenty pre-sets Molly had programmed into it. 'It's two hundred and seventy days till my birthday,' Harriet told Eloise proudly. 'I don't know why it's going off now though and not this morning.'

'Why don't I take you upstairs and read you a story?' suggested Eloise. 'If that's okay with Mommy. It'll leave you two time to catch up and Harriet can show me her books.'

Sydney suddenly found herself feeling territorial. She hadn't been expecting Mary Poppins. 'Supper's almost ready.'

'I'll only be a few minutes.' Eloise gazed down at a now frankly adoring Harriet. 'I love reading stories.'

'She's amazing with kids,' said Dylan, ogling Eloise's miniature backside as she trotted upstairs behind Harriet. 'That's why we're so compatible.'

'Because you're still a child?' said Sydney. She heard Molly telling Eloise that Harriet had just been cast as Mary in the school's Nativity – which was news to her – and that Jesus was to be played by Baby Caca.

'Is that some kind of cockney?' she heard Eloise ask.

'No, it means it wees and poos if you feed it the right food,' said Molly.

Sydney couldn't make out Eloise's response because Harriet slipped on the stairs again. It was starting to be a worry. Along with her car sickness, which seemed to have got much worse recently.

'If you must know,' she turned to Dylan, 'Juanita's here because Charlie got her political asylum.'

Dylan grinned expansively.

'It's true. Her first job was pushing a dust-cart. She told me she'd been an unwilling drugs mule in Colombia.'

'And you believed her?'

'Why not? She's unwilling about everything else. She's the worst bloody cleaner in the world.'

Dylan threw back his head, revealing his long tanned throat, and giggled infectiously. 'Thank God, Syd, you haven't changed at all.'

'There's just more of me.'

'You look wonderful,' he burbled warmly. The room's polar cap finally having melted, he told her how desperate he was to have children. 'And I can't think of a more amazing mother than Eloise. Although you seem to be doing a pretty terrific job too,' he added tactfully. 'Now, come and sit down.' He patted the cushion next to him and watched in amusement as Sydney perched primly on the sofa opposite.

'I want to talk to you,' Dylan's gravelly voice purred. 'It's been such a long time.' A low maple table piled with books stretched out between them like Lake Ontario. 'How long *has* it been?'

'Not sure. Nineteen years?' said Sydney, deliberately vague. 'When did you meet Eloise?'

'Eight months and almost one day ago. I can't believe my luck. So incredibly beautiful. In fact terrific in every way. Brilliantly clever, funny . . . but enough about me. It looks as though life's been treating you well too. Are you happy?'

She nodded extremely vigorously. Why would he assume she wasn't?

'So what have you been up to?'

'Breeding, mainly,' said Sydney dismissively. 'What about you?'

'Brooding. You know – what with you dumping me, then

the débâcle of that final expedition to the Antarctic when Zac Harrington's left bollock nearly dropped off from frostbite.' He looked at her in mock sorrow. 'I almost lost a foot and got pneumonia.' He held up his left hand. One of the nails was faintly discoloured. 'Frostbite. I was delirious for two weeks.'

'How long did it take anyone to notice?' If she had dumped him, it was only after extreme provocation. 'The delirium, I mean.'

'Oh, the delicious English cynicism. How I've missed it.'

She wondered whether she was imagining a genuine wistfulness in his voice. 'So what happened after the frostbite?'

'After the funding for Antarctic explorations dried up in the last recession I got a job with S.B. Steinberg's and moved to New York. Then yes, I admit I got on the dinner-party circuit and did a few ads. Oh, and my father died.'

She looked across and saw a flicker of pain cross his face. Then it was gone, like a passing cloud. 'I'm sorry. I know how much he meant to you.'

'Yes, well, he was never the same after my mother died . . . I did do some quite good ads, you know.'

Sydney smiled. He never had enjoyed charting uncomfortable territory, which was ironic for an explorer. 'I saw the one for watches.' She marvelled at the speed with which Dylan could transform the mood of a room. 'And compasses. Very humorous. And the instant noodles.'

'Which, moving swiftly on, is where I eventually met Eloise. It was hilarious, actually. She hijacked my taxi. I was about to kick her out—'

Sydney was starting to wish he had. 'What changed your mind?'

'Her legs mainly. But also she said she'd call the police and tell them I'd sexually harassed her if I didn't take her home.'

'So you did, and sexually harassed her there?'

'Yes, but only after the second martini. I'm not a complete slut any more.'

'Meaning you were with . . .' Sydney ground to a halt. Whatever else happened tonight, she was determined to keep things light and impersonal. And sober.

'Bluddy hell,' exclaimed Dylan, suddenly sounding very Welsh. He bounded over towards a shelf and pulled out an Elvis Costello CD. He put it into the player and closed his eyes as 'A Good Year for the Roses' soared to its chorus. 'I haven't heard this for centuries.'

Sydney did not close her eyes, otherwise she would have floated off with Dylan to the first time they'd listened to the song together. It was also the first time he'd stayed at her place. She felt an overwhelming desire to get away from him. 'I'd better check on supper,' she said brusquely.

'Again?' asked Dylan. He followed her into the kitchen.

The monkfish was still perfect. Just as it had been five minutes earlier. She needed to cool down and think. She stuck her head in the fridge, where the fifteen mini clotted creams that Tesco.com had substituted for Harriet and Molly's Petits Fromages brought back terrible memories of the time Dylan had tied her to his white chaise longue so that she couldn't go to the morning lecture on infidelity in early Renaissance Italian poetry. She pulled her head out of the fridge and slammed the door. It was five past ten. Maybe Charlie had been run over. Bloody typical. Well, she couldn't hang on any longer. She took the fish out of the oven.

'You don't know how pleased I am to be back.' Dylan scanned a Post-It she'd left for Charlie to remind him to let her know whether he wanted her to bring his dentist

93

appointment forward. 'You do remember the first time we listened to that song, don't you, Sydney?'

Go away, Dylan. She smiled brightly. 'Not long before it's ready now. More peanuts?' Where the fuck was Charlie?

He cocked his head and tapped his temple with his third finger. It made her feel dizzy; it was such a familiar yet long-forgotten gesture of his. She turned away, overcome with nostalgia.

There was a fumbling and rustling at the front door and a squealing from Hamish, followed by a chaotic tangle of coats, briefcase, Harriet and Molly's rucksacks and the light rainfall of discarded sunflower seeds spilling out of them on to the floor. Charlie had finally arrived.

It was extraordinary, how completely someone who charged by the minute could lose track of time. Charlie seemed bliss-fully unaware that he was an hour late for his own supper party. When Sydney met him at the door he seemed to have forgotten about the evening plans altogether. 'For God's sake,' he groaned, when Sydney told them about their guests, 'who invited them?'

Sydney was furious until she took one look at his grey face. He worked too hard. She poured him a glass of champagne and put his briefcase by the front door so he wouldn't forget it in the morning.

They sat down to supper in the kitchen. Dylan marvelled at her cooking and had seconds. Eloise told them about her wheat-intolerance and refused all carbohydrates, reacting as though they were Class A drugs whenever anyone offered her some. And Charlie absent-mindedly picked at some yeast- and gluten-free crispbreads Eloise had extracted from her bag and dipped them in the monkfish marinade.

Calorie-intolerance would be more accurate, Sydney

thought. Eloise looked like the kind of woman who knew how many calories there were in stamp-licking.

'Where did you live in New York once you were married?' asked Sydney, getting up to prepare some finger bowls.

'Upper West Side. We had the best corner restaurants. Now that *is* something Dylan is going to miss.'

'Not with you to cook for me.' Sydney saw his foot work its way under the table up Eloise's leg.

'My God, your streets are so narrow,' said Eloise suddenly. 'How does anyone drive here, Charlie?'

'Charlie doesn't,' said Sydney.

'Never got round to the test.'

Eloise looked at him as if he were some kind of mental defective.

'So why did you come back to London?' Charlie asked.

'Have you been to New York recently?' asked Dylan. 'It's so cleaning-living.'

'You don't smoke . . .' Sydney stopped herself. She didn't want to sound overly familiar in front of Eloise and Charlie.

'It's the principle. Full of politically correct prigs—'

'Do you have kidnappings in England?' asked Eloise dreamily.

'I suppose so,' said Sydney, puzzled. 'But it's not a huge issue for most people.'

'Kidnappings. How quaint,' said Dylan. 'In America it's all about drive-by shootings.'

'Dylan wants to rescue his family's publishing firm.' Eloise rustled around in her bags of Japanese rice-crisp cakes.

'Really?' Charlie's ears pricked up.

'Expand would be more accurate,' said Dylan.

'His family's run it into the ground,' explained Eloise.

'Gosh, how exciting.' Nothing fascinated Charlie more

95

than books, the more arcane the better. If it hadn't been for family pressure, he'd have gone into publishing, Sydney always thought. The only thing he liked more than reading obscure tomes was writing them. Though to be fair, the learned legal doorstops Charlie penned were still in print. Of the six copies Amazon had ordered of *Fiscal Manoeuvres*, his last oeuvre, one had been sold. And according to the reader's review, that was only because the book had mistakenly been listed under Contemporary Punk CD releases.

'What kind of books do you publish?' said Charlie, helping himself to another of Eloise's rice cakes and dipping it into a finger bowl.

'Unreadable ones mainly,' said Eloise. 'Fifteen seventy-two to two thousand and four. That's five hundred years of worstsellers and deadbeats.'

'I don't think it's quite fair to say that the author who got into a fight with the manager of the Oxford branch of Waterstones is a deadbeat,' said Dylan cheerily. 'At one point it looked as though he might even win. Remember when he knocked the manager down one flight of stairs into the basement, Eloise?'

'And you got landed with a bill for forty-two spoiled copies of *Captain Corelli's Mandolin*. Anyway, I'm not talking about the stupid fight but about the sales of *Axis of Weevils*.'

'Waterstones said that as eighteenth-century maritime histories go, it was quite a hit.'

'That's just it, sweetie. From now on, eighteenth-century maritime histories are not us.' Eloise blew him a kiss and smiled fondly at the rest of them.

'Darling, Dylan's family are Glendower Books,' Sydney explained to Charlie.

'No!' Charlie stopped mid-rice cake and grinned in

delight. 'My God, I wrote to you months ago to see if you have another copy of Gilbert Ffleming's *Meditations on Tort.*'

'Did you get a reply?' Dylan asked, looking serious.

'No actually, come to think of it, I didn't.'

Eloise shook her head knowingly. 'That figures.'

'Poor Edith,' said Dylan sadly. 'She was my father's right hand for almost fifty years, but she can't keep up any more.'

'With what?' snorted Eloise. 'Do you know what their biggest seller was last year? Remy de Courcy's *Anatomy of the Bustle*. Ninety-three copies in hardback.'

'That was a bit disappointing,' Dylan said with a sigh.

'It wouldn't have been if you'd marketed it as a follow-up to *What Not to Wear.*'

'I'd have thought ninety-three copies in hardback was rather splendid,' said Charlie a little enviously.

'Do they still have those beautiful pale grey covers?' Sydney loved Glendower Books. Even the feel of them was cerebral.

'Not if I have anything to do with it,' said Eloise. 'You need fuchsia and free offers to compete in the book stores these days.'

'Eloise's best friend is a graphic designer,' said Dylan. 'He's completely redesigned the packaging so they'll leap off the shelves.'

'Packaging?' said Charlie. 'I thought they were books.'

'They still need to be marketed,' said Eloise.

'But will they be academic?' asked Sydney.

'Absolutely. I've helped Dylan put together this terrific list. Academic with a modern twist.'

'Self-help, I suppose you'd call it,' said Dylan. '*Working the Internet for Money*; *Cutting and Pasting Your Own Religion*; *How to Give Birth to Geniuses*, that kind of thing.

97

All with fluorescent covers and win-a-free-holiday stickers.'

'Really?' Charlie looked bemused.

'No, not really,' said Eloise. 'Dylan's being facetious. Or is it ironic? I always get your British humour mixed up.'

'Poor darling. As far as Eloise is concerned, British humour is like British teeth – an affront to normal standards of hygiene and sanity.' Dylan took his wife's hand and kissed it extravagantly.

'So those aren't the real titles. Phew.' After years of bitterly resenting the dust and grime that had gathered on top of Charlie's heaps of obscure Glendowers, Sydney suddenly felt hugely protective of them. And she couldn't understand how someone who worked at Sotheby's could be such a philistine. Unless it was all an act, like Dylan's.

'They certainly are the titles.' Eloise tilted her chin defiantly. 'But he's joking about the free holiday. We're holding out for a car sponsorship deal. I figured that had longer-term appeal, don't you agree?' She looked round the table for support, seemingly reading Sydney's mind. 'The thing about Sotheby's is that it teaches you about selling out in the real world. There's nothing ivory tower about what we do.'

'When you think about it,' Dylan reached for some more wine, 'self-help's just a continuation of what Glendower Books has always done. What's educating yourself about philosophy and literature if not a form of self-improvement?'

'That's true,' Charlie conceded. 'I don't know how I would have got through my degree without A.A. Laforgue's treatise on the Neo-Platonists.'

'Is there a good beauty salon round here?' asked Eloise.

'I assumed you read law,' said Dylan to Charlie.

'Charlie did a degree in Classics beforehand,' Sydney explained briskly. The last thing she wanted was Dylan and

Charlie talking about university. 'At Oxford,' she couldn't help adding.

'Did you know Clinton?' asked Eloise, suddenly seeing Charlie in a new light. It was the first time in what Sydney could only loosely describe as their conversation that she hadn't uttered a complete non sequitur.

'Clinton, Clinton. Let me think. Did he read law?' Charlie took off his glasses and blinked in concentration. 'Nope, it's no good. Can't conjure him up. British chap?'

Eloise looked at him for signs of irony or facetiousness.

'President of the United States,' prompted Sydney, clearing the plates.

'Ah. Yes. That Clinton. Year or so before my time, I'm afraid.'

Eloise lost interest in Charlie and fished in her bag for some dried mango.

'Tell me, Sydney,' she began conspiratorially, 'is it always this warm around fall in London? I bought this fabulous mink in New York and at this rate I won't be able to wear it before it's old news. Mid-November in New York is pretty reliable mink weather.'

'That's because America has weather. Britain has cloud formations. Wow, delicious tucker, Parker,' said Dylan when she brought the next Nicole Farhi dish to the table. For a moment, hearing her maiden name whisked Sydney back to a picnic. A surprise for her birthday. Dylan had prepared it, so it wasn't exactly a balanced meal – champagne and chocolate were all she remembered. Dylan had put on a floral pinny to serve. And then presented it to her. An Ironic Pinny, he'd called it. Then he'd apologized for all the hurt he'd caused her. And she'd cried. Sobbed, in fact. Sitting among the beautiful ruins of Tintern Abbey, wringing her heart out.

She flicked some of the cream towards the middle of the dish. The phone rang loudly, making her jump. It switched to answerphone before she could reach it.

'Hi, Syd. Michael Buerk 999 Rescue Service here,' drawled Miles. 'Sorry I'm late. But you obviously don't need me any more. I'm nipping out for a bite with Jacquie now.' Sydney banged the serving spoons noisily. 'And yeah, since you ask, the situation is okay again. But if I get a chance I'll give you another call. Just in case there's a crisis.'

'Do you like the cinema?' Sydney asked Eloise loudly.

'I adore it,' said Eloise animatedly. 'I can't wait for the next *Legally Blonde*.'

'I don't think I've come across that,' said Charlie.

'They haven't made it yet. But the first two are excellent.'

'That's settled then,' said Sydney. 'Our nanny can't babysit and we have first-night tickets for the Kurdistan Women's Film Festival. Why don't you both have them?'

Eloise nudged Dylan under the table. 'Dairy,' she said, waving away the tart dripping with cream.

'Tell you what,' said Dylan. 'Why don't we babysit, so you can go?'

'We couldn't possibly inflict our little darlings on you,' Sydney began. The last thing she wanted was to see either Dylan or Eloise again in a hurry.

'That's a great idea,' cooed Eloise. 'I love children so much.' She beamed at Charlie.

'And to be honest, Kurdistan doesn't really sound our thing,' said Dylan.

'Are you more of a theatre man?' asked Charlie.

A brittle laugh emanated from Eloise. 'Oh, please. I had to drag him kicking and screaming to see *Chicago*.'

'You used to love Ibsen,' blurted Sydney. 'I remember

you queuing all night to get tickets for *The Lady from the Sea* when it opened at The Bristol Vic.'

'Did you two know each other at Bristol then?' Charlie's eyes blinked behind his spectacles. For a split moment Dylan, Sydney and Eloise locked complicit glances. Sydney looked away guiltily.

'In Sydney's first year. That was when I was young and didn't know the real value of time,' said Dylan. He chuckled. 'Honestly, Charlie, the number of occasions I've sat through *The Doll's House*, which has got to be more depressing, more boring and more lacking in plot than anything in Shakespeare, Dickens or any of those Brontë birds. You may find this staggering, Eloise, but he's even worse than Jane Austen.'

'Is she the one with Colin Firth?' Eloise gazed in disgust at a fleck of cream that had landed near her plate.

'Only Ben Jonson is more boring, more deplete of anything which might even remotely be called a point,' continued Dylan. 'Or a plot. And *The Lady from the Sea* is Ibsen's most boring play of all. Like *Pulp Fiction*, it's about infidelity, but nobody shoots up. Incredible as it seems, they don't really do anything apart from talk about the sodding sea, *for what seems like nine hours*. And to my certain knowledge, Uma Thurman's never been in it. In fact it's so bloody dreary that in the end you want to tell the Lady in question to just get on with it and jump in the fucking waves.'

Sydney felt strangely vindicated. Dylan was back to playing the philistine again in order to get laid.

'That's very decent of you,' she heard Charlie saying. 'About seven?'

'Tell me again what exactly it is you do at the magazine,' said Eloise as Sydney made coffee.

'This and that. It's pretty mundane,' said Sydney hurriedly. She really did not wish to discuss her job at any point, let alone in front of Charlie, with these two.

'It sounds fabulous. Come on, spill the beans.'

'Charlie's the one with the amazing job.'

'Really?' Eloise sounded doubtful. 'What does he specialize in?'

'Tax. He's one of the country's leading fiscal lawyers.'

'In that case,' said Eloise thoughtfully, 'you really should take him to see *Legally Blonde*.'

Fortunately, even hell had to freeze over eventually. At 11.30 they waved Eloise and Dylan goodnight. Sydney finished clearing up and Charlie tried to mend his most recent computer. It wasn't just Eloise who had turned out to be the airhead. What had happened to Dylan? That's what you got for marrying someone who thought San Salvador was the name of the latest catwalk sensation.

At least she didn't remotely fancy him any more, she realized with a jolt that took her by surprise. Had she expected to? For the second time that evening she went upstairs into the hallowed sanctum of Charlie's study and kissed the top of his head, quietly removing the empty KFC tub before he noticed anyone had been in there. Thank heavens she'd made the choice she had. Clever, perceptive Charlie. She couldn't wait to get his take on the evening. 'Coming?' she asked gently, and yawned. He'd taken his briefcase with him. He took off his glasses and rubbed his eyes. In the light from his desk lamp he looked like a bewildered dormouse.

'In a minute.' He frowned, and for a moment he looked exhausted. Then he smiled wanly. 'That was rather jolly, wasn't it?' he said.

As Sydney removed her eye makeup and hung up her dress, she wondered again what she had really been expecting from the evening. Now that she knew she no longer felt anything for Dylan she began to feel a vacuum. She climbed into bed and arranged herself seductively for Charlie. A few moments later she picked up the latest copy of *The Lady* from a pile she kept next to her bed in case the day ever came when she was in a position to employ a proper nanny – should she ever go full-time. And should Charlie ever accept it. In about fifteen years. Ten minutes later she was asleep.

6

The following day Harriet's Baby G watch woke them at 6.30 a.m. and thereafter at a number of strategic, sleep-starved moments, including 7, 7.20 and 7.45 a.m. It failed to give the correct time at any of them. Sydney might have known. It had been a present from Miles, which meant it was probably a fake.

Ten minutes later Charlie announced that he had SARS.

'Shall I get you some Nurofen?' Sydney grappled with the duvet. 'That usually does the trick with your colds.'

'It isn't a cold,' he said icily. 'It is SARS.' He rolled over grumpily.

'The school doors have opened,' Harriet announced at 8.05, as Sydney surfaced from her dreams. She was like a fish caught in nets, slippery in her own sweat. She felt as though she was suffocating. In her dream Charlie had mislaid one of the girls again. She struggled downstairs to make breakfast.

Dylan had been dreaming about being crushed beneath an avalanche again. He opened one eye gingerly and saw Eloise straddled across his chest, her cream and black lace Agent Provocateur half bra hovering at eye level like a particularly dainty bat, waiting to suck his blood.

'Come on, baby,' she whispered, 'what's happened to my big boy?' Her bony legs pressed insistently into his ribs like a novel car crusher and her nipples seemed to sniff the air like frisky hounds on the scent of a fox. Now that he'd opened his second eye he could see she was wearing her crotchless lace knickers with the pearl string. Her pubic hair, as manicured as ever, had been waxed in the shape of a flower. She must have had that done yesterday, he decided. Though God knows how she'd managed to find someone to do it in London. He had to admire her attention to detail. And truly, he appreciated her energy and ingenuity. But he was going to have to go into marathon training at this rate.

She reached across to her bedside table for a bottle of oil, which she upturned over his stomach. Not that there was much need for lubrication. Judging by the dampness between her legs and seeping over his chest, she'd been frotting herself backwards and forwards on him for some time. He closed his eyes again. She'd opened the blinds and the late autumn sun was blinding him.

'Come on, sweetheart,' she said, more insistently.

'Aren't we a tad exposed?' he demurred, blinking again in the coruscating searchlight of the sun. 'I thought you said you caught Mrs Protheroe with her binoculars focused on the house the other day.'

Eloise's mouth curled into one of her feline smiles. 'And the students. Dan's been peeping at us for the past half hour. I think he's got at least one of his little friends watching too.' She arched her back and took his left hand, placing it against her pointed little nipples. His eyes snapped open. 'So let's not disappoint them all.' She moved his right hand down her body. 'You never know. Maybe word will spread and our new friends Charlie and Sydney will join in. Wouldn't that be cosy? Mind you,' he felt her muscles clench round his right fingers with a forcefulness that never ceased to impress him, 'we'd have to put on a good show.' Reflexively, his fingers closed over the perfect orbs – a Madison Avenue special – that had fascinated him when he first encountered Eloise's breasts. He felt her nipples press against his palms and reached up and ran his tongue over them. Truly they were a testament to the surgeon's art. If a little hard and unyielding.

She began to sigh and sway rhythmically. In her black suspenders her beautiful twiglet legs had the spindly grace of a spider, especially when she suddenly span around, and with her back facing him, bent down and took his penis in her mouth. He closed his eyes again and began to moan as she ran her tiny pink tongue up and down and across his balls. Slowly she slid her wet legs along his body, pressing into his chest. She lifted her shiny bob – he sometimes thought she must have been a geisha in another life – and pushed the flower against his mouth. 'Breakfast,' she announced.

The Baby G was bleeping every three minutes.

'We should have set off by now.' Harriet slammed her rucksack against Molly, who slammed hers back. Then she tripped down the last three stairs.

'Do you think her clumsiness is getting a bit worse?' said Charlie, retrieving *The Times* from under Nellie's coffin. Sydney's nerves fizzed. She knew this was another ploy to get her to rethink her Job Situation. She filled the kettle to make more strong coffee. Was Harriet's clumsiness getting worse? And could her job be to blame? And if she really didn't feel anything for Dylan, why had she reacted so strongly to Eloise?

'What do you think of Eloise?' she asked casually.

He looked up groggily from a long speech by Gordon Brown. 'Incredibly pretty.'

Sydney slammed the kettle on. 'Didn't you find her a bit
. . . brittle?'

'Didn't notice really. Any woman who offers to babysit at
the last moment so I can see *Barren Landscapes Barren Lives*
has a lot going for her.'

'You're not saying we should take her up on it?'

'Why ever not?' He lost his place and began again.

'We hardly know her.'

'I thought you knew Dylan at university.'

'That doesn't mean we should automatically trust all his
friends.'

'She's a bit more than a friend.'

The Baby G bleeped again. 'For God's sake!' wailed
Harriet piteously.

'Take who up on what?' asked Molly.

'The nice lady from last night offered to babysit so
Mummy and I can go to see a film,' said Charlie, searching
for his briefcase.

'Eloise?' Harriet's eyes lit up. Sydney felt her elder child
might have had the tact to look as though she felt marginally put out at the prospect.

'Yes,' said Charlie. 'How did you know?'

'I met her last night. She's amazing at drawing. And she
made up this brilliant story right off the top of her head.'

Sydney's children hated her made-up stories. She
retrieved Charlie's briefcase which had worked its way from
his study back on to the piano, next to some mange-ridden
dusters that Juanita had left out as a silent rebuke. Sydney
was going to have to get to grips with Tesco.com which had
brought them a nail brush instead of four new dusters. She
handed him his coat. 'So will you give Eloise a call then?' he
asked.

★　　★　　★

Sydney had already jumped two sets of lights on the way from dropping Charlie at work to the girls' school when her mobile rang. She was tempted not to answer when she saw the name St Francine of Assisi flash up, but that was only putting off the inevitable. Trying to dodge Charlie's mother was as futile as trying to evade death.

'Hello, Francine, how lovely to hear from you.' She was sure Francine timed her phone calls – from Gloucestershire's most perfect village – for maximum inconvenience.

'I'm not calling at a bad time, am I, Sydney darling? Only I thought you would probably have dropped the girls off by now.' Sydney tried to float serenely above the subtle recrimination but it wasn't easy with a police car flashing its blue light behind her. 'I have dropped them off.' She turned the radio up to drown out Harriet, who was attempting to recite her times tables to Molly.

'You're not having to trek all the way over to the East End today, are you?' Francine managed to make it sound as though Sydney was setting off for the Crimea, armed only with a poor maiden's smile and a leaky oil lamp. Actually in Francine's mind the Crimea looked like Switzerland compared with London. It was a constant source of amazement to her that her son had chosen to raise his children there and that none of them had been murdered so far.

'That's right. It's Friday, so I'm not going to the office today, Francine,' said Sydney. Though frankly the office would be a good deal more relaxing than the list of chores she had to accomplish most Fridays, when her 'day off' was spent racing around getting Charlie's drycleaning, picking up rare books, rushing backwards and forwards to Canningtons with bits and bobs he'd forgotten . . . she looked at the flashing police light in her wing mirror and winced.

'All the same, you must be absolutely exhausted.'

'I'm fine.' The Baby G signalled again. 'Doors closing,' said Molly, mimicking Harriet.

'Just because you have absolutely no sense of urgency,' screamed Harriet before hitting her sister.

'Was that Harriet's Baby G?' said Francine.

'It's the radio,' said Sydney. 'It's jammed.' Molly began to sing 'In Jesus We Trust', displaying enviable lung capacity during the chorus.

'The reason I'm ringing is that I'm trying to ascertain numbers for Christmas' – which was still six weeks away. And in any case, Francine already knew numbers for Christmas because they were always the same.

'Only I want to keep it small and intimate this year,' said Francine. 'What with Michael . . .' Her voice trailed off and they both fell into guilty reveries, their own minor quibbles momentarily put into perspective at the mention of Francine and Angus's younger son, who, having waited until he was forty-four to get married, had lost his adored Clare to cancer four years later.

'Yes, of course. It's almost a year ago, isn't it?' said Sydney, aware that she hadn't spoken to Michael for a couple of weeks. 'I'm sure we'll be coming – if you'll have us.' In her wing mirror, Sydney saw a policewoman beckoning her to pull over. Stay calm, Sydney, stay calm. The girls began to weep silently now. 'I'll have to speak to Charlie of course . . .'

'Oh, I've already spoken to him,' said Francine sweetly. 'I know how busy you are.'

Sergeant Ray Gibbons left a message while she was on the mobile to Francine to let her know that Charlie had left his favourite pen at the police station again. Would Sydney like to come and pick it up? Sydney couldn't think of anything she'd like less. She barely stopped all day until four, when she went to collect the girls, listened to their squabbles and times tables, mentally composed a list of stuff they still needed from Tesco's and then remembered Charlie had asked her to be at home at 4.20 to take delivery of yet another new laptop. She almost drove into a lamp-post.

She was nowhere near ready when Eloise and Dylan arrived to babysit. After she had shown them where everything was, she was very late.

By the time the Tube had sat for thirteen minutes between Chalk Farm and Camden Town, she was running so late that Charlie was the last person left in the foyer as she arrived at the National Film Theatre. He looked up from *The Times*'s review of the film and beamed, and her heart folded like a falling leaf because his love for her, usually so well concealed beneath a resolutely unromantic not to say cantankerous exterior, was for a moment transparently obvious, even after all these years.

'*Barren Landscapes* is clearly not one of the festival's most popular offerings.' He gazed round the empty foyer. 'What a shame. Still, it's London's loss. I think we're in for a bit of a treat.'

'Charlie, everyone's already gone in,' said Sydney patiently. He'd obviously arrived only a few minutes before her.

'Marvellous seats.' Charlie squeezed her hand conspiratorially and Sydney dared to hope that this might be his oblique way of saying he was coming round to her job.

They might have been well-placed seats, but they weren't entirely comfortable, thought Sydney ruefully, as she juddered awake for the fourth or fifth time to see the eight-strong all-women cast re-enact a famous battle scene from the nineteenth century, shot in a single take on a camcorder. A small streak of saliva glistened on Charlie's shoulder where she had been resting. She hoped to God she hadn't been snoring. Charlie smiled down at her. 'It's awfully good, isn't it? So clever the way they're playing all the parts and with no scenery or props apart from that tree.'

Sydney nodded sleepily. The film was so long and impenetrable it even had two twenty-minute intervals. During the first one Sydney drank two Diet Cokes and hoped the caffeine would somehow keep her awake to the finale, which seemed several months off. During the second interval she gave up trying to fend off sleep and actively courted it with a gin and tonic.

'What it is,' explained Charlie, in response to her question, 'is an acute observation of kingship, seen from the female perspective. It's fascinating to think how resonant the themes of Shakespeare's most obscure plays are to a former Soviet outpost in the twenty-first century, isn't it?'

Sydney nodded and slung back the remainder of her gin. She almost began to think that perhaps Eloise had a point with *Legally Blonde*.

'You did realize it was essentially a reworking of *Richard II*, didn't you?' Charlie steered her back towards their seats. She noticed with a grim satisfaction that 40 per cent of the audience had decided to cut their losses and leave.

Sydney smiled wanly and nodded off a further six times in the final two acts. The film seemed to be unfolding in real time, which was worrying, since according to the programme notes it spanned three centuries of oppression. She was so tired by the time it limped to its finale that she left her favourite scarf under her seat, and when she stepped blinking into the bright light of the foyer again she saw she'd dribbled on her sheepskin coat as well. She'd give the film director bloody oppression.

The film was so long they'd missed any chance of a romantic dinner. And she would have loved to spend an evening out on her own with Charlie, deftly digging out his sly wit – without Ian and Miranda, without Harriet and Molly, without Francine and Angus . . .

When had it happened, she wondered, as they dashed for a taxi home. When had she turned into the kind of woman who couldn't stay awake through a pretentious art-house film?

Damp and exhausted, they finally let themselves into Clifton Crescent at about a quarter past midnight. Sydney paused in the hall, half expecting to hear snatches of mutual adoration between Harriet and Eloise. But there weren't any, which at least had to mean the children were asleep. A cascade of giggles floated through the door of the sitting room. There was a muffled snorting and some noises that sounded like Dylan imitating a lion. Sydney heard Eloise shushing him and more giggles. She and Charlie stood in the hall sheepishly, not wanting to interrupt. Sydney coughed loudly.

The door to the sitting room burst open and Dylan appeared, his shirt hanging out and an empty bottle in his hand. He looked completely unabashed to see them. 'Hi, you two. They're back, Ellie,' he called into the sitting room. Over his shoulder Sydney could see Eloise frantically buttoning up her shirt and pulling down her mini-skirt. She slid her tiny feet into her sling-backs and padded across the room towards them, smoothing her shiny bob on the way. She twisted her body coyly round Dylan, like a snake coiling round a tree, and took his hand, as if she were a small child seeking reassurance from its parents.

'The girls were as good as gold,' she told Sydney.

'I hope they didn't make you read them too many stories.' Behind Eloise and Dylan, Sydney could see a pair of Eloise's fishnets seeping out from one of the cushions on the very rumpled sofa, like the tail of an escaping cat-out-of-the-bag.

'Not at all. They had to stop me reading to them,' gushed Eloise. 'I adore reading aloud.' Her emerald eyes flashed in the hall light. Sydney might have known Eloise would love the sound of her own voice.

'Molly didn't come down at ten o'clock and say she thought she had food poisoning then?' asked Charlie, slipping some briefs out of his briefcase.

Eloise shook her head.

'Or read to you from Genesis?' He seemed intent on engaging them in conversation.

'Don't tell me kids are still listening to them?' said Dylan.

'The Bible,' Sydney interjected hurriedly. 'She's found God. You must be shattered. I'll get your coats.'

The static from Eloise's hair meant it adhered to Dylan's half-open pink shirt like black rain. *The Times*'s TV pages, which Sydney had helpfully left open on the coffee table for them, had clearly not been looked at. She felt a pang. She couldn't remember the last time she and Charlie had had sex, passionate or otherwise. Either they were too tired, or they got interrupted by Hamish or one of the children burrowing into bed with them. Eloise and Dylan, on the other hand, obviously couldn't keep their hands off each other, even on an evening babysitting.

'Harriet didn't have any nightmares about battery hens?' continued Charlie.

Eloise looked puzzled. 'Nothing like that.'

'How was the film?' asked Dylan.

'Absolutely magnificent,' Sydney and Charlie chorused.

'I'm so pleased,' said Eloise, as if she had personally directed the production.

'Though personally I thought they underplayed some of the more important underlying issues,' said Charlie, leading them into the kitchen. 'Though in other ways it was actually more powerful than *Richard II*, on which it was obviously based.'

Dylan tossed the empty bottle in the air and caught it behind him. 'Fancy a beer, Charlie?'

Charlie followed Dylan into the kitchen. The thought of them on their own together sent Sydney into a panic and she trotted after them, with Eloise wiggling behind her.

'Charlie, I'm sure Eloise and Dylan want to get home. They've been here for hours.'

'We're fine,' said Dylan. 'Aren't we, angel?'

'I think I've got an ancient copy of Professor Mayer's *The Conflict Within*,' said Charlie suddenly. 'That's one of your old publications, isn't it, Dylan? Very pertinent to the film we just saw. Fancy a look?'

'Try and keep me away. Our archives are a bit sketchy. The real problem,' Dylan looked momentarily melancholic, 'is trying to get the same quality now. I'm afraid the print-works we used locally closed down long ago. It's impossible to find anyone who produces a typeface like that.'

'And it was so beautiful,' said Charlie. 'I love that half serif.'

'My great-great-grandfather had it specially designed,' said Dylan. 'It is very elegant.' He followed Charlie upstairs to his study.

'I'm afraid they could be gone some time,' Sydney said anxiously. She hoped their conversation would confine itself to a debate about sans serif typefaces, and switched the kettle on. She was starving. But the only food that Juanita hadn't put in the freezer was two packets of doughnuts, and she couldn't possibly consume those in front of Eloise.

'Dylan adores literature. He loved *Bridget Jones*. That's one of the things that made me fall in love with him. I thought it was, you know, a bit of a chick's movie. Of course he says the only reason he liked it was because of Renee Zellweger's boobs. But I know he's a romantic underneath.'

Sydney was transported back in time again. This time to when Dylan had whisked her off one night to see *A Midsummer Night's Dream*. It had been a beautiful production, performed by a lake dotted with neo-classical bridges and tiny follies, and Sydney had been overwhelmed by the romance and glamour of the evening. She closed her eyes. She could almost smell the lemon and pine essence that Dylan had worn in those days, and the slightly musky aroma of his T-shirt. Afterwards they'd gone for a walk by the lake and he'd pulled her against the wall of a grotto lined with sea-shells, quite roughly – she remembered that she'd scratched her bare arms. And then he'd kissed them and told her that he loved her and she hadn't let herself believe him of course, but she had still felt on top of the world.

'. . . It's so English, this love of literature,' she heard Eloise saying. She wrenched herself back to the present. What were Dylan and Charlie talking about upstairs? 'I love the way everyone's so steeped in history in this country. There's a wonderful understanding of culture . . .'

'Shall we go and find them?' asked Sydney when the kettle had boiled.

Eloise yawned daintily. 'I guess. We have a busy week ahead.' Eloise's small pink mouth curled into a satisfied grin. 'Dylan's whisking me off for a few days – although I don't know where. It's a surprise. All I know is that I need my passport – and something warm to wear on the plane. Isn't it romantic?'

They went upstairs and to Sydney's relief discovered Dylan and Charlie still poring over Professor Mayer's *The Conflict Within* and discussing modern-day kingmakers.

'Can you believe Charlie's got this, Ellie? We don't even have a copy in our archives. It's incredible – an absolute classic,' Dylan enthused.

Eloise gave a mirthless laugh.

'I've got heaps of old books in the attic,' said Charlie. 'If you'd like to see them—'

'Another time,' said Sydney hastily.

They stood at the front door and watched Dylan and Eloise trot across the road, their arms entwined. Sydney reached for Charlie's hand. 'Come on, let's go to bed.' She nuzzled against him.

'In a minute,' Charlie called, as she climbed the stairs. 'I just need to turn the light out in the study.' Sydney undressed and slid between the sheets, waiting for her husband. She heard him open the door of his study, take some more books down from the shelves, pour himself a drink and settle at his desk where she knew he'd sit until three at least, working away on the synopsis of his next but one oeuvre, *The Case for Income Tax*. And then she found herself fretting about Eloise and Dylan's weekend away and wondering when it was that she and Charlie had stopped being infatuated with each other.

'So how was dinner the other evening?' Linda's voice was full of concern. Too full. Presumably to make up for her previous lack of interest.

'Fairly predictable,' said Sydney, trying to sound offhand. She hoped they could move on without too much pathology on Linda's part. 'Eloise has the depth of a bottle of nail varnish,' she added. 'And Charlie – the man who didn't notice Julia Roberts sitting next to him when we went to The Ivy that time – thinks she's incredibly pretty. Oh, and Miles left a message in the middle of it, during which he made it perfectly clear we'd arranged for him to call and rescue me.'

'That good? Don't suppose he's come to his senses? Miles, I mean.'

Sydney shook her head. She felt a moral obligation to make amends for Miles's shoddy behaviour, not least because Linda needed her managing editor back. For the last six months Annabelle had been forgetting things, snapping at the contributors and taking mortal offence if anyone offered to take some of her load off her. She was buckling under the weight of her responsibilities, and so were the rest of them.

'Never mind about him. The big question is, how is the ex-love of your life these days? Still spouting sixteenth-century metaphysical poetry? I never could work out why you were such a sucker for that poetry crap.'

'You love poetry.'

'Not when it's quite so obviously being used as bed-bait. What was that one he was particularly fond of reciting to you? Andrew Marvel's "Ode to His Coy Mistress". Otherwise known as "Shag Me Now, Baby, Before Gravity Claims Your Tits". And looks-wise?'

'Didn't notice much difference,' said Sydney, removing a mound of yellowing press clippings from the chair opposite Linda's and sitting down. 'He's put on some weight though. And there were definite signs of grey hair. But his freckles were very much in evidence, which is odd because you would have expected them to fade a bit. Especially the ones that reached almost to his eyes. That little one, right in the corner – still there. But I think the Antarctic's taken its toll a bit. He's a bit ruddier than he was. And it's laughably obvious that Eloise has influenced his fashion sense. He's definitely been spruced up. I hate it when women do that, don't you? It's so proprietorial somehow. And he's very impressed by status. Kept showing us her huge diamond engagement ring.'

'Same old Dylan then.'

'No,' Sydney paused, trying to identify what had changed, 'not the same old Dylan. More like a shell that looks like Dylan, but something's missing inside.'

'So has he aged well or not would you say?'

'I really didn't notice.'

'Of course you didn't. It's perfectly obvious that you hardly gave his looks a moment's notice.'

Sydney ignored Linda's sarcasm and tried to focus on Charlie's brother Michael's problems. She must call him tonight.

'Frankly, I don't know how you can stomach being in the same room after what Dylan did to you.'

'What did he do that was so terrible, Linda?' Sydney wondered why she was being so defensive. 'He had a fling with someone else. Big deal. Everyone shagged around at university. I'd have thought you of all people know that.'

'If you say so. What about Eloise?'

'A competitive under-eater, impossible to have a logical conversation with, and don't get me started on the name-dropping. She's the Edmund Hillary of social climbers.'

'Perfect for Mr Mills and Boon then.'

Sydney had never discovered why Linda had quite such a downer on Dylan. It must be because she'd never heard him reciting John Donne as the sun rose over Clifton Gorge. They'd only met twice. Briefly.

'I think she might be one of those people who pretend to be more stupid than they are.'

'Dangerous. Like Poppy.'

Not like Poppy, thought Sydney. Poppy wasn't remotely dangerous. Just very vulnerable. She had to be, to put up with the men she chose to wallpaper her life with. One way or another, they all treated her very badly, especially that awful Manley Magus, lead singer with Doors to Manual, currently the biggest-selling band in the world and *Heat!*'s favourite pin-up. None of which had stopped him threatening to kill Poppy if she so much as spoke to another man again. Sydney knew this because recently Poppy had taken to ambushing her in the corridor and confiding to her.

'That reminds me. Apparently Poppy's aunt is that very left-wing vegetarian I told you about during my first week of university.'

'Stalinist Stevie, who organized the veggie protests?'

'The very same.'

Linda looked marginally appeased. 'Maybe in the fullness of time we can expect Poppy to mount a major humanitarian putsch – like a beauty campaign in Rwanda to show amputees there that what they really need is a manicure—'

Dave poked his bullet head round the door. 'Are you dumping this week's motoring column or not?' he asked gruffly.

'Not now, Dave,' said Linda. Sydney tried not to look at the message on Dave's T-shirt, which said Oppressed Minority. He normally wore his Thug on the Street Animal in Bed one on Wednesdays. 'Anything else?'

Dave stomped back to his computer. Considering he was probably in the middle of a chess game against some twelve-year-old in Tokyo, he didn't have that much to complain about, Sydney thought. If he weren't so clever, Linda would have fired him ages ago.

'By the way, he is not the love of my life,' snapped Sydney.

'Not now of course. Charlie is. And you'd be a bloody fool if he weren't the love of your life. But once upon a time you and Dylan were soulmates.'

'No.' Sydney stood up. 'Dylan was never my soulmate,' she said firmly. 'I was in lust, that's all. And now I have absolutely no feelings for him whatsoever.'

'Yup,' said Linda brusquely. 'I can see perfectly well that you're over Dylan. Not that it really matters one way or another, because you have Charlie. And Charlie really is perfect. And you're not a fool.'

Sydney's mound of post seemed to increase exponentially every day. And she loved it. She knew the marriage guidance man would probably say that she was just trying to validate her privileged existence via other people's problems and that she was in danger of developing a God complex. But the marriage guider wasn't around, so he could get stuffed. Why shouldn't she glean a little satisfaction from the fact that not only was she acquiring new correspondents by the sackload, but quite a number of them were turning out to be regulars? Even if it did mean she rarely got a lunch break. She was half-way through a plate of walnut and Stilton sandwiches when the receptionist found her.

'There's a bloke downstairs who says he's come to take you to lunch.' She eyed Sydney's sandwiches enviously.

Beneath his headphones, Dave tossed her a contemptuous look. He made a big deal about never going out for lunch when Sydney was around, even though Helen had told Sydney that he always went out on the days she wasn't in the office. 'I'm not expecting anyone,' she said loudly, for Dave's benefit.

'He's very insistent.'

Reluctantly Sydney took the lift to the ground floor.

'Hello, Miles,' she said coolly. She didn't feel like listening to his sexual exploits today. She wasn't even hungry – and she certainly didn't feel like paying for Miles' lunch after the Selfridges blow-out.

'Yeah, sorry about not phoning back the other night,' he said sheepishly. 'Jacquie and I ended up having a bit of a heart-to-heart and well, one thing led to another. You survived it though, I see.'

Sydney eyed his new leather jacket. It looked expensive, which at least explained why he hadn't yet paid Annabelle his share of Joshie's brace, and at least ten years too young for him.

'I know this great new place I want to take you to.' His eyes raked over the impressive glass-walled mezzanine that loomed over the vast, empty reception area. Sydney glanced at her watch. All the journalists on Schmucklesons' other publications must still be at lunch, idle sods.

'I've eaten, I'm afraid,' she said.

'Doesn't usually stop you.' He bundled her through the revolving doors. Sydney swivelled back inside. 'I'm busy, Miles,' she said firmly.

'Come on, Syd.' He looked utterly crestfallen. Under the merciless foyer lights his skin looked cratered and his stubble patchy. 'I really need to talk.'

It was uncanny, mused Sydney, how even when he was allegedly broke, Miles always kept up with the latest restaurants, bars, clothes, music. And he'd clearly been to Herb!, the slick bar/restaurant which had sprung up not far from the *IQ* offices, before. Still, she did need some fresh air. And she'd just have a black coffee.

They sat in a corner booth, surrounded by skinny young women with long, flat hair, low-cut jeans and brightly coloured thongs. When they stood up to leave they looked like a flock of migrating swallows.

'So what do you think?' she heard Miles saying.

'What about?' Sydney looked at him blankly. Some fettuccine had settled in the dimple of his chin.

'Paris. Do you agree with it?'

'What do you mean, do I agree with it? Do I agree that it exists, or do I agree with how it voted in the last election?'

'Jesus, Sydney, haven't you been listening to anything I've said? Do you agree that I should keep it a surprise from Jacquie? You know, blindfold her at the airport, keep her in the dark? Or would she rather know where we're going in advance, so she can pack accordingly?'

Sydney stared at Miles's badly shaven chin and wondered what it was that apparently made him irresistible to so many women. As far as she could see, his boyish charms were dwindling rapidly. Only last week he'd told Annabelle that he couldn't afford to pay for the twins to have judo lessons. And now he was off to Paris with Jacquie, who never deviated from her uniform of tight skimpy tops, tighter jeans and stilts anyway. So why telling her where she was going would make any difference to her packing plans was a mystery. Sydney wanted to hit him for his insensitivity. Instead she told him that he was starting to look more and more like their father.

'Christ, you really know how to kick a man when he's down.'

Everyone apart from her and Charlie seemed to be going off on mystery weekends. The bill arrived. Naturally Miles didn't even pretend to offer to get it. He might be self-deluding but he wasn't a hypocrite. She got out her wallet and settled up silently. She wasn't going to give Miles her approval over whatever it was he was planning with Jacquie, but one day she would ask him why he always needed it.

'What's the matter, Syd?' he asked as they walked back to the office. 'You seem very tense. Didn't the soufflés rise or is it Charlie who's not rising enough? You should have taken Jacquie's advice about the Myla underwear. She knows how to keep a man happy, I can tell you.'

'I'd rather you didn't,' she snapped. What had gone so wrong the other night? Was Eloise really too gorgeous for her to cope with? Or was it simply that Dylan had spectacularly failed to live up to her memories?

Trust Miles to see everything in crude sexual terms, thought Sydney. Still, what did she expect from someone who gleaned most of his psychological insights from reading *What Car??* She'd told him the truth about the dinner anyway. In the absence of any other interested listeners, she'd had to. She most certainly wasn't attracted to Dylan, she explained – just furious with him for coming to live in Clifton Crescent and jeopardizing things with Charlie.

'But if you're not attracted to him, then how is it jeopardizing things with Charlie?' Miles had asked as they approached the revolving doors of Icon Towers. What a bloody stupid, insensitive question. It was the same question Linda asked her later in the afternoon. And she didn't have an answer for it then either.

At five she remembered to call Charlie's brother Michael. There was no answer. She hoped he wasn't sitting alone in the dark listening to Bach, thinking of his all too brief time with Clare. All that plangent solitude wasn't helping him.

That was the trouble with brooding. It tended to be self-perpetuating.

Dylan and Eloise's romantic tryst away turned out to be much longer than a weekend. Not that Sydney was particularly interested, but she heard from Maisie, who heard from Mrs Protheroe that they'd gone to Rome, somewhere Sydney longed to return. But since the children she and Charlie never seemed to find the time to go anywhere by themselves.

It was made all the longer by Charlie working and Sydney spending all her spare time on her own, sorting out the various broken appliances Juanita had piled up in the hall and chauffeuring Harriet and Molly between play dates. In a rare spare half hour she settled down in the sitting room to catch up on the Joanna Trollope she'd been reading for months, only to find herself overwhelmed by the scent of Eloise's Shalimar, which had seeped its way into the sofa.

Sydney began to think it might actually be possible to be neighbours and not see Dylan and Eloise very often after all. Once Eloise and Dylan got round to rescuing Glendower Books properly and met people who were much more glamorous than Sydney and Charlie they'd probably never see them at all.

Eighteen days later, Sydney arrived at home after work to find Eloise standing on the doorstep in front of her. She was holding a pale green plate with pink roses on it, just like the broken one in Sydney's kitchen.

'For you.' She held it out and smiled. 'I knew I'd seen a similar one before. A friend in New York buys and sells English china. I got her to send it over.'

'You shouldn't have,' blurted Sydney, wishing Eloise

wouldn't keep making her beholden – and feeling ungracious. She turned away sharply, tears smarting her eyes.

'Oh, please.' Eloise watched Sydney fumble with her keys. 'It's the least we can do after your hospitality.'

'Eloise!' Molly slid down the banisters and threw herself at Eloise who scooped her up and twirled her round the hall. Harriet, conscious of her age superiority, was more circumspect but no less pleased to see Eloise. 'I've been practising drawing those pigs the way you showed us,' she said shyly. 'Hi, Mum,' she added, spying Sydney by the door.

'But she put them in chains, and tied them to a thunderbolt,' said Molly.

'Sydney, Dylan and I were wondering if you'd like to come to dinner one night this week,' said Eloise as Molly took her hand. 'It's such a novelty,' she continued. 'In New York no one has dinner parties. You could fit four apartments into the kitchen we've got here.'

'That would be lovely,' said Sydney weakly. 'I'll have to check with Charlie to see when he's free. And also Maisie.'

'Taking my name in vain?' Maisie bustled into the hall in her coat.

'I was just saying Dylan and I want to have Charlie and Sydney over for dinner one night this week and she was saying you're a wonderful babysitter.'

'But a very busy one,' said Sydney.

'I daresay we can sort something out,' Maisie said in a heroic voice.

'That's very kind,' said Sydney, 'but as *I* was saying, this is a hectic time of year for Charlie.'

'Is it?' said Maisie. 'There's nothing written on the calendar.'

'Isn't there?' said Sydney, wishing for once that Maisie would bugger off early. She didn't want Eloise thinking she and Charlie never went out except to see tragically dreary films. Any more than she wanted to have supper with them ever again. 'You know what Charlie's like about writing dates down.'

'About time you two had a proper social life,' said Maisie.

Patience Truelove would probably say she should have mentioned Dylan years ago to Charlie. Which only went to show how bloody easy it was to be wise about other people's problems. If she told him now, he'd assume in that inconvenient, analytical way of his, that she must have had something to hide. Eloise didn't seem to know about her and Dylan either – and she looked the type to go into meltdown over things like that.

'Like what exactly?' Linda asked.

'You know what,' said Sydney. 'It's no big deal. Really. I would have preferred to let sleeping dogs lie, that's all.'

Linda returned to her computer screen. 'Bingo,' she said in a tremulous voice.

'What is it?' asked Sydney, looking out of the window across to Tower Bridge, which was threaded with lights under the dark autumn sky.

'They've found me a baby,' said Linda. 'A little girl. I can't believe it. Sydney, I really think it's going to happen this time. And it's going to be perfect. I know they let me down before but really it was just as well. I wasn't ready. But I'm really going to be there for her. I thought I'd call her Rose – after your mum.'

There wasn't much Sydney could say in response. Her mother, who had been like a second mother to Linda when they were teenagers and had kept in touch with her when Sydney had gone off to Bristol and Linda had been at

Cambridge, would have been very worried about this latest decision. She had always believed children needed at least two parents, which is why she'd put up with Sydney's father.

Sydney was pondering how to ask Linda tactfully if she was really sure she was doing the right thing, because it seemed to her – not that she would have said so in so many words – that Linda would have a hard time being there for a goldfish let alone a child, when there was a call from reception.

'Another handsome stranger to see you, Sydney. You really are a dark horse.'

'I was passing the National Film Theatre when I saw that *Whatever Happened to Baby Jane?* was playing there,' Dylan was saying. 'Do you remember how much we loved that film when we first saw it? I think we must have sat through it about four times.'

Sydney looked at him in disbelief. 'The National Film Theatre isn't on the way to anywhere.' She grinned, despite her misgivings. 'Anyway, I thought you were strictly a *Terminator Four* man these days?'

'Ah, that. As you'll have gathered, Eloise isn't big on art-house culture. So in a bid to get into her knickers I had to make out I wasn't either.'

'I assumed that was all a bit of an act on Eloise's part – to outdo you.' He looked at her wistfully – or perhaps she imagined it – and shook his head.

'So what do you do, read Yeats under the duvet?'

'So you do remember something about me.'

'How can you live like that when you loved books and poetry so much?'

'We all make compromises in marriage, Sydney,' he said meaningfully. 'Anyway, I've got Glendower Books now. It was a bit of a shock for Eloise when I told her I wanted to come back to England and rescue it. But she's taken it amazingly well – frankly, I'm in love with her all over again.' He beamed at Sydney with a dazed expression.

Sydney tried to look neutral. 'Why aren't you taking her to the cinema, or is it past her bedtime?' It had slipped out before she had a chance to realize she was even thinking it.

'Eloise is very good for me,' Dylan said quietly. 'She stops me being a pretentious git.'

'And Charlie's very good for me,' said Sydney. 'He'll be waiting at home if I don't get a move on.'

Dylan smiled. 'You mean that scary childminder of yours will. Eloise has told me about her.'

So they did talk occasionally.

'A quick drink at least?' He looked at her beseechingly. 'And then I'll drive you home. I've been slaving all day over a rich banker in Docklands.'

'Sounds suitably sordid.'

'Just trying to get funds together to invest in Glendower Books.' He raked his hands through his hair and suddenly looked weary. 'It's a bit of an uphill job, to be honest.' He was about to say something but stopped himself. He turned up the collar of his coat. She looked at his cheekbones jutting over the top of it. He really hadn't changed much at all. Not in this light. He bundled her under his coat. 'Come on, it's freezing. One fireside drink and I'll get you home faster than that bloody slug they call the Tube ever will.'

He took her to a cosy pub by the river and over a glass of wine she found herself telling him about the tensions of going back to work and about The Rolling Scones. He laughed and asked if they were an ironic clan.

Sydney shook her head. 'I don't think so. Or facetious.' He grinned. And told her he'd never seen her as the stay-at-home type. Then he asked whether Charlie knew about their relationship.

She shook her head.

'I don't know whether to be offended or extremely flattered.'

'It just never came up,' said Sydney. 'Why should it?'

He looked at her with those tiger eyes. 'Sydney, why are you so scared of us?'

'Us?' She echoed. 'Anyone would have thought we were something out of Euripides.'

'Weren't we?'

'Enid Blyton. Without the emotional maturity or psychological insight.'

'Savage.' He held his hand against his heart in mock pain and seemed to be considering something. 'Well, have it your way. Eloise is a bit sensitive about exes anyway. It'll be our secret. I promise.'

7

Sydney acknowledged only very slowly that Christmas would be slightly different from previous ones in the Murray household. By the time she admitted to herself – and by accident to Mrs Protheroe – that not only had she not got round to making a holly, mistletoe and cinnamon wreath for the front door, but that she was extremely unlikely to, she had a good inkling that things were not going to run smoothly. There were other clues that suggested Christmas might deviate from the norm this year. She hadn't made her own sugar-free organic mincepies. Nor had there been a messy weekend of tangled string, pine needles and glitter trodden into the carpet, at the end of which she and the children would proudly show Charlie their handmade cards. That was because Maisie had beaten her to it, or rather, she bought them Disney ones from Woolworths to colour in.

And she and Charlie hadn't had sex for four months. That was far worse than any previous records. Taking a cue from Poppy, Sydney had investigated Brazilians, leg waxing and an Ann Summers' catalogue, and had even considered buying a lace corset that featured thirty hand-sewn hooks and eyes and cost £200. But she'd stopped herself on the grounds that even if she got round to putting it on, Charlie would never find the time to undo the damned thing.

Even so, Sydney was determined that Christmas would be business as usual. And she did mean business, with all the grim determination to have fun that implied. She wasn't going to give anyone, least of all Francine, any reason to look her sadly in the eye on Christmas Day and ask her if she wasn't driving herself too hard.

As a result she drove herself much too hard. In a bid to prove that her job hadn't impinged in any way whatsoever on anyone in the Murray family, she took on far too much. At work she assumed more and more responsibility – anything Linda threw at her, basically. And at home, she drew up an Advent schedule, drawing a triple circle round 2 December, the last day for ordering the charity cards that she always kept in reserve in case there weren't enough homemade ones to go round when people not on their extensive list took the irritating step of sending them one, and slotting in rehearsal periods for the girls' carol concert. And she completely forgot to book their annual Easter holiday at La Rosa, the gorgeous villa fifteen kilometres from Seville that they'd begun to look on as their own.

Molly was giving a recital on the recorder, guitar, flute and clarinet. Harriet was playing the triangle at the end of 'Ding Dong Merrily on High'. She was also a controversial choice as Mary, which was emotionally draining for all of them as learning her lines was proving to be a nightmare. To cap it all, during a particularly fraught rehearsal in which Harriet kept missing her cue, Miranda had rung to find out if Sydney had managed to find any hessian to make the shepherds' costumes.

'What shepherds?' asked Sydney, knowing the awful answer even before Miranda told her – with a discernible smugness that made Sydney want to punch her – that the teachers had determined this year that all costumes should be homemade to avoid unseemly displays of competitiveness in Hamley's fancy dress department.

'You must have seen the note,' said Miranda, with the predictably sanctimonious efficiency of a founding member of The Rolling Scones. Sydney panicked. Notes came home on Fridays. So she couldn't even blame Maisie. How could she have missed this vital one?

Sydney wanted to lavish perfect gifts on everyone. She knew this was just another way of demonstrating that they had all become winners since she'd gone back to work. But she did it all the same. The most stressful blip on the horizon was selecting a present for Francine, who was impossible to find anything for. Everything that ought to have been just right for her – Nigella Lawson cookery utensils, the complete works of Louis de Bernières – she always turned out to have just bought. If Sydney – and it always was Sydney, Charlie had never yet managed to get all his Christmas shopping done before 26 December – went off piste and bought something a bit more exotic – a day at Spa NK, for instance – Francine would thank her profusely while managing to indicate that she found the gift a little odd. Odd was her favourite word.

To complicate Sydney's schedule further, Linda asked her if she'd consider going full-time, just until Annabelle was back to her old self and could do her job properly. The very thought of Charlie buying this was so laughable that Sydney wanted to scream at Linda not to be so bloody stupid. But figuring she got enough of that sort of treatment from Brian Widlake, she merely said she'd have to discuss it with Charlie.

Linda stared at her with the faux uncomprehending look she resorted to whenever she felt Sydney was betraying the sisterhood. 'Sydney, don't you ever think that sometimes – just occasionally – you might be doing Charlie a disservice?'

'What do you mean?'

'Has it ever occurred to you that you may be a teeny bit responsible for the fact that he can barely locate his own kitchen, let alone operate the dishwasher or the oven?'

Sydney ignored the gross injustice of this slur. This was the first time Linda had ever acknowledged Charlie's domestic shortcomings, so perhaps she was finally starting to see Sydney's perfect life from a slightly more realistic perspective.

'All I'm saying is that sometimes it's useful to infantilize our nearest and dearest. It gives us a role in life.'

That was bloody rich, coming from Linda, who was only too happy to infantilize herself by swanning off to a silver beach where there was no chance of Christmas ever being celebrated every year. But secretly Sydney was exhilarated by this token of Linda's dependence, even if she had as much chance of winning Charlie round as Sylvester Stallone did of starring in the next Jane Austen. Oh, he'd say it was all right *if that's what she really wanted to do* and then make endless jokes about the children having to be taken into care and them all dying of scurvy. And then Francine would swoop in, like an avenging member of the SAS, to take command of the situation and present Sydney with a subscription to *Country Living*.

There were advantages to having neighbours she could trust to take in packages when she was out, but Sydney would have preferred it if one of them hadn't been the first man who had taken her from behind. The regular suppers *à quatre* were getting out of hand. Eloise would never take no for an answer, however, even though she clearly found entertaining guests at home an alien and slightly unhygienic concept. Still, the new kitchen was her pride and joy. She called it the hub of the house and it did look like a hub-cap, partly thanks to Eloise's views, repeatedly explained to her cleaner, that cooking crap cluttering the work surfaces wasn't her style, and partly because the floor was made from industrial rubber. Any existing kitchen appliances were safely concealed behind black laminate doors as if they were somehow deviant.

At least Eloise was brilliant at ordering take-aways for other people. She loaded everyone else's plates with creamy chicken korma, spicy pad plah, and steaming duck pancakes. Then she spent all evening picking at a plate of steamed vegetables.

After their fourth supper in as many weeks, Eloise dragged Sydney into the stark living room. Despite being 18 December, it looked about as Christmassy and uplifting as a stint on Death Row. Sydney shivered. She wasn't crazy about leaving Dylan and Charlie on their own, despite Dylan's assurances that he would never say anything to Charlie about their relationship.

'Damn, we left the wine in the kitchen,' said Sydney. 'Shall I nip back and fetch the bottle?'

'Sit down. I'll open another one all to ourselves. As a matter of fact, I've got something to tell you.' Eloise smiled coyly at Sydney. 'We're planning to start a family as soon as possible.'

'Er, congratulations,' said Sydney, unfamiliar with the etiquette for pre-pregnancy announcements. She wondered where Eloise planned to keep the embryo. Behind the laminate kitchen doors perhaps.

'I don't want to leave it too late.' Eloise curled up in a tight ball in the corner of the white leather Mies van de Rohe sofa. 'I'm nearly twenty-six.'

'That's hardly old.' Sydney took in the huge Precious

O'Dowd flashing traffic-light installation in the corner of the room.

'Isn't it fabulous?' enthused Eloise. 'We just got it. The green symbolizes the Christmas tree. The red is berries. And the amber . . . I've forgotten what the amber represents.'

'Alcohol poisoning?' suggested Sydney.

'The cool thing is that at Easter you just switch the red on to represent Christ's blood. You can work out combinations for Passover too. Precious intends it as an all-year-round installation.' Eloise looked at Sydney earnestly. She had the flawless, porcelain face of an airbrushed doll. 'You were terribly young when you had Harriet. I want to be a young mother like you are. You're so great with your girls.' Sydney felt herself softening towards Eloise. 'I bet you have a wonderful mother.'

Sydney nodded. 'Had. She died. What makes you say that?'

'You're such a natural yourself. I'm so sorry she's dead. What was she like?'

'She was . . . terrific really,' said Sydney, feeling very uptight and English. She liked to keep her thoughts on her mother private, even where Linda was concerned. It was a way of preserving her memory and, she supposed, keeping the bond between them as tight as it had been when she'd been alive.

'My mother's hopeless.' Eloise picked at an invisible thread on her jeans. 'If it hadn't been for an army of nannies I swear we'd all have been taken into care. She barely knew how many of us she'd had, let alone how old we were.'

Sydney smiled at the extravagant hyperbole. 'I'm not exaggerating.' Eloise poured Sydney some more champagne. 'I see her about twice a year on average – Christmas and Thanksgiving. Three the year my brother died.'

'I'm sorry – I didn't know,' said Sydney awkwardly.

'Nineteen. He was a straight-A student and a manic sportsman. He broke his neck in a skiing accident.' Her voice cracked. 'It's hard talking about it.'

'I know – I never talk about my mother. Not even with Charlie. It's like a retreat where I go to when I want to be on my own.'

'Me too,' said Eloise. 'Jed was more than a brother. He filled in all the voids where my mother should have been.'

'My mother was like that – she filled in all the gaps where my father should have been.' Sydney bit her lip. She never spoke about the past. Any of it.

'Do you look like her?' asked Eloise gently.

'Not really – she was tall and blonde and she made lots of her own clothes. Sometimes she could look a bit weird – or at least she never looked like any of the other mothers. When they were all layering their hair like Jane Fonda in *Klute* and wearing mini-skirts, she floated around in these amazing Fifties pouffy dresses she used to buy in Oxfam, like a hippy Grace Kelly. She was a really free spirit. She and my father set up this commune in Wales – well, it was her efforts that kept it going really – and so we, Miles and I, grew up in this ramshackle house in the middle of the Black Mountains.'

'Is that where you got your name?'

'What do you mean?'

'Sydney – after a town there?'

'Sydney was my dad's little flourish. After Cyd Sharisse. My mother wanted to call me Sarah. She didn't like gimmicky names. But Dad was the one who went to register the birth, and Dad was the one who took it into his own hands to change it.'

'Cool name though.'

136

'I was teased endlessly at school. They always said I was really a boy.'

Eloise groaned sympathetically. 'Not good. Still, Wales sounds beautiful and the house was old and rambling? I'm guessing here.'

'We shared it with two other families and tried to be self-sufficient. Years before it became fashionable my mum was trying to find a way to fight corporate globalism.'

'Whereas my mother single-handedly kept it going. If she could have mainlined Christian Dior she would have,' said Eloise ruefully. 'She sounds pretty formidable, your mom.'

Sydney looked at her. How could she be utterly vacuous one moment and so sympathetic and likeable the next? For the first time she began to understand why Dylan was infatuated: Eloise was probably like plutonium – quite rewarding if handled carefully.

'She was – but she was funny too. And much more subversive than any of my friends. She used to take me on marches when I was tiny and if I got tired we would go to the Ritz or Claridge's for tea because she'd worked out that mouthful for mouthful it was the best value in London – plus you could sit there all day. And the waiters were all in love with her. She was so . . . vibrant. And just when you thought you'd got the measure of her she would say something outrageous to confound you.'

'Was your dad a free spirit too?'

'Not really. Just a cheap one. I don't suppose he would have followed any of it through if it hadn't been for her. He's found life a bit challenging since she died.'

'Sounds like your mom would have got on well with my dad. He's funny and interesting too . . . I adore him. But he's completely trampled on by my mother. She's a terrible snob. She always says she's entitled to be, coming from one of the

137

oldest families in San Francisco. But the Fairweathers are pretty grand too, and loaded. And Dad's so darn nice. Too nice. I'm sure my mother contributed to his cancer.'

'He has cancer?' asked Sydney, berating herself for every unkind thought she'd ever had about Eloise. Losing a parent was hell. 'That's what my mother died from – breast.'

'Pancreatic.' Eloise reached her hand out and took Sydney's. 'I'm so sorry. Dad's in remission, but with my mother around it's safe to say being buried alive next to a ticking bomb would be more relaxing.' She threw back her head and groaned. 'Sometimes I think we should just lock her inside Cartier and throw away the key.'

Sydney smiled. 'What does Dylan make of her?'

'They haven't actually met yet,' said Eloise. 'We eloped.' She rolled her eyes. 'She didn't entirely approve of our union.'

'Really?' asked Sydney. Surely the objections hadn't been social? Not with Eloise under the impression Dylan was descended from medieval British royalty.

'My mother was worried he might be gold-digging Euro-trash. I tried to explain the Plantagenets were hardly the same as some two-cents European royalty.' She shrugged. 'But in the end I couldn't put my dad through the saga of it. It would have been so divisive. And what with his illness . . .' She broke off. 'God, listen to me. I haven't even finished feeding you yet.'

Sydney followed Eloise back into the kitchen where Eloise proceeded to serve them all triple-layered chocolate cake with mascarpone, while she nibbled on an orange.

Sydney felt her reservations begin to melt like cream on hot fudge cake. She'd always thought Dylan must have had a good reason for marrying Eloise. He had to be a decent judge of character – otherwise what did it say about the relationship he'd had with her?

But reflecting over Eloise's revelation that she and Dylan were thinking of starting a family, she felt an avalanche of envy that shocked her with its violence. Eloise was about to embark on the adventure of pregnancy when Sydney had put all that behind her. Eloise's life would change dramatically with the creation of who knew how many more small humans, while Sydney's life stretched out in front of her like a bolt of unfurled fabric – she could see all the bumps and nicks ahead. It wasn't the unknown that was so terrifying, she sometimes thought, so much as the deadening predictability of the known.

But there it was. Harriet had been born by Caesarian whilst Molly's umbilical cord had wrapped itself round her neck and the pair of them had nearly died in the ensuing struggle to get her out in time. After Molly Charlie had put his foot down and said he wasn't going through that again. It was his way, Sydney knew, of making light of what had been potentially tragic – and she was touched by his urge to protect her. He said two children were more than enough for any greedy, gas-guzzling westernized family, when she knew he would have liked three or four.

Sydney was very quiet for the next few days. Eventually even Charlie noticed.

'Are you fretting because you haven't made your own mince pies this year?' he said when they'd endured a particularly silent supper together. He'd been even later home than usual and Sydney was beginning to think that a few more dinners across the road might not go amiss. At least Charlie seemed to perk up and make some conversation when he was with Dylan, even if it revolved around issues of kingship and tort.

She looked up and saw him studying her. For one insane micro-moment, she contemplated telling him about the other baby she'd desperately wanted. Then she saw his eyes flick back to the folded copy of the *FT* he'd casually placed next to his plate, and thought better of it. Instead, she went to look in on the girls and count her blessings – which surely included not taking on that extra day at work – until the mad, compulsive longing went away.

But it didn't. And five sleepless nights later she began to wonder how she'd ever managed to convince herself the wound had been cauterized in the first place. There had been twinges before – birthdays were always difficult – but nothing to compare with this overwhelming sadness and longing that had seeped through her bones into her blood-stream – ever since the day, five months earlier, when she'd first got in touch with the Adoption Register – and was leaching into her brain, imprinting itself across her heart so that she was viscerally tormented.

She looked out of the steamy windows on to the sodden streets. She was meant to be on the Circle Line heading east towards the office but here she was heading south in a cab. The insanity made her feel momentarily nauseous. She opened the window slightly to get some air. In the rain, London looked even more untidy than usual. Gradually the untidiness gave way to a defeated air of shabby chaos as the taxi made its way towards Elephant and Castle where the dusty tinsel decorations strung up outside some of the shops juddered under the deluge of hailstones just as much as the handsome Christmas trees outside the multi-million-pound houses round Regent's Park had. The British climate was a great leveller.

The taxi came to a halt on a choked high road in front of

a large self-storage shed painted an eye-tormenting yellow and blue, the dismal cheerfulness of which contrasted so bleakly with the depressing nature of the place that Sydney almost wanted to laugh, but she couldn't because she was crying.

She willed herself to press on. How many of these storage rooms and boxes contained the furniture of people who'd had their houses repossessed? How many were filled with belongings of pensioners who had been forced to move into homes, and were being kept here rather than sold off, in the self-deluding optimism of people who knew in their hearts they'd never again be in a position to reclaim them?

Grimly she walked past the reception, with its bright stickers advertising 15 per cent off the first three months' rental and a huge poster explaining why Storepac was the best value self-storage in the Elephant and Castle. It was certainly the most colourful, thought Sydney, as the flat, grey light bore down on the glass roof of the building like sheets of steel.

Heart sticking to her ribs, Sydney stepped into a lift, her heels clattering noisily on the metal floor. The lift ground its way slowly up past the storage rooms and cubicles on the first floor to the second floor where the smallest units were. Hers was more of a locker really. Sydney studied the plan she'd picked up at the front desk and followed the corridor round, past rows of bright green signs and identical doors spray-painted an absurdly cheery daffodil-yellow. It was like being in a greenhouse full of buried mementos, thought Sydney, as she wove round the antiseptic aisles, her heels clicking on the stud metal floor. Perhaps the owners of Storepac thought this sterile, primitive kindergarten colour scheme was the best antidote to the painful memories shored up behind each door. Her heart was beating so fast she couldn't concentrate properly, and she walked round the entire floor twice before she located the right door. Despite Storepac's chirpy claim to provide access twenty-four hours a day, seven days a week, Sydney hadn't been there for years.

She almost walked past her locker. Even when she forced herself to retrace her steps it was as if an invisible force-field was holding her back from it. She stood in front of it for a few moments, her vision blurring. Her hand shook so violently as she tried to unlock the door that she dropped the key on the floor with a clang. She almost gave up again but the other urge – the one that made her want to tear away at the wound she had fooled herself into believing had healed over – was stronger. She picked up the key and fumbled with the lock. It was so stiff she thought she was going to have to go back downstairs and ask for assistance. Then suddenly the door swung open and she was accosted by a fragile, sweet, musty smell that grabbed her by the throat, the heart and every other internal organ as violently as the stale smell of rosewater on her mother's old clothes did, or the pine and lemon essence that Dylan used. It was like a hand pulling her back into the past. She steadied herself against the door and tried to keep in the present.

Trembling, she reached into the locker. The air around her hand seemed to change and grow heavier. The locker was poignantly bare, apart from a few pathetic remnants and a pile of birthday cards, dutifully bought and posted to Storepac every year. She could have fitted the entire contents easily into a drawer at home, if they hadn't been so explosive. She looked at the pale reddish tuft of hair, soft as thistledown, that lay on top of a cream crocheted baby shawl that had been hers when she was born, and at the forlorn-looking floppy toy dog next to it, with its shaggy white hair that had gone slightly grey with age. Poor stupid toy. Never played with. Sydney stroked it, and the tears that had been pressing behind her eyes all morning streamed down her face. She pressed the shawl against her face and sat down on the floor, her sobs echoing down the deserted corridors.

When she had recovered, she placed the blanket back in the cupboard. But not before she had taken out, and then replaced once more, the crumpled, fading Polaroid of herself that a harried midwife had hurriedly taken that devastating morning nearly eighteen years ago when Sydney had given birth to her baby son and then given him away to strangers.

Dave was almost in a good mood when Sydney got to the *IQ* offices. He'd convincingly trashed Helen in an argument about whether or not Alanis Morissette was crap, and was getting on with the serious business of running his red pen through some freelance copy.

Linda was in a good mood too. The adoption agency had told her she could expect some very good news in January. And she'd just commissioned an exciting piece on Dostoevsky. Sydney was desolate. She must have been mad to come into the office after her visit to the Elephant and Castle.

She hadn't realized how much it would affect her. Ever since she'd had Owen she'd developed her own Black Hole – it was where she pushed all the uncomfortable emotions about her dead mother and her missing baby, a pit locked away where her soul should be, so deep and inaccessible it had become a vacuum. She'd actually convinced herself she wasn't that affected by what she'd done. Naturally she thought about it from time to time – when she was giving birth to Harriet and again when Molly was born, especially when she thought she was going to lose her too. But she'd convinced herself that her feelings at eighteen had only been half formed and that giving a baby away when you were a teenager couldn't possibly be as painful as it would be if you were older and more experienced.

And she had been different then. So sure of herself in some ways that she'd never questioned what she was doing. She hadn't told anyone she was pregnant. Especially not her mother, who had big enough problems coping with her illness. She thought she could deal with it herself, quickly and efficiently. And she was right. She'd been in Milan for the most obvious bits of her pregnancy. She hadn't even had to miss any of her studies – he'd been born at the start of the holidays. She hadn't gone home that Easter, pleading pressures of work. It was better that way as by then her mother was dying. Sydney couldn't face telling her she was pregnant, even though she would have understood, but Sydney needed to keep each unfolding disaster separate before they coalesced and drowned her. With her mother dying, it was unthinkable that she could kill another human being. So adoption – such an unusual step for a middle-class girl, the social worker had beamed – it was.

'You look terrible.' Linda flopped a folder of CVs on to Sydney's desk, making her jump. 'What's the matter? The merry olde Yuletide season making you feel you could murder someone?'

Sydney gazed at Linda mutely. She wanted to slink away and hibernate. To her horror, Linda perched on her desk and kicked a daintily shod foot backwards and forwards, a worrying sign that she was in a chatty mood. Fortunately she mainly wanted to chat about her own problems.

'Fucking Widlake,' she announced conversationally. Sydney peered round Linda's shoulder to see if anyone had heard. They were glued to their computers. Which meant they were all furiously eavesdropping. 'He wants a total relaunch by the end of March. I don't think he has any inkling how much work that actually entails. Oh, and Helen's officially handed in her notice.'

Sensing her name being taken in a not entirely flattering context, Helen looked over towards Sydney and waved sheepishly.

'You can't say she didn't give you sufficient warning.' Sydney reached into her top drawer for a packet of Snowy Doughies. She needed a sugar rush to get her through the morning. 'She's been on about three years' notice.'

'That's just it,' fumed Linda. 'Nobody takes you seriously if you constantly cry wolf. Talk about betrayal.'

Sydney shifted uncomfortably. If Linda felt betrayed by her PA leaving after eight years, what would she think when Sydney told her she couldn't go full-time?

'Would it help if I edited down these CVs for you?' asked Sydney. 'I could interview a dozen and make a short list. You never know,' she lowered her voice, 'Helen's leaving could turn out to be for the best. You're always saying how depressing she is.'

'Be my guest.' Linda slapped the folder down next to the box of Snowy Doughies and stalked off. 'They're all crap,' she added haughtily.

On the morning of Harriet and Molly's carol concert Mrs Protheroe was up and about early, yelling up at the students' house from the road and waking up all around. It was almost like having a cockerel in the neighbourhood. 'Crapulent fraudster,' she called. 'Lombardy pirate. A pox on your puissant shit. The sun will go on shining without your vomitous panhandling.'

Dan leaned out of his window and watched with detached amusement. 'It *is* nice weather for the time of year,' he called down.

'And if you think I'm paying my taxes, you lumpen lickspittle, you've got another think coming. Not a penny of mine shall go to the lackwit bumpkins and dancing whores.'

'Good on you, Mrs P,' said Dan.

Mrs P rolled up her skirt and spat at him.

She was right about one thing though, Sydney thought. It was a gorgeous day. The sky was the colour of a Bel Air swimming pool, with delicate white clouds swaying gently across it like celestial chandeliers – and all hell had broken out upstairs at number 64.

'Where the fuck's my sheet music for "Jesu Joy of Man's Desiring"?' shrieked Molly.

Sydney tried to look appropriately outraged. 'You will not use language like that.'

'I can't help it. I'm stressed.'

Not to be outdone, Harriet's eyes filled with hot tears, which dripped on to the highly flammable-looking Snow White bodice that Maisie, whose sewing skills had turned out to be even more limited than Sydney's, had imaginatively teamed with an old Pocahontas mock suedette skirt. 'That slattern whore has stolen my veil,' she sobbed. Sydney took a deep breath. She was going to have to do something about Mrs Protheroe.

'Once in Royal David's City' always filled Sydney with a deeply enjoyable sense of melancholy. By the time they'd moved on to 'Good King Wenceslas', with a very impressive descant from the upper school, she was fighting back the tears. Having brazened the disapproving looks of the other mothers over her daughters' Hollywood take on

146

the Nativity, she was determined not to embarrass Harriet and Molly by weeping. It wouldn't be fair to heap that on them along with the kipper tie festooned with hunting images that Charlie was sporting, a ghastly joke from Francine. She couldn't stop wondering whether her little boy had ever been in a Nativity play and if so, what part he'd played. She didn't even know what he looked like, let alone whether he was musical.

By the time Molly and the other recorder players walked up to the stage, looking tiny beneath the soaring arches of St Matthew's, tears were coursing down her cheeks. Charlie squeezed her hand. Sydney squeezed back and gave him a watery smile. At the end of 'The Holly and the Ivy', the other girls faded into the background and Molly walked to the front of the stage, suddenly resembling a mutant pixie child and looking terrified as her music teacher struck the first chord of 'Away in a Manger' on the piano. A look of anguish flickered across Molly's normally open, confident face. Sydney wanted to rush to the front and sweep her daughter up in her arms.

It had seemed the kindest thing, back then, to step out of her son's life altogether, leaving an uncomplicated future for him and his new family. The greatest sacrifice.

'*The little Lord Jesus, asleep on the hay . . .*'

'Taking an ungodly long time to tune up, isn't she?' Charlie muttered as Molly came to the end of her solo rendition. Sydney flicked her eyes to see if he was joking. He was deadly serious. She squeezed his hand again. 'They grow up so fast,' she whispered.

'Thank God,' said Charlie. Sydney smiled weakly and wondered what had got into him. She sat back for the Nativity play. Or rather, sat forward because when she looked over towards Harriet she could see she was white with fear. A profound silence descended on the church. In row eight, two of the fathers even switched off their mobile phones. Sydney could hear the rustle of Harriet's blue cape. She held her breath, willing her brain to connect telepathically with her daughter's. What if Harriet's mind went blank and she forgot her words? They'd all be in therapy for years. She gripped the pew to stop herself going over to her.

Harriet, meanwhile, gripped Baby Caca and turned her eyes on the audience as if she half expected to be pelted with rotten tomatoes. One of the teachers coughed a staccato serenade that might or might not have been some sort of secret code. It didn't work. Sydney could see Molly, beneath her shepherd's headdress, which had slipped slightly, mouthing the missing words at her sister. Harriet swallowed and opened her mouth. Nothing came out. A watch bleeped in row four. Charlie glanced at his. The silence was bloodcurdling. And then, just as Sydney thought she was going to faint, out came a torrent of dialogue, with the emphasis in all the wrong places, but with the words in perfect order, at the end of which Harriet gave her audience a beatific smile that almost brought the roof down.

They tumbled out of St Matthew's under a beaming lemon sun. 'Look,' squealed Molly, 'it's the same sun as La Rosa.' Sydney made yet another mental note to book the holiday and dared to hope that it might be a perfect Christmas after all.

Helen was weeping quietly into Linda's cafetière when Sydney arrived in the office. Dave was in a foul mood. Charlotte Rampling's people had delayed the meeting because of her new shooting schedule and he was venting his spleen all over the *Beatles' Greatest Hits* CD Helen had bought her father for Christmas. He had just finished telling her that Lennon and McCartney were the worst lyricists since whoever it was had written 'Daffodils Blue Dilly Dilly' when Sydney sat down. 'Has anyone actually listened to the words of "Nowhere Man"?' He glowered round the office accusingly.

Sydney switched on her computer while Helen retorted that even if Dave would have made the best music critic *IQ* never had, she'd still rather have it off with a gerbil than with him. During the ensuing row an email from a correspondent in Bournemouth called Phyllis flashed up on Sydney's screen. Phyllis was considering a breast job – not to lure her old boyfriend back but for herself. What did Patience think? While Sydney tried to decide what Patience would think, Helen's sobs reached such a crescendo that eventually no one could concentrate and Sydney took her to the canteen to calm down. By the second hot chocolate, not the wisest choice for someone with her skin condition, Sydney had heard the long, tortured tales of Helen's parental suffocation – she was their only, late child – and how much she was looking forward to doing her VSO. Sydney listened for about an hour, and hardly managed to get a word in edge-ways. At the end of her second Diet Coke, Helen blew her nose loudly and announced how much better she felt. 'No wonder you're so good at your job,' she snuffled.

Back at *IQ* HQ Annabelle brandished an article from the *Daily Mail* at Dave. It was titled 'Can We Have Our Balls Back: Why Men Feel Castrated at Christmas'. 'Linda thinks we should get someone to write a reposte to this. Something along the lines of "Why Men Don't Deserve Their Balls". Can you commission one?'

Dave was about to offer several withering reasons as to why he couldn't – and indeed shouldn't – but thought better of it. Nerves were at fever pitch on *IQ* owing to the growing discrepancy between the list of celebrities Brian Widlake kept ordering them to include, and the number who actually made it into the magazine, which was few. And if it was fair to say its celebrity quota was reaching famine proportions, so were its staff's bank accounts. None of them was getting the Christmas bonus, which from now on, the management had informed them, would be awarded on the basis of individual merit.

Sydney retreated into a pile of CVs. What she needed was some time on her own to think things through and work out how she was going to deal with the Work Situation, the Dylan Situation, not to mention the Missing Baby Situation, all or any of which, she was rapidly being forced to concede, might become Explosive Situations that could destroy her indestructible marriage. Perhaps Christmas at Charlie's parents was a good idea after all. Charlie would be locked away with his father discussing rare and sometimes extinct tax laws. The girls would be busily wheeled out by Francine in front of all their friends and Sydney would have some time to herself to work things out, as well as the opportunity to spend some time with Michael, about whom she felt increasingly guilty. For the rest of the day she consoled herself with the prospect of brisk walks and hours of quiet contemplation. Then Miles rang to let her know that Francine had sweetly invited him and Jacquie down for Christmas too.

8

'This champagne is absolutely delicious. And you, Angus, are a naughty, naughty man to keep plying me with it. Specially after I told you I never normally drink.' Jacquie giggled maniacally. Angus muttered something incoherent and bent lower over the tray Francine had given him for Christmas, with its unapologetic depiction of ruddy-coated and ruddier-faced huntsmen chasing a bushy-tailed fox that looked as though it was having the time of its life. Outside the mullioned windows of the Old Rectory, the real-life Chipping Modbury Hunt gathered for its annual Boxing Day meet in all its crimson glory. Sydney looked at the thick dusting of snowflakes settling on the picturesque eaves and thatches of Gloucestershire's most perfect village and wished she could settle with it.

Jacquie batted her matted eyelashes and pouted her frosted coral lips in a gesture that somehow managed to imply a sickly childishness combined with a Cruella de Vil outlook on dumb, helpless creatures. 'Normally I'm more of an elderflower or cranberry juice girl.' She raised her voice to compete with the clattering of stirrups and horse hooves outside. 'But I'll always make an exception for quality, even if it is making me quite squiffy.' Her gaze drifted to the shining flanks of horses pawing the snow outside. 'Does Camilla Parker-Bowles ever canter over to these parts?'

'She rides with the Beaufort Hunt,' explained Angus. 'Although I believe she once—'

'For an energetic woman she's got one hell of an arse on her,' Jacquie interrupted. 'Good job we don't ride, isn't it, Syd?'

Sydney busied herself with some canapés and pretended not to hear. Her not being able to ride had always been a source of great disappointment to Francine.

'Miles says my backside's one of my best assets,' Jacquie continued blithely. 'I put it down to yoga and massage. I've invented this new combination of them both,' she continued proudly. 'Massoga. I'm going to open a studio. You should try it, Angus. Though your bum isn't so bad either,' she winked.

Sydney watched in sympathy as her father-in-law blushed a deep shade of salmon, and felt almost sorry for Francine. You couldn't really blame her for inviting Miles and Jacquie for Christmas, especially after the way Miles had shamefully fed her his sob story about being on his own this year, what with Annabelle carting the boys off to her parents in Yorkshire.

'It's good for emotional stress as well,' Jacquie said loudly in Michael's direction. 'Poor love,' she announced as Michael's nose remained buried in his book. And then in a lower voice that might only be heard as far as the end of Chipping Modbury, 'Still in denial, I suppose. Tragic. He's not that old either.'

Angus coughed and fiddled with the fire. 'Shall I go and fetch the log now?' asked Jacquie.

Sensing that the moment when Jacquie's carob chocolate log would make its grand appearance could be deferred no longer, Francine watched helplessly as Jacquie triumphantly wiggled her way to the kitchen. Sydney made

152

some space among the trays of devils on horseback and salmon vol-au-vents for the imminent visitation and wished the spirit of Christmas would finally embrace her and she'd stop feeling so damn sorry for herself. Even Midnight Mass had left her cold and strangely empty this year. Michael stood up. Sydney smiled gratefully. Not that she needed any help, but the diversion was a relief.

'Need to stretch my legs actually,' he said quietly. 'Been glued to that book for two days now.' He nodded at the volume of Yeats that Sydney had tracked down for him in Camden Passage and looked back at her with such an expression of sweetness and longing that she put all her own problems to one side for a moment.

Sydney heard Miles telling Colonel Tiverton how touched he'd been by Francine's decision to open the Old Rectory, her immaculate eighteenth-century Cotswold home, to him and Jacquie for Christmas, while the Colonel slipped Hamish half a dozen devils on horseback.

'It's pretty devastating to see your family disintegrate in front of you, I don't mind telling you, Colonel. Never mind being banished from the family hearth at this special time,' said Miles, omitting to tell the colonel that he was almost entirely responsible for the disintegration, having spent the previous three Christmases being too hungover and too shagged out by the endless office parties in his advertising agency to appear at the family hearth much before mid-afternoon.

'Ta da,' announced Jacquie, holding up a tinsel-strewn log to which Miles had added a flashing reindeer and four elves. 'Carob log, anyone? Looks a bit too real, doesn't it? But I decided only the best would do for Francine.' She giggled affectedly. 'I'm quite tempted myself. Except luckily I seem to have gone off sweet things lately.'

Sydney absented herself from the sitting room, along with her depleted tray, and ran into Ian and Miranda in the hall. 'Miranda, how lovely to see you,' she lied. She spent most of her time in London not seeing Miranda. And even more not seeing Ian. This despite the fact that Miranda never tired of inviting her to join The Scones, or of inviting her and Charlie round for dinner, in the mistaken belief, presumably, that closer friendship between the wives would somehow promote closer collaboration between the husbands at work.

'You look wonderful,' Sydney lied again, taking in Miranda's pale face and the mottled hollows under her eyes, which were exacerbated by the embroidered purple jacket she was wearing. A jacket, Sydney realized with shame – for both herself and Miranda – that she had casually donated to the Camden branch of Oxfam only a few weeks earlier.

'Where are the boys?' She peered over Miranda's shoulder to make sure they hadn't brought any of their monsters with them. Francine's collection of china King Charles spaniels would never recover.

'We only came with Ezekiel.' Miranda's eyes darted round the hall anxiously. 'I think he's slipped into the garden.'

'The other two are persecuting my parents' housekeeper, no doubt.' Ian allowed himself a fond chuckle and almost asphyxiated Sydney with his Stilton-laced breath. 'Probably tied her to a tree by now.' He looked at his watch. 'Ah yes, should be setting fire to her as we speak.'

'Oh Ian, they're not that bad,' Miranda protested feebly.

'They'd better bloody be. Someone's got to know how to keep the lower orders in their place.' Ian peered into the drawing room at Jacquie, who was demonstrating her

154

massage skills on Angus's neck. 'I hope the new girlfriend looks after Miles better than that first wife of his.' He placed a proprietorial arm on Miranda's drooping shoulder.

'Doesn't the house look lovely?' said Miranda tactfully. Her eyes swept over the burnished parquet floors and handsome staircase with a practised look.

'Yes, well, Angus still does very well for himself,' said Ian acidly. Sydney wondered what he had to feel so bitter about. Like Angus, Ian's father had been a solicitor in Cheltenham, and as far as Sydney knew, was equally comfortably off. But to listen to Ian anyone would think he'd been in service rather than a profitable law firm. 'Like son, like father.'

'Look,' said Miranda, distracting him with some yellow sprigged Nina Campbell curtains hanging across the mullioned hall window. 'Francine's had new curtains made. It's that fabric I showed you from *House and Garden*.'

Sydney followed her gaze. Francine kept an exquisitely cosy house. The elaborate Christmas decorations must have taken her weeks to put up; the mullioned windows were festooned with cartwheel-sized wreaths studded with fruits and berries, and the wooden staircase was threaded with a thick garland of sweet-smelling pine cones, cinnamon sticks and ivy.

'For that price it ought to look nice. It's all right for some.' Miranda tried again. 'I know it's not terribly PC,' she gazed out of the window – there were now about a hundred riders gathered outside, 'but it does look awfully festive, doesn't it?'

'Not if you're the bloody fox,' said Ian in an aggressive, bitter voice that took Sydney aback. She could never quite fathom the Plymptons. He was a terrible snob, but he also seemed to resent his own class and anyone he felt was socially above him. Which must leave him with zero friends, she thought, apart from Charlie, who was too absent-minded to shake him off. As for Miranda . . .

'I always say you can tell someone's well bred by the state of their gym bag.' Jacquie's nipple-cracking voice launched itself towards them from the drawing room with all the finesse of a carpet bombing.

'Entertaining, isn't she?' sneered Ian. 'At least she's more lively than the first wife.' The first wife he'd met once, thought Sydney crossly, when Charlie, in a fit of pity, had invited Ian and Miranda over for supper with Miles and Annabelle.

'Annabelle's wonderful,' said Sydney, overlooking Annabelle's many highly strung periods – mainly brought on by Miles's almost heroic lack of consideration for anyone but himself.

Ian shot her a pitying smirk. 'If you say so. If you ask me, any woman who undermines her husband as much as Annabelle did deserves her comeuppance.' Hamish trotted up, trailing noxious smells. 'Get me another drink, would you, Miranda, there's a good girl?'

Miranda scurried off, hoping no one would notice the appalling state of her scuffed heels.

'Some people are complete gym sluts, you know.' Jacquie's voice rang round the sitting room and into the hall like a claxon. 'You might not believe this, but I've even caught one or two girls frotting themselves in the shower.'

A deathly hush descended on the room. Sydney walked in with another tray, accompanied by Ian.

'There you are, Sydney.' Bunty Maguire's cheerfully raddled face split into an enormous grin. 'Francine's been telling me all about your new job. Sounds fun.'

Sydney smiled gratefully. Bunty blew a series of smoke haloes in Ian's direction. 'Angus and Francine always put on such a marvellous spread at Christmas, bless them.' She tapped her tortoiseshell cigarette holder against her glass and deftly caught the ash on her vol-au-vent. 'I know I ought to invite everyone round to the Moat House. Particularly given that Bertie was the Master for all those years. But since he died I've lost my energy for entertaining and the dogs have got rather used to having the place to themselves. The horses would set them off disastrously, I'm afraid.' She turned her rheumy eyes on Sydney. 'You look lovely by the way, but then you always do.' The smoke haloes began to dissipate and eventually Bunty registered Ian. 'Hello,' she boomed. 'Didn't see you down there. Are your parents and Miranda here too?'

'Indeed.' Ian coughed loudly. 'My parents are two of Francine and Angus's oldest friends.'

'Get any good prezzies?' Bunty addressed herself at Sydney over Ian's scaly bald head.

That was a loaded question, the answer to which depended on your definition of nice. If the thought was what counted, then the annual subscription to Supa-slimmers.com from Jacquie and the shredder that Miles had bought the girls probably weren't nice.

'Some lovely books,' said Sydney, thinking of the set of Louis de Bernières from Francine. And the biography of Catherine the Great and the subscription to *Vogue* from Michael. And the lovely discussion they'd had on the walk yesterday when Michael had told her how much he loved the lines Yeats had written about living in the moment. Somehow they'd fallen way behind the others, and by the banks of the River Chuddle, he'd stopped and for what seemed like quite a few minutes they'd stood in silence contemplating the wraiths of mist hovering over the water like steam.

She didn't mention the present Dylan had somehow slipped into the boot of their car before they left – a frilly, floral apron with a note that said IRONIC PINNY pinned to it.

'You don't seem quite yourself,' Michael said, helping her collect some dirty glasses. 'Is anything wrong? I'm probably the last person you'd want to talk to. But well, if you're completely desperate . . .'

She'd smiled and squeezed his hand, touched that in the depths of his own misery he had the generosity to take in hers. She did need someone to talk to or she'd go mad, and Michael was the soul of discretion. It was very tempting. She shook her head. 'I'm fine. Probably just a bit tired this year.'

'*She bid me take love easy, as the grass grows on the weirs; But I was young and foolish, and now am full of tears*,' he said softly. It was the closest he'd ever come to telling any of them how much he missed Clare.

They took the glasses to the kitchen and Sydney thought how much Michael's grief was undeserved whereas she'd brought all her mishaps on herself.

'How's work?' She wondered if he'd ever resented everyone's assumption that he'd go and work in Angus's solicitors' practice in Cheltenham, while Charlie had gone on to flashier glories in London.

His mouth curved in an angelic beam. 'We've got a really thrilling case at the moment involving someone's river-frontage access.'

'Oh dear. Well, I suppose property rights can be fascinating.'

'Not really. But there is the chance of something taking me to London quite soon.'

'That would be lovely. You must make sure you stay with us. Then I can discuss that beautiful book you gave me.'

'I don't know how they can bear it,' Jacquie was saying. 'But then I was brought up to be very particular. My mother was especially fastidious, you know. She named me after Jacqueline Bouvier Kennedy Onassis.' She looked pointedly at Francine. 'That's why it's Jacquie with a CQ. She loves reading, my mum. She devours all the magazines I bring her from the gym every month.'

'Charlie writes books,' Sydney heard Miranda saying loyally to the room in general, although thanks to Francine's one-woman PR service it was hard to imagine that anyone present didn't already know the titles of all Charlie's oeuvres. Sydney caught the venom in Ian's voice as he instructed Miranda to go to the kitchen to see if she could help. Miranda's life was one long journey to and from the kitchen.

She wondered if Miranda realized how much she antagonized Ian. You never really knew with a marriage. Ian was obviously furious with Charlie for writing his books, which even if they didn't sell, certainly raised his credibility among his peers. Perhaps Miranda goaded him on purpose. Sydney had always felt supremely sorry for her. But she was irritating as hell and Sydney was starting to see why Ian was so unpleasant to her. That was the trouble with being an agony aunt. You saw both sides.

Miles lurched towards the kitchen on the prowl for more drink. His eyes had almost completely disappeared into two mounds of puffy flesh on either side of his face.

'Francine tells me you've got a terribly glamorous new job,' said Bunty, who'd followed her nose towards the sausage rolls.

'It's nothing really.'

'Sounds frightfully high-powered, doesn't it?' said Miranda.

Bunty peered at Miranda over her reading glasses, which she'd forgotten to take off before she came out. 'Is Ian all right, my dear? He looks a bit flushed.'

'That's a super dress, Sydney,' said Miranda, pretending not to hear Bunty. 'Did you get it in Marks and Sparks?'

'Yes,' lied Sydney. Miranda always asked her if she'd got her clothes from M&S. Apart from Oxfam, it was the only place Ian let her shop, and then only as a special treat.

'Why don't you all come into the dining room?' suggested Francine, eager for Miranda to see her new curtains in there as well.

'I hope someone's going to have some log,' Jacquie was saying despondently, as Ian, unable to resist the lure of her breasts any longer, drifted over to the gaggle of men clustered round her. Miranda hurried to the kitchen again, only to return a few moments later in a complete panic.

'It's the hunt saboteurs,' she cried, 'they've pitched up from Glastonbury with all their placards and they don't look happy. They've got their children with them. Some of them have got dreadlocks,' she added anxiously.

'Bloody vandals,' said Miles snidely.

'I don't really agree with hunting myself, I must confess,' said Jacquie. 'And fifty-nine per cent of the country would like to see it banned as well, you know.'

'I think you'll find that fifty-nine per cent would vote to keep it,' said Bunty, sweeping her astonished eyes over Jacquie's white-tipped nail extensions.

'I think you're wrong there, Bunty,' said Jacquie recklessly, ignoring the jaundiced expressions of those around her.

'My dear, I can assure you that I do know what I'm talking about when it comes to hunting,' began Bunty, who could take or leave hunting but always grew ferociously protective when she sensed that her beloved late husband's great passion was under assault.

'The main thing is not to rise to their provocation,' said Francine coolly. Having previously prided herself on the Old Rectory's proximity to Chipping Modbury's annual Boxing Day hunt, she was beginning to see it might have distinct drawbacks. 'The last thing we want is to give them more ammunition.'

The others agreed. Angus went round with the champagne again and everyone set about the business of doing what they always did on hunt day at the Murrays' and got plastered.

Apart from one. From his prime vantage-point behind the new yellow sprigged Nina Campbell curtains in the hall, Ezekiel Plympton fired the first warning shot, a small, lethally sharp arrow aimed from the bow his father had given him for Christmas, at the tallest of the dreadlock heads.

He flunked, grazing the nose of a small child and missing her eye by a millimetre. After that all hell broke loose. For two hours the Old Rectory withstood an onslaught of abuse and rotten eggs from protestors who, once word spread of the outrage that had been perpetrated there, appeared with miraculous speed from all over the county. It took the full might of the local constabulary to bring it to a definitive conclusion. All of which Jacquie could have forgiven, as she later told her colleagues at the gym, if Ian hadn't thrown her log on the fire, *knowing full well that it wasn't really real.*

'I daresay my mother will recover,' said Charlie as they hurtled back down the M4 to London a few days later to the soporific soundtrack of Charlie's favourite Miles Davies CD. 'Eventually. The good news is, thank God we don't have boys.'

'I just don't know what Miles sees in her, that's all,' said Sydney, distracted. She turned the sound of the CD down. Ezekiel's deviant behaviour had unleashed all the longing and doubts she had tried to suppress over Christmas, ever since the trip to Storepac had uncorked them. What if her own son had turned out to be equally delinquent? It would be all her fault. 'Not all boys behave like Neanderthals,' she snapped.

Charlie looked at her in surprise. 'I expect he sees the same thing that Dylan sees in Eloise – a partner in crime.'

Sydney frowned. 'What do you mean?'

'Fond as you – as we both are – of Annabelle, she scarcely shares the same ambitions as Miles.'

'Such as?'

'To have a good time. To get the most out of life with as little effort as possible.'

Sydney sighed. Charlie was right. Jacquie and Miles would probably end up confounding them all by having a wildly successful marriage. She could imagine them still going on mystery weekends and dreaming about opening a Massoga studio when they were ninety. But Eloise and Dylan were different. She couldn't think what Charlie was getting at.

'As for Eloise and Dylan,' Charlie continued, 'there's something odd about that relationship. I can't put my finger on it, but they don't fit together somehow.'

This was news to Sydney, who had reconciled herself to Charlie becoming best friends with both of them.

'I'm not saying I'm not fond of both of them.'

'Even Eloise?'

Charlie turned Miles Davies back up. Sydney turned it down again. 'Come on, Sydney. You know as well as I do that idiotic front she puts on is a sham, just as Dylan's is.'

Sydney knew no such thing. She turned the CD back up. She wasn't in the mood for chatting any more.

Charlie turned the sound down. 'Eloise's so-called philistinism is just a hook for you to hang your dislike on.'

'I don't know what you mean.' Sydney turned the volume up and then turned it down. 'Frankly, I'm amazed that you like Eloise. I wouldn't have thought her politics were up your street for one thing. What *do* you mean?'

'I'd say Eloise is a pretty dark horse.'

Sydney looked in the rear view mirror to check that both the girls were still asleep. 'On that at least we can agree.' She pressed the accelerator to the floor. Ten miles later she asked Charlie what he meant when he'd called them an odd match. But she never got to hear her husband's undoubtedly brilliant evisceration of Clifton Crescent's hottest couple because at 102 miles an hour, they were pulled over by the Thames Valley Police. After Charlie explained what he did and the blue flashing lights woke up Harriet who promptly had a panic attack and threw up, PC Stark let Sydney off with a caution. They didn't get round to discussing Dylan and Eloise again for weeks.

Sydney glanced warily at the job applicant sitting opposite her and wondered whether her plaits were ironic or sarcastic, and decided she didn't understand anything any more. Undertaking to interview the final ten applicants for Helen's old job was meant to take Sydney's mind off her own problems, but it simply added to them. She shifted a pile of papers and one of Annabelle's overflowing ashtrays to one side of Linda's desk, in order to focus better on

Chloë Manners, and then felt embarrassed. Chloë was perspiring so heavily in the full glare of the sun, which was streaming through Linda's grimy windows, that it seemed cruel to look at her. The poor girl must be heartily regretting her baggy, black polo neck and even baggier maxi-skirt, which looked as though it was made from door matting. She looked about as easy in her skin as the Singing Detective. But her CV had been very impressive.

'Well,' Sydney began brightly, 'you've certainly had an impressive academic career. A first in English, from Oxford. What attracts you to this job?'

'I'm just longing to experience the real world,' said Chloë in a clogged voice. She blinked through a pair of wonky spectacles. She looked as though she'd been locked inside a library for ten years and would evaporate in the light. Linda would hate her. She was even less visually appealing than Helen. And all that twitching and shaking. Sydney decided to let her down gently but quickly. It was a shame because on paper she'd seemed a prime candidate.

'An awful lot of it is administrative. And the hours are very long—' she began.

'I don't mind, honestly. I know I have to start somewhere and—' Chloë sneezed noisily and retreated into a bulging plastic carrier bag that was on her knee, emerging with a packet of Kleenex and spilling the contents of the bag on to the floor as she did so. A bag of blackcurrants split over Linda's carpet tiles, scattering to the four corners. Chloë looked stricken and fell on all fours.

'Don't worry,' said Sydney. 'We'll pick them up later.' Linda hovered inquisitively outside. Sydney frowned at her. There was no need to make the experience any more humiliating for Chloë by inviting her to join in. Linda had other thoughts. She barged in and introduced herself.

Chloë blinked like a rabbit sensing imminent annihilation. 'I thought you were the editor,' she said to Sydney, which was sweet of her but not very observant, given that Sydney had explained that she was standing in for Linda when Helen had shown Chloë in.

Linda began pacing the room with a blackcurrant impaled on one of her heels. 'So, Chloë, tell me what you think of *IQ* and how it might be improved.'

Chloë's voice wobbled slightly and her hand shook as she dabbed at some sweat that had collected on her forehead. Sydney's heart went out to her.

'An honest critique,' said Linda, enunciating every syllable. 'No holds barred.'

'Well . . .'

Linda sat down and felt something soft squelch on the undercarriage of her new Jimmy Choo boots. Chloë blushed to the black roots of her aubergine hair as Linda peeled the bag of blackcurrants from her sole.

'You were saying, Connie?' said Linda. Sydney glanced surreptitiously at her diary to check what time the next interviewee was arriving and saw that her name had been crossed out. Another cancellation. What had Helen been telling them all?

'Chloë.'

Linda smiled. She liked to wrong-foot job candidates by getting their names wrong to see how they reacted. Not that this one needed any help, thought Sydney. She was doing a very good job of wrong-footing herself.

Chloë took a deep breath and began chewing on one of her plaits, which at least explained its somewhat singed texture. Either that or she'd been sleeping too close to a gas fire. 'I think it's knowing, ironic, an absolute destination read. But . . .'

Linda's eyebrows shot up her forehead.

Chloë addressed herself to the remaining blackcurrants on the floor. 'You could probably do with broadening your readership a little. I mean, a couple of years ago all my friends slavishly read it, but lately,' she looked up at them furtively, 'you seem to have aged a little. The magazine, I mean. It's still brilliantly written but some of the departments need to address themselves to younger readers a bit more. Without losing the older ones of course.'

'And how might we do that?' barked Linda.

'Recruiting some younger writers for a start,' said Chloë, before reeling off some suggestions. Then, before Linda asked, she offered a few ideas for features she thought she and her peers were dying to read. 'You could start with a piece about sleeping your way to the top.'

'What's the angle?' Linda asked, sounding jaded.

'Post-Ironic. That it's no longer looked down upon amongst my age group to shag your way into a job. Sexual experimentation and openness are widely regarded as a legitimate part of a woman's arsenal of job skills.'

Linda shifted through a pile of CVs until she found Chloë Manners's. 'I see you went to Balliol,' she said.

'For my BA. Then I switched to UCL for my doctorate.'

'Doctorate?' Linda tried not to sound impressed.

'The female orgasm in classical literature.' Chloë dabbed at her forehead with a Kleenex and wiped her eyes, leaving a streak of mascara like a black comet's tail down her cheek. 'You could call it "Come Again",' she added. 'The piece, I mean . . .'

'She's perfect,' said Linda, scratching at a purple streak of dried juice on the back of her heel.

Sydney waved a sheath of CVs at her. 'Don't you want to

166

see the others?' Sympathetic as she felt towards Chloë's over-active sweat glands, there was something not right about her. One minute she could barely look Sydney in the eye, she was so shy, the next she was slyly challenging the award-winning editor of *IQ* to a debating match on equal terms.

Linda held up a page of closely typed notes that Chloë had left for them to look at. It contained at least ten feature proposals Linda would love to commission instantly. Miraculously, it was unblemished by blackcurrant stains.

'This girl's got it all. Look at all these ideas she brought with her. She's bright, obviously hard-working, and best of all she's not remotely Brian Widlake's type.'

'She's not anyone's type,' said Sydney crossly. Linda needed to learn to trust other people's judgement occasionally, otherwise it was a waste of time delegating.

'You're just miffed because she played it one way with you, and then upped the ante with me.'

'You're just keen because she so obviously isn't someone Widlake would hire. It makes you look as though you still have some independence.'

'Look, I didn't mean she didn't think you were her intellectual equal. You're gentler than I am, that's all.'

'She wants your job,' said Sydney stubbornly. She hated seeing Linda smitten by fakes.

'So should anyone with drive. Honestly, Sydney, I'm not so insecure that I won't hire someone just because they're ambitious.'

Perhaps it was time Linda was a bit more circumspect about the people she employed, thought Sydney. She tried another tack. 'I thought you liked your staff to look attractive. You've always said it helps when it comes to getting quotes out of people.'

'The whole point about Chloë is she's going to be chained to her desk doing all the stuff no one else wants to.' Linda pushed away the CVs Sydney had placed on the desk. 'We should snap her up now, before someone else does. Girls like that – brainy, original and unassuming – are like gold dust.'

Sydney decided to let Chloë dangle a little, however. She spent the next day trying to come up with kindly rejection notes for the other candidates, attempting to make them as personal and encouraging as possible. Two days later she rang Chloë to let her know the good news. A cool, clipped, very deep voice instructed her to leave a message in tones that didn't sound at all like the ones she'd used in the interview.

A postcard of a kitsch St Bernard in sunglasses arrived from St Moritz on 5 January to let them know that Eloise and Dylan were having such a good time they were extending their skiing trip for another fortnight.

'All right for some,' said Sydney. She didn't know whether she felt relieved they weren't around for most of January or strangely let down.

'We could have gone skiing if you hadn't had to rush back to the office,' Charlie reminded her.

'You hate skiing,' said Sydney. Before she could savour that small victory, Mrs Protheroe began pummelling their front door down. When Sydney went to see what was wrong she told her aliens had landed in Clifton Crescent.

Sydney invited her in for some tea, although when she saw that she had Betty, her incontinent mastiff, with her, she wished she hadn't. They both trotted down the hall ahead of her before she could change her mind. In the clear light of the kitchen, Sydney could see Mrs Protheroe was agitated. The purple tint on her hair hadn't been retouched for weeks and the roots were snowy white. It turned out she'd received a letter over Christmas from her daughter's solicitor demanding she vacate the house.

'But she can't do that,' said Sydney gently. 'Where are the deeds, Mrs P? Charlie will check them for you if you like, won't you, Charlie?'

Mrs Protheroe looked blankly at Sydney, her faded blue eyes suddenly frightened and lost. 'I don't know where they are,' she said hoarsely. A fat tear fell on her liver-spotted hands. Then she whispered that there were no aliens. Charlie patted her hand and said that was a pity because he'd always wanted to meet some so that he could discuss tax policies in a parallel universe. He told her to be sure to let him know if any did land. Then he asked her to show him the deeds when she found them. It was at moments like these, thought Sydney, that she realized how much she loved her husband.

Unfortunately such moments were shortlived. Ever since they'd got back from Charlie's parents, he'd become increasingly irascible, which wasn't really like him. Sydney almost started to miss Dylan's irrepressible Tiggerishness. When Mrs Protheroe mentioned that she'd seen Satan's Chariot – aka Dylan's red Ferrari – roar up the Crescent one night she felt a stab of excitement. But the sighting turned out to have been a mirage.

'How long can a skiing trip last?' she asked lightly, one morning.

'Oh, for God's sake stop bleating about your lack of holidays,' snapped Charlie. 'Christ knows how many times I've asked you to accompany me on my work trips.'

So that I could sit on my own by the pool while you slave over suspect tax forms all day, thought Sydney. One look at

Charlie's gnarled forehead told her to keep this observation to herself.

'Anyway, there's Easter to look forward to. The girls are desperately excited about Spain, even if you're not.'

Spain! With a sinking heart, Sydney got on the phone to Paradise Regained and experienced anything but bliss when they confirmed the inevitable by telling her that La Rosa was fully booked for the rest of the year, along with all their other villas of repute.

'But we've been going there every Easter for the past five years,' she protested.

'I might be able to do you a week in August,' offered an insensitively cheery voice.

'But my husband gets heat rash. That's why we always go at Easter. Really chronic heat rash,' she added. It would be about 103 degrees at La Rosa in August.

'That's a shame. But it's absolutely chocka. It's only free that week because the couple who were planning to take it then have had a fatal car crash. Ever so sad really. But a window of opportunity for you. Although I must tell you that I've given their daughter-in-law first refusal. Tell you what I can do,' the voice said brightly. Sydney's heart leapt. 'And that's offer you a two for one on Ambre Solaire. They've got a special deal with us this summer.'

What the fuck was she going to tell Charlie and the girls?

Chloë started in the last week of January, and with each passing week, her look metamorphosed into something different. First the hair shifted from blotchy aubergine to a rather savage blonde. Then the glasses shifted altogether, along with a tiny bit of weight, Sydney noticed enviously. She was so obviously a work-in-progress she could probably qualify for an Arts Council grant.

'You want someone with goals, Sydney,' Linda reminded her. 'They usually work like slaves. And she's no exception. I'm feeling so renewed I thought I'd take us all on a brain-storming weekend somewhere nice.'

'Won't that be expensive?' said Sydney, wondering how Charlie would take her absence. Badly, would be her guess.

'No one ever remembered an editor for coming in under budget,' said Linda loftily. 'It'll be a bonding exercise. Shall I tell Annabelle to sort out the details with her or will you?'

It was 14 February when Dylan called her at the office.

'Any chance you and Charlie are free tonight?' he asked, sounding a bit short of breath, but failing utterly to refer to the long absence. 'I've got some news.'

Eloise is pregnant, thought Sydney. To her horror, she felt her hand shake.

'I hope no one minds, but I've opened all the mail,' said Chloë. 'Everyone's so busy they don't get round to opening their post for days sometimes. Quite educational, some of it, especially yours, Sydney.' She smiled up at Sydney. 'There's a whole magazine's worth of stuff just in this little pile. You should have more pages.'

Sydney narrowed her eyes thoughtfully and tried not to feel violated. Her correspondence – from Richard and Phyllis and all the others – was private. Or at least it was private until it appeared in the magazine.

'Can I make you some tea or coffee?' Chloë cocked her head to one side. She'd stopped wearing plaits and had a trim from the looks of things. 'Or I could nip out and get you a proper cappuccino.' Sydney glanced out of the window. It was snowing. 'Better than the muck they serve in the canteen,' said Chloë.

'Chloë,' Sydney began, 'it's freezing. And you're not very warmly dressed.' When had she stopped wearing the shrouds?

'Don't worry about me. I got in at eight so I could get ahead. And now I'm at a bit of a loose end. A walk would wake me up.' The way she managed to imply that she was loving her job while somehow being much too good for it was really quite impressive, thought Sydney. 'Some of your correspondents have pretty torrid lives, don't they? However do you keep a straight face?'

'Not having a sense of humour helps,' said Sydney. She hoped Chloë wasn't going to spend her whole career at *IQ* patronizing her.

Her waspishness appeared to have floated over Chloë's head. 'By the way, Dave called earlier to say he missed the bus from Dalston,' she said.

'I see,' said Sydney, wondering if she'd imagined Chloë's gloating tone.

Sydney easily made it home in time to see the girls, have a bath and change for Dylan and Eloise's supper, thanks to Chloë who had transformed her corner of the office and made significant headway with the backlog of correspondence. Sydney could even begin to see how with less of the coal-face to chip away at, she might actually find some time to help Linda and Dave plan the next evolutionary stages of *IQ*. It was quite an exhilarating thought.

Dylan darted round her and Charlie in his gadget-free kitchen, crashing drawers and burning his fingers. If anything, thought Sydney, letting the champagne Dylan had poured her fizz on her tongue for a few moments, he looked a bit drawn. The angles of his face cast eerie

172

shadows and from where she was sitting, his flashing eyes looked almost haunted. She wondered where Eloise had got to.

She wasn't the only thing missing. The house looked even barer than it had before.

'The Precious O'Dowd's gone,' said Dylan, following her eyes.

'But I thought Eloise loved it,' said Sydney.

'She's gone too.' He paused casually, almost relishing their blank expressions.

'What do you mean, gone?' asked Sydney with mounting foreboding.

'Left me. Moved out. Returned to America. We're getting divorced.'

'Bit sudden, isn't it?' Charlie looked up from an article in the *Economist*. 'Only been married five minutes.'

Bit sudden? Sydney was reeling, now that the impact of what Dylan had said had sunk in. It was ludicrous. Unbelievable. And shockingly inevitable.

'Nine and three-quarter months,' said Dylan. 'That's the equivalent to twenty years of marriage in New York.'

'Are you sure it's not just some little misunderstanding?' asked Charlie. 'They do arise in marriage from time to time.' He looked pointedly at Sydney, who found herself unable to articulate anything. It had absolutely nothing to do with her and Dylan. There was no her and Dylan. Never had been. He'd made the wrong choice, that was all.

Dylan smiled bitterly. 'The little misunderstanding was me thinking she was sane.' The same old flippancy, thought Sydney.

He looked out of the window across the concrete Zen garden Eloise had had installed, and switched tacks. 'I know

173

it probably seems very shallow to both of you,' he said wistfully. 'Not to mention abrupt. But we did try and make a go of things, honestly. But towards the end we were just keeping up appearances. To be honest, it hadn't been working for ages.'

'How could a nine-and-three-quarter-month marriage not have been working for ages?' Sydney asked finally. Her voice sounded breathless. She looked across at Charlie to see if he'd noticed.

Dylan shrugged helplessly. 'You know me, Sydney—'

'Not very well.' She tossed him a warning look.

'I'm just a foolish, old fashioned romantic. I fell madly in lust. Story of my life – ever since the girl of my dreams jilted me.' Now it was Dylan's turn to look pointedly at Sydney.

'You don't strike me as the unrequited type,' said Charlie thoughtfully.

'Still waters, Charlie, and all that. Do you know that poem by Tennyson?'

'I think the curry's burning,' said Sydney.

'I must seem very callous. But you have to remember I've had longer than you to get used to the idea.' He looked over at Sydney again, broke off, and for a moment seemed almost downcast, broken even. He'd got quite thin and his eyes seemed to have sunk beneath his bushy eyebrows. He looked like Shelley all over again. 'I really did give this marriage my all, you know. But you can't breathe life into a corpse.'

'When did it go wrong?' asked Charlie, sounding concerned.

'Shall I serve?' said Sydney hurriedly. She was desperate to find out more but had the uncomfortable feeling she was sitting on unexploded uranium. 'Darling, I don't think Dylan wants to talk about it.' Now she looked at Dylan pointedly. She laid a hand on Charlie's shoulder. It was the first time they had voluntarily touched in weeks.

'Can we do anything to help?' she added neutrally.

'Join me in a toast?' said Dylan, raising his glass. 'To divorce. It's bloody marvellous.'

9

Thud, thud, thud. Sydney gripped the sides of her mattress and willed her eyelids to part. There were two explanations for the noise worth entertaining. Three if you had a strong stomach. Either Linda was already on the phone having one of her lively discussions with Brian Widlake or Dave had turned up the volume on his headphones again.

The third option – that the monotonous banging was Dave *in flagrante* – was too horrible to contemplate just yet.

As was Charlie's reaction to her polite request that he consider letting her go on the brainstormer. Sydney couldn't think what had got into him lately. She knew he had a lot on at the office and – rightly or wrongly – she instinctively blamed Ian for some of it. It wasn't as if there wasn't a long history of Charlie bailing Ian out. However, work pressures had never got to him before. But he'd flown off the handle so violently the minute she'd broached the issue that she'd more or less decided not to go, when Linda had got to her, pleading desperation, desolation and despair. Sydney had to come or they were all doomed, was the gist of Linda's none-too-subtle argument. So in the end, Sydney had cooked Charlie steak Béarnaise, which he'd hurled at the floor, telling her to fucking well go if that's what she fucking well wanted. To which she'd responded – admittedly more in shock than wisdom – that she fucking well would.

They never rowed. They never swore either. At least, not

in front of each other. She fumed silently in bed for several nights while he hunched over his laptop in his study. And the more she fumed, the more he hunched and the worse the atmosphere between them got. What right did he have to refuse her? He was living in the Dark Ages. It was all Ian's fault. And Francine's. And Charlie's. But most of all it was hers for letting him get away with it for so long.

Not going, once a distinct possibility, was no longer an option. Linda needed her and she needed this job. Other women went back to work to fill the space once they'd decided not to have another child. She'd gone back because she needed to escape the hauntings of the other child she'd had. If only she could talk to Charlie about it she might start to find a way to heal. But that was about as likely as talking to Mary Queen of Scots. Less, in fact, because lately Mrs Protheroe had had several lengthy conversations with the Queen – in French.

A shaft of sunlight, sharp as a spear, penetrated a chink in the rose-patterned curtains and Sydney's semi-sealed left eyelid. She bitterly regretted last night's intake of organic elderflower champagne. But at least Annabelle had finally accepted that Sydney hadn't had anything to do with inviting Miles and Jacquie to Gloucestershire, though it had taken a lot of careful explanation on Sydney's part and fist-banging on Annabelle's.

Sydney put one foot out of the bed, felt her stomach lurch like a clapped-out washing machine, and gingerly reached for the curtains. Outside, the rolling Dorset countryside, dotted with taupe sheep, glistened under a coating of frost like a giant velvet pin-cushion and rolled a bit more. Butely, the enchanting country spa Poppy had booked them into for the weekend, was certainly set in some ravishing scenery. She had to pull herself together, for

Linda's sake. She was relying on this strategy weekend – as recommended by Seismic!, a young, modish consultancy who'd choreographed the whole thing in return for some free publicity – to turn *IQ* around.

Half an hour later, as Sydney fought back her nausea in Butely's exquisite dining room – the finest example of Gibbons's panelling in the county, as someone, she couldn't quite recall who, had informed them the previous evening – it was painfully clear that Annabelle, Linda and Dave had also consumed the organic wine liberally. Linda was staring morosely out of the French windows towards a trio of stone lions. Annabelle's left hand was shaking so badly she looked as though she had been plugged into a socket. And her eyes were swollen again, so last night's champagne high had obviously worn off, leaving her feeling terrifically low.

Dave was wearing the same clothes he'd worn the night before. There was still no sign of Poppy. She was meant to have caught the same train as Dave and Chloë from Waterloo. But there had been an issue over luggage – Poppy's Vuitton, to be precise, which she'd asked Dave to keep an eye on while she went to buy some magazines. As the train pulled out, she'd noticed it was still on the platform. Keeping an eye on it, in Poppy-speak, turned out to include carrying it on board. Poppy had called Dave a stupid bastard as she watched it receding. He had called her a fuckwit. Then she had jumped off the train. All this had been somewhat gleefully explained over dinner last night by Chloë, who had been far more restrained in her drinking than the rest of them. Sydney forced down a mouthful of apple and cinnamon crunch and felt it scrape against the furred-up sides of her oesophagus and land somewhere around her kidneys.

Chloë breezed into the room carrying a new Anya

Hindmarch bag with a naked picture of herself aged four, that she'd bought on one of Poppy's hefty discounts. Her lank hair, normally clamped round her face like damp nylon curtains, was swept back into a pony-tail, and without her orange makeup she looked almost normal. She'd already been jogging and was dripping with positive endorphins. 'Hi, everyone,' she beamed. 'What's the matter with your hand, Annabelle?'

'I must have slept on it,' said Annabelle hoarsely. 'Do you think there's anywhere in the grounds where smoking is permitted?'

'Only the lane at the end of the drive,' said Dave bitterly. He had not been consulted on this weekend, and if anyone had had the courtesy to ask him – although why should they, he was only the features editor? – he would have told them that he would rather pluck out his eyes, shit melons or even fill out two years of VAT forms than spend five seconds at a sodding health farm. But he was just a bloke. What did he know?

A jug of freshly squeezed blood-orange juice was placed on their table. Linda turned green and excused herself, saying she had to make a quick phone call.

'Does anyone know where Poppy is yet?' asked Annabelle, attempting to sound businesslike, calm and firm, and failing miserably.

'I think she may still be looking for her luggage,' said Chloë. Her cheeks flushed delicately.

'It wasn't my fault,' snarled Dave.

'Have I missed anything?' asked Linda, returning to the room looking even paler.

'No,' said Annabelle and Dave quickly.

'In that case shall we make straight for the library?' Linda suggested valiantly. 'I hope everyone's feeling energetic.'

'I would have got off the train to help Poppy,' said Chloë to anyone who would listen, 'but I didn't want to let Linda down.'

Sydney picked up the brand-new pencil that had been placed at an angle of ninety degrees in front of her and began tapping nervously on the notebook that Annabelle had considerately provided. All right, so she had gone away leaving Charlie and the children. But it wasn't as if she hadn't left him comprehensive instructions on where everyone was meant to be and when, from Harriet's ten o'clock Saturday tap class to the project on mummification that Molly was meant to finish by Sunday night. Maisie was coming on both days – on double pay – for a few hours to ease the way. And Juanita was due on Sunday afternoon to clear up. Sydney looked at her watch nervously. 9.30. Perhaps she should have called already but she thought it might make things worse. Or more to the point, she thought it might make Charlie worse. Anyway, by now, with any luck, he would be reading the notes Sydney had left next to his bed. They were identical to the ones she'd pinned to the wall above his desk, on the pinboard in the kitchen, by his binoculars and on the mirror in the bathroom.

And when he opened the fridge he'd see the arrows pointing to the freezer where she'd left a heap of Tesco gourmet meals in the order in which they were to be eaten.

But maybe she shouldn't have come.

She heard Linda saying her name.

'Sydney?' Linda repeated.

'Yes.'

'So you are still with us. How nice. Even nicer if you'd stop the percussion.' She stared at Sydney's pencil. Sydney put it down with elaborate precision. She most certainly didn't need any grief from Linda on top of everything else.

'As you probably all know by now,' Linda gazed down the table in Butely's exquisite old library with a fixed smile that reached as far as her nose, 'we're under a certain amount of pressure to re-align *IQ*'s position in the Saturday supplement market-place.'

'What does that mean in laymen's terms, exactly?' asked Chloë.

'We're selling out,' said Dave.

If only they could sell out, or at least hit the regular 80 per cent sell through targets Brian Widlake had set them they'd be laughing, thought Sydney.

Linda ignored them both. 'I happen to think there's an enormous amount of satisfaction to be derived from adapting a product to changing tastes.'

'Is that what you meant when you collected your award and said *IQ* was the best place in the world to work because it was allowed to be a bastion of quirky individuality?'

'I don't think the two statements are mutually exclusive,' said Linda testily.

Annabelle opened her notebook, which she'd already colour-coded into different topics, and looked longingly at a packet of cigarettes she'd hidden in her lap for comfort.

'We should begin with Issues of Diversity. We'll move on to the fun things later. That's when we'll be set projects like role reversal, when we put all our names into a hat and play each other's parts.' Annabelle gazed at them all encouragingly, just as she and Linda had been advised to do by the bright blonde with perfect breasts from Seismic!. 'But for now I feel we must stick with Issues of Diversity.' The air throbbed with apathy. 'That's where we feel free to express exactly what each of us feels personally about the magazine. And don't just say it pays our rent.'

'No fear of that. Because it doesn't,' muttered Dave.

'It might do if you didn't fritter most of it in the pub,' said Linda.

'Or you didn't fritter the budget on weekends in ludicrously expensive health farms,' countered Dave.

'It's actually very reasonable. Poppy's doing a write-up, so they'll knock some of the bill off,' said Chloë helpfully.

'That's typical of the rigorous journalistic standards of our new regime,' snapped Dave. 'Are any of the new generation of journalists familiar with the concepts of truth and accuracy?' He slumped back in his chair, looking as belligerent as the buffet staff had on the train when he'd asked if they had any milk that didn't have curds in it. Sydney couldn't altogether blame him. The *IQ* staff had been so battered by confusing directives from different management initiatives over the past year it was hardly surprising if they felt jaded. But she wished he wouldn't take it out on Linda. She began to regret her own testy performance with the pencil.

Issues of Diversity proved to be rather stormy. Annabelle wondered whether to have one of her strategic coughing fits or whether it might be better to save it for later. Before she could decide, Chloë piped up to ask whether there would be time to discuss features ideas before lunch.

Annabelle looked at her notes doubtfully. 'We're meant to build up to that bit. After we've discussed models for constructing a magazine teeming with socially concerned yet populist features.'

'That's okay,' Chloë said brightly. 'I have been building up to it.' She reached into her Anya Hindmarch tote and pulled out a file. 'I've got some ideas I've been working on here.'

Annabelle looked for guidance on this departure. Linda nodded gracious assent.

'Here goes then,' said Chloë. 'Shoot me down if they're bad.' She tossed them a nervous smile, revealing unusually pretty teeth. 'Okay, um . . .'

Dave sighed loudly and pretended to read the *Private Eye* that was stashed on his lap.

'. . . I've titled them all, because that way I think you get a better feel for the sense of playful irony that I think is going to be the key to our reversal of fortunes.'

Linda smiled encouragingly.

'For instance, the first one is called "No, you can't drive by his house to see if he's home . . . or rummage through his dustbin . . . or call him and hang up when he answers".' She paused to gauge their reactions which ranged from disgust (Dave) to amused curiosity (Linda) to recognition (Annabelle) and astonishment (Sydney).

'It's meant to be slightly jokey in tone, but to strike a chord at the same time,' explained Chloë nervously. 'Another one could be called, "If he's so bloody great, why don't I fancy him?"' Linda chuckled. Chloë continued, 'Then there's, "I am a busy woman. I don't have time to do everything. Too bad no one else can do it as well as me."' She looked up from her notes. 'I guessed you probably wanted to make the magazine more feminine, Linda, without resorting to the clichés of women's magazines.'

'So you thought you'd just take the piss out of them instead,' said Dave, furious he hadn't thought of it himself.

'It's not taking the piss.' Chloë's pale blue eyes looked wounded. 'They'd be seriously researched pieces.' She turned her back on Sydney and Dave and directed herself to Linda and Annabelle. 'The thing, as you know, is that the magazine supplement market is completely devoid of a relevant voice that women can relate to while experiencing a break-up, or for that matter, any life change (work, friendship, getting married, motherhood, etc.). My mission has always been to find one that spoke to the experiences of modern women—'

Mission? She was a PA, for Christ's sake, Sydney was shocked to find herself thinking.

'And now –' Chloë looked adoringly at Linda – 'there's a chance to create one.'

Dave glanced at his watch. 'Any more?'

'Dozens,' said Chloë. 'Those are just for one section.' She began handing out neatly typed lists of bullet points. 'Naturally I don't think *IQ* should entirely be taken up with female emotional issues. We need to rev up the car column.'

'I think it's fine as it is,' jumped in Annabelle, who felt personally responsible for the motoring section of the magazine.

'I've got some thoughts on beefing up our arts coverage too . . .' Chloë reached into her Anya Hindmarch again and pulled out four more lists of bullet points which she handed round. 'But in the meantime I thought we should have a karmic page – all the latest spiritual and health trends.' She paused. There was a silence while the others came to terms with the fact that Chloë's torrent of ideas had trounced all of their paltry suggestions.

'You'll see there's some ideas for fashion too,' Chloë rushed on. 'I think I may have found a way to do it that pulls in lots of advertisers and fits in with our brief. And there's something on a new stocks and shares column. I think we could make finance really sexy.' She blew aside a hunk of hair that had fallen across her face and crossed her eyes self-mockingly. 'You'll probably think it's all crap. But – well, I'm just so grateful to have been invited on this weekend. I want you to know how much I appreciate your support.' This last was directed at Dave, who pretended to find something stuck under the Chippendale table they were sitting at.

Linda scanned the lists. 'These are terrific. Absolutely spot-on. And fresh.'

'Yes. However did you think of them?' asked Sydney quietly.

'They're really just expanded from your problem pages,' said Chloë sweetly, 'which I think you do brilliantly, by the way. I'm hoping we'll get to role-swap,' she said under her breath. 'But you probably noticed that they had some overlap with the letters you get sent.'

Sydney was saved from answering by Poppy, who clattered through the double doors with uncharacteristic haste. 'Shit, shit, shit. Hi, everyone. Christ, I'm glad to see you. This place is impossible to get to.'

'Couldn't you find a taxi from the station?' asked Annabelle, taking in Poppy's flushed cheeks.

'Couldn't you find any clothes?' asked Dave, taking in her white hotpants.

'Couldn't even find a train. Has anyone done a piece about how bad the rail system is in this country?' She directed a reproachful look at Dave. 'Luckily I'd noticed a garage on the way to Waterloo so I nipped in and bought a Smart.' She took in the jaundiced expressions, particularly of Annabelle, who was bracing herself to tell Poppy the company would not be paying for this particular travel expense.

'Don't worry,' said Poppy, misinterpreting her concern. 'I didn't have to drive it in the end. I got a ride in Alvaro Zapporto's helicopter.'

Sydney smiled at her sympathetically. Alvaro Zapporto was a leathery billionaire polo player, much favoured by

Poppy's mother who was keen for him to marry her daughter, despite him being old enough to be her father and bald enough to be her baby.

'Did you find your luggage?' asked Annabelle nervously. 'Only I'm not sure the company would turn out to be liable for lost clothes under the current travel insurance policy' – especially as she'd almost certainly forgotten to renew it, thought Sydney with a sympathetic pang.

Poppy shook her head. 'Someone accidentally put it on the train to Southampton before I reached it. It should turn up next week. The keys to my flat were in there and everything. I had to nip into Dorchester to buy some stuff for the weekend and I can't say I'm impressed with the shopping. I don't think they'd ever heard of Earl Jeans before.'

'They probably think they're a bunch of local aristos,' joked Chloë.

Poppy pretended not to understand. 'I don't think so, Chloë. I noticed the Butelys died out yonks ago. Good job too, judging by some of their portraits. Have you seen the undergrowth on the fifth Countess's upper lip?'

'I take it you ended up in the children's department.' Dave peered at Poppy's shrunken T-shirt.

Ignoring him, Poppy sat down, craning a look at the bullet points in front of Dave and smiled radiantly at them all. 'Well, what are we waiting for? Let's get started.'

'I've just been suggesting some ideas. They're not very good. There,' Chloë pushed a list of bullet points towards Poppy, 'you can see them if you want.'

'They look terrific to me,' said Poppy generously. 'I've always said this magazine needs more sex and glamour.'

'What about an Out of the Closet feature?' said Chloë. 'We could photograph individual items of clothing on one spread and on the next page readers would find out who they belonged to. And Oliver James could do some kind of psychological piece about what their clothes say about them.'

'You could do my uncle on my mother's side,' suggested Poppy. 'He's been in the closet longer than one of Joan Collins's debutante dresses. Although no one's supposed to know. He's the Shadow Home Secretary.'

Sydney's eyes widened. So Stalinist Stevie was not only a nob, but related to a Tory grandee.

'If you could put some of this stuff on your gossip page instead of the half-baked crap about how good this party was and how fabulous that face cream was, we might have a magazine worth reading,' said Dave.

And Linda might be able to deliver Brian Widlake what he wanted while still doing a tongue-in-cheek magazine her friends wouldn't turn their noses up at, thought Sydney.

'I've got tons more fashion ideas,' boasted Chloë, ensuring the spotlight shone on her again. 'If Picasso were alive now he'd be working at Dior, is one.' The others eyed her with grudging admiration.

'I've got quite a few for fashion as well, as it happens,' said Poppy, suddenly rattled by Chloë's rampant colonialization. 'Like getting Mario Testino on board. And glamorous socialites. I thought if I could schmooze Mario and ran a huge glowing profile of him, he might agree to shoot some of my friends for the mag . . .'

'We could have some astrology as well,' enthused Chloë. 'I've got this gay friend who's an amazing star reader – very funny and waspish.'

'That's settled then, isn't it?' said Dave. 'Shall we rename it *Cosmic-olitan* while we're at it?'

'Funny you should mention that,' said Linda defensively. 'Because our esteemed editor-in-chief is very keen on an astrology page. He was telling me only the other day how much he valued the journalistic totems of some of the women's glossies. I wasn't going to tell you this because I knew it would distress you, but since some of you are still reluctant to descend from your ivory towers, you might as well know that from now on every piece in *IQ* has to fulfil the three Fs.'

'Which are?' Annabelle's cheery good spirits were starting to sound demented.

'Fun, froth and fuckability.'

Chloë's hand shot up. 'I've got one for that too: "How Do Siamese Twins Have Sex?"' The grudging admiration of a few moments ago turned to fascinated revulsion. There was a silence. Then Annabelle rang the bell for an early lunch.

Lifted by the organic lunch-time stew, they came up with an array of ideas, none of which on closer reflection seemed quite as sparky or fresh as Chloë's. Linda said they needed more sensationalist scare rants masquerading as socially concerned articles, and Dave irritably suggested an 'Is your bed killing you?' feature. 'You know, is the mattress giving you scoliosis? Might one of the springs spear you through the brain? Or how about, "How contaminated is your hairbrush?"'

There was another pained silence, which was only broken when Linda told him there was no need to be childish. Dave stared round the room belligerently, then reverted to his original plan and delivered a slew of ideas for stodgy art pieces that made no concessions whatsoever to Brian Widlake's three Fs, but were so obviously close to his heart that Sydney almost felt sorry for him. It must have been soul-destroying to see the way the magazine he loved was going. But at least he could see it.

The mood, which had threatened to blossom into something close to optimism shortly after lunch, sank like an infected gall bladder. And they hadn't even reached the role-swapping stage.

'So we're all agreed that there needs to be less depressing stuff about testicular cancer and male menopause,' said Dave pointedly as the herbal tea arrived.

'I don't think anyone actually went that far,' said Linda, torn between wanting to make *IQ* as upbeat and glossy as possible and not wanting to get rid of her main means of tormenting Dave.

'So what *are* you saying exactly?'

Linda sat back wearily. They'd been thrashing over ideas for eight hours, going round in circles for seven of them. And her head was throbbing. 'I'm saying that two thousand words on Alzheimer's, even if they are written by Iris Murdoch from her sodding grave, won't cut it any more. But that doesn't mean we can't do what we do with style and panache.'

Dave looked at her as if she'd just told him she'd voted for George Bush.

They decided to leave the role-swapping for the evening, when they visited The Hung, Drawn and Quartered, Butely's local pub. Annabelle went up to the bar to buy them all drinks.

'I have to tell you, Dave, that if you're still pretending to be me, then he's not your type,' said Sydney, watching him studiously observing the blond Adonis behind the bar as he flirted outrageously with Annabelle.

Dave reddened, right up to his ears, and shot her such a poisonous look that she wondered if she hadn't touched on a raw nerve. So much for trying out some Poppy-like banter.

'You're not secretly gay, are you, Dave?' asked Poppy. Then, remembering who she was supposed to be, she changed tacks. 'Have you got a problem you'd like to share? Is that how you'd do it, Sydney?'

'Not exactly. But I think the idea is to reinterpret the character you're playing from a different point of view. I must say, I'm not entirely getting to grips with being you, Poppy, but I suspect when I do it'll be great fun.'

'I'm having a lovely time being Linda.' Chloë hugged her knees. 'Who'd have thought I'd get to experience life as an editor so soon?'

Linda pulled up a chair, fresh from another lengthy call on her mobile. 'Don't enjoy it too much, Chloë,' she said in a voice that didn't quite achieve the jokey tone she was hoping for.

'Did you say that as you or you as me?' said Sydney. Thank God. Linda was finally on to Chloë.

'I thought *I* was Sydney,' said Poppy.

'It is slightly complicated.' Chloë smiled at Poppy condescendingly. 'But you get to be me, for your sins.'

'Yeah, for once you get to see what it's like to be a nobody,' said Dave. Chloë flushed and then recovered her composure. 'In my role as Linda can I say you're fired?'

Dave ignored her and turned to Sydney. 'Shouldn't you be phoning your kiddies now? Or rather, the nanny?'

Sydney, who had been warming to Dave with every one of his rebuffs to Chloë, felt betrayed. After all her efforts not to mention her children all day to anyone, when it was all she could do not to catch the next train back to London, something in her snapped. Annabelle went on about Joshie and James much more than she ever mentioned Harriet and Molly.

'Shouldn't you be lighting up a packet of cigarettes?' she asked Dave, who was playing Annabelle.

'Very sisterly, I must say. Is that all you think Annabelle does?'

Annabelle, who'd thrown herself into her role as Dave by borrowing one of his Smash the Establishment T-shirts, teetered up to the table with a tray of drinks. 'Isn't it funny the way you and I got to play each other?' she said, handing Dave a pint of Prince William. 'I mean, of everyone we probably have the least in common.'

'That's the point, isn't it?' beamed Chloë. 'To get under each other's skin.'

The others eyed her with varying degrees of opprobrium.

'I know,' said Poppy, whose tempestuous family life had made her exceedingly well versed in avoiding atmospheres. 'Let's play capitals.'

'Of countries, do you mean?' asked Dave. 'Okay. This one's a bit tricky, Poppy. What's the capital of England?'

'No, not countries. Film capitals. Like who was the capital of *Moulin Rouge*?'

'No one was. It's a film.'

'That's why it's film capitals. The answer is Nicole Kidman and Euan Macgregor.'

'So it's not about countries. It's not about capitals, and you can have two of them as the answer.'

'Got it.'

'Irresistible.'

'Actually, you could have three of them. Like in *Charlie's Angels* it would be Drew Barrymore, Lucy Liu and—'

'Yes, I think we're with you now,' said Dave.

'I think it's a good idea,' said Linda. 'It would improve our knowledge of popular culture. Brian's always going on about that.'

'Is he now?' snapped Dave, who thought his grasp of popular culture was perfectly flawless already. 'I'll start. Name the capital of Kurosawa's *Ran*.'

It took fourteen guesses before they conceded defeat.

Poppy was next. 'Okay, I'm going to turn this around and name the capital first. So you've got to guess the country. That's the film, really.'

'Yes, yes, I think we're just about still with you,' said Dave.

'Leslie Ash.'

'*Quadrophenia*,' said Dave.

Poppy giggled. 'Yeah, right.'

'Well, what else has she done?'

'*Men Behaving Badly*,' said Chloë, letting the neckline of her jumper slip past her shoulders.

'That's not a film.'

'*Scandal*,' said Linda.

'That was Joanne Whalley-Kilmer.'

'Yes, as Christine Keeler. But Leslie Ash played Mandy Rice-Davies.'

'I think that was Bridget Fonda,' said Sydney.

Dave looked at her with a tiny glimmer of respect in his eye. Despite everything, she was enjoying herself. It was so much less complicated than home.

'Surely not,' said Linda. 'It came out way before her time.'

'Is she related to Jane?' asked Poppy.

Dave scowled into his beer. 'It's like working with amateurs.'

'I loved *Scandal*,' said Chloë, leaning over the table to reveal her bottomless cleavage.

'I really don't think it was Bridget Fonda,' said Linda. 'It was a British film.'

'Yes, but even in those days we were busy selling out to

Mammon and casting Americans if we thought it could help at the box office.'

'As I recall, it wasn't a particularly good film,' retorted Linda.

'No, you're right, actually.' Chloë back-pedalled frantically. 'The script was very soggy. But I just love that period, don't you?'

'Which one?' said Poppy, feeling the game slip from her control.

'The Sixties,' said Sydney.

Poppy beamed, reassured to be back on familiar territory. 'Now you're talking. Eye-liner, Pop Art. It's all back, you know.'

'I suppose it could have been the other redhead – the one who played Dorothy Parker, what's her name?'

'Jennifer Jason Leigh,' said Sydney, 'who played opposite Bridget Fonda in *Single White Female.*'

'The most accurate portrayal of the female psyche ever,' said Dave maliciously.

'Have you commissioned that piece on testicular cancer by the way?' said Linda.

'Do you give up?' asked Poppy.

'I loved that film too,' sighed Chloë. She caught Linda's expression. 'Even though it was ridiculously misogynist. You had to laugh at the dystopic male view of females and take it as a compliment.'

'That's one way of looking at it, I suppose,' said Linda. 'Except that Hollywood didn't see it as dystopic.'

'*The Bill,*' said Poppy loudly.

'Actually, I did part of my dissertation on it,' said Chloë.

'More good use of the taxpayer's money,' commented Dave.

'The country-stroke-film that Leslie Ash is capital of is *The Bill*,' repeated Poppy loudly. The game was not fulfilling any of her requirements tonight. Which was odd, because it was always such fun when she played it with her proper friends.

'Not a film,' snorted Dave.

'And not right, I'm afraid,' said Sydney as tactfully as she could. If nothing else, handovers with Maisie had taught her the difference between a Leslie Ash police vehicle and all the others. 'The answer's *Mersey Beat*.'

Dave looked at her again. Poppy giggled. 'You're really brainy, you know, Sydney.'

They played on with similar results, becoming more and more tipsy and raucous. Poppy, who turned out to be a brilliant mimic, had them all in hysterics with her impersonation of members of the Shadow Cabinet, most of whom it turned out she'd known since she was a baby. Then, when Chloë left early, pleading a headache, she offered them a wickedly accurate rendition of Chloë's new drawl. It was a blessed relief to be away from Charlie and Dylan, Sydney realized with a start, though where it was getting the magazine was a moot point.

'I think that was brilliantly productive, don't you?' asked Linda as she and Sydney meandered nervously along Butely's dark, empty lanes from the pub. The frosty, black sky was smothered with tiny stars. Sydney was about to ask whether this was Linda still in character as her, engaging in a grotesque parody of her own even-handedness, when she realized that questionable as the weekend was in many ways, she was still having the time of her current life.

As promised, the following morning was given up to pampering. Chloë had a massage, a yoga lesson and a facial.

Dave went for a swim and a secret back scrub. Annabelle had acupuncture to help her give up smoking. Linda, who was getting very angsty because she still hadn't heard from the adoption agency, spent the morning meditating. Sydney went for a walk and tried not to think about home. It was hopeless. For seventeen and a half years she had managed to lock away all thoughts of her baby. Now she couldn't stop thinking about him. She rang Clifton Crescent but all she could hear was the girls squabbling in the background.

'Harriet started it – again,' snapped Charlie. 'I really think you should book a meeting with her teacher.'

Sydney was tempted to point out that if he spent more time at home he might realize squabbles were a normal part of his daughters' lives. He might also have time to book an appointment with Miss Cavendish himself. But she felt guilty for being away, so she didn't. And even though Poppy showed her her new mink Tod's clutch bag later on and offered to lend it to her whenever she wanted, she continued to feel bad. Normally she could accommodate both the luxurious and grim aspects of life without too much problem. But not today. All she could think about was the girl who gave away her baby on that dazzlingly sunny morning all those years ago.

On the drive back to London it became clear to Sydney that Linda was so convinced the weekend had been a tremendous success – both as a bonding exercise and as a stimulating catalyst that would send them all into creative overdrive – that she was talking about turning the magazine around by March when they reached Reading. She was still babbling with the glee of a zealot when they got to Chiswick.

'I've found a new route on the adoption front,' she continued breathlessly. The lights on the motorway fizzed a milky white like Alka Seltzer, making her eyes glint like flashing knives.

Sydney steeled herself. 'What happened to the orphanage in Romania?' she asked carefully.

'Too slow. I've abandoned that path. I'll be ninety and needing *my* nappies changing before they find me anything.'

'There's a lot to sort out.'

'Plus I felt I was coming up against the same old prejudices.'

'Such as?'

'The point,' Linda continued airily, 'is that in China you can literally buy a baby and cut out all the crap and the waiting. It's fantastic. Think of the wasted lives of all those children who linger in grubby cots for years while social workers piss around with the bureaucracy and all that ridiculous paperwork. It's far, far more humane this way.'

'And what happens when you get back to England?'

'Do you mean nanny-wise?'

'No, Linda, I mean reality-wise. You can't just bring a baby to Heathrow and show the authorities a till receipt.' The weekend had been a complete waste of time, Sydney realized suddenly. Linda was as ostrich-like as ever, and Sydney now had to face Charlie's seething resentment.

'So do you think I should go with Whitney?' persisted Linda.

'Witney, Oxfordshire?'

'No,' said Linda patiently. 'Whitney the waitress in Tennessee who's volunteered to have a baby for me. God, Sydney, she's a wonderful person. The kind who restores your faith in humanity. I mean, truly altruistic.'

'What's she charging?' snapped Sydney. She was in no mood for Linda's delusions.

'The going rate. But she's got a sperm donor lined up

already and everything. His name's Wade and he's a prison officer. Actually, I think he was her boyfriend and he's dumped her. But he's big and strong and very handsome in the photographs.'

They drove on through the suburbs in silence. When the snow started to fall, muffling the silence until it seemed almost frightening, Linda switched on the radio to listen to the news.

When she arrived home Sydney was still brooding on Chloë's performance at Butely and the sheer gall of delivering a stream of ideas more or less directly lifted from the letters and notes that had crossed Sydney's desk in the past few weeks, many of them marked confidential. The moon bathed Clifton Crescent in a fairytale light, turning the stucco on the terraces to Christmas cake icing. Mrs Protheroe was out with her tape measure watching Sydney park. When Sydney turned off the engine, she scuttled between her bumper and the car in front. 'She-Devil,' she hissed.

'Lovely evening, Mrs P,' replied Sydney, feeling exhausted after dropping Linda back at her flat. What was wrong with her? Health farms were meant to be invigorating.

'The were-wolf's home.' Mrs Protheroe's milky eyes slithered over Sydney. She was wearing her old mink jacket; the one Mr Protheroe had given her in 1954. 'A pox on you all,' she added darkly, before scuttling across the road to measure Dylan's bonnet again.

'You look well,' said Dylan, opening the front door to her and Charlie's house. He picked up her case and carried it through the hall.

'Do I?' Sydney followed him into the kitchen and tried not

to look in the least bit rattled by having the were-wolf in residence in her house.

'Mmm, all sort of glowy.' Sydney took off her coat and looked at him warily.

'Don't worry. I haven't moved in. I popped round to see if you and Charlie fancied coming round tonight, only to find Maisie on the doorstep in a panic. Apparently her mother's been taken ill and she couldn't get hold of Charlie who's had to make a quick dash to chambers.'

'So you held the fort?' asked Sydney incredulously. She hung up her coat and ran upstairs to see the girls.

'You can thank me profusely later,' Dylan called up the stairs. 'By the way, supper will be ready in half an hour. Charlie said he'd be back by then. End of the Road Hot Pot okay – or green curry as it's more mundanely known?'

Charlie got back late of course, and barely registered Sydney's return. After all her efforts to keep Dylan at arm's length from Charlie, they made an almost surreal threesome, Sydney thought as they sat down to a surprisingly delicious meal.

'Don't look so amazed,' said Dylan good-naturedly, ignoring the chilly atmosphere between Sydney and Charlie. 'I wouldn't have survived in the world's remotest televisual opportunities if I hadn't learned to rustle up something warming.'

'What was so urgent that you had to go to chambers on a Sunday?' Sydney asked Charlie, squeezing any trace of resentment out of her voice.

'This and that.' Charlie appeared absorbed in spearing a prawn. 'Nothing very interesting compared with your brainstorming weekend, I'm sure.'

'How's the case going?'

Charlie frowned. 'Which one would that be?'

'If you told me a bit more about what was going on, I might know,' said Sydney, straining to keep the mood light. She couldn't understand how she had ended up spending the first night back after her first-ever absence sharing green curry with her husband and her ex-lover.

'More wine?' asked Dylan awkwardly.

In the weeks after the brainstorming weekend Dylan drifted in and out of number 64 as if he half lived there. Whatever overhaul he was engaged in at Glendower Books, it must have been a very gentle one, given how much spare time he seemed to have. At first he only popped in when Charlie was bound to be there, but gradually he came whenever he felt like it.

Sydney supposed he was lonely and that all the off-handedness about the end of his marriage was bluster – which she found touching, even if the frequency of his visits unnerved her. He was extraordinarily good with the girls; he never seemed to tire of playing Cluedo with them, even though Molly always won, or of listening to her endless God-squaddy stories, or of spinning Harriet all kinds of yarns about his explorer exploits – so far-fetched that Sydney decided they must be true. She was pathetically grateful when he began teaching Harriet to tie knots, especially when she turned out to have quite a talent for them. She came home one day to find him showing her his Swiss Army knife.

'There's been another saga at *Mellow Moments*,' said Molly, in response to her mother's slightly panicked expression.

'So I've stepped into the breach,' said Dylan. The children had already eaten – some of Dylan's green curry, which was extraordinary in itself, given that they normally hated spicy food.

Dylan and Sydney waited as long as they could for Charlie, and then Sydney called him and he told her he wouldn't be back until eleven. He sounded worn out and dejected. Sydney offered to come to the office with some supper but he said that would rather defeat the purpose of staying late. So she and Dylan ate on their own and for the first time since he'd come back they discussed their mutual love – for literature.

'Have you noticed that left-wing writers tend not to be able to write?' Dylan dished up some more curry.

'With the notable exception of Zola and Graham Greene and George Orwell, Mayakovsky, Stephen Spender, Sartre, Dickens—'

'My point entirely. Take their counterparts and compare literary merits. Ezra Pound, T. S. Eliot, T. E. Lawrence, Jean Cocteau, Wyndham Lewis – hideous politics, I grant you, but who would you rather read? And don't obfuscate, Sydney, because I know what a soft-spot you had for T. S. Eliot, while I never once saw you actually enjoy anything by Sartre.'

Sydney's nerve ends tingled. She hadn't had a conversation outside the office that didn't somehow involve school, The Rolling Scones, the logistical running of her and Charlie's lives or the advisability or otherwise of extra-strong cleaning agents for what seemed years.

It was harmless banter. Nothing like the old days, because she was so much more resilient. Resilient and resistant. And desperate to ask what had really happened between him and Eloise, but she sensed it would be wiser to steer away from anything too personal. One night while Charlie was missing in action at the office again, Dylan pulled some Rizlas out of his pocket and began rolling a joint.

Sydney hadn't been stoned for years. By the time she and Dylan had smoked their way through three spliffs she was on the ceiling, with two of Juanita's cobwebs, and finding everything hysterically funny, even *Newsnight*. She still didn't get any further with her quest for Eloise knowledge. But he made her laugh.

She was still giggling the morning after – and decidedly tetchy and ravenous by the time she got home that evening. As usual, the fridge contained nothing that might usefully be combined into a conventional meal. She picked up the phone and asked Charlie if he could pop into the all-night corner shop near his chambers on the way home. They'd run out of bread for the girls' toast in the morning.

'I could do,' Sydney heard Charlie sigh irritably, 'but I wasn't planning on leaving until midnight. I doubt if it will be open then.'

'I'll be off then,' Maisie trilled from the hall.

A bleak prospect opened up before Sydney, involving driving with children in their pyjamas to get some bread. It wouldn't kill Charlie to nip round the corner for five minutes. He probably hadn't stretched his legs all day. No wonder he was starting to look like Liberace.

'Couldn't the shopping wait until tomorrow?'

'Don't be ridiculous,' said Sydney, surprised at her own anger. She must finally be coming down from the spliffs. 'Don't worry,' she heard herself adding in a martyred tone, 'I'll go.'

'You wouldn't have to if you didn't insist on shopping on the Internet.'

'I wouldn't have to shop on the Internet if you ever

thought for a single moment about pulling a quarter of your substantial weight around the house.'

There was a stunned silence. From both of them. 'Are you all right, Sydney?' Charlie asked eventually.

'No, I'm sodding well not all right.' She was tired, a bit stoned, and she was having a row about bread.

'I don't wish to deal with this right now, Sydney. I've got a mountain of work to get through. In two days I have to be in Bermuda with a watertight case for an out-and-out crook.'

'Bermuda?'

'Yes, Bermuda. I'm sure I told you before. Something needs sorting out there.'

'You didn't mention Bermuda.'

'Does the destination make a difference? Look, I'm rather busy.'

'You always are.'

'It pays the bills.'

'And my sad little job doesn't?'

'Frankly not after you've paid Maisie and Juanita.'

'I don't see how you can possibly know anything about our finances since you haven't actually bothered to look at a bank statement for nine years. Or a mortgage statement. Or anything else that keeps this show on the road.' She was shouting now. She never shouted. She pulled herself together. 'How long are you going for?'

'Ten days, initially. Though I may have to keep going back. Can't be sure.' It was so spiteful of him to keep on punishing her for the brainstorming weekend like this. She said nothing.

'I'm not going to have this conversation if you can't be rational. It's a waste of my time.'

'You will not put the phone down on me,' said Sydney furiously.

He put the phone down on her. He'd never put the phone down on her. She rang him back and got through to the clerk who told her Charlie's line was engaged.

Half an hour later she was up to her elbows in flour – the stigmata of the martyred working mother – and pummelling every last bit of air out of some dough. She was still so furious that she knew she was going to have to smash something. What? Not her beautiful china. She hurled a milk bottle on the floor and then another. Then she took a full one and threw that on the floor. Then she burst into tears and began to mop up the mess. She was still swabbing when the phone rang. Her heart lurched. Charlie.

'Hello, is that Sydney Murray?' For a moment the brittle transatlantic voice on the other end of the line sounded like Eloise.

It was Virginia Horwell, one of Fleet Street's most formidable journalists, currently an associate editor on the *Daily Mail*. 'I've got a piece here about women married to enablers and it's crap,' drawled Virginia. 'I'm trying to sex it up.'

'I'm sorry?' asked Sydney, struggling to be polite. She looked at her watch. Ten o'clock.

Virginia Horwell adopted the voice she always used to use when she was a rookie reporter stalking old, frail people. 'Enablers. Men who hold down high-powered jobs but still find time to back their wives up at home. Someone here suggested you'd be an ideal candidate. I gather your husband's a saint.'

One worthy of crucifixion, thought Sydney. 'I think you have the wrong number,' she said coldly. Then, shaking with anger, she bundled the dough into the oven. For some non sequitur of a reason she wished Dylan had never reappeared in her perfect life.

The following morning, equally illogically, she looked up the number of the Adoption Contact Register which she kept in a tiny lined notebook at work. It was nine months since she'd first contacted them and suddenly she desperately needed to know if they'd heard from her son yet.

10

The look on Miss Cavendish's translucent, twenty-seven-year-old face, as Sydney panted into her classroom at 4.20 just as she was putting on her jacket, left Sydney in no doubt as to where Miss Cavendish stood on irresponsible, unpunctual parents.

She wondered where she stood on irresponsible, unpunctual parents who went out dancing all night with their exes. Not that she'd meant to. Dylan had turned up on her doorstep with a leek in his mouth and two tickets for Aretha Franklin. To celebrate St David's Day and commemorate the first time they'd seen Aretha Franklin together. Miraculously, Maisie had been free to babysit at the last minute again. Sydney decided she had an uncanny nose for trouble, but since she adored Aretha and she had been getting lonely without Charlie, she'd grabbed the invitation. Unfortunately they'd missed the last Tube home, couldn't find a taxi, and had ended up in a smoky club in Clerkenwell on blues night.

'I don't really believe in beating around the bush,' Miss Cavendish told Sydney with a babyish sternness that made Sydney feel almost maternal. No teachers at her daughters' school ever wanted to beat about the bush, just as none of them looked as though they'd graduated from the Lower Sixth yet. They'd obviously all been to a teacher training college that thought beating around bushes was very bad for children and that Informal Chats were a much better policy. So far Sydney had been to three of these in the past eighteen months.

Miss Cavendish picked up a yellow exercise book with the word Histree written on it and traced her finger across it. Sydney smiled. She was used to Harriet's creative spelling. She noticed that Miss Cavendish's hand was shaking. This was beginning not to look like a standard meeting.

'I wouldn't use the word disturbed about Harriet,' Miss Cavendish began, perching daintily on the miniature plastic chair opposite Sydney. 'Not exactly, but there's some kind of short circuit in her behaviour. I don't know what it is precisely. But she's being very disruptive in class.'

Not *disturbed*, exactly? *Disruptive*? Sydney suddenly felt nostalgic for the days when the entire country did nothing else but beat around bushes.

Miss Cavendish's eyes widened nervously. 'What I meant to say is that she's been exhibiting a lot of behavioural abnormalities lately.'

'Behavioural abnormalities?' echoed Sydney. She gripped the seat of her chair and suddenly wished Charlie was with her instead of in Bermuda. She had expected a routine discussion and suddenly she was being informed that her daughter was on the road to Borstal.

'Exaggerated lack of concentration – even more than usual; extreme unwillingness to apply herself to any task that involves reading or writing. Mrs Murray, Harriet seems to have a lot of anger.'

'Isn't that normal in a dyslexic?'

'Yesterday,' Miss Cavendish continued nervously, 'she trimmed the plait of the girl in front of her.' She looked sternly at Sydney now. 'You didn't hear about it?'

'Perhaps she felt she was being helpful. You know what

children are like when there are scissors around. I once—'

'With a Swiss Army knife, Mrs Murray,' said Miss Cavendish. Sydney made a note to take Harriet to a shrink. And then she made a note to kill Dylan.

'Mrs Murray, there *is* a problem,' persisted Miss Cavendish with infuriating calm. 'We've had a number of complaints from other parents about her behaviour towards their daughters. We were trying to contain them. But then she punched a child.'

'I see.' Actually, a shrink was a ridiculous over-reaction. What about the child she'd punched? Why did no one think *she* might be a provocative brat?

'Harriet is a very bright child, Mrs Murray.' Now Miss Cavendish was getting to the good bit. 'And obviously it's very important for Harriet's sake that we try to get to the bottom of her anger so that she can begin to realize her potential. You've probably noticed how frustrated she's become.'

All Sydney had noticed was what she assumed was a normal ten-year-old with normal ten-year-old foibles. 'Maybe she's pre-pubescent.'

'Mrs Murray, are there any problems at home we should know about?'

Problems? How could there be? She had the perfect life. Sydney pretended to rack her brains. Miss Cavendish folded her hands in a prayer-like gesture. 'I don't want you to think you're being bulldozed into anything but I've spoken to the Head and if you agree, we'd like to get Harriet assessed by a behavioural psychologist. Your decision, of course, but we think it would be extremely helpful in enabling us to get a handle on what's wrong.'

A handle. How typical. 'Why is everyone in our education so obsessed with putting a label on every single child that comes through the system?' asked Sydney angrily. Then, feeling she'd stepped way out of line, as Miss Cavendish appeared visibly to shrink away from her, she began back-pedalling furiously.

Outside, Sydney dialled Charlie's number and tried to work out what time it was in Bermuda. She needed to re-gurgitate the entire conversation as quickly as possible so that he could analyse it properly with his cool, forensic logic and tell her she was panicking unduly. Instead she got his voice mail. Shaking, she left a terse message for him to call her and tried not to feel resentful. But she did. She was so shocked by the meeting that she almost didn't notice the smoke billowing out of Mrs Protheroe's kitchen when she got to Clifton Crescent.

It was all under control, the shortest of the giant fire-fighters told her. A silly accident with a chip pan. But it would leave some nasty scorch marks on the stucco. He shook his head sympathetically and sucked his teeth. Probably cost a fortune to put right. When Sydney asked him how Mrs Protheroe was, he looked almost affronted, as if he wasn't used to neighbours in such architecturally cherished areas being more concerned about the in-habitants than the buildings. As it happened, Mrs Protheroe was a bit dazed. Apparently she'd gone to bed shortly after putting on the pan and was now recovering in the Royal Free.

Sydney stepped round the yellow cordons, and made a note to go and visit Mrs Protheroe and also somehow to track down her daughter and see if she couldn't mediate some kind of reconciliation between them. She'd barely put her foot through the front door when her phone rang. It was Dylan, asking how the meeting with the teacher had gone.

She couldn't even remember mentioning it to him. But if she had, that would be good. That wouldn't be remotely romantic, flirtatious or misleading.

'I'll be off then,' Maisie called from the hall.

'So on a scale of okay to marvellous, how did it go?'

'What's the phrase for the pile of shit that lies beneath several tons of crap?'

'I see. Well, look, I'm at home. On my own. You're at home. On your own. Let's say we get morose and maudlin together.'

'Let's say we don't.' Suddenly she really needed Charlie at home. But that was the problem. Even when he was in the country he seemed to have difficulty locating his house these days. 'Dylan, did you give Harriet your Swiss Army knife?'

'Of course not.'

'Well, have you checked recently that you've got it?'

There was an uncomfortable pause. She heard him feeling in his pockets, then he offered to call her back when he'd had a proper look for it. Five minutes later he rang, sounding contrite.

'Look, I think it's best if you don't come round here so often. Harriet's disturbed.' She put the phone down and felt much better. For five minutes.

And then Dylan pounded on the front door. He was kneeling on the pavement with a geranium in his mouth. He spat it out. 'I couldn't find a rose, so I pinched this from 73's window box. Forgive me?' He gazed up at her imploringly. Déjà vu, again.

Sydney looked at him disapprovingly. 'You are childish, irresponsible and utterly, utterly in love with your own shortcomings.'

'I know. I blame my ex-girlfriends.'

Inevitably she let him in. And inevitably, over some wine,

she confided in him, mainly, she supposed, because there was no one else.

'Miss Cavendish asked if I'd noticed any behavioural abnormalities,' she said, tears stinging her eyes. 'Of course I hadn't,' she went on bitterly. 'I'm too busy dealing with strangers' abnormalities.' *Not exactly bullying.* And to think how often Sydney had thought Harriet's problems were all academic; that she was baffled, exhausted and frustrated at having to master concepts that were as impenetrable to her as the theory of flight – when all along it was her emotional state that was the real disaster. Then Sydney thought of a small, hazy boy who had no one at all to help him with his homework or his abnormalities. The saddest thing was that she didn't even know what he looked like, let alone whether or not he was still at school.

Dylan put an avuncular arm round her. 'Teachers love playing the guilt card. You hadn't noticed any abnormalities because there aren't any. Harriet's a great kid. Look, do you fancy a bite to eat? I'm famished.'

She mustn't be disarmed because of a simple geographical quirk that meant he was here and Charlie wasn't. Or that he seemed genuinely concerned. Or that all things – and knives – considered, he had a real gift for communicating with children. Dylan had always been good at touching, meaningful, childish gestures. He was so incontinent with his touching, meaningful gestures that actually they were meaningless. But touching all the same.

They had a take-away, then she told him she needed to do some work. Then she called Charlie to reassure herself she was doing the right thing. But he still wasn't answering.

Sydney found an address for Mrs Protheroe's daughter in a chamber-pot Mrs Protheroe kept under the dining-room table. And Charlotte Rampling's people finally agreed that rather than writing the fifteen hundred words on euthanasia herself, it would be much easier if a journalist from *IQ* came over to Paris and let her dictate it. 'Paris, here I come,' said Dave, rubbing his hands in glee. 'City of light, city of dreams.' His pudgy features were so pleasantly animated that he looked almost boyish.

'City of shite, more like,' said Poppy. She'd just had another row with Manley Magus the godlike lead singer from Doors to Manual whom she'd accused of being a religious bigot, after he'd suggested she accompany him to a kabbalah class. Manley had promptly vanished – if making the headlines every day with his sell-out round-the-world tour with Doors to Manual could be called vanishing.

'Have you seen the state of their pavements?' Poppy said grumpily. 'I can't believe they market it as the city of lovers. Still, I suppose it's worth it if you think people are interested in Charlotte Rampling these days. Personally I would have thought she was more suitable for *Saga* magazine.'

Dave looked crestfallen, like a small boy who's just discovered the articulated Tonka lorry his father gave him for Christmas is a cheap copy that breaks whenever you try to make it articulate. No, that would have been Miles, Christmas 1975.

'I think Charlotte's fascinating, Dave,' said Chloë, arching her neck into a yogic position that was meant to stretch the throat and had the advantage of making her breasts look even bigger. She'd been going to Bikram yoga ever since they'd got back from Butely and it had clearly paid dividends. She was also, now Sydney came to look, wearing an almost identical shirt-dress to the ones Linda wore. 'And you don't write enough for the magazine.'

Dave offered her a tentative grimace, which Sydney

recognized as a smile. Her stomach dipped. She was almost as irked by her suspicions of Chloë as she was by everyone else's apparent naïvety.

'With any luck you might get something quite interesting. I think it's great Linda's letting you go,' Chloë purred. 'She's so brilliant at taking punts on people.'

- 'Try these, Annabelle.' Poppy handed her a box of face creams that had just arrived from a convent in Tuscany. 'Made by nuns and brewed for a hundred years,' she said proudly. 'And Sydney, these shades just came in.' She flourished a pair of huge black Chanel sunglasses at Sydney.

'Don't you want them?' asked Sydney, embarrassed. Nobody could say Poppy wasn't generous with her freebies.

'They've got your name on them. Anyway, I've got hundreds. I'm going to need to move to a bigger place at this rate.'

'I don't know how you have time to do any work,' said Chloë, 'with all the unpacking you have to do.'

'Here you go, Chloë.' Poppy handed her what looked like a carved model of the Leaning Tower of Pisa. 'It's a wooden dildo, made from sustainable Wenge wood.'

Chloë bit her lip. Sydney thought she might be about to cry, but she managed to laugh it off instead.

'How can you brew a cream?' asked Dave, though slightly less acidly than usual, Sydney thought. In which case she was beginning to see why Linda had agreed to his doing Charlotte Rampling. If it put him in a good mood for the rest of the year it was worth it, even if the finished piece was unprintable.

'It's excellent for fine lines,' persisted Poppy. 'But then so's not smoking.'

'Annabelle, would you like me to see if I could try and get us some more exciting cars to drive for the motoring column? Only I've got a few contacts in the car business . . .'

To Sydney's satisfaction, Annabelle pretended not to hear Chloë. Finding cars – and automobile industry contracts – was her job. It wasn't her fault that everyone was a bit wary of lending *IQ* cars at the moment, following the latest multiple pile-up.

'My doctor said it would be more dangerous for me to give up cigarettes than to carry on.' She lit another Marlboro. 'She says I need to be in a reliable relationship.'

'With cigarettes?' asked Poppy.

Annabelle laughed. It was the first glimmer of her old humour Sydney had seen in years.

Dave's moon face broke into a huge, wrinkled smile – he must have been ecstatic about the interview – and Poppy and Annabelle subsided into silly office giggles. Chloë sloped off towards Linda's office carrying a large ring-binder stuffed with glossy car brochures.

It wasn't like Charlie to sulk. He didn't need to when he could effectively ignore her most days of the week by burying himself in his work and newspapers.

She went to visit Mrs Protheroe in hospital to prove to herself what a wonderful, capable person she was, but Mrs Protheroe didn't recognize her for the first ten minutes and when she did, she called her a harlot. It was very depressing. And her daughter, whom Sydney had managed to track down, didn't want to know.

Anthea Protheroe wasn't the only stranger Sydney was working on. A week after Charlie had gone to Bermuda, a letter arrived from the Adoption Contact Register. It reminded her to be patient, explaining, again, that even if her son did want to contact her, he couldn't do so legally without his adoptive parents' consent.

Dylan announced he would have to go to Paris to meet with a Patrice Brougier who was interested in investing in Glendower Books. 'Now that Eloise is off the scene, I badly need an injection of dosh,' he said glumly. For one wild, idiotic moment Sydney contemplated putting her measly savings into Glendower Books. She was heart-sick of being such a parasite on Charlie: if they took off it might give her some financial independence. Then she came to her senses.

Linda still didn't understand how there could be anything wrong in Sydney's charmed existence, not even when Sydney marched into her office with the letter from the Adoption Contact Register, finally desperate to come clean about her past. 'So Charlie's a little uncommunicative.' Linda's attention strayed reluctantly from the BMW brochure she'd been studying. 'You want to try dealing with Brian Widlake who is more than communicative. Honestly, sometimes I think it's better when they ignore you.'

Sydney wondered, not for the first time, how someone so intelligent could be so emotionally unintuitive. Stupid question. She was married to the prototype. She thought about explaining to Linda everything her marriage guidance counsellor had told her about sublimating rage into skewed rationalism and using anger denial as a mask for fear of loss of control. Instead, she asked her where she'd bought her new chocolate suede boots.

'Poppy got them for me,' said Linda vaguely, clearly not wanting to endorse any suggestion that Brian Widlake's pet appointment was turning out to have her uses. A BMW coupé beckoned voluptuously from the brochure in front of her. 'He's insisting we cut our staff, by the way.' She raked her hands through her newly highlighted hair.

Sydney felt her palms go clammy. 'That's ridiculous. We're pared right back to the bone as it is.'

'From now on anyone who doesn't pay their way is out.'

'I suppose Chloë could go? She was last in.'

Linda shook her glossy head with the mournful air of a defeated gun dog.

'What does Chloë do exactly?' persisted Sydney. She began folding the letter she'd brought to show Linda into tiny squares. She suddenly realized how much she loved this job.

'What doesn't she do? You know she's helping to call in some decent cars? As well as coming up with most of the good ideas. She's even submitted a few synopses of pieces she'd like to write. I wouldn't be surprised if she turns out to be another Julie Burchill.'

Sydney's heart pounded. Linda wouldn't be offloading Chloë. Who then?

'He wants Annabelle to go.'

The letter from the Adoption Contact Register slipped from Sydney's fingers and fluttered to the ground. She scooped it up and waited for the tiny, shameful shaft of relief to be replaced by anger and righteous indignation. 'But that's so unjust . . .' she began weakly. She was flooded with self-disgust. What would Annabelle do now? It couldn't be allowed to happen. She'd take voluntary redundancy herself.

'I know. Somehow if Widlake had recommended sacking Dave or even you, it would have been okay because it would have proved he didn't know what he was talking about. But with those fucking infallible antennae of his he's spotted the weakest link from four floors away.'

'What do you mean?' asked Sydney unconvincingly.

'Come on, Sydney. Annabelle's hardly the sharpest heel in the wardrobe right now.'

'Maybe not. But she's been loyal to you for thirteen years. And it's not as if we don't all know why things have been a little rough, not to mention complete and utter hell, for her lately. This would devastate her emotionally and financially. You can't seriously agree to it, Linda.'

'All right, Sydney. Calm down.' Linda scowled at Dave who was hovering outside her box. 'Jesus. I'm just telling you what I have to put up with these days. Every day, if you must know. On top of everything else . . .' A note of something Sydney had never heard in Linda's voice before. Self-pity? 'Of course I'm not going to fire Annabelle. I'll find some other way of making cut-backs.' She glanced round the office furtively. 'In the meantime, if you have any ideas, I'd be grateful if you passed them on.'

The longer Charlie took to return her calls, the more explosively resentful Sydney felt. The compression in her chest was a cancer of anger, the size of Jacquie's chocolate log, and almost unbearably visceral. Eventually she decided to be adult and ring him. Again. This time he answered. She could hear people splashing around in the background and the unmistakable sound of ice tinkling in a silver bucket. 'Bullying,' she repeated loudly.

'That teacher's obviously hysterical,' said Charlie with maddening serenity. Sydney stabbed her pen on her palm. She'd wanted calm rationalization, not cold indifference. 'Harriet punched a girl at school. How's your heat rash?' she enquired sulkily as she heard someone three thousand miles away dive into a warm pool.

'Sorry, I missed that. The fourth Mrs Vilovich just jumped off the top board. Except it turns out her husband never officially got round to divorcing the third Mrs Vilovich.'

'They want to get in a psychologist,' said Sydney.

'I can't hear you.'

'Tell the fourth Mrs Vilovich to stay away from the diving board then,' said Sydney crossly. 'Is it because of bigamy that you've had to delay coming home?'

'Not exactly.' He lowered his voice. 'I can't explain now, but this is quite a complex situation that I'm having to extricate Canningtons from. It's not quite as simple as was originally suggested to me. I will fill you in when I get home.'

'When will that be?'

'I'll call you when I know for s—' The line snapped, along with Sydney's patience.

'Whitney's changed her mind,' said Linda bleakly when Sydney poked her head round her door the next morning.

Sydney racked her memory for the alphabetical list of *IQ*'s stroppy freelancers she'd begun to store there. She lost track after the Bs.

'That fucking waitress,' snapped Linda.

'Linda, I'm so sorry,' said Sydney, suddenly picturing Linda sitting alone in her flat at night prostrate with longing for a little bundle to fondle. She felt shabby, guilty and somehow responsible for everyone's woes. Coming on top of everything else, this would be a devastating blow for Linda. 'Is she absolutely sure?'

'Yeah. Apparently Wade has come back to her and promised to raise the baby with her.' She shook her head at the perfidy of men. 'I despair of the male race sometimes. They're all such bastards.'

'Perhaps it's for the best,' said Sydney gently.

'What do you mean?' Linda turned her tear-streaked face towards Sydney and conjured an expression that was both accusatory and martyred.

'You must admit the timing's not great at the moment. What with pressures at work.'

'I've certainly got no time to meet a man and conceive the natural way, if that's what you mean,' Linda said bitterly. 'God, Sydney, I'm so tired of waiting for someone to love.'

She pushed the already crushed blinds to one side and craned her neck out of the window, scanning the street below.

Sydney took a deep breath. 'That's another thing – maybe you need to start thinking laterally about the men you date.' And try not to select ones with the same *IQ* as your waist measurement. But Linda appeared not to be listening.

'Oh my God, Sydney. A BMW convertible has just pulled up! On indefinite loan, if I'm not mistaken. I told you you'd misjudged Chloë.'

Dylan returned from Paris with the promise of long-term investment from Patrice Brougier, a spring in his step and a bottle of Shalimar for Sydney. He also gave her the address of The Learning Pool, which specialized in diagnosing children with unspecified behavioural problems, which a very nice woman he'd found himself sitting next to on Eurostar had passed on to him. Then he'd invited himself in to watch a DVD of *Whatever Happened to Baby Jane?* which he'd just bought. He stayed far too long. By the time they'd rewound their favourite bits and reminisced about the time they'd first seen it at the Arnolfini in Bristol, it was almost one in the morning. Which meant that when Charlie arrived from the airport at 8.30 a.m., the routine which Sydney and the girls had fallen into in his absence had gone completely AWOL.

But even if the routine had been running perfectly, the home-coming would have been bumpy. What she probably should have done, Sydney realized as she leafed through the catalogue of designer sex toys and fetish designer lingerie that Poppy had left on her desk, was meet Charlie at the airport in a push-up bra, crotchless panties and her best slutty stilettos, ready to service her man – en route for their house if need be. But since she didn't possess any of these apparently indispensable items of clothing, and since Charlie had gone straight to chambers from the airport, it was all a bit academic. Besides, sex wasn't the be-all and end-all in marriage. But perhaps relegating it to somewhere between taking Hamish for his annual flea injections and remembering to change the soil in her terracotta tubs was underplaying things too much.

She resolved to make amends that evening by cooking steak Béarnaise. But Charlie had gone straight up to his study, wearily removed some papers from his briefcase – an early proof of an updated version of *Hypothecation: The Wrinkles Within* he was working on, Sydney noticed belatedly – in a halo of put-upon patience and begun proof-reading them.

Sydney followed him upstairs with a cup of tea, determined to get things at least back to normal. She could work on making them good later.

'I don't know why you're still angry,' he began in his saddened but close-to-exasperated tone. He placed the tea on the cherry-wood bureau where it would no doubt leave an interesting patina of concentric circles if she didn't move it on to the mantelpiece.

'Sydney,' Charlie repeated carefully, 'what are you so angry about?'

She stopped in her tracks as if he'd lassoed her. 'I'm not angry. You are.'

His long face looked preposterously incredulous. Sydney was shocked to realize that although of course she wasn't angry, she would quite like to punch Charlie's lights out, or at least send his precious anglepoise crashing to the floor. Anything to dislodge him from his complacent nest of superiority.

'We really cannot have a rational discussion while you're being so unreasonable.' He sighed, clearly itching to get back to *The Wrinkles Within*. 'Perhaps you'll feel better after the holiday.'

She walked out of the room and marched down into the kitchen, kicking a box of Charlie's papers he'd left lying in the hall on the way. Then she tore it open and tipped all its contents upside down in the hallway. Then she picked them all up again and carefully rearranged them, making sure to get all the pages that had fallen out of the file marked Mikhael Vilovich. After which she went into the kitchen and poured herself a glass of wine to steady her nerves while she worked out what the hell to do about the annual holiday they always took in Seville – the holiday they always had to take at Easter because of Charlie's heat allergy. The allergy that didn't, she noted, stop him going to Bermuda.

At eleven the following morning, Annabelle approached Sydney's desk with a concerned look on her puffy face.

'Rampling's on hold again,' she began balefully. 'Are you all right, Sydney? You look a bit frazzled. There's nothing wrong at home, is there?' she asked, not entirely managing to keep the optimism from her voice.

Sydney's eyes flicked towards Dave to make sure he was otherwise engaged. She couldn't start bleating about how she'd screwed up on the annual holiday, even though she knew Charlie would go ballistic – in his non-ballistic way – when he found out. So she told her about Miss Cavendish's diagnosis of Harriet instead.

'A bully. My God.' Annabelle sank down on Sydney's pile of papers and lit a cigarette.

In the absence of any moral support from Annabelle, Sydney tried to buoy herself up. 'She was exaggerating, I think. But when I remember all the times we've got cross with her for not trying in her work. And all the time she was a psychological mess. Maybe we pushed her into it . . .' Sydney's voice shook.

Annabelle put her arms round Sydney's shoulders. 'Don't blame yourself. If I thought like that I'd have to jump out of this window. At least you've got a supportive husband.'

'The really frustrating thing is not knowing why she's so angry. I mean, obviously the dyslexia doesn't help . . .'

'You would tell me if there *was* anything up – in the marital department – wouldn't you?'

'Of course there may not be anything wrong with her. You never know these days . . .'

'Who's dyslexic?' asked Poppy, sauntering over with a large jar and picking up fag ends. 'Have you seen Chloë? I thought I'd get her to try out this new acne cream.'

'She's not in,' snapped Annabelle, who was furious with Chloë for not even phoning in to warn them she'd be late.

Sydney began to cry softly. She pulled a small scrumpled note with '*Hello Kitty*' on it that she'd found by Harriet's bed that morning. '*Ples help. Don't mek me go to scul eny moor. My lif is hel.*'

Poppy studied it in silence for a few moments. 'The good news is that her grammar is impeccable. I had a ghastly time at school,' she added cheerfully. 'I was always getting into fights. One time I tried to flush this girl down the loo.' She placed two gel pads tenderly on Sydney's eyes and then sat down to gaze lovingly at her endless, bronzed legs. 'I've always been able to think laterally.'

*   *   *

The Learning Pool said they'd do their best to find a cancellation for Harriet and in the meantime made an appointment for her in June, three months away. Charlie, meanwhile, was apparently too busy for any appointments now or in the future. Sydney tried. She truly did. But whenever she suggested that they needed to talk, he said he was tired or waiting for an important phone call. And when she went into the kitchen and telephoned him from her mobile and said this *was* an urgent phone call, he wasn't remotely amused.

'Why won't you discuss this with me, Charlie?' Sydney tried to keep her voice calm.

'Discuss what?'

'Your inability to discuss.'

'That's a nonsense, Sydney, and you know it. You're the one who's angry. And until you calm down there's no point in us having any conversations.'

'But I can't calm down until you let me tell you what's bothering me.'

'Aha, so you *are* angry.'

'Probably,' she conceded wearily. 'But so are you.'

'Rubbish.' His voice hardened, the way it did when she'd heard him talking to policemen in court when he thought their sloppy practices meant that someone Charlie knew was guilty was about to slither off the hook.

'You are. But you won't admit it. You see anger as losing control, whereas it's a normal human reaction.' She swallowed and forced her voice down an octave. 'You do your utmost to wind everyone up so you can sit back and play Solomon.'

'This is psychobabble and I'm going to put the phone down.'

'Don't you dare hang up on me!'

'It's not hanging up if I tell you in advance that I'm going to do it.'

'You're a passive-aggressive, Charlie.'

'For heaven's sake.' She pictured him rolling his eyes. 'Sydney, listen to me. You're overtired. And you're overtired because you've taken on too much. Now go to bed and get some rest.'

And then he hung up.

'Please don't say no to this next request.' Linda's voice had the tropical warmth it always acquired whenever she was about to ask a big favour. Sydney braced herself.

'Bring your passport to work.'

Relief flooded Sydney. For one moment she'd thought Linda had been about to ask her to hand in her notice after all.

'And take it to Paris with you this morning. Dave's gone down with flu and I need you to do Charlotte Rampling.'

'I thought she'd postponed.'

'Her film's been delayed and she's got some spare time.'

'Why me?' Sydney asked in horror. 'What about Chloë?'

'God, Sydney, I'm not that besotted. She needs years at the coal-face before I let her anywhere near her own piece. Anyway, Brian Widlake's got her running some errands for him.'

'I didn't think he knew she existed.' Sydney was even more astonished that having established her existence, Brian was interested. The whole point of Chloë, as far as Linda had been concerned, was that she was precisely the kind of plain bluestocking Widlake loathed.

'Apparently not only does he know she exists, he's quite a fan.' Linda sounded mildly peeved. 'Anyway, you're a brilliant listener and people really open up to you.'

'But I don't write.'

'Tape it and we'll cobble it together between us.'

'What about style and panache?'

'I've got those. You just need a tape recorder.'

'I'll have to speak to Charlie. I'll need to ask Maisie to cover tonight as well.'

'It's only a day. And you'll be back by seven. He'll hardly notice. Please,' said Linda. 'And drop the I'm-not-worthy act, Parker. No one else remotely literate is free at such short notice.' No one else, apart from Dylan, called her by her maiden name.

By the time the train entered the Tunnel, Sydney was a ball of nerves. As soon as they plunged out of the darkness and into the flat plains of northern France, her phone rang again for the third time. She wished Linda would stop calling. It was just making them both nervous. Sydney couldn't shake off an awful feeling of doom, but she attributed it to the date: 20 March. Owen's birthday. He'd be eighteen. Old enough to contact her. As usual, she'd posted the card to Storepac. As usual, it had made her cry. In some ways she was lucky to have a distraction this year, even if it was one that could end in disaster.

The call wasn't from Linda but Miranda, ringing to find out whether she and Charlie were renting La Rosa this Easter.

'By the spookiest of coincidence,' Miranda's voice sounded eerily chirpy, 'I think I might be renting the villa in the next olive grove. With some friends – the Grangers. Do you remember?'

Sydney didn't remember but she had a suspicion that like most of Miranda's friends, they'd be ghastly and some considerable distance to the right of Mussolini.

'I didn't book it personally, you understand,' Miranda explained hastily. 'The Grangers did. Will you be at La Rosa as usual? It would be so nice to meet up.'

'I'm not too sure,' said Sydney, wishing she'd remembered to ask Linda if she was meant to ask Charlotte Rampling about her divorce. She hoped not. Surely *IQ* still needed to preserve some of its tact and integrity.

'Gosh. It's terribly late still to be unconfirmed, isn't it? I'm not surprised though, given how busy you are these days. You could always stay with us. It's an absolutely huge villa from the sound of things. There's plenty of room for three families.'

Sydney knew there was. She even knew the villa. It was the same size as La Rosa, which made her and Charlie's failure ever to invite Ian and Miranda to stay all the more glaring.

'That's very kind of you, Miranda, I'll speak to Charlie.' Or rather she wouldn't. In his current contrary mood he might want to go. And if she pointed out how grim it was likely to be, he'd point out – not in so many words but in a fashion no one could misinterpret – that if she didn't have a job, she wouldn't have forgotten to book and the situation would never have arisen. It was all right for him because he always buried himself in his work on holiday. He wouldn't notice if they went to Magalluf with Osama Bin Laden and 400 lager louts. She looked out of the window as the northern French plains flashed past, flat as billiard tables. 'I'd better go, Miranda,' she said hurriedly. 'I've got a call waiting. But thanks so much for ringing.' Gratefully, she switched lines.

'If I didn't know better I'd think you were stalking me, Parker.'

'Dylan?'

'I had to make sure it really was you over there.'

'What are you talking about?'

'Check out the ruggedly handsome beast in seat forty-three.'

Sydney peered behind her towards the far end of the compartment. Dylan's tanned features twinkled from seat 43. He waved and grinned at her.

I I

Sydney pulled up the neck of her black jumper and put on the dark Chanel sunglasses Poppy had given her as she and Dylan strode along the platform at Gare du Nord. She was beginning to feel the effects of the champagne they'd shared.

'Ah, Gay Paree. Cradle of art, literature and *l'amour*,' said Dylan as they sped past the station's Burger King.

'Is that sewage I can smell?' Sydney sniffed the air accusingly. She had to wrench proceedings back on to an even keel. It had been bad enough on the train, when their conversation had skittered between bad jokes about literature, Dylan's concerned enquiries about Harriet, and a discussion about their favourite poets. Dylan had a new Glendower volume of obscure English verse he was taking to show Patrice. Then he had asked why she was so nervous and she'd let her guard down about the Rampling interview. By the time the steward wheeled over the coffee and chocolates, Dylan was reciting Andrew Marvell to her. And now she couldn't get his wretched 'Ode to His Coy Mistress' out of her mind. Linda was right. Dylan's sub-text was about as subtle as a plane crash. But while they'd been in a bit of no-man's-land on the train, with no-man's-rules, she was prepared to sit back and enjoy it. Now however, it was time to erect some barriers.

'Goodbye, then,' she said as they approached the taxi

queue. Dylan, she knew, had a chauffeur-driven limo meeting him at the front of the station.

'I don't think you'll be going anywhere for the next hour or two,' said Dylan with a smack of satisfaction. Sydney felt the fist round her bowels tighten. The disgruntled queue was massive, and growing longer by the second.

'Hopefully Charlotte Rampling's a very patient woman.' Dylan looked grave and Sydney's mobile rang again.

It was Linda. 'I've just sold Rampling to Brian Widlake as the most revealing interview she's ever done.'

'Slightly premature,' said Sydney crossly. She was starting to find the pressure intolerable.

'He's using it in the TV ads on Friday. So try and keep the euthanasia on the light side if you can. The photographer will meet you there.' A woman in an ankle-length sable barged in front of Sydney in the taxi queue. Sydney wanted to cry.

'Oh, come on, Parker, hop in.' Before she could think up a suitable rebuttal – which would have taken some time as there weren't any – Dylan threaded his arm through her elbow and marched her across the concourse again towards a navy blue Mercedes and a uniformed chauffeur.

Sydney slid over to the far corner of the back seat. Dylan watched her with a twinkle of amusement. 'You ought to wear heels more often,' he said.

'I thought you were trying to save money these days.' She fondled the leather seats and tried not to sound flattered.

'I am. But luckily Patrice's budgets are bottomless. Along with his vanity. Which makes him the perfect sleeping partner in a vanity publishing project.'

'Let's hope Sleeping Beauty doesn't wake up in a bad mood one morning.'

The limo screeched down the narrow streets of the 10th

arrondissement, a steady stream of expletives exploding from the front. Sydney thought of Princess Di and began searching for the buckle of her seat-belt. Typically, there wasn't one.

'What's he saying?' asked Dylan.

'That the only way to get anywhere in this fucking city is to kiss everyone's bumpers and then stick your tongue up their arses.'

'And they say romance in Paris is dead.'

Sydney gazed out of the window as they skidded along the Seine, glittering like an olive satin ribbon under an aqua-marine sky. High above the Eiffel Tower a doily of lacy clouds parted like Can-Can bloomers. The sun was rising rapidly and showering the gleaming domes of the Grand and Petit Palais in the kind of golden light Hollywood actresses would kill for. Which meant that hopefully they'd get some fantastic portraits of Charlotte. Today at least, Poppy was wrong about Paris: anything less resembling a hell-hole of dog shit was hard to imagine. Sydney for once felt disconcertingly aroused. It must be nerves.

'Just look at the gilt on Les Invalides,' said Dylan. 'They say La République Glorieuse almost went to the wall trying to pay for it.'

Sydney turned her head towards yet another grand cupola. Jesus, was every building in Paris shaped like a breast?

'God, this city's phallo-centric,' said Dylan as they buckarooed in sight of the Eiffel Tower. Thanks to their driver's tireless use of the accelerator pedal and imaginative deployment of the hand-brake, the rest of the journey up the Champs-Elysées was a stomach-lurching blur. As they skidded into the Place Charles de Gaulle their driver slammed on the brakes and Sydney felt herself slithering across the seat towards Dylan like a magnet. She reached for the hand-strap and winched herself back into the corner, wishing fate – or whatever it was – would stop hurling her and Dylan together. It was really very difficult maintaining a briskly efficient, sexless front with someone you'd had sex with in every conceivable position, including front, side and upside down.

The corners of Dylan's mouth twitched. 'Sydney, you'll do yourself an injury if you carry on like that, not to mention pulling the strap out of Patrice's very smart Merc. What's the matter?' he added drily as Sydney frowned. 'I'm not going to try and seduce you, you know. I'm not that foolish.'

At those few crushing words Sydney felt herself turn scarlet – and deflate. What an utterly ridiculous fool she was making of herself. Why couldn't she treat the whole thing as an amusingly sophisticated Gallic sort of joke, as Dylan obviously did? She wanted to say that she had never suspected any such thing, but that would be making too heavy work of Dylan's comments, which were a stream of unedited consciousness half the time anyway.

They pulled up in the 16th arrondissement outside a gorgeous example of nineteenth-century baroque Parisian architecture. She stared up at the balcony above her, which billowed out from the first floor like a pregnant belly, gathered her notes together and thanked him politely for the ride.

Dylan stuck his head out of the window. 'Listen, if you have a problem with a lift back, or find yourself at a loose end, give me a call. I'm free after four.'

Sydney smiled graciously. She had no intention of spending any longer than necessary in Paris. She was booked back on the 20.19 train which should allow for plenty of outfit changes, awkward silences and tantrums from the photographer.

What it did not allow for, however, was a spontaneous demonstration on behalf of Paris's 350,000 shop workers, which brought the city's cash registers and most of the twenty arrondissements to a standstill. Sydney was stuck in a jam near the Arc de Triomphe for forty-five minutes before anything moved at all. Not that she noticed initially. She was too busy marvelling at how well it had all gone with Charlotte Rampling, who had been charm personified: warm, frank and funny and a testament to how reviving a divorce could be. Even the photographer had behaved reasonably well, only making Sydney hold his light reflector for an hour before he decided to do away with it altogether.

By the time they were making painfully slow progress round the Arc de Triomphe, she was in a panic. It was quarter to eight already and given that the gates closed twenty minutes before the train was due to leave, the chances of her making it were almost non-existent. She'd have to break the news to Charlie, and then she'd have to do something about finding a room in a small hotel somewhere, and then she'd have to deal with the persistent voice somewhere in the back of her head which kept telling her that whatever her thoughts on the subject, fate had something quite different in store for her. She fished in her bag for her phone but it was already ringing by the time she found it. It was probably Maisie wanting to find out what time Charlie would be home.

'How did it go?' Dylan's voice reverberated down the line like a thunderbolt.

She gave him a dutiful, short report, although inside she was beginning to feel reckless. Outside the car, a roar of protest rose from the crowd like steam. A drum began beating and the marchers started blowing their whistles and chanting.

'You're not stuck in that bloody *manifestation* are you, Sydney?' He sounded quite concerned. She thought about lying but just then a protestor waved a football rattle so loudly next to her window it would be obvious she wasn't on the train.

'Where exactly are you?'

She craned her neck for a street sign. 'Quite near the Georges V. I could make a dash for it on the Mètro, I suppose.'

'Hardly. The last train from Gare du Nord leaves in nineteen minutes. There's no way you'll make it. Hop out of your taxi and meet me in the lobby of the Georges V hotel for a drink. It's the only sensible option currently.'

'I might have known you'd be staying somewhere flashy and tasteless,' said Sydney, a small curl of excitement unfurling in the pit of her stomach.

'Cruel, Parker. But true. Actually, they've redecorated. It's terribly chic. Shall I see if I can get you a room for the night?'

Sydney could just imagine Annabelle's face if she presented a bill from the Georges V. There wouldn't be a packet of cigarettes left unsmoked within a ten-mile radius of Icon Towers. Breakfast alone at the Georges V would cost more than her daily allowance.

'Something smaller and nearer the station would be more appropriate.'

'OK. We'll get the concierge here to find something. In the meantime, I'll organize some champagne on ice. Oh, and Sydney, don't let the whiff of cordite turn your head. I don't want to find you taking part in a French sit-in.'

Sydney eyed the swelling mass of marchers pressing

against the lines of cars which had ground to a halt again and were stacked up along the Champs-Elysées like matchbox toys. Dylan was right. She didn't have many options.

She got out and paid the driver. She walked past the glittering shop windows and let the cold drizzle run down her flushed cheeks. She turned into the Avenue Georges V, feeling like Anne Boleyn walking towards Tower Green. Then she reminded herself what Dylan had said that morning about having no intention of trying to seduce her. Perhaps she'd misjudged him. It wasn't as if they hadn't had dinner on their own together on a number of occasions in the last few months. Just because they were in Paris didn't mean she was about to be ravished. She was a happily married woman. Actually, she was an unhappily married woman at present. But affairs didn't happen to people like her. So why did a small swarm of mischievous butterflies keep fluttering about inside her? She rang Charlie to break the news about the demo and he received the news with his expected icy sangfroid.

'And darling' – she hadn't called him darling for months – 'what do you think about us going on holiday with Ian and Miranda at Easter? You're always saying we ought to be more sociable with them. You know how many times they've hinted about coming to stay with us at La Rosa. And now it turns out they've booked the villa next door. And it also turns out, as I've just discovered, that La Rosa has just been sold and the new owners don't want to lend it out to anyone but personal friends any more.' And she hadn't lied to him – explicitly at least – ever. It was a foolish lie at that – one he could readily check out if he had the inclination. And one he was also likely to contest on a legal basis. She waited for the inevitable line of questioning. But there wasn't any.

'Do whatever you think best,' he said wearily. She

switched her phone off. And then she tried not to run towards the Georges V.

Lionel, the concierge at the Georges V, was charmingly accommodating about finding Sydney somewhere more modest to stay. It wasn't easy because it seemed a lot of other travellers had had the same idea, but in the end he found her something adorable-sounding on the Left Bank – miles from the Gare du Nord but the best he could do in the circumstances. Sydney and Dylan, both on their second glasses of champagne and comfortably ensconced in a dimly lit corner of the bar, agreed that Lionel had done brilliantly and ordered another round. Sydney had taken off her coat and half-way through her third glass now, was starting to feel at one with her situation. Not that there was a situation. And even if there was, she was entitled to a little harmless flirtation.

'You mustn't get too worked up about anything the school tells you,' Dylan was saying. 'Harriet's a great kid. Probably just a bit too original for them. They invariably get it wrong. My school was convinced I'd be a drop-out.'

She smiled gratefully. It would be nice if Charlie made himself this available for comment on his daughters' futures. 'Now what I want,' continued Dylan, 'is dinner. I suggest we walk to the Victor Hugo on the other side of the river. It's a bit of a trek but it will get our appetites going and at least we'll be close enough to your hotel to walk to it later if the traffic's still at a standstill.'

Even the cacophony of honking horns, the curses of thousands of surly drivers, the beating drums of the protestors and the filthy sleet couldn't disguise just how breathtaking Paris was at night. The lights that had been put up for the Millennium celebrations still gyrated round the

Eiffel Tower like demented fire-flies, and the buildings along the Seine glowed with the self-satisfied radiance of the ecstatically beautiful.

'I love this bridge, don't you?' said Dylan, as they reached the graceful curves of the Pont Alexandre III, with its crazily opulent lamps that sprouted leaves and four twisted Neptunes that had turned mint green over the years and now looked as though they were the same colour as the moon in the darkness. The bearded mermen coiled about the lamps gazed over the bridge imperiously, as if they could make the tide turn. Sydney stared into the fast-flowing river below and was shocked to find herself wishing she could be swept along in its current. She pulled herself together and tried to remember what Linda had said when she'd first told her Dylan had come back into her life. Something about women like her never committing foolish acts and about it not being in their terribly sensible DNA.

The Victor Hugo was a jewel of wood panelling, candlelight and discreet service tucked away in a cobbled corner by the River Seine. Dylan, Sydney was glad to see, was as ravenous as she was and they were soon tucking into oysters, which they washed down with more champagne. Then Dylan ordered a bottle of Château Margaux – there was nothing much wrong with his credit rating, Sydney decided – and recommended she have the steak Béarnaise which, he said, was matchless.

Emboldened by the wine and the oysters, and puzzled by Dylan's behaviour, which was uncharacteristically impeccable and completely devoid of innuendo, Sydney sank back in the leather banquette and eyed him slyly. He was looking particularly rugged after their walk. And he had on a Gauloise-blue shirt which brought out the periwinkle of his eyes. She wondered if he had deliberately talked about

Harriet's problems to lull her into a false sense of security. There was nothing like a school discussion – even when it concerned your own children – to dampen any thoughts of passion. Suddenly she wanted to feel aroused. She realized with a stabbing sense of shock how much Dylan's flirtatiousness had buoyed her up over the past few months. Think DNA, Sydney, she told herself.

'How was Patrice?' It was a suitably businesslike start.

'Frisky. He wanted me to go speed-dating with him tonight. And when I said I was too tired, he sent the chauffeur round to the hotel with a colossal amount of porn for me to watch. I was about to get stuck in when I heard the marchers and thought of you.'

'I would have thought speed-dating was right up your street.'

'I am rather an expert at speed-marriage, it's true.' He tried and failed to dampen down the twinkle in his eyes. 'But I can barely understand French when it's spoken slowly. The only full sentence I know is *Voulez-vous coucher avec moi?* And there's probably a new slang for that. Think how gutting it would be to get the offer and miss out through *entente discordiale*.'

'Hm. How are the business negotiations going?'

'Marvellously. He's agreed to all my proposals. So saved from the brink again.' His mouth curved into a slow, satisfied smile.

'Were things really that shaky?'

'Put it this way. Our bestseller last year sold two thousand copies.'

'Isn't that quite respectable for a hardback?'

'It was on our paperback list.'

Concentrate, Sydney. 'So how do you sell more without selling out?'

'Haven't a clue, but I've a feeling it's going to involve sex – somewhere down the line. Patrice is particularly keen on us chasing the pink pound. He's convinced it's going to be the only part of the book market that booms in the next few years.'

'The *Iliad* – for all Homer-erotics?'

'That sort of thing.' He grinned. 'Or Keats's "Ode to Mist and Mellow Fruits"?'

'Why did you and Eloise really break up?' Sydney asked suddenly, deliberately leading the conversation on to the kind of intimate terrain that usually made her so nervous.

'Incompatibility. I'm a reasonable human being and she's a monster,' he smirked.

'But what was the turning-point?' asked Sydney, determined not to be fobbed off. She wondered whether Dylan had ever shared any of his Welsh myths and legends with Eloise.

He put down his knife and fork and looked at her intently. 'She's sick, Sydney. She can't help it. In the end I couldn't tell what was true and what was in her head. But I could even have lived with that,' his blue eyes clouded, 'I wanted to help her. But she wouldn't have it. You see, she was convinced I was still in love with you.'

'But that's ridiculous,' said Sydney, appalled. She felt her appetite evaporate immediately. This was suddenly too intimate too quickly for her liking. She was playing with fire and the heat was starting to frighten her.

'Is it?' His eyes bore into her and she felt her heart crashing against her ribs.

'Sydney?' He reached for her hand but she managed to move it towards the salt just in time. 'Some things never go away completely. I think that's why I fell so utterly and heavily in love with Eloise when really we had nothing in

237

common. I just desperately wanted to be in love again after all these years. I'm very tired of serial dating.'

Sydney felt a lump in her throat. Why was she here, now, with this man and not her husband? Then, to her amazement, he laughed.

'That doesn't mean it has to ruin your life.' He stared at her intently and she stabbed at her steak. 'Now, perhaps you'll tell me, Parker, what exactly your job at that magazine is? I may not know much about the workings of a newspaper but it seems to me that glorified secretaries don't usually get to zoom out to Paris to interview Charlotte Rampling.'

'Come on,' said Dylan, leaving a massive tip for the waiters, 'let's get you home.' He bundled her out of the door and stepped round her so that he was on the outside of the pavement. They walked past the tiny art galleries and furniture shops along the Quai Voltaire. He was so close she could smell the sharp citrus tang of his aftershave. There were no taxis to be had, needless to say. To her confusion, Sydney's heart leapt.

The Henri IV was tucked away in a tiny backstreet and by the time they'd found it the receptionist had locked the doors and dimmed most of the lights. Gingerly, they rang the bell and were ushered into a dark lobby that smelled of beeswax and mimosa.

'Seems all right,' said Dylan, 'but you never know with these places. Let's inspect the room. If it's a flea-pit you can always come back to the Georges V. Don't worry, it's a suite,' he added, catching her petrified expression. 'And I'll sleep on the sofa.'

At least he probably had some toothpaste, thought Sydney, remembering with a pang that she didn't even have a change of clothes.

The room was like a doll's bedroom, but perfect – a bower on the fifth floor, with *toile de Jouy* wallpaper and two sets of French windows opening on to two tiny balconies that overlooked the courtyard.

'Will this do?' He walked to the windows and flung them open. Sydney hung up her coat and looked at his back silhouetted against the moon, and to her horror found herself desperately wishing he'd turn round and take her in his arms. Get a grip, Sydney. She mustn't tumble into his muscular, Mills and Boon's arms just because he'd shown traces of considerable pride in her achievements when she'd told him what she actually did on *IQ*, whereas Charlie would have been furious. It wasn't the same thing. First, Dylan wasn't her husband, so he couldn't feel threatened. Second, she had deceived Charlie, so he had every right to be peeved. Third, Dylan was far too easily impressed by tawdry, shallow achievements and sexy actresses of a certain age. Fourth, she didn't think she could bear for him to see her naked. She shivered, even though it was baking in the room.

'You need a warm bath,' he said gently. He went into the bathroom and turned on the taps. 'The toiletries aren't much cop, I'm afraid, but at least the water's piping hot.' A sweet rush of synthetic jasmine drifted towards her. 'Right then, I'll be off.' He buttoned up his coat. To her utter consternation Sydney was flooded with disappointment.

There was a knock on the door. The ancient receptionist was standing outside with a tray of tea.

'How very, very inconvenient,' said Dylan, when he'd left them. 'I suppose it would be rude not to drink it now he's gone to all that trouble.' He poured two cups and brought one over to her. He was so close she could hear him breathing, see the fine hairs on his throat rising and falling. She longed to reach out and touch him.

She moved away to perch on the little chair by the writing desk. 'So do you have any more meetings tomorrow?' she asked brightly.

He didn't answer for what seemed aeons. Then he looked at her gently. 'Sydney, tell me to mind my own business if you like, but is everything okay between you and Charlie?'

Crossing the tiny room, he folded her in his arms and pressed her tightly against him. She could hear his heart beat and smell the citrus. She buried her head against his wool jacket and allowed herself a little snivel. Slowly, he tilted her head up and dabbed her tears. Equally slowly, he began to kiss her, almost stealthily at first, as if he were testing the waters, even though there was nothing to test. There was an inevitability about it all, thought Sydney, as she closed her eyes, that filled her with as much joy as despair.

She felt Dylan's hands under her jumper, edging up towards her bra. She pushed him away gently. His eyes gleamed with longing and she felt a curl of desire between her legs. She pulled his hands on to her and slowly lifted her arms, waiting patiently for him to remove her jumper. He kissed her nipples until they were hard as buttons. She pulled off his jacket. His body was at once strangely familiar and shockingly different from Charlie's. He guided her back on to the crisp white sheets. She ran her hands under his clothes and along his taut body until she felt the jagged scar on his left shoulder.

'Where d'you get that?' she asked, desperately wanting to stop touching him.

'Plane crash in the Andes.'

Sydney tore at his shirt and tugged at his trousers, desperate now to get it over with.

'Not so fast,' panted Dylan. 'I've waited half a lifetime for this. I don't want to rush it.' He rolled on to his side and stared at her with his probing eyes, gently unbuttoning her skirt until she lay almost naked beside him. His eyes lingered over her body. She pulled up the sheet shyly. He pulled it away again and stroked her breasts. 'Where d'you get that?' He ran his tongue over her Caesarian scar, kissing the hairs that sprang out of the top of her knickers.

'Royal Free,' she said ruefully.

'You're beautiful,' he whispered in the moonlight, working his hand down between her legs while Sydney groaned with the unexpected pleasure of it all, breathing in citrus. 'My lovely Seren,' he whispered while she wrapped herself around him. His skin felt like a cashmere blanket enveloping hers. This absolutely could not be happening, thought Sydney, rearranging the sheet over her thighs. Dylan immediately removed it.

'You're like the Lady of Caerphilly, the beauteous Alice,' he murmured.

'Did she have stretch marks too?'

'She had copper-coloured hair like yours. And two lovers. Her husband and the handsome Prince Gruffydd. He was also very sensitive to the needs of women.'

'What happened?' gasped Sydney. It wasn't too late to stop. She tried to think unerotic thoughts. Miss Cavendish. The Rolling Scones . . .

'Gruffydd was hanged and Alice was banished to France.' Dylan licked her nipples. 'But they had great sex.' Sydney sighed ecstatically as he buried his face between her legs, exploring every inch of her with his tongue and fingers until she wanted to cry out. He touched her in ways Charlie never had. Or perhaps she had encouraged Charlie not to. It hardly mattered. He hadn't touched her at all for months.

'I always loved you, you know,' said Dylan. At least, she hoped it was Dylan who'd said it and not her.

241

Sydney couldn't remember such intense, dark pleasure. Afterwards she lay curled in his arms looking at the rooftops while he stroked her. 'It's just the same as all those years ago,' he marvelled.

'How can you say that?' She wished she had a cigarette to hand.

He nuzzled her neck. 'Do you ever wonder what would have happened if we'd had a child together?'

Then she told him about Owen and felt him go rigid with shock. 'His eighteenth birthday was yesterday,' she said quietly.

His voice when he finally spoke was so quiet that she feared he was in a cold fury, but he held her more tightly than ever and questioned her until a pale sun, anaemic as goat's cheese, slithered above the grey roof tiles. No recriminations, just surprise that she'd given the child a Welsh name. Then eventually, still clasping each other, they fell asleep.

He had already gone when she woke up – for another meeting with Patrice, he wrote in the note he left her. He had also left his watch and set its alarm for nine so that she wouldn't be too late back to London. Next to the watch he'd left the anthology open at a poem attributed to Henry Constable.

Sydney brushed the hair out of her eyes and pulled the sheet up around her breasts that were still tender from Dylan's touch.

> Blind were my mine eyes, till they were seen of thine,
> And mine ears deaf by thy fame healèd be;
> My vices cured by virtues sprung from thee,

My hopes revive, which long in grave had lain:
All unclean thoughts, foul sprites, cast out in me
By thy great power, and by strong faith in thee.

She pulled the sheet further up around her chin, not yet sure how much of the previous night was a dream. It was hard enough accepting that she could have let another man see her, cellulite, untended bush and all, without contemplating the other issues. For one moment she wondered if she'd dreamed the whole thing. Then from out of the book the Bristol Cathedral bookmark fluttered on to the bed like a falling leaf.

12

Even the sky seemed unseasonably azure on the journey back to London, like the inside of a lava lamp. Sydney's senses, like the nerve endings in her skin, were throbbing. The Kentish fields, sprinkled with daffodils and tulips, had undulated like a jewelled belly dancer's stomach. She took a taxi straight to the office from Waterloo. It was better to keep busy, she'd decided.

It was three o'clock when she arrived on the sixth floor, sunglasses still pressed firmly against her eyes. Clothes the same ones she'd been wearing yesterday. She ought by rights to feel grubby and cheap but she felt bizarrely calm – and rather desirable. Perhaps it was the effect of twenty-four hours in Paris, among men who didn't ignore you if you were over the age of thirty. Or perhaps it was the effects of the previous night with Dylan – she'd forgotten what it was like to be bedded by an athlete – and the ensuing twenty minutes of pummelling under a surprisingly powerful French hotel shower. Sydney glided purposefully towards her desk, head high, mind focused on the Charlotte Rampling tapes. As well as keeping busy, she decided it was probably better not to think too deeply.

'Love the shades.' Poppy looked up at Sydney with astonishment. 'You should wear them more often, Syd.'

Disconcertingly, Dave appeared to have made a miraculous recovery and was tapping his computer screen, on which he'd been editing Poppy's article on how to feng shui your hair. Poppy returned to the computer despondently.

'As I was saying before,' Dave sounded almost jovial, although he clearly hadn't fully recovered from his flu, 'it would be nice to find the occasional scrap of evidence that you had actually been educated. See here. You've got the object and subject mixed up. It's easily done, but it makes your Light Entrapment Illuminator sound as though it's just spent three hundred quid at Selfridges, and scientifically advanced though it might be, I don't think even it's up to that.'

'All my notes must have got muddled up in Alvaro's chopper,' said Poppy apologetically. 'What's the probs this time?'

'The probs, Poppy, is punctuation,' said Dave. 'Complete lack thereof. Look at this endless sentence. God knows how far you have to travel to find a verb in it.' He sighed. But less belligerently than usual. Or perhaps Sydney was projecting her euphoria on to everyone else. She fingered Dylan's watch in her pocket.

'Do you actually know what the basic components of a sentence are?' he asked more gently. 'The nouns, verbs and correct tenses and sub-clauses? Because having mastered the admittedly impressive art of home waxing, Poppy, it would be almost as great an achievement to learn to write English.' He opened a dog-eared copy of Fowler's *English Usage*.

Poppy sighed. 'Mummy always said grammar didn't matter just as long as one didn't marry anyone who'd been to one. Ooh, sorry, Dave. Actually, Mummy's a bit out of touch. She's terrible politically incorrect. You should hear what she calls foreigners behind their backs. And to their faces, come to think of it. She's starting to be a bit of a liability in public. Luckily she prefers her pigs to most people. So she doesn't get up to Harrods as much as she used to. Especially since it was bought by a Moroccan.'

'Egyptian,' said Dave, appalled but fascinated.

'She didn't want me to have a career. She says it's common to take jobs from people who really need them.'

'Yes, well,' began Dave slightly stiffly, 'Mummy won't have anything to worry about if you don't make your copy a little clearer. So listen up. A verb is a doing word. Every sentence needs one.' He cracked his knuckles, a sure sign he was enjoying himself. 'And a noun is a thing. When you're more experienced as a writer – in about three thousand years' time – you can start experimenting with grammar and doing away with it altogether ultimately. But in the meantime, let's get this into something akin to English.'

Dave and Poppy's strangely comforting babble washed over Sydney. She found Dave's love of language and his enthusiasm to communicate it unexpectedly touching – and the fact that his social conscience had moved him to help an educationally disadvantaged girl from a large estate to better herself. She looked slyly at their two downturned heads and wondered what Mummy would say if Poppy turned up to introduce Dave to her prize Gloucestershire Old Spots.

She prised apart the window blinds, which appeared to be covered with something brown and glutinous, and stared out at the cobbled street and the wharves opposite. Below, three journalists from *Silage Monthly* and *Rat Poisoner* were scuttling back from a late lunch, casting short, stubby shadows that moved across the pavements like a slow flood. The bright blue sky had turned a dull rat colour and the moon had already risen over the river.

A shout came from Dave and Poppy's direction, but a reasonably good-natured one. 'For God's sake, Poppy!

What do you mean, you've left your notes in the car? You treat that Smart like a glorified handbag.'

'It's about the same size as the latest Prada Poppy just got.' Chloë sidled over with a packet of biscuits and offered them round. She didn't, Sydney noticed, take one herself. She didn't appear to be dyeing her hair such a virulent strain of daffodil any more either. It was more of an expensive silver birch. Nor did Dave and Poppy include her in their conversation. She was like the girl who never got picked for the team. From behind her black lenses Sydney cast a surreptitious look over Dave's putty-coloured features. If she wasn't mistaken, he almost seemed to be happy. So much for being too ill to go to Paris. What was he playing at?

'I think I preferred you when you were on your death-bed with Singapore Flu,' said Poppy.

'It wasn't Singapore Flu in the end, as you know,' said Dave through gritted teeth. 'Just a nasty cold that reacted badly to a kebab.'

Sydney slunk into her seat. Dave must be feeling doubly resentful at being done out of a trip to Paris. Her in-tray seemed to have doubled in size in the forty-eight hours since she'd been in the office; she was having problems concentrating and she was desperate to know if there was anything usable on her Charlotte Rampling tapes. Concentrate, Sydney, concentrate.

Her phone rang. Her heart stopped. Dave's drone echoed round her head.

It was Michael, who had come up to London for a meeting with one of his clients and was now at a loose end. He sounded bereft. 'I couldn't get hold of Charlie,' he said apologetically. 'So I'm bothering you, I'm afraid. I need to stay overnight to finish some research. They're putting me up in a jolly nice hotel. But I just wondered if by any chance you and Charlie were free for a bite to eat?'

Sydney's balloon of euphoria, which until a few moments ago had been soaring miles above Icon Towers, felt as though it had been run through by a bayonet. Until Michael's call she'd kept herself going by thinking – and trying to feel – in the abstract and telling herself that sex with an ex almost didn't count. When you thought about it only the timing made it adulterous.

'. . . that's if you're both not too tired,' she heard Michael saying.

'Of course not,' she said faintly. On the train back she'd done nothing but reflect on the previous night. She'd decided that she and Dylan could never, ever repeat what they'd done in Paris. They could never refer to it either. Eventually it would melt into history, like a dream. Perhaps what they'd done would even prove cathartic for them all. She'd have to break with Dylan. If there was anything to break. But until Michael's call, she hadn't thought about herself and Charlie as a couple. 'We'd love to see you. Eight-thirty?'

She had barely placed the phone down when it rang again. Charlie. She steeled herself.

It was Dylan. 'In case you're wondering how the poem ends, from memory, I think it goes like this: "Dear Joy, how I do love thee! When can I see you again? Are you free at all today, tomorrow or for a fraction of a nano-second the day after?"'

'That doesn't sound very authentic to me.' He was fatally easy to banter with. 'I can't speak now,' she said hurriedly. Her phone flashed. There was a call waiting. 'Thank you for the beautiful book by the way. I'll always treasure it.' Her hand hovered over the second call button.

'Whoa. That sounds a bit final.'

'It's the editor-in-chief,' said Sydney, taken aback by how desolate Dylan sounded. 'I have to take it.'

It wasn't quite the editor-in-chief, but it was Linda, on the warpath. She asked Sydney to meet her in her office in fifteen seconds.

Things were pretty grim. Widlake had brought the deadlines forward by another week so that he could personally check every line that went into the magazine. Yesterday evening he'd taken the unprecedented step of visiting Linda in her box. The glutinous mess on Sydney's blinds were where his coffee had been hurled in a gesture that suggested he wasn't completely impressed by what he'd seen there.

'He's a Neanderthal, a philistine and a thug,' wailed Linda. 'How's the Rampling going?'

Sydney was saved from having to reply by Chloë, who peered round Linda's door at the same time as she knocked.

'Sorry to interrupt,' she said with inappropriate sunniness that Sydney found extremely vexing. 'But this needs a rapid response.' She swished towards them in yet another low-cut shirt-dress.

'What is it?' Linda asked sharply. Sydney felt a little curl of triumph.

'U2 have agreed to let me go on tour with them.' Sydney and Linda stared at her simultaneously.

'You're not leaving?' Linda sounded disappointingly aghast.

'No, of course not. It's for a piece.' Chloë smiled graciously and perched on Linda's desk. 'I didn't want to tell you before in case I got everyone's hopes up for nothing. I've been talking to their people for weeks. The idea is that I get exclusive access to the band and write it up as a tour diary. They've promised me unrivalled access as well as photos of anything we want. It'll be real fly on the wall stuff.' She paused tremulously. Linda was frowning.

'I understand if you feel someone more senior should do it,' Chloë continued, lowering her lids. She was desperate to do this assignment. It was written across her face in 72-point capitals. Sydney had to admire her strategy. Reminding Linda of her inexperience was a huge risk. 'Maybe Dave would be better. He's far more experienced.' That was an even bigger one. 'He's a brilliant writer. And he was so disappointed about not being able to do Charlotte Rampling.'

That was a master-stroke. Even if Linda had been considering Dave for the piece, she wouldn't want to give it to him now in case it was interpreted as a sympathy gesture. Linda was painfully aware that she had to be seen as someone who could make tough decisions based on hard-headed sales calculations rather than emotions.

'It's not that,' said Linda sharply. 'I couldn't spare Dave from the office right now. But maybe a freelancer—'

'Ah.' Chloë crossed her legs and rotated her foot, just as Linda always did. 'That might slow things down a bit. You see, the band agreed to this on condition that someone from the magazine – a staffer – did it. They love *IQ*, you see. And well, I've met them a couple of times. That's why I was late a few weeks ago. I had a bit of an all-nighter in Dublin.'

Linda seemed dumbfounded.

'It wasn't that big a deal. I nipped over for a friend's birthday and when Bono heard I was going to be there he got me some backstage passes and,' she shrugged helplessly, 'you remember that morning I was late in – I felt so guilty especially as I couldn't say anything, and Annabelle was furious. Rightly so, of course,' she looked directly at Linda with adoring, forget-me-not eyes, 'but I had been up all night talking with the band and persuading them to do the piece.'

It was a masterclass in disingenuous ambition, which would have been entertaining if it hadn't been so effective. Sydney couldn't believe Linda was falling for it all.

'It does sound promising,' she said. 'Wall to wall voyeurism. Plus classy celebs. But how long will it all take? I think I can spare you even less than Dave.'

'Don't worry about that. I can dip in and out of the tour and pretty much do it on my weekends. And don't worry about the cost. They've said they'll pay the travel expenses.'

'The thing about getting outside sources to pay,' Linda was saying, 'is that it could be construed as compromising. You can't really be objective if the subject of your piece is footing the bill, can you? It's not something we've ever done before and frankly—'

'– it's something we should absolutely consider from now on,' said Annabelle, walking in with a mountain of invoices for Linda to countersign. She beamed at Chloë. 'Well done.'

Sydney felt utterly isolated. She hadn't seen Annabelle look this pleased since Joshie had decided at the last minute not to be a breech birth. Chloë had them all wrapped round her newly manicured fingers.

Charlie was furious with her for getting stuck in Paris. Not that he said so in so many words. Instead he was affability itself for the two and a half hours that Michael stayed. But the moment Michael retreated politely back to his hotel, insisting he'd imposed quite enough on them already and adding that he'd never have come round if he'd realized that Sydney had just come back from what must have been an exhausting trip to Paris, Charlie stormed off to his study where he stayed up working until Sydney went to bed and finally turned out the lights. In a way it was a relief. She didn't know if she could really lie next to Charlie having so recently lain next to Dylan. He'd already gone by the time she woke up. Her bayoneted bubble lay well and truly in shreds on the floor.

She didn't hear from Dylan for most of the following day, which at least gave her plenty of time to transcribe the Rampling interview, which seemed to contain some quite good stuff, and to polish her kiss-off speech to Dylan. By the time he called she felt almost faint from neglect.

'I've got to go to New York.' He sounded uncharacteristically subdued. 'Unbelievably, the divorce is proving a bit more complicated than I'd ever in my worst moments thought it could be. At this rate it'll drag on considerably longer than the damned marriage. Bloody lawyers. With apologies to Charlie,' he added.

They owed Charlie a bit more than an apology, thought Sydney with a sickening pang of something that felt uncomfortably like guilt.

'Sydney darling, I'm so sorry.'

'When will you be back?' she heard herself asking.

'Not quite sure. Could be a few weeks. Could be a few months.' This wasn't how she'd imagined sending him packing at all.

'I see.' She should be feeling relieved. She *was* relieved. She also felt she was being abandoned.

'You don't see at all, you ninny. I'll be back. I'll call you every day. And everything will be fine.'

Sydney swallowed her pride and antipathy and asked Dave for help with the Rampling interview. And while he was busy working the confidences she'd got out of Charlotte

Rampling into a slick, polished masterpiece, she spoke to Linda about revamping the problem pages, using some of the letters as a basis for features and hiring a new photographer to spice up the look of things.

'But I think those illustrations are so beautiful,' said Chloë, placing a cappuccino in front of Linda. Sydney waited for Linda to slap Chloë back in her place. She could never bear people interrupting.

'Maybe we should hang fire on the illustrations,' said Linda thoughtfully. 'Though I love all your other ideas.'

At home Sydney overcompensated madly for working, for forgetting to retrieve the girls' school notes from their rucksacks and for having a one-night stand with the father of her first child by reading *Black Beauty* over and over again to them, checking their rucksacks every evening and every morning and sitting on the phone for hours trying to coax a cancellation out of The Learning Pool, the place Dylan had put her on to. What she didn't quite manage to pull off was a conversation with Charlie.

Dylan called her five days running from New York, but only to swap jokes about New York lawyers, or come up with more suggestions for chasing the pink pound. Sydney wanted to ask him to stop phoning, but it seemed a bit of a heavy-handed way to deal with such light-hearted banter. She sometimes wondered whether Paris had ever happened. But she had the anthology, the watch and the bookmark in her drawer at work, where the packet of Snowy Doughies had been.

Apart from the times she was with Dylan, Sydney had never done anything in her life without thinking seriously about it. She was the sensible, wise one, the prescient one. The one who'd found Mr Right when she was twenty-two and been sensible enough to marry him, even if sometimes she felt meeting Mr Right had been the worst thing that had happened to her.

And now she didn't want to think beyond the next hour. When she was in the same room as Charlie, she couldn't think beyond surviving the next few minutes. His seething, silent refusal to admit that he *did* feel resentful, let alone discuss it, made each portion of a second an ordeal. It was like being a child again, with the mood swings to match. At work she manifested all the symptoms of a hyperactive compulsive. Even Linda noticed and told her to go and get herself sorted out with some Evening Primrose oil. Then a bottle of Floris rose geranium oil arrived on her desk one day, with a note from Dylan apologizing for not being able to fill her bath with real roses but hoping the next best thing would do. Charlie naturally appeared oblivious.

And all the time the Easter holiday loomed, heavy with the terrible promise of not finding anywhere to stay in the whole of Spain and then subsequently being on the receiving end of yet more pained, martyred looks from Charlie, who was silently but very obviously putting it to her that everything that went wrong from now until infinity was all her fault.

So when she wasn't slaving over the Rampling, bolstering Harriet, petting Molly who was getting increasingly miffed at all the attention Harriet was getting and increasingly turning to religion for solace, or stroking the many egos of Dave, who'd worked miracles on the Rampling, and working on new layouts for her pages, she was frantically surfing the Net into the small hours searching for a villa that looked and felt like La Rosa. Preferably in the same location, with the same name. She might as well have looked for food in Eloise's fridge. So when Miranda, uncharacteristically buoyant after a filo pastry session with the other happy clappies from The

254

Rolling Scones called her to find out if she'd had any luck finding a villa as gorgeous as La Rosa, she was caught at a low ebb. And when Miranda shyly reminded her that they were all still welcome to stay with them, she heard herself, in a defeated voice, agreeing it was a good idea.

Then she presented it to Charlie, hoping, more out of dogged optimism than any realistic expectations, for a perfunctory thank you for her efforts, followed, ideally, by a refusal to stay with Ian and Miranda. Instead he muttered something about having quite a lot of work to take with him and asked her if she could have a word with Miranda about those boys of hers and keeping the noise down.

'Is Charlie all right?' Miles, jauntily unshaven as ever, popped in to see Sydney at work a few days later. He pulled up a chair at her crowded desk and started playing with some PVC underwear that had been sent in by an enterprising PR hoping for a recommendation in one of Sydney's advice columns, along with a pair of marabou handcuffs, now missing.

'Shouldn't you be somewhere, Miles? Let me think. Ah yes. Work. You do still do some occasionally, I take it?'

'On my way between clients,' he said cheerfully. 'So I couldn't resist popping in to see my favourite sister.'

Chloë sashayed past with a tray of coffees and a plate of Hobnobs. Miles looked at her longingly. 'Any chance of one of those?' he asked, directing his gaze at her breasts, which were shown off to their fullest glory in a purple, lace-trimmed V-neck shirt-dress. Chloë smiled and handed him a mug and some biscuits. 'I can see you're going to go far,' he winked at her.

'She already is,' said Sydney, watching Chloë and her Hobnobs make a bee-line for Dave.

'I'd love to read the Rampling when you've finished it,'

Chloë said to Dave huskily. 'I've got no idea how to structure things properly yet and you're such a brilliant editor.' Sydney felt nauseous. Chloë's much-vaunted feminism was so subtle it was undetectable most of the time. At least she'd stopped fluttering her eyelashes at Dave and begun appealing to his sense of intellectual superiority. Judging by Dave's grudging acceptance of a Hobnob, it was beginning to work.

'You want to watch it, Sydney,' said Miles, following her gaze. 'You're starting to sound quite bitter. And you want to look after Charlie. I called him today about something and he was definitely not pulling out the stops to be charming.'

'Thanks for the advice.' The irony of Miles attempting to lecture her on marriage couldn't be lost even on him.

He shifted uneasily in his chair. 'Actually, one of our clients is getting a bit bolshy about some work we did. Doesn't want to pay for it.' He sniffed. Sydney passed him a packet of Kleenex from her drawer.

'Frankly, I'm amazed you got through to Charlie,' she couldn't resist saying.

'Yeah, well, I only did because I pretended to be calling on behalf of some sodding great conglomerate who were looking for new lawyers. And he was very curt, I don't mind telling you.'

'And you're surprised? Honestly, Miles, you are incorrigible.' She wondered whether she ought to try the same tactics to speak to Charlie. 'Are you all right for money?' she asked anxiously. The last thing Annabelle and the boys needed, on top of Miles's expensive infatuation with Jacquie, was an excuse for him not to contribute to at least some of the bills. Now she was working, she could probably help out a bit without having to go cap in hand to Charlie.

'Yeah, yeah. We're fine.' He blew his nose loudly. 'Maybe

256

not up to your lavish standards. But as soon as Jacquie's studio is up and running we're going to be swimming in the stuff. And,' he added, eyeing Sydney's concerned expression, 'I'll make it up to the boys, I promise.'

'Studio?'

'Yeah, the Massoga. The bank's finally okayed it all.'

Sydney braced herself. 'How much are you borrowing?'

'Fifty thousand. Peanuts really. But she's very stylish, my little Jacqueleene. She can make a place look a million dollars on a couple of quid. It's all a question of draping lots of white sheets all over the place and lighting a load of candles.'

'Preferably not near the sheets,' said Sydney.

'Anyway, never mind about our finances. You want to think about your future, Syd. You're not getting any younger. If you don't nurture that marriage of yours you could find yourself outside in the cold with the rest of us. Men need servicing, you know. Much as most women seem to resent it.' He sighed, then sniffed. 'It's a cruel, cruel irony that even women who start off wearing red lacy thongs gradually progress to chastity belts. I wouldn't mind, but fifty-seven per cent of women are kept by their men. Yet they act as though they're Mother Teresa when you suggest they might like to provide the occasional blow-job on a strictly quid pro quo basis. Honestly, what do they think we keep them for?'

'Thank you for sharing those enlightened views.'

He grinned lopsidedly, baring one of his little nicotined fangs. 'Any chance of another coffee?' He looked round for a bin that wasn't overflowing into which to chuck the dregs of his last cup, settled on a relatively empty one by Poppy's desk and lobbed his cup over. Sydney looked up in horror. 'Yessss!' He pummelled the air with his fist. 'Striker Parker scores again.'

'That bag cost two grand.'

'What bag?'

'The one you just threw your coffee into.'

'It looks like a rubbish bin.'

'That's why it costs two grand.' Sydney handed him the packet of Kleenex again. 'It's the season's must-have.'

'What is it exactly you do here?' He dabbed the bag unenthusiastically. 'Because I have to say, Sydney, your desk doesn't look like the desk of an assistant. It's far too messy.'

'That's because I get everyone else's crap dumped on it.' She removed Annabelle's ashtray. 'And don't worry about us,' she said hastily. 'Charlie and I are just fine.'

'If you say so.' He grabbed another biscuit from Chloë's tray as she waltzed past. Her big red lips curved into a luscious sleeping cat-shaped smile. She was looking more and more like a Fifties starlet every day, Sydney thought. Over by his screen, Dave was hammering away on the keyboard, still adding lustre to the Rampling. When Miles had more or less finished cleaning up Poppy's bag, he made a great play of cleaning Sydney's desk, and when her phone rang he picked it up.

'Hello, Sydney Murray's office. Her PA speaking. How may I help? Oh, it's you, Miranda. Yes, it's Miles. Yes, Sydney's brother.' Sydney watched Miles preen in front of his reflection in the window. He'd flirt with a turd if he thought it would get him somewhere. 'Tell me, how are The Rolling Scones? That's marvellous news. I'm sure the confit tasted wonderful. Ian's a lucky, lucky man – a fabulous wife with superb legs. Now there's a combination. Yes, just popping in to see the old girl. Help her pass some time. No, it's not distracting – she loves it. You know how little work journalists really do.'

Sydney gesticulated frantically at her pages which had

to be finished today and drew her finger across her neck.

'She's in a meeting at the moment with the ed. Just got called in. Hold the front page and all that. Can I take a message? The Grangers have pulled out of the holiday. Why?' He whistled. 'He's been having an affair. That's very careless of him. To get caught, I mean. Just teasing. Yes, I can see his wife must be gutted. Yeah, I can see that leaves you up the swanny. No, you must be desperate. So you're looking for another family to take their place. At a reduction, you say. What sort of reduction? Would a childless couple do?'

Sydney began to make wild hanging motions but to no avail. Five minutes later the holiday she thought couldn't get any worse did.

Miles meanwhile had put the phone down and looked like the cat that had got the Crème de la Mer. 'Fate works in mysterious ways.' He clicked his fingers like castanets. 'This is just what Jacq needs.' He sat down again and put his feet on Sydney's desk, on top of a letter from Richard, who had taken Sydney's advice about not giving up everything to go and live in Belize and now wanted to know if she thought he should have a sex-change. She'd spent ages drafting her reply and now Miles had left a sludgy footprint over Richard's address. She wished Richard would learn to use email.

'Really? Wasn't the weekend in Paris enough?'

'That was before the baby.' Sydney's coffee cup hovered mid-air. Miles beamed down at her with manful pride. 'The one me and Jac are going to have,' he added, somewhat needlessly.

Sydney was lost for words. Not that Miles seemed to notice. 'She's five and a half months gone. Not that you'd know. It's all that exercise she does. I would have told you earlier but we had to keep it quiet because of the banks. We reckoned they wouldn't have lent to us if they'd known. And what with keeping it from them, we sort of forgot to tell anyone. Actually, we were hoping you'd be its godmother. So don't go pissing Charlie off. We're counting on you for top prezzies.'

13

The only tickets they'd been able to get were for four days after the villa was available, at 7 p.m. on Thin Air, a no-frills – and they really did mean no frills, thought Sydney, as she cast a lugubrious eye over the mange-ridden velour seats – line that had just been bought, coincidentally, by Schmucklesons. Not that there was any discount for employees, naturally.

Owing to a slight misadventure earlier in the day with Hamish, who'd disappeared just as Sydney had tried to ferry him into the car to take him to the kennels, they were hellishly late checking in and even later boarding. The only seats were right at the back, next to the lavatories. Molly held her nose for almost the entire flight. Charlie stuck his head into *The Times* law pages for the duration and Sydney pretended to be engrossed in Antonia Fraser's *Marie Antoinette*. Occasionally they exchanged pleasantries. When Sydney passed him something that purported to be orangeade – the flight attendants had sold out of wine, coffee, water and fruit juice – he thanked her. When he picked up her handbag for her, she thanked him. To anyone looking they must have seemed a model of dull, contented complacency. But as their plane bounced down at Malaga airport, Sydney experienced the queasy sensation of her life spinning out of control.

★   ★   ★

'Well, well, well.' Ian's palms were rubbing together so glee-fully it was a miracle they didn't ignite in the April sunshine. 'This is a turn-up for the books, isn't it?' Sydney nodded politely and gazed back out of the kitchen window towards the pool where the girls were already swimming – and had been since eight o'clock that morning.

'Fancy us welcoming you here,' crowed Ian. 'After all the times you were at La Rosa. Still, we got here in the end, didn't we? Sorry about last night, not being up to meet you, but those charter flights come in at such ungodly hours, don't they? I told Miranda you'd understand if there wasn't a reception party but she insisted on staying up. Couldn't manage it myself, I'm afraid. Charlie still asleep?' he added hopefully.

'No, he's upstairs working,' said Sydney wistfully. She was starting to wish she'd never come downstairs. Miranda must have been scrubbing the already spotless floors and filling every chest and dresser with lavender-scented drawer liners since seven o'clock. Which meant that Sydney had had to as well.

The news of Charlie's industriousness sent Ian into a decline. Then he brightened again. 'No sign of the love-birds? It's amazing how much some people sleep. Waste of a good holiday if you ask me.'

Sydney didn't.

'Jacquie was down at seven-thirty doing her sun saluta-tions,' said Miranda brightly. Her husband looked at her venomously and wandered outside despondently, his hair glistening like nylon in the unforgiving sun.

Sydney looked at her watch. 10.30. She wondered when they could stop cleaning. 'Is there anything else I can do?' she asked weakly.

'I was just going to cycle to the local butcher and then I

262

thought I'd get some vegetables in the market in Santa Cruz – it's a bit of a hike but much cheaper than the one in the village. Ian does so like it if we can get fresh produce daily. And at some point I need to get more drawer liners. Ian does like the smell of lavender. And it takes away the odour of his ciggies and cigars. Then I was going to come back and start on lunch. I thought paella, if that's okay with you and Charlie and the girls. It's rather a palaver, but it's so nice if we can introduce the children to some authentic fare, don't you think?'

'We could buy some in the market, there's a stall that sells it fresh out of the pan,' suggested Sydney, taking in Miranda's pinched mouth and sunken cheeks and wondering if she'd ever had a proper holiday.

Miranda bit her lip. 'I don't know . . . Ian thinks food should always be home-cooked. Especially with shellfish.' She ran her pencil down a list. 'Then for supper I thought we could have roast beef. Ian likes to eat early on holiday. Six okay?'

'Great,' Sydney smiled weakly. 'And we should try out some of the local restaurants while we're here. There are some excellent ones.'

Miranda looked wistful. 'Ian doesn't really like to eat out. But you and Charlie can always go. We could babysit the girls.'

Sydney wondered why Ian was so mean. Even though he wasn't as senior as Charlie – as he frequently reminded them all – he must be on a good salary. But he was tighter than a hangman's noose and – she gazed through the window where he was screaming at the closed shutters to wake up his boys – marginally less fun. She began to wonder whether the housekeeper on whom they had agreed to split the costs really had gone down with something, as Miranda had told them last night. Or whether Ian had been too stingy to chip in. No one could accuse Charlie of being ungenerous. She must remember to count her blessings the next time she was at a loose end.

She heard the girls squealing with pleasure as they squirted each other with water-guns. At least they were having a lovely time. As soon as someone came to relieve her of sentinel duty she'd take Charlie some coffee and see if she couldn't get into his good books. She wondered whether Miles was up yet and went upstairs to check. While she was there she switched on her mobile. There were three messages from Dylan: two indecent, one incredibly romantic, telling her he couldn't live without her, that he understood that like most women, she might need a hundred years to decide what she wanted, but that she should remember Andrew Marvell.

Outside Ian was attempting some small-talk with the girls. 'Hello, Molly, how's school? Won't ask you, Harriet. Us thickies must stick together.' He smirked. Molly looked at him in disbelief. He turned away. Molly stuck up her middle finger as Ian began to frog-march Ezekiel around the pool terrace, his ruddy nose slicing through the air like a pick-axe. At least, Sydney assumed it was Ezekiel. He was so heavily camouflaged in a snorkel and a wetsuit at least two sizes too big for him and bent double under the weight of an oxygen tank that he looked more like some kind of mutant aquatic hobbit.

'I'll count to five,' said Ian loudly.

Ezekiel objected half-heartedly.

'Five!' said Ian.

Ezekiel stood defiantly by the edge of the pool.

'Come on, Ezekiel,' said Ian with a bullying undertone.

Ezekiel remained glued to the water's edge.

'He looks a bit frightened,' Harriet called up, her sense of fair play drummed into action.

Ian ignored her. 'I said five, Ezekiel. Did you hear me?'

Ezekiel muttered something else and drooped even more dejectedly under the weight of his tank.

'He says he doesn't want to,' said Harriet, squinting in the sun.

'Thank you, Harriet. But don't interfere, there's a good girl,' said Ian nastily. 'Now, Ezekiel, there's absolutely nothing to be frightened of, is there, you little wimp? You know the hand signals, don't you?' Ian ran through the diver's code-book and made his son repeat them.

'He must be frying in all that rubber,' Molly said loudly.

Ezekiel nodded miserably, and while his father momentarily turned his back to light a cigarette, stuck two fingers up at him. Harriet and Molly looked on with rapt attention.

'Shouldn't you be doing some reading, Harriet?' said Ian. 'I believe it's not exactly the jewel in your academic crown.'

Inside the kitchen, Sydney flinched. She couldn't bear to watch. But if Ian didn't stop ranting at Ezekiel and insulting Harriet, she was going to punch him. She began to make some coffee. She didn't think she could bear ten whole days of Ian's bullying. She looked over at Miranda, on her knees again, this time in the process of emptying one of the immaculate saucepan cupboards, and found herself suddenly despising her for not speaking out on behalf of her boys. No wonder Ezekiel behaved like a monster half the time and the older two, Gideon and Samson, appeared to be on a mission to get expelled from every institution their father deemed admirable.

She took some coffee up to Charlie who glanced up briefly from his work and thanked her with scrupulous politeness.

'Any chance of getting the noise down?' The muslin curtains fluttered as Sydney closed the windows slightly.

''Fraid not just yet,' she smiled ruefully. 'Unless you want to tackle Ian.'

Charlie ignored her and she felt very lonely. She went back downstairs and heard an almighty splash outside and a heart-wrenching scream. She ran on to the terrace and saw Molly and Harriet clinging to the sides of the pool with horrified expressions and Ezekiel flailing around on his back at the bottom.

'He's bleeding,' screamed Molly, pointing to a thin but steady red wisp that eddied round the turquoise waters.

'That's one way of learning to get in quickly,' chuckled Ian. 'Don't make a fuss, dear,' he said to Harriet, who was starting to weep. 'She's very highly strung, isn't she?' he added to Sydney.

'He can't breathe,' shouted Molly. 'And he can't turn himself the proper way up.'

'He'll be fine once he remembers how to correct his oxygen pressure,' said Ian. 'Don't worry, everyone,' he looked at Sydney steadily, 'I'm not going to let him drown. But he has to learn the correct procedure.'

'His tube's come out of his mouth,' sobbed Harriet. Ezekiel's small body was floundering manically now. Sydney ran to the water's edge.

'Maybe it's time for your daughters to get out of the pool,' said Ian, his skin glistening like a half-cooked sausage, 'so that the lesson can continue without further interference.'

Sydney tore off her caftan but before she could jump in somebody else had dived into the water. It was Gideon, his tall, lanky body streaking towards Ezekiel through the sun-dappled water like a silver fish. He pulled his brother to the surface and swam to the side where Ezekiel lay gasping for air. Gideon gently lifted his small frame on to the terrace where he was immediately sick.

'You fucking arsehole,' he screamed across the pool at his father. 'You know he's petrified.'

'He's a bloody drama queen. Look, he needs to know how to do it properly for when we go out to sea,' said Ian, attempting to sound like a reasonable but wounded father.

'He doesn't fucking want to go out to sea, you bastard.' Gideon held a towel to the gash on Ezekiel's forehead where his oxygen tank had struck him. 'And if you weren't too fucking tight to pay a proper instructor who would tell you that, the poor sod might actually start to enjoy his holidays for once in his miserable little life. If he hasn't lost all ability to enjoy anything, that is.'

Ian looked defiantly at the gathering audience – Sydney could see Miranda cowering by the kitchen window. 'Temper, temper, Gideon.' He glared at his son with something like hatred – perhaps because he recognized that Gideon was now too big to be bullied and therefore beyond his power. He marched towards the boys. 'Christ, I was only trying to get the lazy little bugger into the pool. God knows the greedy sods who own this place have charged enough for the privilege.'

Gideon turned away in disgust and began stroking Ezekiel's forehead.

'Very well,' said Ian in a belated attempt to be conciliatory. 'We'll postpone this lesson till tomorrow when you've pulled yourself together, Ezekiel.' Harriet was sobbing quietly in the pool. Ian picked up the snorkel and threw it at Gideon. 'For Christ's sake,' he spat, 'the little fairy needs some character-building. And some muscles.'

'You make me sick,' screamed Gideon. 'Now, for fuck's sake just leave us alone.'

267

Ian looked momentarily cowed. 'Very well.' He walked stiffly back to the house, and tossed Sydney a baleful, put-upon expression. Then he shrugged. 'I'm surrounded by prima donnas. They all take after their mother. More coffee, Sydney?'

Sydney went inside and texted a message to Dylan telling him not to get in touch with her again. She would never work things out with Charlie with Dylan hovering permanently on her network like an overly energetic fly.

Upstairs, the shutters on Miles and Jacquie's windows rattled and Miles, wrapped in a tiny towel and only just decent thanks to the bougainvillea veiling the villa, appeared on the balcony.

'Morning, everyone.' He yawned. 'Sounds like we've been missing quite a party.'

It would have been hard for the holiday to get worse after that inauspicious start, but somehow it managed to.

'Tell me, Mand, what is the point of The Rolling Scones?' said Jacquie two evenings later. She sucked daintily on some of Miranda's crackling.

'Yet another way for my wife to justify staying at home,' said Ian. Sydney looked at him in astonishment. She had always assumed Ian had kept Miranda in the kitchen at home deliberately, especially after he'd made his feelings on working mothers perfectly clear at Christmas.

'I just think a family is better off with a mother who's there for them all,' said Miranda firmly.

'That sounds a bit retro, Miranda. You don't believe in Fifties values, do you?' Jacquie's bronzed, iridescent features glowed like sparklers in the outside garden lights as she flapped her eyelashes at the table, canvassing support for her argument. Sydney pulled her shawl round her shoulders. Ian and Miranda had wanted to eat outside but it was getting quite chilly. Miranda appeared not to hear, so Jacquie repeated herself more loudly, which, Sydney had noticed, was her favoured tactic when dealing with the locals.

'I believe in Fifties hourglass figures,' Miles chortled. 'Anyway, Mandy, if the idea is to perfect your cooking, it works.' He sloshed some more of the cheap sangria he'd bought into everyone's glasses. 'This crackling is fabulous, isn't it, Jacq?'

'Certainly is. Honestly, my appetite these days is ferocious.' She stroked her small six-and-a-bit-month bump proudly. 'I never thought a cheap cut could taste so good.'

Miles coughed loudly and Sydney saw him nudge Jacquie's ankle with his toe.

'Eating early helps,' burbled Jacquie, oblivious to the rapidly freezing atmosphere. 'I haven't had supper at six since I left home. Miles thinks it's terribly non-U. Yes you do, Miles. But actually I'm with you, Miranda, it's much better for your digestion, isn't it? Keeps the weight down too.' She gazed lovingly at her swelling breasts. 'The thing is, Miles, we couldn't afford for me not to go out to work.'

'My point precisely,' said Ian. 'It's all very well for fifty-seven – fifty-seven, mind you – per cent of women to give up work and stay at home, but it just means men have to work their bollocks off to keep the dears in the idleness to which they're accustomed.'

'Language, Ian,' said Miranda, ladling some more gravy over his potatoes.

'And is it because they're so dedicated to their families, or is it because they're just bloody lazy and have fuck-all ambition?'

'They do say women were much thinner in the Fifties,' mused Jacquie, slapping a fly on her neck. 'According to the *Daily Mail* they were at least two stone lighter. Because of all the housework.'

'It certainly keeps you quite fit,' said Miranda, clearing the plates. Sydney stood up to help her.

'I can see that,' leered Miles.

Jacquie threw a crust of bread at him and giggled. 'Trust you. I wonder if there's a way of incorporating housework into a studio routine?'

Sydney followed Miranda into the kitchen and began loading plates into the dishwasher.

'Let me rinse those first.' Miranda squirted some liquid under some water and began brushing them until they were clean. Then she handed them to Sydney. 'Do you mind taking over while I beat up some cream? It's the only way to get them really sparkling.'

Miranda's bacteria phobia meant it was at least twenty minutes before they returned to the terrace with a trifle that Miranda had whipped up sometime during the afternoon when Sydney hadn't been looking. God knows it felt as though she'd been in the kitchen all day, when she hadn't been outside trying to stop Samson dive-bombing Molly and Harriet. All day Sydney had been feeling alternately exasperated by and desperately sorry for her. She tried to tease some confidences out of her and offer her a sense of solidarity. But Miranda wouldn't venture an opinion about Ian's treatment of her youngest son, apart from saying that he did have a point about them all getting the most out of the pool. 'Although, frankly,' she added, 'it's so luxurious and there are so many rules about it in the handbook I'm a bit frightened of spoiling it.'

Here was a woman so browbeaten, thought Sydney, she

couldn't even comment on the weather until her husband had. But perhaps that was because she didn't have anyone she could trust. Sydney suspected that apart from the smug, equally repressed members of The Rolling Scones, Miranda didn't have any friends. Why else would she make such an effort to court Charlie and her?

But now, after what Ian had just said, Sydney began to wonder whether Miranda wasn't somehow complicit in her own destiny after all. When she said Ian thought this, and Ian wanted that, perhaps what she really meant was that she did.

Sydney wiped a few more dishes, but her heart wasn't in it. That was the trouble with trying to analyse anyone, especially when you hadn't met them. What if Richard really was cut out to be a surf bum after all? Who was Sydney to sit in judgement over anyone, including her *IQ* correspondents? You never truly knew all there was to know about a relationship, even your own. All she knew was that it would have been nice if Charlie could find at least a letterbox if not an actual window in his diary over the next week when he could spare his family a quality moment.

'Are you all right?' Miranda looked at her enquiringly. Sydney smiled weakly and followed her outside with the plates, shivering as the cold night air nipped at her skin. Even Jacquie had put a cardigan on. Ian had lit a cigar and was breathing gusts of foul-smelling smoke over her. They were still discussing the work ethic – or rather, the female race's lack of it.

'Are you trying to get us all fat, Mandy?' Jacquie ran a white fingertip along the edge of the bowl and licked the cream off.

'Better do some housework, Jacquie,' said Ian. He was clearly on a mission to humiliate Miranda and the 57 per cent of women who didn't have careers. 'My wife swears by it. Though why she can't do some proper work as well beats me. What have you got to say on the matter, Charlie?' Ian turned to the opposite end of the table where Charlie had been quietly contemplating a second helping of potatoes before Miranda whisked away his plate.

'Not that my nan was exactly sylph-like,' continued Jacquie. 'And she was a Fifties housewife, with her own confectionery business on the side. But there're always exceptions to the rule, aren't there? Your boys are very athletic looking. Not at all lardy like a lot of teens these days.'

'That's 'cos Ian frog-marches them round the pool every day,' joked Miles.

There was a stark silence, relieved only by the sound of slapping as Jacquie tried to swat another fly.

'I said, what do you think, Charlie?' said Ian pointedly.

'About what?' Charlie looked up, his eyes narrowing dangerously.

'Oh, for God's sake, man, women working. You've got it made financially, of course, with a wife who manages not only to run an office but more or less keep the family on the road.'

Charlie cocked his head in the old familiar gesture of engaged enquiry that had made Sydney fall in love with him. Her heart juddered with hope.

'If Sydney's work was financially worthwhile, that would indeed be true,' he said eventually, eyeing her coldly. 'But from where I'm sitting it looks like a rather expensive hobby by the time you've factored in the childminder, let alone all the extra organic foods she keeps ordering in the erroneous belief that it will make amends to her children for not being there.'

★ ★ ★

Sydney felt utterly humiliated. Not that she could have it out with Charlie because he wasn't talking to her in private, other than the basic functional requests that she pass him his book as they got into bed, or open the window. She lay next to his apparently blissfully sleeping form stiff with rage, sorrow and the occasional flash of repentance. She tossed and turned, railing against her husband; against Francine, for whatever it was she'd done to Charlie to make him so chauvinistic, Ian for being chauvinistic in a completely different way, Miranda for being so wet and yet so manipulative, Dylan for taking her last text too literally. Then she cried for Ezekiel who was obviously a deeply unhappy little boy, and for Owen who, she prayed to God, had found better parents, wherever he was. Then, when she couldn't bear the sleeplessness any more, she went downstairs, shivering in the early grey light. She sat in a corner next to the range in the kitchen trying to read *Marie Antoinette* until the sun rose and she could hear Miranda's footsteps on the stairs. But all along she was thinking about Dylan; longing, but not quite daring to ring him.

The next seven days got worse. Miranda and Ian didn't want to go out at all. Charlie seemed to work non-stop, Sydney did more and more cleaning, especially as Miranda had taken it into her head to skim the pool every three hours. There was no escape. Miles and Jacquie certainly didn't want to eat out without Sydney and Charlie to pick up the bill. So the six of them were trapped like passengers on the *Titanic*. Sydney couldn't sleep at all and her moods flip-flopped like baby dolphins. Sometimes she was convinced that all she felt for Dylan was lust and a sense of unfinished business. At other times she was certain he had changed; that missing bit of emotional hardware that had made him so flippant twenty years ago had been slotted into place

273

when Eloise left him. She wished her sixth sense hadn't deserted her, and she wished, above all that she was at home. She must have been mad to think she and Charlie could sort anything out on this holiday; but she was determined to make things right when they got back.

Then one night, the urge to hear a sympathetic voice – Dylan's sympathetic voice – was so overwhelming that she crept out to the pool with her mobile. Jacquie, who had taken to texting her gym night and day, was there in the lotus position, with her mobile pressed between her shoulders and her left ear.

'No, no, Elaine. What you want to do is tell him you can't go out 'cos you're cleaning your gutters. No, wait. Tell him you're trimming your cuticles.' She cackled softly in the moonlight, and waved at Sydney, who decided that Jacquie was God's way of protecting her from doing anything else stupid, and slipped back inside.

At least Ian had finally given up on Ezekiel's diving torture, presumably deciding that letting him terrorize small girls was equally character-building. At least the girls were having a reasonable time, however. And after witnessing Ian's treatment of his sons, she had a feeling Molly would drop the threats to phone Childline for a while. And at least she and Charlie managed to look like a normal couple in public.

Even Miles was relatively containable, until the last but one night when he led Gideon and Samson on a break-out, sneaking out of the villa at midnight to get hammered in the local bars until three. At which time they turned up noisily at the villa, waking up the entire house just in time to see Miles throw up in the pool.

As usual Sydney felt responsible and arranged for the pool to be professionally cleaned at her expense. While it was out of action she drove Miranda, the boys, Molly, Harriet and Miles to southern Spain's largest water park where Samson was escorted off the site for squirting some shaving foam he'd smuggled in with him into the floating tea-cup pool – but only after they'd been there for five hours and Sydney had developed what later turned out to be a nasty bout of cystitis.

When they got back to the villa Charlie and Ian were upstairs having a ferocious-sounding row. Sydney had never seen her husband, who regarded anger as a symptom of failure, so livid or contemptuous. But she never got a chance to ask him why.

True to form, Thin Air got them home four and a half hours late. The wait at Malaga was excruciating. Charlie sank into an impenetrably morose silence. The girls bickered non-stop and Sydney couldn't put Owen out of her mind. It was a month since his eighteenth birthday. In theory, of course, it could be years before he contacted the Adoption Contact Register – if he ever did. But 20 March had been a milestone. There could be a letter from them waiting for her at home.

Outside 64 Clifton Crescent, Charlie discovered he'd lost his keys but insisted on searching through all his luggage even though Sydney, now she came to think about it, could picture them lying on the desk in their bedroom in Spain – the desk from which he'd barely stirred in ten days. She eventually found hers in the bottom of her beach bag.

Once in the house, it felt as though everything was conspiring to delay her from finding a private corner to go through the post. Assuming, that was, Juanita hadn't filed it in the compost.

It was two in the morning when she finally sleepwalked

the girls up to bed and returned downstairs to find Charlie sorting through the mountain of letters that Juanita had left by three empty bottles of Cif. She watched, with a sickening sense of foreboding, as an envelope from the Adoption Contact Register fell to the floor in slow motion. She ran from the foot of the stairs to the table in the hall, reaching to scoop it up from the floor. Charlie put his foot on it, trapping her fingers.

'You're hurting me.' Her voice shook.

He kept his foot there. 'Would you like to read that out? It's obviously very important. I've never seen you move so fast.'

Sydney's heart pounded in her ears. She told herself to keep calm. What could Charlie possibly know?

'It's been a long time since the first letter they wrote to you, hasn't it – nine months, would you say?' He stared at her contemptuously. 'Almost as long as the length of a pregnancy.' His heel ground into her finger.

'Let me go,' she said feebly. Her brain reeled. She had had no idea Charlie had seen that reply to the letter she'd written to the Adoption Contact Register. Nine months since Charlie had changed; fallen out of love with her. Nine months that he'd been waiting for her to confide in him.

Sydney's brain whirred furiously as the blood drained from her fingers. 'I can explain,' she said hoarsely.

'I daresay you can,' he said icily. 'But it's a bit late.' He moved his foot and picked up his case, piled on top of the others by the table. 'I hope you and your son will live happily ever after.'

She heard him close the door behind him and walk down the steps and along the length of Clifton Crescent.

14

All night she tortured herself over the wasted months of silence. So Charlie had known abut Owen for ages. But how? Had he put two and two together when he saw that first wretched reply? She racked her brains trying to remember how long it had sat in one of Juanita's new filing systems before she'd got to it. Or had he known even before then? And why had he never said anything? Probably for the same reason she hadn't. People thought marriage brought security, but she could see that hers had been bound by fear.

She was still lying in bed, Harriet's thin, hot body curled into the curves of her own, when she heard Juanita rattle her keys in the front door, then pause in the hall, waiting for the alarm to go off.

Gently, Sydney extracted her right arm from under Harriet's head. It felt numb, like the rest of her. She pulled on her dressing-gown and padded downstairs.

'Morning, Juanita,' she whispered. 'The girls are still asleep. Charlie's gone to work though,' she added, conscious that her eyes must look like dark red worm holes. She hadn't slept a wink.

Juanita squinted at her quizzically. 'You tired?' She gave a brittle laugh. 'Always the same with bloody holidays. You keep those girls at home today. School is so stressful. Is like cruelty to kids. Teach load of crap too.'

She hung up her coat and marched into the kitchen,

presumably in search of Glade and Mr Sheen reinforcements. She poked her head round the door. 'Holiday must have done Charlie good. He don't forget his briefcase. Bloody turn-up for books.'

Sydney walked slowly back up the stairs. She couldn't tell Juanita about Charlie. She couldn't tell anyone until she'd come to terms with it herself. She raked over the previous few hours for the millionth time, picking for clues amongst the detritus of what hadn't been said. Nothing felt real any more. She was desperate to know how much Charlie knew, whether he'd guessed about Dylan's role in everything and if he knew about their night in Paris. She looked guiltily at Harriet, still asleep, her thick hair streaked across her face like fronds of ivy, and felt an overwhelming surge of panic.

Juanita had started on the stairs when Sydney came to and realized that she ought to have been at work. Given how late they'd gone to bed, she didn't have the heart to wake the girls up and pack them off to school. Stiff with exhaustion, she went downstairs to call Maisie.

Maisie's answerphone informed her that she was either on another call, in which case she'd get back to her very shortly, or that she was doing *Maisie's Mellow Moments*, in which case she'd be gone some time.

Half an hour later, Sydney still hadn't heard back, so she called Linda, hoping to avoid speaking to Annabelle or anyone else who might pick up Linda's office line if she happened to be out at a meeting. She already felt bad for taking ten days out of the office in the darkest hour of her need, as Linda had put it. Now she was letting her down again.

Chloë picked up Linda's phone. 'Hi,' she said casually. 'I'll pass on a message if you like.' There was a new excitable, breathless tone to her voice.

'It's probably better if I speak to her myself,' said Sydney warily.

'I'll get her to ring you,' said Chloë. 'How was your holiday by the way?' Before Sydney could answer, Chloë told her how much they'd missed her. 'And if there's anything else I can do for you while I'm on the line, do let me know.' Sydney began to wonder whether she hadn't got Chloë all wrong. She couldn't trust anything any more, least of all her own judgement.

'Wait a moment, Linda's just appeared,' said Chloë. 'I'll hand you over.'

'Linda, I'm so sorry.' Sydney could feel the constriction of shock that had been holding her together for the past few hours buckling under the force of a familiar adult voice.

'It's fine, Syd. Honestly. Don't worry. I'd have taken this job even if things hadn't descended into the cesspit of celebrity so-called culture here. How did you find out by the way? He hasn't sent out an official release already?'

'Find out what?'

'About me moving to New York.'

'You're moving to New York?' repeated Sydney dully. Her pummelled brain was no longer processing information properly.

'I know it seems sudden.' Linda sounded momentarily guilt-stricken. 'I would have told you first, honestly. But it's all happened so fast and you were away. I'm still pinching myself. Editor of *Quantum Leap*. Can you believe it?'

Linda wasn't making much sense, but eventually Sydney gleaned that she had been offered the editorship of *Quantum Leap* twenty minutes before Brian Widlake had fired her. Linda was so excited at the prospect of getting her hand on the highest of America's high-brow literary magazines, one which regularly ran articles on authors almost no one apart from their publishers had heard of, and yet for some reason – one that was rumoured to have something to do with tax write-offs – was awash with cash and highly regarded thanks to its lavish parties and extravagant marketing budgets, that she barely gave a thought to her sacking, or to Sydney, who was getting fainter and fainter on the other end of the line. On the upside it meant that Linda didn't bat an eyelid when Sydney exaggerated quite how late the plane had got in and told her she wasn't coming in to work.

'I suppose my getting the editorship in the face of historic – and violent – competition isn't that extraordinary,' Linda gabbled on, happily oblivious to Sydney's plight on the other end of the phone. 'You know how crazy Americans are about British journalists, once they can get past the teeth. Not that I didn't win it fair and square.'

'When are you leaving?' asked Sydney, wondering how many weeks' grace she had before Linda's replacement, hand-picked by Widlake presumably, was installed.

'They're clearing my desk as we speak,' said Linda ecstatically. 'I didn't think this sort of thing really happened in this country. It's quite thrilling.'

'It happens all the time in America so you'd better get used to it,' said Sydney.

'Whoops. Here's me celebrating my good fortune and you must be wondering what it's going to mean for *IQ*. Not that it's that big a deal to you, let's face it. It's Annabelle I worry about. But what can you do? If it's any consolation, I'm going to write a letter to whoever takes over here telling them all what a truly brilliant team you are. You do know I'd take you to New York like a shot if you weren't married to Charlie, don't you, Syd?'

It was no consolation at all. Sydney couldn't imagine anything being less welcome to an incoming editor than a list of recommendations from a predecessor. Especially one who was widely deemed by the new powers that be to have failed abysmally.

Sydney desperately needed to hear Linda say something – anything – banal about Charlie's departure being for the best. But all Linda told her was that she was having an impromptu leaving party at The Ivy later that night and that she hoped Sydney would move heaven and earth to be there.

It was probably just as well. She knew that Linda would tell her she was crazy for even contemplating life without him. So she congratulated her again and rang off. What she feared more than Linda's disapproval, she realized, was her pity. She was used to being seen as the one with the golden life and she had become tremendously fond of the illusion.

The next few hours dragged even more slowly than they had on the dismal Spanish holiday. Sydney felt she was being flattened by a fleet of tanks. First life without Charlie, which was so shocking it had purged her mind of all thoughts of Dylan as if it were one of Juanita's cleaning agents. Now life without Linda. Not that she could bring herself to believe Charlie had actually gone, although she could see that he had checked out emotionally months ago. He couldn't stay away for long. The small suitcase he'd taken on holiday and walked out with last night would hardly sustain him through what was turning out to be a bitterly icy April. He'd be back. And he would forgive her for having kept her first child a secret, especially when she explained that she'd done it to protect them all. He'd forgive her for Dylan. He'd . . . Sydney looked down at her left hand and saw that her right one had been digging into it so hard there were gouge marks. Because of course she knew Charlie would do no such thing.

★　　★　　★

281

She resisted the urge to crawl back into bed. Instead she got up and made shaky progress unpacking the heap of luggage sitting by the door. At eleven the girls woke up and she began to regret not sending them to school. Harriet taught her how to make Nigel Slater's macaroni cheese for lunch, and Sydney remembered the countless times Harriet had made it for them before and how she'd taken everything for granted, even the sad, dull ache buried in the bottom of her heart.

'What do you mean, you won't be able to make my leaving party?' asked Linda incredulously when she called back later that day.

'It is quite short notice,' said Sydney uncertainly. Her life seemed to be unspooling at two different speeds. There was Life Without Charlie speed, which unravelled in slow motion, and Life Without Linda, which was God with His finger on the fast forward. 'Most people don't hand in their notice, vacate the building and have their leaving party all within twelve hours.'

'But you must be there. You were there at the start of my career. You need to be there now. Surely Charlie could get one night off work to babysit?'

Sydney eyed the girls tucking into their macaroni cheese. So far they seemed happily unaware of Charlie's absence. But then it was only a quarter to two and he wouldn't normally have been home until after nine anyway. She wondered briefly whether she could get away indefinitely with not telling them he'd left.

'Tonight's a bit tricky,' she began. 'Charlie's exceptionally . . . tied up. And Maisie's doing her show.'

'I see. I'm sorry I failed to plan my career around Maisie's radio commitments. Do you know how difficult it is to get

282

a big table at The Ivy at short notice? Perhaps I'll see you before I leave for New York. On Friday.'

Charlie's keys didn't get jammed in the door later that night and Sydney didn't make it to Linda's leaving dinner. Instead, she read three chapters of *Black Beauty* to the girls and pretended everything was normal. At ten o'clock Mrs Protheroe pressed a freckled, arthritic finger on Sydney's doorbell and didn't lift it until she had gone downstairs and let her in. Only faintly registering that Mrs Protheroe was in full stage makeup, wearing her favourite sequinned cardigan, Sydney listened patiently while she told her that the forces of evil had released her from captivity and enquired whether Sydney had seen the latest copy of *Hello!*.

'The She-Witch is in it.' She pointed to a scratched and folded photograph of Eloise in the arms of some dashing actor at a sparkling fund-raiser in New York. Sydney studied the date on the front cover. Eloise certainly hadn't wasted much time getting over her heartbreak. It wasn't even the very latest copy of *Hello!* but one that was several weeks old, and stamped with a Royal Free Hospital frank. And they'd got Eloise's name wrong.

'And he's no better than he ought to be,' Mrs Protheroe gesticulated meaningfully across the road at Dylan's house, 'up all hours and out for a good many others. The Devil makes work for Those Who Cheat,' she muttered.

Sydney briefly considered correcting her but let it pass. She offered her a hot toddy instead and watched her toddle off with the glass. It was only later that she realized Mrs Protheroe had been wearing only one slipper. She'd have to call the Royal Free tomorrow. They clearly had no business letting her out so soon.

*   *   *

'Where's Daddy?' asked Molly sleepily the following morning.

'At work,' said Sydney, as breezily as she could manage on twenty minutes' sleep in a vast, Siberian bed. She felt even more terrible than she had the day before, which, given how lousy she'd felt then, was some kind of achievement.

Molly fondled the artificial silk flower on Nellie's coffin and Sydney pretended to focus on the congealed scrambled eggs, sausages and bacon she had been tending for the last quarter of an hour, although it might have been more usefully deployed to dam the Thames than feed her children. She watched Molly out of the corner of her eye. She seemed to have accepted her mother's explanation.

'Are you and Dad having marital problems?' asked Harriet. Sydney tossed a perfect pancake and made a big deal of catching it again. 'Ellie's parents are having a trial separation. But Ellie doesn't think they'll get back together. Her mum says they're incompatible. Her dad's a sex addict, apparently.' Her large, serious eyes, the same thistle colour as Charlie's lingered on Sydney. 'Do you think you and Dad are incompatible?' Sydney managed a squawky, false-sounding laugh. 'Because when you think about it, you are very different.' Harriet kept her gaze on her mother, who seemed to be very distracted by her pancakes.

'That's not necessarily a bad thing,' said Sydney. She was being evasive, but it was nearly eight o'clock and they'd have to leave for school in ten minutes. Anyway, Charlie might be back tonight. Sydney had checked his wardrobe and he didn't have a single warm jumper with him.

She scrapped the eggs and bacon and concentrated on the pancakes instead, serving them with a triumphant flourish. Why hadn't these simple pleasures been enough? Even though Charlie had made it clear he'd left because of what

284

had happened with Owen and Dylan, somehow Sydney couldn't shake off the conviction that what had really sealed her fate was Charlie's sense of rejection that the perfect life he'd provided for her hadn't, in the end, been sufficient.

She sat down in front of her own plate and felt suddenly nauseous. Harriet wasn't eating anything either. Her eyes probed her mother's face anxiously. 'You are all right, aren't you, Mummy?' she asked shakily.

'You look absolutely terrible, if you don't mind my being brutally frank.' Poppy was speaking in a theatrically loud whisper. 'Was it the food in Spain?'

Sydney shook her head, a reckless expenditure of energy given her current depleted levels. Standing in the decidedly utilitarian, dark grey corridor leading to the *IQ* offices, Spain seemed a million years ago.

'Are *you* all right, Poppy?' asked Sydney, suddenly aware that Poppy was in the office on a Tuesday before noon.

'Not really.' Poppy's football-sized lips trembled. 'It's the new editor.' Her eyes stopped darting and began to bulge dramatically. She looked like a beautiful exotic fish dangling on the end of a line.

'They've appointed one already? That's a bit hasty, isn't it?'

Poppy nodded miserably. 'Not only that but she's here. Chloë thinks Brian had her waiting in the wings all along.'

'Who is she?' asked Sydney, bracing herself.

'Virginia Horwell.'

'Are you sure?' Sydney felt sick. It was hard to tell what Virginia Horwell was most famous – or notorious – for. Firing women who had the temerity to get pregnant, fat, married or old. Or hiring men who were ruthlessly, blindingly and futilely (she wasn't named after the Virgin Queen for nothing, apparently) in lust with her and would do all her dirty bidding unquestioningly. She was also known to be ferociously un-PC and permanently on the Atkins Diet, an unhappy combination that made her aggressively toxic and prone to monstering various hapless celebrities in screeching headlines for the edification of her readers. If they were gay, marginally to the left of Genghis Khan, or a member of an ethnic minority, so much the better. *Private Eye* called her Verucca Whoremoan in celebration of her short skirts and her high-pitched nasal commands, and had introduced a column called DeathWish, lampooning all the demeaning tasks she made her staff do. She was also the most successful woman in journalism, having doubled the circulations of the last two publications she had taken on, and went everywhere with two secretaries and a doppelgänger.

'Of course I'm sure. She's wearing a red jacket with gilt buttons and shoulder pads, if you can believe it. It's as if deconstruction never happened. And her skirt's so short you can see her thong.'

Sydney could believe it. Only recently she'd seen Virginia wipe the floor with David Dimbleby on *Question Time* in a most inappropriately cut-away crimson halter-neck top and leather biker jacket.

'She must be at least forty,' Poppy added in disgust. 'She's brought all kinds of horrible-looking sidekicks with her. One of them actually called me lovey and asked me to go and fetch Virginia's drycleaning from Jeeves.'

'What did you say?'

'I'm on my way there now,' confessed Poppy.

A few months ago Sydney might have cleared her desk then and there. But she was a one-parent family now. She needed this job.

Poppy looked pensive for a moment. 'It's enough to make

you question your choice of career, isn't it? I'm starting to think journalism's rather brutal. They even took Linda's car. And it didn't even belong to them. There were no taxis to be had for love or money. She had to get the Tube.'

She wandered disconsolately towards the lift, leaving Sydney pondering the hitherto unconsidered possibility that Poppy viewed her twelve-hour week as an actual career.

'By the way,' called Poppy from the lift, 'we now start work at eight-thirty a.m.'

Sydney looked at her watch. 10.15. What with the traffic outside school, things hadn't exactly run to plan. It was enough to make her nostalgic for the old days of forty-eight hours ago, before Virginia and her evil Armada had sailed in, when Dave had been bolshy but fundamentally a push-over; Linda had been losing her judgement but was still talented; and Annabelle's questionable future at Icon Publishing seemed slightly less perilous than it presumably was now. Taking a deep breath and bracing her shoulders, she marched down the corridor and through the swing doors into *IQ* land.

Virginia's strident tones hit her from the far side of the office. 'And this is?' She drummed her ox-blood talons on Sydney's desk, where she appeared to have been poring over some proofs with Chloë. At least Sydney assumed it was still her desk. Heart thumping, she continued her grim progress. Chloë, wearing a dark red mini-skirt almost as short as Virginia's, looked up at Virginia admiringly.

'These are the problem pages, Virginia,' she replied, with a faint but discernible sneer. Virginia had been viciously ripping apart every item slated to appear in the forthcoming issue all morning and Chloë had been doing her utmost to distance herself from all of it.

Virginia ran her thickly lined eyes down the proof, which Sydney now realized were the ones she'd been working on just before she'd gone on holiday, taking in every word while everyone in the office held their breath. Savouring the tension, Virginia looked up eventually and held her hand out for the black coffee that one of her henchmen had been following her around with.

'Not bad,' she said when she'd finished perusing it thirty seconds later. 'Could do with a punchier headline and you can dump those few little illustrations right now. I want something graphic and bold with a lot of red in it. Get Terry O'Neill on the case.'

'I'm so glad you like it,' Sydney heard Chloë say. 'And you're quite right about the illustrations. I always thought a proper photograph would be much stronger. It will make editing these pages so much more rewarding.' She looked up and reddened as she saw Sydney approaching the desk. 'Virginia, this is Sydney Murray,' she said, suddenly sounding nervous. 'She . . . works on the problem pages too.'

At 12.30 an email flashed up. It was from Linda. She'd just heard the shocking news about Virginia from Dave and wanted Sydney to call her at home. Not that there was any chance of that. As the day ground relentlessly on, Sydney felt more and more like Alice in Wonderland; everything at *IQ* – or *VIP* as Virginia informed them it was henceforth to be called – had been turned on its head, including Linda's bedraggled office, which, shorn of its mountains of books, old clippings and manuscripts, looked even shabbier, but was already in the process of being redecorated. Virginia didn't believe in scruffy chic. She didn't believe in time-wasting niceties either, such as civility, remembering people's names or chairing features meetings, preferring to bark orders at random minions as she teetered round the office. She told Annabelle to go out and buy her a new pair of tights. She ordered Dave, whom she insisted on calling Damien, to commission an investigative feature on the cellulite-giving properties of carbonated water, and she screeched at Poppy to find her a lunchtime Brazilian.

'Isn't she invigorating?' said Chloë nauseatingly.

'Isn't she a fucking bitch?' grumbled Dave, sounding less belligerent and more put upon than ever.

'The budgets won't take the strain,' said Annabelle, wringing her hands and somehow managing to light a cigarette simultaneously. 'Terry O'Neill indeed.'

'There are no budgets,' Virginia declared imperiously as she approached their little huddle, which immediately scattered like skittles. 'Brian has given me carte blanche to turn this train wreck around.' Her shiny red lips twisted into something that might very loosely have been described as a self-satisfied, eviscerating smile – in the Chamber of Horrors. 'Budgets are for losers.'

That was Annabelle out of a job then, thought Sydney in dismay.

The irony was that Virginia's Reign of Terror achieved in a few short days what Linda's well-intentioned stabs at democracy, bonding exercises and trip to Butely had signally failed to. It united the original rump of *IQ* – that is, *VIP* – into a loyal core.

Sydney decided she could live with Virginia's graphic new photographs, including the one of herself – she didn't have a lot of choice – much more easily than she could with the lies she'd been living. On the fourth day after they'd got back from holiday, she told the girls gently that Charlie had temporarily moved out to give them both a rest from each other.

'Is it a trial separation?' asked Harriet dourly. 'Because we all know they never are temporary.'

Molly climbed on to Sydney's lap and turned her enormous blue eyes on her mother. 'I believe you.' She squeezed Sydney's hand and tried not to cry. 'As long as he comes back very soon.'

Sydney kissed the top of Molly's blonde head, which smelled, as always of marzipan. She reached her arms out for Harriet. 'Come on,' she said, shifting Molly on to one knee and pulling Harriet next to her. 'There's plenty of room.' Actually there was more room than usual. Sydney hadn't eaten for days. Harriet glared at her mother fiercely. And then she began to sob.

On Friday night Charlie called. Sydney's heart, which launched itself into her mouth every time the phone had rung, was so overwrought it could barely muster a defeated twitch.

'I've found quite a nice flat not far away,' he said quietly. 'I'd like to come round and pick up some things on Saturday morning if that's all right. And see the girls of course. Shall we say after lunch?'

Sydney suggested they say before lunch but Charlie muttered something about work. Then he asked her how she was and she answered politely that she was fine, because somehow sticking to a moronic script of unemotional clichés seemed the mature thing to do.

Five minutes before Charlie was due on Saturday, Dylan turned up, his cheekbones jutting above his turned-up collar like shark's fins. Her stomach somersaulted. It was almost a month since she'd seen him and the depths of her feelings for him hit her with the force of an Exocet.

'Mrs Protheroe said Charlie had moved out.' He tilted his head to one side and gazed at her enquiringly. His eyes glittered. He seemed exhausted and exhilarated. 'Has he? Christ, Sydney. Why didn't you tell me?'

She looked at him helplessly. 'We don't belong together,' she suggested eventually.

'Why ever not?' He looked at her with his uncomplicated optimism and she wondered if he was missing that piece of emotional hardware after all or was just a very accomplished actor. 'I don't suppose there's any chance of not freezing to death on your doorstep? It's so cold I can feel my balls shrivelling out here. Not even you could want that.'

'Charlie's coming round any second.'

'I won't be long.' He followed her into the hall.

'Some explorer.' Sydney deliberately kept her back to him. She didn't want his scrutiny.

He grabbed her wrist and twisted her towards him. 'Sydney, what's going on?' he asked gruffly. He pulled her closer. She could smell lemons. They were so sharp they stung her nostrils. 'Does Charlie know about us?'

'Please.' She wrenched her arm from his grip. 'The girls are in the kitchen.'

'I've missed you,' he said tenderly. 'You don't know how many times I dialled your number.'

'I take it you forgot part of it then? Mrs Protheroe said you came back a few days ago.' She remembered his watch – in her drawer at work – and wished it was here so she could return it to him.

'Mrs Protheroe's quite right.' The light, flippant tone that was never far from his voice returned. 'I nearly came round then but she – the Purple Oracle – told me you were still away. And then I had to go to Paris. Where I thought about you incessantly.' He smiled, and his face illuminated the hall.

He drew her into his coat. 'Sydney, I know you said you never wanted to see me again – and most men might take that as a bit of a blow – but . . . well, for one thing, I need to know if you think about our son as much as I do.'

She pointed towards the kitchen, imploring him to be more discreet. Then he kissed her forehead gently. To her shame and confusion she felt a familiar and unwelcome tingle between her thighs.

'All right. But promise me you'll see me soon.'

She promised, and watched him bounce across the street again, wondering why someone so apparently straightforward could leave so much confusion in his wake.

Charlie was only half an hour late to collect the girls, which was his equivalent of being an hour early. He rang the bell and they both stood awkwardly on the steps for a few moments, before settling for courteous, distant hellos. She offered to fry him a steak but he said he'd already eaten. He hovered by the front door and asked whether she'd mind if he took the girls to an art gallery that afternoon.

'Of course not. They'd love that,' said Sydney, half hoping he'd invite her along. If they couldn't have the perfect marriage, perhaps they could have the perfect separation.

15

Sydney spent the 183 minutes that Charlie was out with the girls wondering whether the agony of watching your children and your possibly-soon-to-be-ex-husband going off together ever got better. Because right now the pain was so eviscerating she spent the first hour lying curled up on her bed. Not even a phone call from Linda, newly arrived in New York, roused her. Eventually she hauled herself up and tried to make a cake to welcome the girls back, but it sank. At four o'clock she poured herself a glass of wine and lay down with some slices of cucumber over her eyes. At a quarter to five she seriously considered phoning Dylan and begging him to bring round some marijuana. At five she poured herself a large brandy. By five-thirty she had anaesthetized herself enough to be wreathed in one enormously fake smile, in time for the girls' return.

The following weekend wasn't any better. She was shattered from putting in twelve-hour days at the office thanks to Virginia's habit of screeching orders at everyone the moment they arrived and then screeching contradictory orders as they were about to leave. She floated around on permanent red alert, hollow-brained and hollow-eyed from lack of sleep.

Her Fridays off went by the board. Now her days were a blur of editing, rewriting, directing photo-shoots in order to get at least four layouts completed each week to present to

Virginia, who liked to have lots of choices. According to the vast-bottomed, bow-tied doppelgänger, whose name turned out to be Alun Coxham, she always worked like this, and Sydney could count herself lucky that Virginia only made her prepare four choices. 'It must mean she rates you,' he said, sweeping his bulbous, jaundiced eyes over Sydney's exhausted face.

It was Harriet who worried her most. Molly looked sad, and held Sydney's hand protectively a lot of the time, constantly asking questions about when the trial separation would be over. But Harriet had retreated into herself and barely spoke at all. Her paintings, always on the dark side, were becoming demonic. Her latest was a portrait of battery hens having their throats slit. Sydney kept making new lists of positive action, at the top of which was ringing the school to let them know what was happening at home. But somehow there was never time.

Judging by the despairing, lifeless expression in Charlie's eyes and the huge pouches beneath them, he wasn't faring much better than she was. Worse, possibly. Then again, since he wouldn't take any of her calls and waited outside for the girls in a taxi when he came to collect them, there was no way of knowing for sure.

Despite having precisely no one to confide in – Linda, high on New York euphoria, was impossible – Sydney nobly did her best to keep Dylan at arm's length, which wasn't easy when he called and sent flowers all the time. But following an extremely tense telephone conversation with Francine in which they both tried not to make it too obvious that they blamed each other in some as yet unspecified way for what had happened, and Francine managed to mention the fact that Charlie was single and grieving three times, Sydney felt all her old frustrations with the Murrays' refusal ever to confront their emotions bubble to the surface.

So when Dylan arrived on the doorstep one night, she let him in without demurring. She demurred even less when he bustled into her kitchen with two shopping bags and set about making a surprisingly delicious-smelling curry. 'If I can't woo you with flowers, I get to you via your stomach,' he announced. 'And you can be sous-chef.'

Sydney was tired of fighting Dylan off, especially when the fight made her feel like a falling leaf struggling against a hurricane, but she couldn't sleep with him again. It would make deciding what she felt about Charlie even more complicated.

'What are we making?' She peered over his shoulder appreciatively, feeling the steam revive her.

'Mountain Reviver.'

'Which is?'

'Green curry.'

'Mmm, my favourite.'

'Don't commit before you've sampled Polar Warmer.'

'And that is?'

'Green curry. And then there's Indomitable Stockpot.'

'Green curry?'

'Yup.'

'Delicious.'

He stooped down to kiss her neck. She dodged just in time. 'You always were so easy to please.'

She closed her eyes. Charlie would probably disagree.

'What I'm really trying to say,' he said another evening, 'is that I'll always be here for you.'

She hardly cared whether or not she believed him. She had been endlessly cautious with Charlie and look where it had got her.

'I would never have left you if I'd known about the baby, you know.'

She felt a familiar pain shooting down the left side of her temple. It was the same sensation she'd felt when Charlie had left. The same feeling when she'd caught Dylan in bed with that girl from the Architecture Faculty all those years ago. Why hadn't she ever been able to acknowledge how much that had devastated her before?

'Sydney. Answer the question.'

'What question?'

'The implicit one – the why-didn't-you-tell-me one.'

'Because I thought you might come back when you found out. I couldn't use my decision to keep the baby as a hold over you.'

'She meant nothing, you know. I was an arsehole with a giant ego.'

'Still are.'

'True. But an older, wiser, much more celibate arsehole.'

'You can't be much more celibate. You either are or you're not.'

'Well, at this rate I am, my little pedant. I certainly don't want to get laid by anyone else apart from you. And since you're not exactly throwing yourself at me at the moment I'm holier than the Pope. It's killing me.'

She couldn't help smiling at his forlorn expression. He was contagiously ebullient.

'That's better. God, Sydney, I admire you so much. Most girls would have just nipped out between parties and got an abortion.'

'Don't admire me too much,' she said, trying to dampen his gusto, which threatened to sweep her over the crest of a waterfall. 'I told you before. I wasn't thinking straight. I'm sure if my mother hadn't been dying I would have got rid of the baby.'

'I don't believe that for a moment . . . I keep dreaming about him, you know. Owen, I mean. Don't you wonder what he's like? I've been thinking of this Welsh legend my mother used to read me when I was a child. The one about Prince Llewelyn who had to leave his newborn child, and instead of a babysitter he chose his faithful dog, Gelert, to look after the baby.'

At least a dog would probably take his ward for a run in the park occasionally, unlike Maisie, thought Sydney.

'All right, so a dog's an unorthodox choice,' said Dylan. 'I don't suppose Esther Rantzen would approve. Anyway, off Llewelyn toddles, leaving Gelert in charge of his child. Llewelyn's been gone for less than an hour when Gelert and the baby have an unexpected visitor. A vicious, starving wolf from the woods tears into the room where the baby's sleeping. Fast as a Ferrari, Gelert takes the baby in his mouth and gently lays him on the floor with a blanket over him so that he can fight off the wolf.'

Dylan poured them both some more wine. 'Llewelyn returns to find the baby missing and Gelert covered in blood. It's not looking good for the dog. Llewelyn thrusts his sword into Gelert and kills him. But as Gelert falls with a thud to the ground, blood spurting from his severed throat . . . '

'You're overdoing this.'

'. . . he hears his son cry. He lifts the blanket to find the baby safe and well with not a scratch on his body. Llewelyn then realizes his mistake as he sees the wolf's dead body by the cot.' He paused. In the dim light his eyes flickered and he looked rather vulpine himself.

'Then what?' asked Sydney, curiosity getting the better of

her. Dylan's myths and legends always worked their magic on her eventually – along, she was sure, with most of the females he tried them out on.

'Llewelyn bitterly regrets his actions and arranges for Gelert to have a burial service and a gravestone with his name and achievements carved upon it.'

Sydney put down her knife and fork. 'Not much consolation, is it?' She stood up and began loading their plates into the dishwasher. Clearing up was not Dylan's forte. But at least he cooked, unlike Charlie, Sydney was shocked to find herself thinking. She couldn't be getting over Charlie already, surely? Eleven years of marriage had to count for more than that. She scraped the leftovers into the bin.

'I suppose I'm Llewelyn,' she said bitterly, 'giving up his baby to something he doesn't really understand.'

'That's not what I meant.' He twisted her round to face him. 'It's not an allegory for us,' he said softly. She wished he'd stop saying us. 'It's just that I've been thinking about him a lot. And you. And us. I've started dreaming about him at night. Only he doesn't have a face—' He stopped abruptly and turned away. 'I'd better leave,' he said gruffly. 'You're tired.'

It was a typical Dylan tactic, she reflected, climbing into bed next to the girls. Withdraw early and leave them panting. It wouldn't work with her, obviously. She nuzzled closer to Molly who had wrapped herself in one of Sydney's shawls. She wished she could see things more clearly. She wished she missed Charlie more and lusted after Dylan less. She wished she knew whether her refusal to go to bed with Dylan was making things more or less intense between them. She wished she had someone over the age of ten to discuss things with.

A willing confidante turned up outside her front door the

following Sunday in the form of Miranda, bearing an enormous box of provisions. 'I've brought you some supplies,' she said, standing expectantly on the doorstep. 'We're all so sorry to hear about Charlie. And you.' Her Alice band wobbled in sympathy as she peeked over Sydney's shoulder into the hallway, hoping, presumably, for signs of carnage.

'All?' asked Sydney, alarmed.

Miranda giggled nervously. 'Sorry. When I say *all*, I mean just Ian and I of course. Charlie's been the soul of discretion, as you might expect. But Ian suspected something was up when he heard him ordering a taxi the other night in the office to take him to his new flat. I hope you like the food. There's some homemade steak and kidney puddings and pickles. A box of chocolates to keep your endorphin levels up. I don't care what they say about calories. At times like these you learn what really matters. A big Stilton and some Duchy of Cornwall oatcakes – perfect for when you're eating alone. Ideally it would go very well with a nice bottle of Merlot . . .' She trailed off. 'But I didn't pack any wine in the end.' She paused awkwardly. 'Not good. When you're drinking. Alone.' She paused, waiting for Sydney to ask her in.

Sydney wondered briefly whether the new, out-of-control her might suggest Miranda make one of her mercy calls on Mrs Protheroe.

'Would you like a cup of tea?' she asked when it became painfully clear Miranda wasn't budging.

'Only if it's not any trouble.' Miranda stepped past Sydney before she could reconsider the offer. At least the house looked tidy. Since Charlie's departure, things had been running like clockwork. Once Juanita had guessed what had happened – and a life larded with tragedy and catastrophes had given her an unerring sixth sense for these

299

things – she had rallied round and even overcome some of her allergies.

While Sydney brewed some tea, Harriet and Molly watched with increasingly wide eyes as Miranda unpacked the food supplies.

'They're not from Nestlé, are they?' asked Molly, as Miranda lovingly placed the Duchy of Cornwall oatcakes next to the bread bin.

Miranda laughed playfully. 'Dear me no. Everything's either homemade or organic.' She eyed the girls as a missionary might once have gazed pityingly upon Biafran refugees. 'This is for you to have tonight.' She nodded towards the steak and kidney pudding. 'You'd probably like something hot for a change.'

Harriet considered the overwhelming smugness of this. 'Since all that meat in Spain I've become vegetarian,' she announced haughtily.

Sydney didn't think she'd ever felt prouder of Harriet. God knows she'd tried to feel grateful to Miranda for her charity. She'd even had a stab at answering all her nosy masquerading-as-concerned questions as politely as she could. As well as attempting to coax Miranda into dropping her own beatific mask. But to no avail. Miranda was even more wedded to her own idealized version of her marriage than Sydney had been.

Later that night, after the girls had gone to sleep – in her bed again – her doorstep was graced with yet more provisions. This time from Dylan – a bottle of Dom Perignon and a dummied-up Glendower book entitled *Ode to Divorcees*. When she saw how cheerful he was looking she began to worry that, in his own way, Dylan might be as deluded as Miranda. What else could explain his insane – and insanely attractive – optimism? He'd never been the type for morose introspection, but years of tackling barren icy wastelands had robbed him of what little scepticism he'd ever possessed and instead imbued him with an unshakeable and often entirely baseless faith in fate. Which was why, presumably, although his own track record in the family stakes was not exactly impressive, he seemed to think he could take on Sydney, Harriet, Molly and quite possibly Owen without any problems.

'That's not funny, by the way,' she said as he followed her into the kitchen. 'I'm not actually divorced.'

'Yet. But you will be once you see sense. What's this?' He gazed at the box Miranda had brought, which Sydney hadn't quite got round to finishing unpacking.

'Air lift. Welcome to Baghdad.'

'Nice Stilton. Crying out for some wine though. We'll just have to make do with this.' He uncorked the champagne and handed her a huge glass, then grabbed the box of chocolates. 'May I smear these over you now or later?'

'I take it you're inviting yourself to supper?' said Sydney, not entirely appalled at the prospect. Miranda's saccharine condescension had left her in need of cheering up.

Dylan hung up his coat and sat down, his sprawling limbs filling the room. 'Thought you'd never ask.'

By the time they had worked their way through the champagne Sydney was incapable of cooking, so they dined on chocolate, Stilton and Duchy of Cornwall oatcakes and toasted Miranda with a bottle of rosé Sydney found on the bottom shelf of the fridge. Then Dylan kissed her and she kissed him back and just as he was leading her towards the sofa in the sitting room the phone rang. It was Miranda reminding her not to put the Stilton in the fridge.

'Are you all right?' she asked as Sydney struggled to do up her bra and Dylan got down on his knees and made begging noises.

'Just a bit tired,' said Sydney, trying to sound put upon.

'Oh dear.' Miranda's syrupy sympathy was so thick she could have knitted blankets for the needy out of it. 'I can imagine,' she lied. 'Never mind. If you look in the bottom of the box, I've packed some herbal sleeping pills.'

'She's right,' said Sydney after she'd put the phone down. 'I'd better go to bed. Alone,' she added as Dylan brightened.

He looked at her earnestly. 'I do love you, you know, Sydney. With all my heart, spleen, kidney and future excess weight. But if I'm moving too fast, just tell me. I'll wait as long as you want. Go as slowly as you want. I'll hobble after you on crutches if that's what it takes.'

She felt herself burning up in the intensity of his gaze. 'I have had a letter,' she said suddenly. 'From the Adoption Contact Register. That's why Charlie left. He'd known for months, you see. It's from Owen. He's been in touch with them. He wants to see me. If I – we – agree, they'll pass on the details and then organize a meeting.'

Forgetting his previous protestations about moving slowly, Dylan bounded over and swept her up in his arms, holding her so tightly she had to fight for breath.

Legally Dylan had no rights as far as Owen was concerned. As the helpful woman at the Adoption Contact Register had explained, Sydney didn't have to consult or even inform the father of her child about her intentions to meet him. After all, when she had first approached the Register, Dylan was little more than a blurred memory. But her life had changed unimaginably since then. And she had a feeling it was about to change again. The nice woman told her that she would be offered counselling and that in her opinion she should take whatever was going.

'Charlie has left me,' Sydney repeated calmly. Saying it twice didn't make it any more real. She still couldn't feel it as much as she should.

'Don't be ridiculous,' said Linda.

'Which is the ridiculous bit?'

'He can't have. You're exaggerating.'

Sydney considered her options. She could tell Linda some of the truth. She could tell her none of the truth. She certainly couldn't tell her the whole truth.

'You haven't slept with Dylan?'

It looked as though she didn't have much option. 'Only once.'

'Sydney, in God's name *why*?' Linda's lofty disapproval was the final straw.

'Because I had a baby with Dylan nearly eighteen years ago, gave him away and forgot to tell Charlie.' It was quite a lot for anyone to digest in one go, especially someone who was convinced Sydney led a blameless existence. Waves of silence roared across the Atlantic.

'Say something please,' Sydney said eventually.

'You bitch,' said Linda, slamming the phone down.

On Monday morning at two minutes past eight The Learning Pool telephoned Sydney to say there had finally been a last-minute cancellation. They could see Harriet at 10.30 if Sydney could get her there in time. Sydney did a rough mental calculation. Mondays were now the layout days for her pages. But so were Tuesdays, Wednesdays, Thursdays and Fridays. She couldn't pass up this opportunity, especially with the way Harriet's work and behaviour at school appeared to be heading in a downward spiral. She left a message on Annabelle's mobile saying she'd be late.

Harriet looked terribly small wired up to all their machines. Sydney waited with her for two hours during which she was scanned, quizzed and placed on a tilting floor in a tiny cubicle with walls that closed in on her to test her sense of balance. At the end of it all she and Harriet were called into a small office containing a desk, a sheaf of graph paper pertaining to Harriet, and a petite, neat-looking woman with efficient-looking hair and the warmest smile Sydney had seen in a long time.

She pointed to one of the charts in front of her. 'If you look here, Mrs Murray, you'll see that Harriet's cerebellum never properly developed. That's the bit of the brain that controls all her reflexes,' she explained. 'The cerebellum takes care of all those things we supposedly do automatically. When we walk upstairs, it's the cerebellum that measures the first tread so that once we've taken the first step, we know the distance between all the others. That's why if one of the treads is slightly out of kilter we stumble.'

'Is this why Harriet's always falling down the stairs and bumping into things?' asked Sydney, relief washing through her.

'Exactly. Normally the cerebellum is functioning at birth. But if you look at this graph, you'll see Harriet's is barely registering. Let me demonstrate something to you.' She turned to Harriet. 'Could you stand on one leg, Harriet?'

Harriet did as she was asked, balancing perfectly.

'Excellent. Now, do you think you could stay like that, but say your two times table at the same time?'

Harriet began reciting and immediately fell over.

'You see, Mrs Murray, in a normally developed cerebellum, a person would be able to recite their tables and balance on one leg because the cerebellum would automatically kick in and take care of all those automatic reflexes. But Harriet's doesn't do anything automatically. So she has to work twice as hard. It's exhausting and it can cause terrific mood swings as well as playing havoc with the learning functions.'

The suggestion that Harriet's aggression had a physical cause was the first good news Sydney had heard in months.

'The even better news is that the cerebellum is a part of the brain that can be developed like any other. It's a long process of course. We're looking at a good two years of exercises that need to be done morning and night, without fail, every day. Are you ready for that, Harriet? Even on Christmas Day?'

Harriet's pale face nodded with relief. Sydney felt the tears stinging the backs of her eyes.

'Good girl. They're very special exercises by the way. They were developed by NASA for astronauts. Not a lot of people know this,' she pulled a face at her appalling Michael Caine impersonation, 'but when astronauts return from space and anti-gravity, their cerebellums are completely out of whack. Sometimes they find they've become dyslexic or unpredictable. These exercises were devised to put them right.'

Harriet looked as though she'd just been told she'd won a scholarship to Harvard. 'So what exactly is the label for this?' she asked.

'Label? We don't believe in those, Harriet. We believe in individuals.' She turned to Sydney. 'And you, Mrs Murray, are you ready for this punishing regime? I warn you that roughly four weeks into this programme the novelty definitely wears off, and fifty-six weeks into it you'll both want to kill me. But we do get extraordinary results.

Harriet's a very bright little girl and it must be extremely frustrating that she's not achieving her potential.'

Sydney wanted to kiss this woman for finally offering her a solution to Harriet's mood swings, even after she asked her whether she was sure, as a single mother, that she would be able to see it through. 'It is a hell of a commitment,' she repeated. 'I won't pretend that some don't fall by the wayside. And Mrs Murray, you work four days a week, don't you?'

Sydney nodded meekly and crossed her fingers under her chair. Lately she'd felt as though she was putting in a forty-four-day week.

'Well, far be it for me to discourage any mother from working.' She beamed at Sydney and Harriet. 'I've got four myself. But it's going to be very, very tough.'

Twenty minutes later Sydney and Harriet floated out of The Learning Pool clutching two files of exercises, two small juggling balls, a bean bag, a giant inflatable ball, and an appointment for two months' time. It was only after Sydney had dropped Harriet off at school that she realized it had never occurred to her to ring Charlie to ask him to come with her. No change there then.

Sydney stepped out of the lift and collided with Poppy. 'Jesus, Sydney, where've you been? Virginia's spitting pins. She's laid out your pages with Chloë.'

'But I left a message with Annabelle,' Sydney protested indignantly. She'd already all but given up her four-day week. She wasn't going to sacrifice what was left of her home life to Virginia's vampiric delectation as well.

'That would explain it. Virginia sent Annabelle out first thing this morning to The Heavenly Banana.'

'Is Annabelle all right?' asked Sydney, alarmed that this was some kind of It-girl slang for being fired.

'The Heavenly Banana's the new organic deli in Notting Hill,' explained Poppy. 'Virginia's been put on a low-stress diet by her bio-chemist – the same one as Gwyneth Paltrow. No meat, no dairy, no carbs, no onions. Or was it parsnips? She's in a foul mood. Annabelle isn't thrilled either. She called to say that the Tube got stuck at Marble Arch. She's still in Notting Hill. Oh, and *Breakfast Time* are in to film a segment on the way Virginia's turning *VIP* around. And Chloë's already nipped out to buy a suit like Virginia's. Even though I told her it's all about jeans and jackets these days.'

Sydney followed Poppy down the corridor, past a tangle of cables and two sound technicians.

'Stop!' Alun Coxham pranced into the corridor and waved his arms in front of them like a Railway Child. 'Don't take another step,' he ordered dramatically. 'Virginia's lost one of her contact lenses. She can't possibly do the interview without. I suggest you all start looking – and next time,' he added viciously, 'I recommend that you leave the bright ideas well alone, Poppy.' He tiptoed back down the corridor, his enormous bottom practically dragging along the loose carpet tiles like a mine-sweeper.

Poppy stared up from the floor defiantly. 'Virginia kept screaming at me to find her an eye cream that worked. She's always complaining that everything I give her is useless. So I told her the only thing that really works is haemorrhoid cream. And when that didn't go down too well I suggested some facial exercises.' She shrugged. 'Short of plastic surgery it was all I could think of. She must have dislodged one of her lenses when she was doing the Brow Waggle. Oh God,' she wailed, 'could you help me write a CeeVee or whatever they're called, Sydney? I think my days here are numbered.'

'Come on. It won't come to that,' said Sydney staunchly.

She was starting to realize how much she valued the old *IQ* team. She gazed down the corridor and saw Dave, who had done an amazing job on her Charlotte Rampling notes, on his knees as he squinted at the carpet tiles looking for something small, blue and rubbery. It was Sydney who eventually spotted Virginia's missing contact lens impaled on the tip of Poppy's stiletto heel.

It was lucky that Poppy had been sent a set of clear contact lenses the previous week. They weren't prescription, but there was always an outside chance that the clear ones might act as a placebo. The interview with *Breakfast Time* went better than expected, given that Virginia could hardly see out of her left eye. Alun told her it gave her a seductive come-hither look. Virginia told him he was a useless wanker and sent him out to buy her some corn plasters. But, Sydney noticed, she was smiling, so she clearly responded to compliments.

It was just as well, because the proofs of Sydney's – or rather, Dave's – interview with Charlotte Rampling were lying on Virginia's desk when she summoned Sydney to her newly revamped office, which had been painted Blistering Scarlett and furnished with tiger-striped velvet upholstery. Virginia was hunched over the article like a polecat waiting for a small, vulnerable animal to scuttle in. She swept her matted lashes over Sydney as she came in.

'Please don't imagine in the future we'll be making a habit of interviewing actresses who appear in Frog films with subtitles. But in the meantime, since there's nothing else to fill its place, we'll run it. The proper relaunch is next weekend by the way. In the meantime you did a pretty reasonable job, considering what an old broiler you were dealing with.'

Recognizing this for the gushing praise it was, Sydney seized her chance to show Virginia that the old *IQ* rump was nothing if not committed to one another and pointed out that Dave had done most of the serious writing part. 'I just asked the questions and pressed the record button.'

Virginia looked at her with distaste. 'From now on, pressing the red button's all it takes. I want all our interviews to be Q & A.'

Annabelle arrived back from The Heavenly Banana laden down with organic produce and every vitamin and mineral from A to Zinc, vowing never to give up smoking. 'Have you seen the prices in there?' she asked Sydney rhetorically. 'Four quid for a loaf of spelt. It makes fags look like the bargain of the century.'

An email flashed up in Sydney's inbox. It was from Linda.

I can't believe you watched me go through the trauma of an adoption for all those years without telling me you'd given away a child.

Only Linda could get competitive trauma syndrome, thought Sydney. And if she remembered correctly, the trauma had been somewhat assuaged when Chloë had organized the extended loan of a BMW.

Given the level of stress they were all under, the mood in the office had become surprisingly buoyant. Virginia might be terrifying, but there was never any ambiguity about what she wanted. And as the relaunched *VIP* began to take shape, they could see a hypnotic albeit horrible logic to it all. Chloë of course was thrilled because under the new budgetless budgets, Virginia had no problem about her going off every weekend with U2 and with any luck, as she put it, shagging the lot of them. Dave seemed to be flourishing under firm command, and even came up with some rather good punning headlines. And once Annabelle had pointed out to Virginia that she was paying way over the odds for her vitamins and minerals at The Heavenly Banana and explained she could source the same thing for her in Brick Lane, her short-term future also seemed assured – at least for as long as Virginia stuck to her new diet. And Linda sent her another seven emails saying she was working through her anger but until then Sydney was not to contact her, unless she could remember where Linda had left the essay on The Future of Molecules, which she knew would go down a storm with the readers of *Quantum Leap*.

Sydney fell into bed every night between the girls and felt herself sucked into a storm-tossed world of half-forgotten memories and dreams. When Charlie came to take his daughters to his flat, Sydney waved them off as usual, having carefully packed all Harriet's exercises with instructions to Molly to monitor her sister, in case Charlie turned out to disapprove – it was a very alternative programme after all. An artificially sunny smile plastered across her face, she watched until the taxi had disappeared round the corner and then padded disconsolately back into the house where she lit the fire and the little antique chandelier table lamps and lay on the sofa while it grew dark outside, listening to Elvis Costello, wallowing in her loneliness and remembering occasionally to congratulate herself for not falling apart. Wasn't the house tidier? Weren't the mornings simpler now that she wasn't always having to pop into the police station to collect Charlie's lost property? Was it not infinitely more serene in the house without the constant hum of his laptop? It was good to be on one's own sometimes. She was glad that Dylan had had to go back to Paris to woo some more cash out of Patrice. It meant she finally had some peace and quiet in which to think.

It was some time before she realized there was someone at the door. Not Mrs Protheroe. She always pressed her finger on the bell and kept it there. Whoever was outside was knocking. Probably a delivery of some kind – one of Charlie's obscure almost-out-of-print law books coming back from the warehouse perhaps. She swept her eyes over the stocky, thuggish-looking figure in front of her, vaguely taking in the crooked front teeth and sprinkling of angry-looking acne, and the battered leathers, and chastised herself for not using the intercom. Judging from his red, blotchy skin he'd been shivering in the vicious wind for some time.

'Sidnoy Murroy?' A nasal Brummie accent pierced her reverie.

Sydney nodded, a slow realization creeping up on her. The youth stepped towards her clumsily. For a moment she thought he was going to mug her. But instead he threw his arms round her. 'At last,' he sighed, resting his lank hair on her shoulder. 'Mum, it's me. Jison.'

16

Jason's zircon ear stud pricked a staccato tattoo into Sydney's collar-bone while a number of unworthy thoughts clotted her brain, chief among them whether or not this was one of Dylan's practical jokes. Ever since she'd first written to the Adoption Contact Register all those months ago, she'd been mentally preparing herself for this moment. But somehow she had never envisioned it happening quite like this. Or Jason looking quite the way he did.

Or, for that matter, for Jason being called Jason. It occurred to her fleetingly that Dylan had hired a stripagram to pretend to be their son, but with something shockingly close to regret, she realized that wasn't quite his style. She opened her eyes and glanced over Jason's shoulder as he pressed her closer to him. He was encased in black leather biker gear that squeaked every time he moved. He also seemed rather short to be a son of Dylan's. But even as this ray of hope flitted through her mind, a darker recognition chased it away. Jason was standing on the step below her.

'Owen!' she exclaimed, folding her arms gingerly round him. She felt the stubble on his chin graze her cheek and waited for the tidal wave of maternal love that had instantly overwhelmed her at his birth. This was not how she'd imagined their reunion. Where was the formal introduction? The counselling? The induction video?

'Yeah, I always wundered about that name?' He let go,

stood back and squinted at her. He had a huge duffel bag with him which suggested a visit of some magnitude. And a black eye, which was worrying. The ignoble part of Sydney wondered how on earth she'd explain him to Charlie and the girls when they came back.

'Come in.' She peered into the street for signs of Mrs Protheroe. He followed Sydney out of the biting wind into the house, creaking down the hallway behind her. She paused uncertainly and he put his duffel bag down, all the while paying close attention, she noticed, to the gilt-framed paintings and the lamps in the hallway. She led him into the sitting room with its huge sash windows, large creamy fireplace and piles of books everywhere.

'It's very exotic. Is it foreign? The name, I mean,' he asked hopefully.

'Welsh,' said Sydney. He really wasn't that tall, even when he wasn't standing on a lower step. But he had to be Owen. How else could he have tracked her down?

'Oh.' He sounded momentarily deflated. 'I'm an Aston Villa man meself.'

There was so much Sydney wanted to ask him that she hardly knew where to start. 'Please make yourself comfortable. Can I get you a drink?'

'That's very kind of you?' He coughed nervously and directed his gaze into his helmet, which was cradled in the crook of his arm. 'If you don't mind me stopping a while, could I just change out of me leathers?'

He appeared a few moments later in a pair of ripped jeans and a baggy T-shirt and sat down carefully on one of the sofas, eyeing Sydney's glass of wine. She leapt up to get him one and he seized his chance.

'I don't suppose you have any lager?'

Sydney disappeared into the kitchen to look for some,

crouching by the oven to eye herself critically in the reflection of its door. If Jason wasn't quite what she'd been expecting, God knew what he made of her. She hoped she wouldn't disappoint him.

'They didn't even tell me that was my birth name?' Jason, having followed her, stopped by the French doors to the garden, hands in his pockets, gazing round the kitchen. She stood up, embarrassed. She wasn't sure when he was asking her a direct question and when his voice was simply shifting up a pitch. 'Mum and Dad, I mean? That is, my adoptive mum and dad,' he added tactfully. Sydney could see he was struggling not to offend her and felt her heart warming.

'At least not for ayges? I must of been about thirteen when they finally got round to telling me everything.' He pulled a none-too-clean hankie out of his pocket and blew his nose loudly using one hand. 'I don't blame them though. They tried their best – you know, to make me feel at home and that.' There was a throbbing silence, while Sydney grappled with the thoughts rushing in on her. He took his hand out of his pocket and she saw that it was bleeding. He'd wrapped a bandanna round it but the blood was seeping through.

He caught her looking at it. 'Came off worst against a lorry in the service station.' He grimaced. 'Sum people have no manners.'

She found some antiseptic cream and got him to wash his hand. Then it occurred to her he must be starving, having ridden all the way from wherever he'd come from. 'Would you like some supper?' she asked.

He perked up. 'Wouldn't say no.' He blew his nose again, not that it seemed to make much difference. Either he had terrible sinus problems or his accent was so thick it amounted to a speech impediment, Sydney was appalled to find herself thinking. She took some marinade out of the fridge. 'Salmon pasta?'

'Grite?' he said gamely. 'Or I could nip out and get us sum fish and chips?'

Sydney smiled and reached up for a frying pan. 'No need. I'm pretty sure I've got the ingredients for batter.'

'Nice pictures,' he said, examining Harriet's latest one depicting a mutilated monkey bleeding to death while two men in white coats appeared to be cutting it open and extracting what looked like a bottle of shampoo from its stomach. Sydney had had her doubts about putting it on display but Maisie had pinned it up while Sydney was at work, thinking it was a picture of fireworks. She handed Jason a lager and assembled some flour and water.

'Abstract, is it?'

'Not exactly.' She smiled weakly and wondered where to start. 'Harriet's very concerned about animal rights.'

'Bloimey,' said Jason, running his finger over the limestone counter. 'She's your daughter, I take it? Which makes her my half-sister.' He shook his head sagely. 'It's a bit of a mind-cruncher that one, isn't it?'

Sydney nodded. It certainly was. 'I hadn't expected things to happen quite so fast.' She began whisking the flour and water and invited him to sit down. She noticed he'd put his jacket on again.

''Fraid that's my fault.' He rubbed his nose sheepishly. 'I jumped the gun? I couldn't be doing with all that to-ing and fro-ing and waiting about. You know, you write to them, I write to them, they write to you, they write to me . . .'

'But how did you know where I was?'

He tilted his chair on to two legs and appeared to be ruminating deeply. For a moment she thought he was going to go flying backwards but he'd obviously honed the skill over years. She dunked the fish in the batter and lowered it into the sizzling frying pan.

'I originally wrote to them a year ago, to see like, if you'd registered. At the time they wrote back to say they couldn't help me till I was eighteen. So when I turned eighteen on March the twentieth, I decided to go and see them in person. In Southport loike? Anyway, I got chatting to the lady there. She was very nice and she got out your file. I was dead chuffed because it meant you wanted to see me? But then she started going on about how I had to be patient and stuff? Because you might always change your mind. And I thought, uh-oh, here we go. Any excuse not to deliver, loike. And after I'd paid a tenner as well. Then she said what they normally did was arrange for me and you to have some counselling loike before we finally met. Then she starts going on and on about the psychological ramifications? And I thought, sod this for a game of cards. I wasn't keen on the counselling to tell the truth because, you know, life's too short, isn't it? So what I did was, I pretended to come over faint? And while she was getting me sum water I had a quick recce of your letter. I hope you don't mind.' He gulped the last of his lager. Sydney chopped up some potatoes and poured him another one. 'I did feel bad loike, her being so kind and everything, but over the years I've had me fill of bureaucracy, if you know what I mean.'

In an odd way Sydney did empathize. At any rate she admired his apparent lack of neurosis. But she could have done with the counselling sessions, even if Jason didn't need them.

'I think you're very brave, coming here by yourself, when you had no idea how I might react . . .' She trailed off.

'Not as brive as you. The minute they told me you'd been in touch I knew it meant you still had . . . feelings for me.

But you couldn't know how *I* felt loike. I mean, I might have been really miffed with you. Not that I am,' he added hastily.

Sydney focussed on the chips and began to feel highly ashamed that she'd ever looked askance at his appearance. How could this child she had given away to strangers apparently harbour no bitterness towards her? A particularly vindictive spot to the left of his nose began to bubble, probably from being in the cold so long. It was an unseasonally cold day. Perhaps he didn't get enough vitamin C.

'Would you like some salad with this?' she asked, laying the table and arranging the battered salmon and chips in one of the big white Nicole Farhi bowls.

'Nah, you're all right.' He looked up apologetically, as if afraid he'd transgressed some as yet unfamiliar boundary of politeness. 'I don't really do salad?' He studied the fish inquisitively. 'This stuff looks like it came from one of those Michelin tyre restaurants,' he said approvingly.

Sydney opened another bottle of wine and sat down opposite. She moved the corners of her mouth into what she hoped was an encouraging smile. 'I think it's brilliant that you came. And I'm dying to hear all about you.'

'I'm pretty curious to hear it meself?' he said laconically. He bit into the fish as if it were pigeon scrotum. 'Nice.'

Sydney felt a curious displacement of weight about her shoulders: the immense worry about the fate of her son floated off into the ether, to be replaced by the dawning certainty that she didn't have a clue where to take things from here. She tried one of her experimental smiles again, as Jason munched on a chip.

'Any salad cream?' he asked hopefully.

Sydney fetched some. 'Right,' she said when she'd sat down again. 'Where shall we start?'

★   ★   ★

They talked for hours. He told her all about growing up in Dudley with the Watsons – Maureen and Barry – the couple who'd adopted him when he was two weeks old and taken him to live in their snug semi in a leafy cul-de-sac. She learned that he'd loved playing football at school and that he quite liked climbing but that even though he'd been quite interested in history, English and geography, something had gone wrong: academically he hadn't exactly shone and now he was working as a courier for DHL. He'd driven down from Dudley on his motorbike, which explained why the circulation still didn't appear to have kicked into his reddened extremities. Normally riding the bike in the cold was okay, he assured her, but it had seemed to take a long time today, what with the anxiety and his stereo being on the blink. She was more touched than ever by the thought of the wind slicing through his spots like a cheese-cutter.

He had no other brothers or sisters, though Maureen and Barry had bought him a beagle called John when he was twelve. Unfortunately John had got run over which had clearly left its scars on Jason. He – Jason, not John – liked Monopoly and heavy metal, believed devoutly in the rights of motorcyclists and had only been abroad three times, always to Calais, which didn't, Sydney couldn't help thinking, suggest a hugely inquisitive mind or much of his father's lust for travel, and went to show how important nurture was compared with nature. She quizzed him further, hoping for evidence of Dylan's genes. It wasn't a very fruitful line of enquiry. She didn't get the impression that he was a huge fan of Shakespeare or poetry, although he quite liked Harry Potter and he had a passion for science fiction, especially black holes, the lost city of Atlantis, the Knights Templar, UFOs, Bible Codes and a *Blue Peter* manual he'd got years ago containing a long list of bulletins from Nostradamus, to the effect that the world was about to end in a vast cataclysm.

'Earth is going to be consumed in an epic environment disaster, and pretty soon by my reckoning?' He mopped up the last of the fish. 'I don't want to depress you, Sidnoy, but the threat of a giant asteroid strike is increasing daily. Either that,' he was warming to his subject, Sydney felt, but it was hard to tell because his voice still sounded slightly less animated than the speaking clock, 'or there's going to be a massive re-alignment of the planets which will increase solar activity, thereby unleashing a complex chain of events causing the Earth's crust to slide and poles to shift. Quite frankly, it would be a geological Armageddon? You'd have volcanism going on on a global scale. The thing is, Syd—' He eyed up the remaining fish hungrily. 'What do I call you by the way?'

'Sydney's fine.' She helped him to another serving. 'If that's what you'd like.'

'Is that a Welsh name too? I only know one other Sidney and he played centre forward for Dudley Comp's First Eleven.'

'No, it's not Welsh. My dad – your grandfather – had a thing about an actress called Cyd Charisse. But I grew up in Wales too. That's not where I met your father though.' She told him about Dylan and watched his small, beady eyes darting from side to side of her head like hyperactive tadpoles grow wider as she told him about his father's exploits.

'Is he famous then?'

'In exploring circles, I think.'

'So, famous and Welsh. You win sum, lose sum,' Jason chuckled.

'Quite a few of his expeditions were followed in the news-papers. But he gave it up before he actually got to lead any of them, so he's not as well known as someone like Sir Ranulph Fiennes.'

'So my real name's Owen Glendower.' He rolled the name around his mouth. 'Bloimey, an explorer. Did he know about me?'

Sydney shook her head. She could see the extent to which she must seem the guilty party to Jason. She'd rejected her son and hadn't even given Dylan the chance to decide. But amazingly, he didn't appear to hold it against her. 'An explorer,' he marvelled. 'It's a bit more interesting than working in the bought ledger department at John Lewis. Don't get me wrong? Barry, that's my dad, or rather my adoptive dad, is very nice,' he added loyally.

Sydney wanted to reach out to him, but refrained for fear of embarrassing him. 'It's all right,' she said gently. 'You don't need to worry about hurting my feelings. I'm sure Barry is extremely nice. And your mum. The social workers were very, very careful about finding you wonderful parents. If it hadn't been for that sense of trust I'd never have been able to . . .' She tripped over the lump in her throat, aware that she was probably coming across as an odious hypocrite. The bottom line was that in his eyes at least, she'd rejected him.

Jason reached out a reddened hand for hers. 'Were your mum and dad really strict?' he asked.

Sydney looked into the tiny greenish-blue marble chips that were his eyes – the exact colour you would get if you mixed hers and Dylan's – and felt herself opening up like a forced hyacinth. She told him about her mother, his grand-mother, and about Miles. And how she'd been in love with Dylan but that she'd realized that they were both too young – or at least he was too young, but she didn't say that part – to settle down together. She didn't tell him the bit about walking in on Dylan as he was reciting John Donne to that other girl while she wriggled elegantly on top of him all those years ago. But she found herself confiding things she hadn't confided to anyone else, finally admitting that she had once hoped to spend the rest of her life with Dylan but that after a litany of misunderstandings they had parted for good.

'So you don't see him any more?' He sounded disappointed.

'Well yes, actually I do. Now.'

Jason let out a low whistle. 'Crikey. What about your husband? What's his name? How did he feel about it all?'

Sydney flushed. 'Charlie. We're having a trial separation,' she said quickly.

He looked at her sympathetically. 'My ex, Kelly, told me she wanted a trial separation. Then she ran off with Karl, this bloke she used to go out with? She told me although she still loved me she just wanted to be friends now. Not that I'm saying it's loike that with you and Charlie.' He broke off to ruminate dolefully for a moment. 'I expect temporary separations are different down here.' He sniffed. 'I'm sure Charlie will forgive you in the end. What does he do by the way?' he asked casually.

'He's a lawyer. A barrister. Specializing in tax.'

'That's a coincidence, because I've got quite good with tax meself. Bit creative with me self-assessment, if you know what I mean. In fact some of the other lads at DHL have asked me to have a look at their forms. I was thinking maybe of charging . . . Charlie does know about me, doesn't he?' he said suddenly.

Sydney nodded.

'How did he take it?'

'Brilliantly. In his way.' She told him how she'd given up her job on the magazine when she'd had Harriet. How the first five years after that had been more or less blissful and how grateful she'd felt for having the chance to throw herself into full-time motherhood. But how, gradually, she'd realized there was a void in her life, especially once Molly had started full-time school and needed her less, and how, after taking the job at *IQ*, she'd recognized that it was a hole the same shape and size as Owen.

'Tell me to mind my own business if you like, Sidnoy, but did you volunteer the information about me to Charlie, or was it more or less forced on you?' Jason's chippy eyes narrowed to tiny peep-holes.

'I suppose you could say it was a bit of both really.' Sydney began to wilt under Jason's cross-questioning. He was a lot more astute than he looked, she was proud to discover.

'When?'

'About three weeks ago.'

'Do you think he'd ever suspected anything?'

Sydney looked at him thoughtfully. 'No, absolutely not,' she lied. She'd been racked with pain at the thought that Charlie might have known – and suffered – about her and Dylan and Owen for years.

'Are you really positive about that, Sydnoy? It's a big thing for someone not to guess. I mean, I always thought there was something different about me, even before I understood what adoption was – and I'm not even clever loike Charlie.'

Sydney winced. Jason was quite perceptive for a boy. 'Charlie's very . . . distracted sometimes. He's probably the best tax lawyer in the country. But in his personal life . . .'

Jason looked a mite sceptical. 'Do you want this separation to be temporary?' he asked suddenly. 'Tell me to mind my own business if you loike.'

'Charlie was so different from everything Dylan was,' said Sydney wistfully.

'Meaning he's not now?'

'I was twenty-two when I met him and at the time he was exactly what I needed.' She smiled sadly. 'Sometimes you make compromises in life because it seems the most sensible thing in the world, but being sensible isn't always wise . . .'

Jason looked pensive and asked Sydney if he could have another lager. 'If you don't mind my saying, Sidnoy, twenty-two seems a bit young to be making compromises.' He stared round the kitchen appreciatively. 'Not that this house seems much of a compromise to me.'

Sydney poured him his lager. She hadn't heard anyone talk with this kind of neutral clarity about her and Charlie before. 'What about you?' she said brightly.

'Kelly always said I was a lot more reliable than Karl. Which wasn't hard frankly, seeing how he's a complete dickhead. To this day I still think his car had a lot to do with her decision – and I don't think I'm kidding myself there, Sidnoy. But now that I think about it, Kelly probably thought she was compromising herself by being with me. I can be a bit too sensible, you know.' He made little quota-tion signs with his fingers as he said the word sensible. 'Karl's a lot harder than me . . . more reckless. Personally I think I'm just what Kelly needs.' He flashed his small, pointy teeth. 'But needing isn't the same as wanting, is it?'

Sydney told him about Dylan's hasty, short-lived marriage to Eloise, who Jason agreed sounded like the ultimate nightmare. 'So you see, much as I love – loved – your father, I'm not sure I could ever truly trust him again. I couldn't face being that hurt again.'

'Maybe you just need to let go of the guilt you feel about Charlie.' Jason's flinty stare took in the empty wine bottles lined up next to Juanita's empty cans of Pledge.

Sydney started to explain that wasn't really the problem.

But she realized it probably was. It was perfectly natural that Jason should want her to get back together with his father. But it wasn't going to happen, she decided. She needed to be without men for a while.

'Jesus, Sydney. Any more bombshells lurking in your handbag?' Linda was so titillated by Sydney's latest revelation that she appeared to have forgotten that she wasn't officially talking to her. 'Where is the lovely Jison now?'

'Upstairs,' whispered Sydney. 'Sleeping.'

'Sydney!'

'What else could I do? He'd had an exhausting journey down here. It's freezing cold and pitch black outside. I could hardly tell him to get on his bike and go back to Dudley, could I? And he doesn't know a soul in London. Besides, I'm all alone here. It's quite nice to have some company,' she added pointedly.

'How do you know he's really your son? Have you got a sample of his DNA?'

'No I have not. I know you've been in New York three whole weeks already, but DNA tester-kits are not yet must-have accessories here.'

'Just make sure you lock your bedroom door. Can't you get Dylan to come round?'

'I thought he was the Devil's sperm.'

'That's why he can deal with Owen. Christ, Sydney. Owen! What were you thinking of?'

'I think it's a beautiful name,' Sydney retorted indignantly. 'It means well-born warrior.'

'That's all right then. Pity he hasn't had much success battling against acne. Maybe he needs to enlist St Clearasil. It's a good job love is blind from the sound of things. What are you going to do with him?'

Sydney already regretted giving Linda such a shallow account of her son's appearance. She hadn't wanted her to think she was overly doting and she'd clearly gone too far the other way. Now Linda was deliberately not grasping the point. Owen – or rather Jason – wasn't hers to do anything with.

'Have you told Harriet and Molly about him?' Linda asked sharply. Once again Sydney felt that her perfectly controlled life – the one she had felt so guilty about – was being tossed down a waste disposal unit.

'That's all under control,' Sydney replied.

Linda snorted. 'Is it too late to say you don't want to continue the relationship?' she asked. 'Can't you tell the Adoption Contact Register that having met Jason – sorry, Owen – without, may I remind you, due warning from them, you don't feel it's going to work out? I'm sure they could find a subtle way to dump him. It's the least they can do in the circumstances. You could probably sue them, you know.'

Sydney's maternal hackles began to rise. Who was Linda to decide that just because Jason – Owen – was a bit spotty and spoke like a nasally challenged bingo caller, he wasn't up to scratch? 'There's someone at the door,' she said coldly. 'I'll call back later.'

'Biggest lie in the world,' said Linda, 'after all the ones about maternal love.'

Jason – she would have to come to terms with his name and that was all there was to it; she had given up any parental rights she might have had the moment she had handed him over to the resolutely cheerful nurse on that sunny morning eighteen years ago – slept the blissful sleep of the innocent. Or, as Linda would have put it, the gormless. Meanwhile Sydney lay on her bed watching first the moon rise, then the dawn break across a sky whose colours seemed to mirror her own contradictory emotions. Since the arrival of her son several hours earlier, her life had become incalculably more complicated; its tonal variations had shifted from black and white to a thousand shades of cream and grey. She had, she could admit it now, been a bit taken aback by him at first. And by the lack of any warning. But part of her felt euphoric – it was almost the same charge of endorphins she'd had when she'd given birth – and was busy making plans for the bonding they were all going to do.

She tiptoed into the spare bedroom to gaze on him while he slept. She wanted to reach out and touch his skin, so different from Harriet and Molly's downy perfection, trace his features into which the mysteries of his character had already been etched. Her beautiful son. A trickle of dribble dangled from his mouth off the bed, glistening like a slug trail. Sydney turned softly and went to her room. But Linda had made one pertinent point. How on earth was she going to break it to the girls? Who – she glanced at the clock next to her side of the bed – would be home in ten hours.

She must have dozed off eventually. When she woke a pale, almost white light was struggling through the crack in her blinds and Jason was silhouetted in the doorway, holding a mug of tea for her.

'I hope you don't mind?' he snuffled. 'I helped meself to a bit of toast and stuff. I waited as long as I could, but it's nine o'clock and I'd better be off.'

Sydney sat up hastily, rubbing her eyes.

'Do you have to go so soon?' she said blearily, secretly flooded with relief.

He shrugged philosophically. 'Yeah, I've got an afternoon shift? I'd better get a move on actually.'

Sydney hurriedly pulled on some clothes and followed him downstairs.

'Well, bye then.' He stood awkwardly in front of her, one arm hanging stiffly by his side like a rifle, the other curled protectively round his helmet.

'Goodbye, Jason.' She looked at his pale face which behind the curtain of stringy hair suddenly seemed so young and vulnerable, and flung her arms round him. She hugged him silently, feeling the helmet pressing against her heart and magnifying its beating.

'I've left me mobile number on the kitchen table,' he said shyly. 'Just in case you want to meet up again.' He trotted down the steps, pausing briefly to gaze up at the front of the house, taking in its creamy contours in the thin, clear light before tossing her a wave. She watched him straddle his bike which, like him, seemed rather smaller than she'd imagined, and roar off down the road, trailing small, black puffy clouds in his wake.

It was only later, as she ground herself a rather lonely pot of coffee for one and sat in the blossoming garden drinking the bitter-tasting brew, that it occurred to her that perhaps he didn't have an afternoon shift after all but had diplomatically departed early to leave the way clear for the girls' return. She shivered. The nearly white sky was turning a dirty charcoal. She went inside to while away the hours until the children came back, nervously rehearsing the explanation she would have to give them – and sooner rather than later.

As usual, Charlie didn't come inside when he dropped the girls off on Sunday afternoon. Sydney watched his taxi chug down the street and thought he must still be very angry. She made a big effort to seem bright and cheerful for the girls, dabbing on some makeup for their benefit and putting on the long rose-pink velvet skirt with the sequined hem that Molly loved. She had cooked them their favourite: stuffed peppers and fruit salad. But they could only manage a few mouthfuls. Harriet had got a bag of sugar out of the cupboard and was about to sprinkle it on her fruit when Sydney gave her one of her looks.

Harriet glared at her. 'Dad lets us.' She kicked Sydney's chair. Molly got up and put her arms around her mother.

'It *is* delicious, Mummy,' she lisped, her mouth smeared with raspberries. 'It's just that we had a huge lunch. Daddy took us to Pizza Express. My choice,' she added proudly.

'That's right, make Mum feel bad.' Harriet mashed a strawberry with the back of her spoon. Sydney offered her some ground almonds and felt a bittersweet pain tearing at her chest. So this was what broken families felt like. She thought of all the times she'd wished she could empathize more strongly with some of her correspondents. How unbelievably smug she'd been. 'Don't ever worry about making me feel bad,' she said softly. 'I'm glad you had a lovely time with Daddy.'

They looked at her with, Sydney couldn't help feeling, a certain amount of cynicism. Molly was about to say something when Sydney saw Harriet kick her under the table.

She ran them a bath with her favourite oils and lit lots of tea lights, and even Molly said it was relatively enjoyable when she got in. Afterwards, when they snuggled up in her bed together, with Hamish sandwiched between the troughs – the demise of her nuclear family was working out very nicely for him – she told them about Owen. She didn't hold back very much at all, trying not to flinch when they asked her uncomfortable questions concerning his precise parentage, why she had given him away, and why, exactly, she hadn't told them before.

'Are you going to marry Dylan now?' demanded Harriet, two vivid bursts of angry red colour on her cheeks.

'Of course not,' said Sydney. 'I know this is hard to understand but I was very young when I had Jason. What happened then doesn't change the way I feel about both of you.'

'So we've really got a half-brother?' said Molly, round-eyed. 'Cool! Can we meet him?'

'If you want to. He has a motorbike.' Sydney wondered with a certain sense of poignancy whether this might be his strongest selling point as far as they were concerned.

'It is cool to have a brother,' Harriet whispered later as she pressed against Sydney for reassurance again. 'Even if he is really only a half-brother. But if you don't mind me saying, Mum, I can see why Dad's pissed off.'

Sydney couldn't wait to tell Dylan about Jason. But before she got a chance, a tropical bushel of flowers arrived with a note telling her he'd had to go to Paris again and that after that he'd be going to Belgium to look at a factory that sounded as though it might be able to print Glendower books with the same typeface and paper as had traditionally been used, for a very competitive rate.

He was gone for three weeks, during which time he sent her romantic notes and sounded increasingly harassed, although he said he couldn't wait to see her and meet Jason.

Jason, however, seemed to have gone incommunicado. Perhaps he had decided he didn't want to pursue a relationship with Sydney after all. She couldn't blame him. Ashamed, she remembered how she'd watched him itemizing everything in the house, certain he was either planning a robbery or working out how much of it he was entitled to. The prospect of not seeing him ever again made her feel desperately sad, but the sadness, although she didn't want to admit it, was tinged with relief. She didn't call him: it was better to let him decide for himself.

The notes for Harriet's next set of remedial exercises arrived in the post and all Sydney's energy was used up trying to coax her into doing them, feed Virginia's rapacious demand for copy and work out an appropriate response to the latest food parcel that had arrived by post from Francine. She collapsed most nights on the sofa at ten o'clock in front of a glass of wine and the news. She tried very hard to keep upbeat, steering through the weekends with grim cheeriness and a coathanger smile whenever the children were around. She wished Charlie would at least talk to her. She must have said something to Harriet or Molly because he stopped waiting in the taxi when he dropped them off and actually walked them to the door and waited for her to open it before saying a terse goodbye. They were making progress.

She was still sleeping fitfully and dreamed repeatedly that she was drowning. Once, when she was tossing on the sofa, Charlie was under the water with her, pulling away from her no matter how fast she swam after him or how tightly she tried to hold on. A foghorn sounded eerily in the distance – in the gloomy oppression of her dream she instinctively knew it was the sound of the *Titanic* going down. It kept on sounding, its lugubrious toll somehow tied up with her own fate. The harder she held on to Charlie, the louder it sounded, until eventually she woke up and realized someone was at the door.

'Jesus, I've heard of playing hard to get but this is ridiculous. I've been standing outside for ages.' Sydney shrank in the dazzle of Dylan's cheerfulness and felt rather as she imagined Cherie Blair must have when she was first snapped by the paparazzi opening the door in her nightie.

'A more fragile, sensitive soul might have been hurt that you hadn't returned any of the fifteen messages I left for you today and yesterday.' Sydney looked sheepish. She had deliberately not picked up the phone all weekend. 'And the really paranoid might assume you were deliberately trying to avoid them.' He flung his coat over the banisters. 'Luckily for you, I'm a totally insensitive bastard.' Sydney's tiredness and depression evaporated in the blast of his good nature, which was even more ebullient now that the last piece of finance had been agreed by Patrice, he'd got agreement from all the major booksellers to give prominent-ish space to the top five Glendower classics, and the Belgian print-works had come up trumps. In the four weeks since she'd last seen him, he seemed to have changed: his bravura now seemed backed by a sense of solid achievement. He was more like the old Dylan, minus the mocking philistinism.

They finished the bottle of wine and he showed her a beautiful finished copy of the anthology he'd chosen as Glendower's first new book. Then she told him about Owen's visit, carefully evading Dylan's questions about his appearance. Dylan looked ecstatic at the thought of finally meeting his son. She did tell him he was called Jason, where-upon they opened another bottle of wine. Then he asked if he could stay the night and she told him the girls were in her bed and anyway it was too early to drop another bombshell on them. So he ran her another of his special baths and then he left her to it. When she went into the bathroom she saw that this time he'd come prepared and had scattered hundreds of rose petals in it.

As she lay in Dylan's arms the following Saturday night, Sydney conceded there might be certain advantages to the children staying with Charlie every weekend. Not that she and Charlie had officially agreed that he should have the children every weekend. They hadn't officially agreed anything, because they hadn't officially had a proper conversation. But they were starting to fall into a routine and Charlie was becoming increasingly more punctual. Once she even thought he'd smiled at her, but it could have been a trick of the light. Sydney encouraged the girls to discuss their weekends with their father with her – she didn't want to feel he was out of bounds, either to them or to her. It transpired he'd found himself a very nice flat and was even talking about getting somewhere bigger. So sooner or later he'd have to talk to her, Sydney found herself thinking, because he was bound to want to sell the house.

The more deafening the silence from Charlie, the more clamorous Dylan's declarations of undying love, until one night he asked her to marry him. Taken aback, she burst out laughing. He looked so hurt, she really thought he might have meant it, so she reminded him she wasn't actually divorced yet, and then he'd opened a bottle of champagne and toasted lawyers.

She didn't tell Linda about the proposal. Actually, she didn't mention that she saw Dylan almost every day, even when Linda rang when she and Dylan were in the bath. 'Are you alone?' Linda asked suspiciously. 'Christ, Sydney, don't tell me the Hell's Angel has pitched up again.'

Sydney didn't answer. At some point she and Linda had swapped roles. Linda was now slightly maternal and disapproving and Sydney had become the wayward child. It irked and liberated her at the same time.

17

Having been somewhat economical with the truth in discussions at the office about her privileged life prior to Charlie's departure, Sydney found that now that she really was a single mother struggling to be all things to all people and in all places at all times – most notably when it came to last-minute meetings with Virginia that clashed with school appointments – she dreaded other people's pity more than their envy. It was bad enough fending off Linda's incredulity that she had let Charlie go, as Linda put it, as if Charlie was a particularly precious parrot that she had carelessly allowed to escape but Francine's pained but scrupulously balanced concern about the crack-and-alcohol hell she was certain Sydney must be stumbling towards was worse.

At least Annabelle was far too distracted not to believe Sydney when she told her that everything was all right, couldn't be better, and that Charlie seemed to have come through his bad patch (she had added the bit about Charlie's bad patch to provide a bit of social realism to what she knew seemed like an absurdly sunlit existence to Annabelle).

But then, everyone in the office was distracted. They were working insane hours to meet the new deadlines and to satisfy Virginia's insatiable hunger for backup copy and sweet liqueurs, which she liked to crack open at nine, just before she left the office for dinner. When she wasn't screaming for copy, fresh supplies of booze and Tampax – privately, Sydney thought Virginia ought to see a doctor but she was buggered if she was going to suggest it to her – she was simply screaming. Unlike Linda, who had always returned from her encounters with Brian Widlake looking as though she'd done ten rounds with Mike Tyson, Virginia stalked back into the office, sleek as ever, looking like the cat who got the crème de menthe. But that didn't stop her tongue-lashing everyone else.

One particular noisy and harassed morning, Poppy, who as a desperate survival tactic against Virginia's constant tongue-lashings had decided to give kabbalah a go after all and was exuding a concentrated air of calm, was summoned for another verbal beating. She paused outside Virginia's office and smiled at her colleagues bravely. 'Wish me luck.'

'Why do we put ourselves through this?' said Chloë, trying vainly to be comradely.

'Because it keeps a roof over our head,' snapped Annabelle.

'Not much of a roof,' grumbled Dave. 'Mine's sprung a leak. It's like living under Niagara Falls. And do you think I can get hold of my thieving landlord? Can I bollocks! I wouldn't mind,' he added ruefully, 'but it's starting to drip on my old CDs.'

'Haven't you finished downloading them all on to that iPod you forgot to return to the press office?' asked Chloë with mock concern. Since Virginia's arrival, she'd stopped trying to ingratiate herself with the rest of them.

Ignoring Chloë, Annabelle smiled at Dave in a motherly fashion and said that if he wanted he could always store them in her loft until he'd got round to selling them all off on ebay.

In the old days Dave would have demolished Chloë for breakfast for her sly attempts to get him into trouble over purloined freebies. But Virginia's foul temper tantrums meant there was no time for time-wasting diversions. As well as having to write or commission far more features than were actually needed, all journalists were expected to write across every Icon Publishing title according to a new law instigated by Schmucklesons. That meant that at any moment every journalist, no matter which title they nominally worked for, could be required to write a piece for *Big Babes*, *Cement Monthly* or *What Rodent?*. There was never a moment's respite. Even the Charlotte Rampling piece proved a mixed blessing because it meant Virginia was dumping more and more articles on Sydney. And as Sydney was the first to admit, she was a very slow writer at best. And at worst, she wasn't always a very good one.

Miraculously, her success under the new regime didn't seem to alienate Dave – any more than Sydney had already managed to alienate him simply by existing. He even offered to help her with some of her other pieces, and commiserated so sincerely when her tape recorder failed to record a single word during one interview that Sydney almost felt the débâcle was worth it just to make her peace with him. Predictably, Virginia took a different view. She fired her on the spot, then relented when Sydney managed to grovel with the PR to let her have another slot and even told her she admired her balls. So all was well that ended well – except that a nagging genie inside Sydney's head kept reminding her that it was Chloë who'd been dispatched to buy the batteries for the tape recorder before the interview.

At least Virginia's notoriously short attention span meant they were never kept in suspense very long. Poppy burst out of her office seven minutes later, fuming and plucking furiously on her now very frayed kabbalah bracelet. 'She says I can only do make-overs from now on,' she thundered.

'Like Susannah and Trinny. Only she wants me to grab people from the street. Anyone would think this country was bulging over with naturally gorgeous people just waiting to be touched by the hand of a stylist, instead of cursed with people who are just bulging. I'm going to have to go for a walk and think about this.'

She didn't come back all afternoon. At five o'clock she rang Sydney from one of Alvaro Zapporto's horseboxes and told her she didn't know whether it was worth staying on at *VIP* any more.

'At least Linda appreciated me.' Sydney tactfully stayed silent. 'I don't want to be snobbish,' continued Poppy, 'but one of the reasons I loved doing my old column was that it was proper, investigative journalism.'

Sydney heard whinnying in the background. 'Where are you?'

'Windsor Great Park. Alvaro's got a rehearsal thingie. But it's all right this time, Sydney. Honestly, he says he's totally reformed.'

He couldn't reform his age though, which was far too old for Poppy. Sydney found herself wanting Poppy to stay with the magazine. She wanted them all to stay. She had invested too much in *IQ* now to give it up.

'Make-overs *are* proper journalism,' she said. 'Consumer journalism, anyway. Readers love them. You'll probably end up with the most popular item in the entire package. You'd find yourself in a very powerful position on the news-paper if you did them.' All of which was true up to a point, thought Sydney. So she wasn't conning anyone.

'Do you really think so?'

'Definitely. And with your contacts you could pull off some amazing coups.'

'You've got a point, I suppose.' Poppy paused. 'But Mario

Testino definitely wouldn't want to shoot real people, would he?'

'Probably not.' Sydney grappled for something else to say that would encourage Poppy to come back, without giving her completely false hopes. 'Unless you got some really big political names.'

'I could do, I suppose, through Mummy. That would show that bitch Virginia. Whoa, Flapjack, calm down.' There was more whinnying and stamping of hooves. 'Sorry, just been head-butted by an aggressive stallion.' Sydney heard Alvaro's unmistakable gravelly drawl and the sound of Poppy's mobile being dropped. Sydney felt uneasy. She seriously doubted if Alvaro had turned over a new leaf. He was a serial womanizer, manizer and, so legend went, horsizer. But at least it sounded as though Poppy would be back at work soon.

Just as Sydney was thinking about leaving for the day, Virginia summoned her into her box. Sydney hovered by the door where Virginia's red stilettos had been kicked off – or more likely thrown – and shivered. Virginia kept her glass box at sub-zero temperatures, all the better, it was rumoured, to burn off the calories she didn't shift on her new diet, thanks to her weakness for sweet cocktails. Given that she exuded the warmth of the world's most feared dictators, it was inevitable that her office had quickly been dubbed the Ice Bloc.

'I need you to be in New York this Friday,' said Virginia without looking up from her proofs. 'There's an interview with that gorgeous lead singer in Doors to Manual. What's his name?'

'Manley Magus,' said Sydney instinctively.

Virginia looked up suddenly and smiled. In her new snakeskin jacket and the pool of light from her anglepoise she looked like nothing so much as a hungry python. 'I knew you'd know.' She leant back and her mini rose up to her knickers, which Sydney was obliged to observe were python printed. At least she was wearing some today.

'About twelve hundred words. All the usual stuff. Drugs, debauchery, the size of their dicks.'

'Anything else?' asked Sydney icily.

'Not really. I don't care what you do so long as you get the lowdown on their sex lives. It's probably worthy of a cover story. He's supposed to be a horny little bastard, isn't he?' she cackled. 'Well named, evidently.'

Flattering though it undoubtedly was to be in Virginia's favour, Sydney suddenly remembered they had Harriet's check-up at the centre on Friday.

'I'm sorry, Virginia, but I'm really not very experienced when it comes to interviews,' she said firmly.

'I'll be the judge of that,' said Virginia crisply. She hadn't made her name as a mentor for countless journalists without developing a certain pride in her ability to spot raw talent. 'You might not be the most accomplished writer, that's for sure. But you've got a way of listening that draws people out.'

'What about Chloë?' Sydney realized with a sickening clarity that if she told Virginia about Harriet's appointment she was sufficiently sadistic to find another article for her to do out there that would keep her away even longer.

'She's still working on U2 in case you hadn't noticed,' said Virginia. 'Frankly, I'm going cold on the whole idea. She's been working on it for four weekends in a row. Why she can't just get gang-banged and get it over with in one go, I don't know.' She flashed her nicotine-flecked teeth in a manner presumably meant to indicate that she wasn't being entirely serious.

'Surely it would be cheaper to get someone based in New York to write it?' said Sydney, casting around desperately for alternatives.

'Not really,' Virginia replied, sweeping her broomstick lashes over the proofs again. 'The hacks there are all so bloody overpaid. Flights are unbelievably cheap at the moment. And presumably you're not expecting to stay at The Four Seasons.'

'You know he used to go out with Poppy . . . sort of? Perhaps she . . .' Her voice trailed off, along with Virginia's waning interest.

'Sydney, you know as well as I do that airhead could barely spell Manley let alone work out what to do with him. Really, anyone would think you weren't keen on this feature. I know hundreds of journalists who'd give their right tit to get this opportunity. You could become our star celebrity interviewer if you play your cards right.' She looked up briefly, her face contorted by a reflex round the mouth that could have been a smile or a grimace. You could never quite tell with Virginia. All Sydney knew was that the meeting was over.

'I think it's brilliant,' said Dylan when she told him. 'The start of a really stellar career. And before you say anything, I can take Harriet to the centre on Friday. God knows I've watched you do the exercises with her enough times, so I know the drill. And then Charlie will take them for the weekend anyway, won't he?'

Sydney's stomach churned queasily as she pictured Dylan doing the Saturday hand-over to Charlie and how badly that would go down with Charlie. Just as they were developing a civilized routine as well. So far she had successfully managed not to let Charlie bump into Dylan at the house. Just as she

339

had successfully avoided telling the children how close they'd grown. So much for honesty being the best policy.

'And that's another thing.' Dylan leant over and kissed her shoulder. 'When you get back I want us both to meet up with our son. And then we'll introduce him to the girls.' He squeezed Sydney until she was almost breathless. 'Just like one big happy family.'

'I can't believe how much weight you've lost,' Linda repeated accusingly as they drew up outside her apartment on West 82nd Street. 'You're looking a bit gaunt actually.'

'Thanks.' Sydney followed Linda under a red canopy that ran the width of West 82nd Street into her block.

'Don't worry, gaunt's a compliment in this city. What have you been doing?'

'Trying to keep Virginia more or less satisfied.'

'I see,' said Linda as the doorman whisked Sydney's luggage out of the boot and into the lift. 'Not only does that cow unite you all, drive up circulation and stem the haemorrhage of advertising. She achieves the impossible and stops you eating.'

Sydney leant back on the dark wood panelling as the lift whooshed them to the eighth floor. She felt giddy from jet-lag and over-activity. She'd taken a taxi from the airport straight to Linda's laughably plush offices on Broadway, which had been designed at vast expense by some fashionable architect Sydney had never heard of. They'd had lunch in the latest restaurant, then Linda had packed Sydney off for a triple-oxygen facial, pedicure, manicure and leg wax while she did some work. Now she was taking her back to her apartment.

'Much you need to care. Your life appears to be panning out nicely.'

'That's because I've learned about the divine nature of forgiveness,' said Linda, as the lift stopped opposite a carved mahogany door which swung open to reveal an enormous room overlooking Central Park. 'The quality of mercy is not strained, and all that.'

'Nor is the quality of this flat,' exclaimed Sydney, taking in the lavish furnishings, and book-lined walls, the lamps that bathed the dark red rugs and heavy red curtains in twinkling lights. She rushed over to the window and gazed out at the trees below. 'Look at that view.'

Linda basked in satisfaction. 'We couldn't have you staying in that flea-pit Virginia had you booked into, could we? Tight cow. Anyone can make the accountancy books look good if they're a cheapskate—'

Sydney stared longingly at the well-upholstered bed that beckoned her through an open door. 'You've got so much . . . stuff,' she interrupted. Linda's flat in Belsize Park had taken minimalism to pitiful levels of deprivation. 'It looks as though you've been here for centuries.'

'Not me. Clayton,' said Linda. She threw down her bag on a huge red sofa strewn with tartan cushions and beamed. 'It's gorgeous, isn't it?'

'Clayton?' said Sydney, slipping off her coat.

'He's the guy sub-letting it to me. His sister's a contributing editor at *Quantum Leap*. Actually he hasn't been here for centuries, just thirty years. It's rent controlled. Costs him about three dimes a month. Incredible, isn't it? And Clayton's so talented he's made it fabulously glamorous. It's been featured in all the magazines. But then he is a set designer, so what do you expect?' She padded off towards what Sydney assumed to be the kitchen. At any rate, she returned with a chilled bottle of champagne.

As the bubbles slipped down, cold as ice chips, Sydney stretched her legs out on the sofa and felt extraordinarily relaxed, all things considered. She was glad Linda wasn't in one of her forensic moods. She couldn't face an inquisition about Charlie. Or Dylan. Or even Jason. Especially not Jason, because then Linda might articulate what Sydney had been trying not to acknowledge to herself: namely, that since she'd met her son her feelings had been decidedly ambivalent. She braced herself for a Spanish Inquisition.

'Sydney, tell me truthfully. Did you ever love Charlie?'

'Of course.' The force of her reply almost took Sydney by surprise. She realized she'd been subconsciously wondering the same thing.

'I don't understand how you can have loved two people who are so different.'

Sydney looked at her carefully. 'That's just it. I loved Charlie because he was so different from Dylan. He was everything I wanted then.'

'And now?'

This was dangerous, thought Sydney. 'You look fantastic,' she said lamely. Luckily Linda took the bait.

'It's just drinking two litres of water a day,' she said. 'And a bit of botox. And eyebrow-threading. Regular skin peels. Vitamin injections. Dermabrasion. Restylane. N-Lite. And the teeniest little demi-lift. Just round the jawline. Clayton's idea. The boy's a genius.'

'Boy?'

'Man really. He's sixty. Now I know why you never minded hanging out with all Charlie's old friends. They make one look so youthful.'

'Gay?'

'Makes Graham Norton look like Mike Tyson.'

'I never really noticed the age difference with Charlie until recently,' Sydney said quietly. 'It's as if he suddenly skipped into another generation.'

'About the time Dylan came on the scene. What a coincidence.' Linda shook her head. 'Honestly, Sydney, wake up. Whatever makes you think Dylan could ever compete with Charlie? It's perfectly obvious he's a sex god and all that. But what makes you or him think he could ever take you and the children on?'

'Who said anything about that?' said Sydney crossly. They each had another glass of champagne. 'And what exactly did you mean earlier about learning to forgive?'

'Among other things, I've forgiven you for having a baby when I couldn't. For giving it away when I wanted one. And for not telling me about any of it all those years. Cheers.'

'One, being pregnant and eighteen wasn't the most fun I've ever had,' began Sydney. 'Two, giving my baby away wasn't a barrel of laughs, and neither – and this may come as a shock to you, Linda – was it done with the express intention of hurting you. Three—'

'Come on, Syd. You must see it from my point of view. Discovering my best friend had kept such a huge secret from me all that time was a bit freaky.' She leant her head on one side and let the caramel fringe fall in her eyes. 'You have to admit it's odd. I was almost convinced you were a bit sick in the head.'

'There were periods when I wondered the same.' Sydney thought of all the times she had almost come clean with Charlie. 'But once you've gone down a certain road, it becomes very hard to turn back.'

Linda took her hand. 'Let's not quarrel yet. Especially not before I've told you my big news. I'm getting married. To Clayton. And you should see the ring. It's gorgeous.'

*   *   *

Of course the ring was gorgeous. Clayton had designed it himself. It was being altered to fit Linda at the moment but when it was done it would be perfect. As indeed was Clayton, who, as Linda reasonably pointed out, being gay, if not technically speaking entirely perfect for her, was at least perfectly at ease with strong, overbearing women. He seemed to make her very happy, so Sydney decided not to interfere – she'd doled out enough advice to everyone and when it hadn't been ignored, it had turned out to be defective. Besides, Linda told her it was all down to her. 'You were the one who first told me to think laterally where men were concerned. You were so right. He is everything I could want.' He was also away, overseeing the first out-of-town runs of a new production of *La Cage aux Folles* in Minneapolis.

'You're going to love him, Syd. He's funny, smart, has brilliant taste – unlike *moi*,' she added ruefully, 'and he takes the piss out of me something rotten.' Her face was suffused with pink joy and she looked ten years younger. Any remaining rancour Sydney had felt about Linda's blinding self-obsession evaporated, although she couldn't resist asking whether she had given up on the idea of having children.

'No way. Why do you think I've just ordered Martha Stewart's giant turkey baster? You've got to get over this little hiccup with Charlie. I want you all here together at my wedding which, incidentally, is going to be the happiest day of my life. Apart from anything, having Charlie there will make Clayton seem not quite so ancient.'

It was strangely reassuring to see that Linda's make-over had left her self-obsessions fully intact. Sydney yawned. 'If you don't mind, I won't come out for dinner. I've got to be up early for the interview tomorrow, and I need to go through some notes.'

She also suddenly needed to hear Dylan's voice. He told

her everything was fine; that the girls were happy and that he missed her. She fell asleep thinking about him and how Linda would just have to get used to the idea that Charlie wouldn't be at her wedding after all.

Given that only a week before Sydney had never heard any of Doors to Manual's music, the official interview with them went about as well as could have been expected. Which was to say terribly. At least the tape recorder, from which Sydney hardly dared drag her eyes, seemed to be functioning properly this time, which was more than could be said for the band's responses to her questions. After two hours of the most brain-numbing anorak talk about the relative merits of Yamaha pianos versus Bechsteins Sydney regretted ever raising a single musical query. It had only been to get them warmed up. And she definitely regretted taking the time to listen to their entire output on the plane when she'd really wanted to watch *Cold Mountain* for the 900th time. Fortunately they turned out to be fabulously unprolific, with only two albums – both of which had been monster sellers – to their name in almost five years.

This, Manley explained over wheatgrass juice in their record company's offices, was because they took their music very, very seriously. Sydney glanced at her watch furtively. Harriet would be going into her assessment any minute. Manley rambled off on a long, complex discourse about the band's famous use of swooping chords and his personal love of A minor in the ascendant.

'It's true,' said Apollo, the band's drummer, wandering over with a wholemeal muffin. 'He loves that sodding note more than any chick.'

As the minutes ticked past, paranoia and the jet-lag combined to make Sydney very jittery. At this rate she'd never get any of the dirt Virginia wanted. Apollo wandered off with the rest of the band in search of more wheatgrass. Sydney racked her brains for a bon mot that would resuscitate the interview.

'Tell me about your name,' she began unpromisingly. 'Is it after the poet – Gerard Manley Hopkins?'

Manley unleashed one of his rare, famously languid smiles, and for the first time Sydney began to see what had attracted Poppy – and millions of other girls – to him.

'Man, how d'you know that?' He shook his head incredulously. 'No one ever gets that. No one's ever heard of him. Specially here.'

'My first real boyfriend used to read me poetry. In bed,' she said, feeling underhand. Dylan had never read her Gerard Manley Hopkins, dismissing his poems as second-rate. 'It's a beautiful name,' she added guiltily.

'It's a fucking albatross of a name,' said Manley, his astonishingly soft, lilting voice coming perilously close to animation. 'Specially when you're gay.'

Sydney's ears pricked up.

'Which I'm not, by the way,' added Manley. 'But what if I had been? My parents didn't even take that on board.'

'Try being named after a city founded by convicts.'

He smiled again and his face lit up like a star. 'My first girlfriend said she'd only go out with me if I changed my name to Douglas and grew a foreskin.'

'It's hard to trust people when you've been so badly hurt,' she said, feeling increasingly underhand. Poppy and Manley's affair had never leaked out to the public, and here she was about to use insider information from Poppy to prise open this very private man.

His lovely grey eyes flashed wide open. 'What do you mean?'

'It's just that you look like someone who's very trusting. Who when he gives his heart to someone, gives it completely.' She was just making it up as she went along now. Poppy had said he was overbearingly possessive and incapable of expressing his true feelings. 'Sometimes that can get misconstrued as possessiveness. And if you're not used to communicating your emotions that can lead to all sorts of misunderstandings.'

For a moment she thought she'd overstepped the mark. A cloud passed over Manley's angelic features, and remembering what Poppy had said about his deep, seething anger, she thought he was going to thump her. He put his head into his hands for a moment and then he stared into her eyes for at least a minute. 'Oh my God,' he said eventually. 'How did you know? I haven't told anyone.'

'I sense the pain in you,' lied Sydney. She was so tired she sensed almost nothing apart from pins and needles in her foot.

For someone who wrote endless dirges about love, hate and passion, Manley was appallingly bad at communicating his emotions, but over the next few hours the floodgates opened and he told Sydney everything. How he'd been packed off to boarding school at eight. How he'd learned to close himself off. How meeting Poppy had changed his life and how they'd ended up having a ridiculous row after he'd asked her to come with him to a kabbalah class and she'd accused him of trying to control her life and brainwash her, when all he'd wanted was a bit of company. How he'd dedicated his recent songs to her and – this shyly – he really thought the new album might contain some of his best compositions. And if Poppy would only give him a second chance, he'd chuck it all in to devote his life to making her happy.

347

At five Linda called to find out where Sydney was. 'Don't forget we've got the *Quantum Leap* party tonight. You won't let me down? Clayton's twin sister, Millicent, is hosting it. I'm dying to introduce you.'

'That could be a bit tricky,' whispered Sydney. 'I can't get away.'

'You're not missing my party again,' said Linda. 'Bring them with you. Millicent loves an eclectic mix.'

At 5.30 Sydney rang Dylan. 'We've just got back,' he said. She heard gales of laughter in the background and a groan from Dylan. 'That was Molly,' he said, sounding winded. 'She's taken to using my left shoulder as a launch-pad for the trampoline. Honestly, Syd, it went brilliantly this morning. Harriet's a star. They're thrilled with her progress.' A loud guitar wail shattered the air. 'Where are you by the way?'

'In a recording studio. The band insisted on playing me some samples from their next album.'

'Wow. Well done you. What a coup. That third album's been in mysterious limbo for ages. God, two stars in one family.' He chuckled goodnaturedly. Sydney realized with a start that he'd been there for both her big career breaks so far.

'Man, he's really opened up to you,' marvelled Apollo. 'I haven't seen him this forthcoming in twenty-seven years. How you gonna edit all that stuff into one article?'

Sydney smiled weakly. That was exactly what was starting to worry her. Manley had told her some deeply personal secrets that she could just imagine Virginia spattering all over the front cover like road kill. Somehow she was going to have to write an article that would please her boss without betraying him.

*　　*　　*

'Welcome to journalism, baby,' said Linda when Sydney explained her dilemma later. She gazed lovingly at the theatrical crowd pressing against the bookcases of Millicent's apartment, which was almost an exact replica of her brother's, but on the opposite side of the park. According to Linda, Millicent was almost identical to her brother too – which meant that he must be very portly, incredibly camp and exhausting.

Linda drifted off to collar Salman Rushdie for a piece for *Quantum Leap*. Seeing Sydney unoccupied, Manley slipped away from a crowd of middle-aged admirers and joined her.

'I hope you and your friends really didn't mind us crashing.' He smiled timidly. 'We so rarely get to meet real people these days.' He scooped two more orange juices off a passing tray. 'Do you really think Poppy would give me another chance?'

Sydney looked at him wistfully. 'I'm sure she will. She's taken up kabbalah, you know . . .' She shivered despite the warmth and reached behind the sofa for her shawl.

Millicent swirled up in front of her in a mist of beaded and feathered caftan. 'You darling, glamorous things. It's so fabulous to have someone under eighty here for a change,' she stage-whispered. She reached up and grasped a hunk of Manley's cheek. 'You twenty-something males are just so . . . smooth. By the way, I have someone I'd really like you to meet, Manley. She teaches poetry at Brown and she's just written her first play, which is how Clayton knows her. She also happens to be about your age, Manley, though God knows you never can quite tell these days.' She looked about her capacious caftan as if she were searching for a small dog. 'Oh, there you are, you gorgeous little thing. Manley, meet the auspiciously named Caroline Lamb.'

Manley held out his hand shyly. A tiny girl with a pale

349

urchin cut and eyes fixed firmly on Manley's stepped forward just as Sydney turned round and did a double take.

'Eloise!' she exclaimed.

'You two know each other?' asked Millicent incredulously after what seemed hours.

'No,' said Eloise firmly. She gave a brittle little laugh, showing her small, sharp teeth. She had dyed her hair red and changed its style and was wearing an inexpensive-looking cheong sam – the kind that can be picked up in any Chinatown – but Sydney would have recognized those pointy little incisors anywhere. She shook hands firmly with Manley and turned her clear green eyes to meet Sydney's puzzled gaze. 'No,' she smiled politely, raking her up and down. 'We've definitely never met. You must have taken me for someone else. Don't worry,' she smiled graciously, 'it happens all the time. I guess I just have one of those faces.'

18

It was the brazen coolness with which Eloise had reacted to being caught in a clear case of identity theft that unsettled Sydney most. She brooded about the chance encounter – she was certain it *was* her – all the way on the flight back to London. Somehow she couldn't help feeling it reflected badly on Dylan. How had he ever got caught up with someone like Eloise, let alone married her? She wished she'd had a chance to confront Eloise properly. But having point-blank denied meeting Sydney before, and gone on to say that she'd only ever been to London once when she was a teenager, and how much she'd love to visit again one day when she could afford it, Eloise had made it clear the subject was closed. Sydney couldn't contradict her without making a scene in front of Millicent and Manley, and when she looked for Eloise later she had melted into the crowd, always slightly beyond Sydney's reach, until an hour or so later she had evaporated altogether, like a wraith.

Virginia was desperate to get her hands on the Doors to Manual piece the minute it was finished. Sydney was desperate in case it turned out there was nothing worth writing up on the tapes. There was plenty, of course, which made her even more desperate in case she messed it all up trying to write it down. There was no Dave to help her out this time. Virginia had got him working on the captions for a spread of pictures by a legume artist who specialized in celebrity portraits made from vegetables, and keeping things concise yet vacuous was testing all his ingenuity. And there wasn't time to do anything – not even to phone Poppy and tell her how much Manley loved her, and play her the tapes; or phone Jason to try to gauge whether he'd like to see her again; or phone Dylan and get to the bottom of whatever he knew about his ex-wife. To stop anyone distracting her she unplugged her phone.

At seven o'clock she emailed the finished article to Virginia who'd been screaming for it since four. Then she listened to her messages. There was one from Poppy telling her that Alvaro had proposed, and since her mother was very keen and Poppy was looking for an excuse not to do any more make-overs on size eighteens, she was thinking of accepting. There was one from Dylan asking her what was going on. And there was one from Jason apologizing for not being in touch and telling her he was thinking of moving to London.

To her eternal shame this last bit of information filled Sydney with mixed emotions, as everything to do with her son seemed to. She rewound the message. 'Yeah,' continued Jason lugubriously. She also thought she could hear him revving his bike. 'Things are a bit quiet up here? And what with the whole situation between my girlfriend Kelly and her new boyfriend Karl, it might be a good idea to get away.'

She rang him back immediately, careful not to quiz him over his previous silence, about which he seemed happy to fill her in on only very sketchily.

'What do your mum and dad think about you moving to London?' She wondered if he expected to live with her.

'My adopted mum and dad you mean? They're wun hundred and ten per cent behind it,' he said. She heard his engine spit. 'Sort of. More to the point, what does my birth-mother think?'

Sydney swallowed. 'It's terrific. You'll stay with us of course. At least to begin with.'

'No need for that. Don't want to outstay me welcome, Sydnoy. Specially not with me new sisters.'

'Is your bike all right?' she said, feeling warmly disposed towards the Fates again.

'Fine.' She heard a small explosion. 'It's just a bit tempera-mental, that's all. It loikes to give me a bit of gyp now and then. Loike women.'

'So when will you be arriving?'

'I thought I'd come down and spend a day doing a recce for bedsits sometime this week.'

'That soon?' It didn't give her long to prepare the girls. She heard his engine backfiring. 'You must come and see us the minute you get here. You could stay until you find some-where more permanent. That's if you'd like to.' She must be mad.

'I was hoping you'd say that. You must be telepathic.' He chuckled. 'Or me mum. How about tomorrow night? I could pop by for some tea.'

The last time Sydney had felt this nervous about a dinner was when Charlie had invited Dylan and Eloise over that first time last autumn. She could barely credit how much her life had turned upside down in the intervening months. Back then all she'd had to worry about was whether a meal might qualify as dinner or supper. No wonder Dave had thought her a smug bitch.

She called Dylan to invite him round as well, on the grounds that the more of them there were, the less intense it might be. Although it might also have been for moral support. He'd been in a meeting when she'd rung so she kept it brief – no Eloise discussion. Then she rang Poppy and played her the part of Manley's interview where he'd told Sydney how much he loved her. Poppy was ecstatic and resolved to fly to his side immediately, just as soon as she knew where he was. 'And you can put that in your piece, Sydney. As a world exclusive, and to hell with Mummy.'

'What's Jason like?' asked Harriet, laying the table for the five of them.

It was hard to know where to begin. Sydney didn't want to oversell him. 'You'll see for yourself,' she said, eyeing the clock nervously. 'Shit, we haven't done your exercises, Harriet.'

They were still hurling beanbags in Harriet's bedroom when Sydney heard the ominous roar of Jason's bike outside. The three of them watched through the window as he creaked up the front steps, his face mashed inside his helmet, like one of the headless Riders of the Apocalypse. Molly, ignoring everything she'd ever been told about not answering the bell, rushed to open the door.

Jason hovered anxiously on the steps for a few moments. His leathers looked grimier than Sydney remembered. She'd forgotten how small and vulnerable he was.

'Let him in, Molly,' she said gently.

'Are you our brother?' asked Harriet in disbelief.

'You must be Harriet?' He gripped his helmet tightly. She frowned at his untidy features.

'Is that your bike?' asked Molly. 'It's not that big.'

'Big enough,' he said defensively. He flapped his gloves nervously against his chest.

'You must be starving,' said Sydney. 'Would you like to eat straight away? I know the girls are desperately in need of some glycogenic adjustment.' She shot them both a warning glance as they stared at Jason's bow legs.

'That'd be grite?' He sounded relieved. 'I thought you all ate really late in London. I'll just take me leathers off if you don't mind.'

The girls watched him peel off his top layers, then Harriet led him into the kitchen and pulled out his chair, which Sydney noticed for the first time had been strategically placed on one side of the table, along with one for Dylan, opposite their three.

'I've cooked fish and chips,' she said in an absurdly upbeat voice. Jason perked up. The girls sat down in silence on their side of the table. Sydney wondered whether she ought to move her chair. If the three of them sat in a line on one side poor Jason would feel he was facing the Inquisition. On the other hand, it might look a bit pointed to start shifting things around now. She'd just have to hope Dylan arrived soon. She dished up. 'What would everyone like to drink?'

'Elderflower cordial,' said the girls in unison.

'Ooh, do you like that stuff?' said Jason chattily. 'I used to love cola when I was your age.'

'What do you like now?' demanded Harriet.

Jason winked at Sydney. 'Don't suppose you've got any more lager?' She looked in the fridge. Damn, they'd run out.

'Not to worry,' he said cheerfully. 'I'll try some of that elderthingy stuff.'

'There isn't much left,' Harriet announced rudely.

The phone rang. It was Dylan letting Sydney know he was stuck in another meeting but would get there as soon as possible.

Molly briefly averted her eyes from the clump of gingery tufts that were arranged round a large angry spot on Jason's jawline like anemone fronds and poured him a very weak

355

glass of elderflower cordial. 'Does it hurt when you ride your bike?' she asked suddenly. 'Only your chin looks as though it's bleeding.'

Molly and Harriet sipped noisily on their drinks during the conversational lulls that blossomed into a cavernous silence. Sydney could only assume that the children had peaked too early. She knew she had. The full extent of her jet-lag seeped through her body like a sedative. Molly began softly humming 'With Thee By My Side I Shall Not Stray'.

'Molly, we don't sing at the table,' said Sydney, beginning to wish they did sing. Anything to break the quiet. She conducted a very stilted conversation with Jason through the first half of the main course, mainly about his move, Mrs Protheroe and the great divide between Dudley and London, which according to Jason boiled down to the service stations being pricier the closer you got to the metropolis. They rapidly ran out of topics and they still had the pudding to get through. What had happened, Sydney wondered. All Jason's chirpy observations and the girls' native inquisitiveness seemed to have disappeared along with the bubbles in their elderflower cordial.

Dylan's ring at the doorbell literally saved her. She flew down the hall to let him in. He hugged her and asked her how it was going. 'Like a house on fire,' she lied. He looked sceptical.

'Okay, it's more like hell now I come to think of it. I was probably mad to expect anything else,' she said despondently. 'The girls were so excited at the prospect of meeting him but now that he's here, they're being a bit uncooperative. And he's changed. He was so sweet and funny the other day. Now he's like one of those people you see in silhouette on *Crime Watch*. I expect he's very nervous, poor thing. But it's not easy. And I'm like a wet blanket.'

'It'll be fine.' He pulled her towards him and kissed her, cupping his hands over her buttocks. When she opened her eyes she saw that her children – all three of them – had lined up behind the door in the corridor.

'This is Dylan,' said Harriet sullenly to Jason. 'The bloke Mum's pretending not to be shagging.'

Molly kicked her. 'Don't be mean,' she said. 'Especially now that Daddy's got a girlfriend.'

'Look on the bright side,' said Dylan later, when Jason, Harriet and Molly had all finally been persuaded to go to bed. 'Now that the girls know about us, we don't have to bother with all that creeping around any more.'

Sydney was finding it increasingly difficult to see brightness on any side. She must have been insane to think she could ever introduce a long-lost son into her family without a hitch. The evening had been so far from fine that even Dylan had found making conversation with his son about as easy as trying to climb Kilimanjaro in plimsolls, especially when he discovered that Jason's exploring genes had so far only taken him to Calais. To be fair, Jason said he was hoping to make it to Dieppe next time. Then he'd asked Dylan for travel tips and whether or not he should call him Dad. And every time he opened his mouth it only emphasized the difference between Dylan's mellifluous tones and his adenoidal drone. She'd probably traumatized all of them for life. And how the hell had Charlie found time to get a girlfriend?

'The other bright side,' continued Dylan, pulling her closer towards him on the sofa, 'is that Jison's obviously not going to last more than five minutes in London. He's got all the sense of adventure of a carpet tile. Less if you include the loose ones.'

'Don't be such a snob,' snapped Sydney, all her frustrations and disappointment coming to the boil. She was so tired she was wilting like a daisy at night. Not that she wanted Charlie to be unhappy, but he could have had the grace to wait a few more months before shacking up with someone else.

'Come on, Syd, it's got nothing to do with snobbishness. Let's face it, we've got about as much in common – common being the operative word, I think even you would concede – with our son as Chanel Number Five has with diesel. It's probably all to the good. Clean breaks for everyone.' He kissed her ankle. 'Don't look so downcast, my little peach. We can all exchange Christmas cards and send him a nice fat cheque when he finally marries the delightful-sounding Kelly.'

'You're not serious. Surely you're not going to reject your long-lost son, simply because he talks funny and has a few spots which by the way – as I think even *you* would concede – will eventually clear up?' She struggled from his arms, and in her haste knocked her shin against his chin.

'Christ, Syd.' He sounded quite winded. He rubbed his chin ruefully. Even in her frustration Sydney couldn't help thinking that Charlie would have reacted far more grumpily to being socked in the jaw. 'All right, you win. A prezzie when he hits twenty-one wouldn't go amiss either.'

She wrenched her wrist from his grasp.

'Sydney,' he remonstrated, 'I apologize for my shallow behaviour. I'm sure everything will work itself out somehow. Just don't forget that you were the one who brought up the spots and the funny accent.'

'Drop the bloody accent business, will you?' She glared at him.

He held his arms up in a gesture of surrender. 'Okay. How was New York?'

Having spent the last forty-eight hours rehearsing how to take the next hurdle, she went at it full tilt. 'I saw Eloise. At a party. Only she had changed her hair, her clothes. Oh, and her name.' Her voice hardened. 'Have you any idea why that might be, Dylan?'

He looked, just for one moment, as if he were going to confess something. 'I told you. She's not well.'

'Who isn't?' she demanded. 'Eloise or Caroline Lamb?'

He laughed mirthlessly. 'Oh dear, is that what she's calling herself? That's my fault I'm afraid. I told her about Byron – predictably she loved the part about him screwing his sister. She always did like me to talk dirty when we were fucking—'

Sydney winced.

'That's all it was, Sydney. And equally predictably, she loved the part about Caroline Lamb dressing up as a boy.'

Sydney didn't really want to hear any more, although she had the distinct feeling he was holding something back. She felt weak for not having discovered after all these years who he really was: the airhead who'd married Eloise, or the man who was struggling to resurrect a rarefied publishing house and who held her in his arms at night and told her he'd never let her go again.

'So you're not surprised?' she asked him, unable to bury this particular bone.

He tapped his temple. 'Nothing she does surprises me. Though obviously I didn't know any of this when I married her.' He got up suddenly. 'I don't know about you but I'm beat.' He kissed the top of her hair. 'Thank you for a lovely tea. Or supper.'

*   *   *

Next morning, as she and the girls set off for school, Sydney asked, 'What does Dad's girlfriend do?' with a studied casualness that no one, not even Molly, could mistake for the real thing.

'Plays gin rummy. She's brilliant. She spent a whole afternoon teaching us,' said Harriet. 'Daddy played too. They get on very well,' she added viciously. Molly glared at her.

They found Jason sprawled on his back outside number 64 Clifton Crescent, beneath his bike. Judging from the 101 small pieces lying about him, it was playing up again.

'What's the problem?' asked Sydney.

'She's just sulking.' He peered up at them, squinting in the early morning sun. His face was covered with black grease and lit up by a smile so sweetly good-natured that Sydney felt herself fall in love with him all over again.

'Looks like me dad's had second thoughts,' said Jason, gesturing towards a sign plastered across Dylan's bedroom window. On it was simply scrawled in red ink, 'Forgive me, I am but a shallow bastard.' Sydney blushed, and then she felt a small shaft of pride. Whatever else, Jason wasn't stupid. He knew exactly what his father had thought of him.

Having had her U2 odyssey curtailed slightly earlier than originally planned, and expecting to be showered in glory – had she not, after all, slept her way round most of the roadies and made promising inroadies with the band itself – Chloë was not best pleased to find all the attention momentarily focused on Sydney's Doors to Manual piece.

'Christ, they're so middle-class and middle-brow,' she rasped, kicking the coffee machine to which she'd been dispatched by Alun. 'Sydney said in her piece that the most rock and roll thing they'd done was miss a flight to Canada once. Even their sodding manager despairs of their clean living. Well, fuck this place.' She banged the machine again and a volcanic gush of hot water spluttered out of the valve, scalding her hand.

Chloë's bleak expression made Sydney feel almost sorry for her. Her ambition was so palpable you could almost reach out and stroke it, along with the luminous Virginia-type bouclé suits she'd taken to wearing; so rampant it was almost like a deformity. Sydney had been dying to confront Chloë about those batteries for weeks but now she realized that she'd known all along that Chloë had sabotaged her interview. It didn't even matter. Virginia had loved her article on Manley, particularly after she added the exclusive about Poppy.

'It's not really fair, is it?' mumbled Annabelle, sidling up to Sydney with two cappuccinos from down the road. 'She so badly wants to do well here and Virginia's just told her she has to carry on being her secretary for a while.' She sat down and smiled. 'Which is actually a demotion. Apparently Virginia thinks Chloë lacks the necessary experience to forge ahead as a features writer just yet.'

'Maybe Virginia has a point. Chloë's very young. And painful as working as Virginia's skivvy will probably be, she'll learn a hell of a lot.'

'I don't think Chloë sees it quite in those terms,' said Annabelle. 'In her view, Virginia's jealous of her youth, rather than protective of it. Chloë said only a few weeks ago that Virginia was telling her how much she reminded her of herself when she was twenty-three.'

That would explain why Virginia had been relatively supportive of Sydney then. She was clearly no threat. 'Do you think she's talented?' she said suddenly. 'Chloë, I mean.'

'Hard to say.' Annabelle closed her eyes and exhaled three perfect smoke rings. Sydney noticed that lately she'd become very dedicated to acquiring the kind of useless skills men usually sat around cultivating in pubs. 'Her ambition is so consuming it's hard to know if there's room for anything else.'

'Only – it sounds ridiculous – but I think she gave me four sets of dud batteries for that interview.' She looked across to see if Annabelle's expression had changed to one of incredulity. But she was watching Chloë spit into the coffee she'd just made for Virginia.

'Wouldn't surprise me,' said Annabelle matter-of-factly. 'Mendacity is a fact of life for Chloë. I started making a chart of her lies weeks ago, but after a while there didn't seem any point. You know as well as I do that Chloë's a ruthless, scheming little bitch. But Virginia's a bigger, even more scheming bitch. So it's hard to know who to root for.' She shrugged. 'Dave and I reckon we'll both be out on our ears by the autumn. We've talked about setting up something together. Maybe doing some contract publishing.'

'Really?' For some reason Sydney felt slightly hurt at being excluded.

'Yes, he's got loads of ideas for music magazines.' She looked at Sydney thoughtfully. 'It's about time I salvaged my old managerial skills before it's too late.'

'So you and Dave have been doing a lot of talking about this, have you?' said Sydney slowly. Finally things began to fall into place. What a self-obsessed idiot she'd been.

'Yes, we have actually.' Annabelle reddened. 'And we need to discuss it quite intensely this weekend as it happens. In Rome. Dave's found us a really great deal on the Internet.' Her hand began to shake and a slug-sized dollop of ash fell into her cappuccino. The next words came out in a rush. 'So what I was going to say, Sydney – *kind, thoughtful* Sydney, nicest sister-in-law anyone could ever hope for, especially given that the male link between us is such an A-class shit – is that if you still love me at all, could you possibly take the twins for the weekend so that I can have the first proper, uninterrupted shag I've had in oh, about ten years, somewhere romantic with someone who can't keep their hands off me? And I promise, promise, promise to pay for anything they break.' She took a gulp of her coffee and looked up nervously to gauge her soon-to-be-ex-sister-in-law's reaction. To her huge relief, Sydney was laughing.

But not for long. Sydney was shocked, frankly, by how vexed she was at the idea of Charlie having a girlfriend. So vexed she told Linda, waiting for the inevitable dismissal which she knew would make her feel better.

Instead, she heard an unpromisingly sharp intake of breath at Linda's end. 'Are you sure?'

'Fairly,' Sydney said, sounding more casual than she felt. 'Molly and Harriet have played gin rummy with her. It might not be serious though.'

'Sydney! With Charlie it's always serious. He's hardly the type to be casually entertaining women in his flat, is he?'

Sydney knew this was true. She knew she was on shaky ground complaining. She knew she should feel happy for him. She just wished he could have had the grace to remain single and grieving for a few months at least. He owed that much to his mother.

She changed the subject. 'Any Caroline Lamb sightings?'

'Have you told Dylan about seeing her?'

Sydney watched Chloë angrily wiping something from her eyes. It looked like tears. Again. She wished she hadn't broached the Eloise subject now, because she didn't want Linda knowing how evasive Dylan was being. The sun, which had dappled the sky a deep blush-pink earlier in the morning, like a rose that had been left in the bath, now looked like a bloodied egg. She told Linda Virginia had just ordered her into the office and put the phone down.

It was true that Virginia was in a particularly rancid mood, screamingly informing them that they were all fucking morons and that in particular Chloë's piece on U2 had sent her into a coma. Then she announced that from now on they were going to be running a new feature called Me and My Pets, which she was putting Sydney in charge of.

Then when Sydney got home she had a stormy session with Harriet who was tired and refused to do her exercises. Harriet was screaming so loudly that it took about five minutes for them to hear the doorbell. Dylan was standing outside holding a magnum of champagne and an over-flowing ice bucket and wearing a rueful smile.

'I'm a shallow, snotty, snobby shit.' She followed him into the kitchen and watched while he opened the bottle and handed her a glass. 'I've decided to do something rather radical: grow up.'

Sydney let the champagne fizz on her tongue, her body tensing in anticipation of one of his big gestures. 'Isn't that a bit hasty? You might go into shock.'

'Don't be tart, Sydney. It doesn't suit you.' He reached into his inside pocket and passed her two business-class tickets to Venice and a fax from the Cipriani.

'For the weekend after next.' It was one of the most romantic moments of her life, apart from the time she'd discovered – about two years after it had been published – that Charlie had dedicated the first imprint of *Fiscal Wrinkles* to her.

'I am trying not to be tart, Dylan, but I thought you were watching the pennies – what with the divorce and so forth?'

He held up a hand. 'No, no, Sydney. Please don't thank

me. And please don't worry about the money, my little chancellor. Patrice is pumping money into Glendower Books like there's no tomorrow. Just say you'll come and show me the beauty of Venice. Or if not that, at least help me find Harry's Bar. Can you believe I've never been?'

'I'm not sure I've got time,' said Sydney, wishing she could respond to his gestures in kind. It wasn't even as if she was still properly cross with him about his attitude towards Jason. Why, when Dylan was so busy forcing life back into her existence, did she still feel numb? His face fell. She suddenly wanted to wipe away some of those worry lines that seemed to have furrowed his skin in the past few months.

'I deliberately booked next weekend rather than this one so that you've got plenty of time to sort whatever it is you need to sort out. And Maisie's got plenty of time to record her *Mellow Moments* in advance and I've got plenty of time to bond with Jason.'

Sydney looked at him tenderly. 'Really?'

'Really. I've got it all planned out. I'm going to the Midlands this weekend so he can show me some of his haunts. We'll spend some quality time together, my son and I, going to Slade concerts, pelting each other with phlegm and eating lots of Balti curries – or whatever it is Brummies do.'

'Nice to see you're taking it all seriously then. I suppose Charlie could have the girls for slightly longer than usual if Maisie won't pre-record. Of course I'll come.'

His face folded into an enormous smile. 'Really?'

'Really. And the good news is, you don't have to go to Birmingham. Jason's moving to London this Friday.'

'Don't tell me he's found somewhere to live already. You haven't offered him a permanent room, have you?'

'I'd be very happy to have Jason move in, but I think it's a bit much for the girls to take on.'

'Harriet and Mol still hopping mad then?' said Dylan sympathetically.

'I wouldn't say they were hopping mad, exactly,' Sydney replied evasively. 'Dan's offered him a room. It seems they got chatting when Jason was fixing his bike in the Crescent the other day. So you see, Jason's obviously got charm. Isn't that great, Dylan? Your son's going to be a permanent fixture in Clifton Crescent.'

That weekend, while Dylan attempted to bond with the son of whose existence he had – as Sydney kept reminding herself – been blissfully unaware until the last three months, Sydney tried to love, then like, and then at least not want to murder her nine-year-old twin nephews, Joshie and James, who made Beelzebub and Pol Pot look like the Angel Gabriel and Florence Nightingale. When they weren't waking up at 5 a.m., or punching each other or head-butting Molly and Harriet, they were setting fire to the wings of tiny butterflies and small, bilious-coloured plastic ponies, blocking the loos with mounds of old copies of Maisie's *TV Times* which until now no one had dared throw away, torturing Hamish and vandalizing as much furniture as they could before Sydney ordered everyone out of the house and marched them all round Hampstead Heath.

Alas, London's wildest outdoor space could only contain the twins for so long. It was a positive relief when Charlie came to collect the girls at midday on Saturday because it meant Sydney would no longer have to worry about them being set alight, drowned or suffocated. She jotted down a note on a Post-It reminding herself to have stern words with Annabelle when she got back about the twins' diet.

'Come on,' she said, excavating Joshie from beneath the pile of books that had crashed down on him. 'You're going to help me tidy up. And then we're going to make lunch. Together.'

By two o'clock, Sydney was ready to climb the walls, which was handy because Joshie had hurled two-thirds of Jamie's wholemeal macaroni cheese at three of the kitchen ones. In return, Jamie had taken the bag of compost hanging by the fridge door and tipped it over Joshie's organic ice-cream, at which point Sydney began to wonder whether changing their diet was really the solution. They needed Ritalin. Before she could stop him, Joshie, having eyed the pottery on Sydney's dresser and caught her warning look, had reached for Nellie's coffin, which he hurled at his brother's face. He was a good aim, Sydney had to give him that much. It hit the corner of Jamie's eye, causing a spectacular spurt of blood which very nearly made Sydney pass out, and bounced on to the stone floor so violently that the lid actually came unstuck. Inside was a large plastic sack containing an unfeasible amount of ashes, clearly labelled Tango: born May 1990, died 2004, which certainly solved the mystery of the extra-large coffin, even as it raised some vexatious questions about the reliability of their vet. But Sydney couldn't deal with that problem just now.

At 3.15 they pulled up outside Casualty. At 6.15 she called Dylan's mobile.

'Having a hard time?' It was impossible not to detect a gleeful edge to his voice.

'Eventful.' Sydney pulled Joshie away from one of the front tyres on the car which he was trying to bayonet on a syringe he must have purloined while his brother was being stitched. 'How about you?'

'Interesting. Jason's just taken me for a whirl on his bike.'

'That sounds fun.'

'We're currently stuck on the Newbury bypass.'

'Bad traffic?'

'The traffic's great. Not another vehicle in sight. It's the bloody bike that's the problem. It's broken down. Sydney, did you know that our son had smashed someone's jaw in a pub not a million miles from Clifton Crescent?'

'Don't be ridiculous,' said Sydney. 'He's hardly been in London.'

'Well, he's a fast worker. Because apparently it happened the night before he first came to see you.'

That might explain the cut on his hand, the bruise, and probably the hasty retreat the following day. Then again, he could have been telling the truth when he said he'd scraped his fist on a lorry. Either way, Sydney wasn't going to engage with Dylan when he was clearly in a bad mood.

'Where is he?' she asked.

'Under the bike. Where else?'

She asked Dylan what time he thought they'd be back and whether he'd like to stay for supper with the twins. One big happy family. Even to her ears this sounded slightly implausible.

'Love to, if you can hold off till midnight,' he said grumpily.

Sydney felt that somehow Dylan blamed her for the way his weekend was imploding, but it was hardly her fault. Anyway, thanks to the RAC truck which Dylan called out on his own account, they arrived back in Primrose Hill by 10 p.m. Sydney was dozing, having given the sedative the doctor had given her for Jamie to both boys, and taken a shot herself.

Perhaps it was the ignominy of having to travel by RAC,

but Jason was taciturn throughout supper. At 11 he excused himself and popped round to sleep at Dan's. Dylan and Sydney faced each other glumly across the table. Sydney must have looked the more dismayed because Dylan suddenly snapped out of his mood and took her hand in his. 'I'm not going to give up on Jason, whatever you think. We will make this work. All of it. You have my promise.' He kissed her tenderly and went home.

Thanks to the effects of the sedative it was 9 a.m. when Sydney woke the following day. When she went downstairs, more bliss awaited her. Jason had nipped in, fixed Tango's coffin as good as new, and was making the boys' breakfast.

'Couldn't sleep,' he said ruefully. 'Always get like that when me bike's poorly. Oive been fiddling with it since six. And I think she's okay?'

She considered probing him about the fight he'd been involved in. But a pan of milk he'd forgotten boiled over. Sydney switched it off and told herself not to mind the mess, not even the bits of macaroni still imbuing the walls with such interesting texture. After that, events overtook them.

'That bloke from the RAC must have been a roight pillock?' Jason began mopping up apologetically. 'He said it wasn't worth mending. Eat your bacon, Jamie.'

Sydney glanced warily at her nephews. They still seemed a bit groggy. Thank God, Annabelle and Dave weren't due back for hours.

Jason followed her gaze. 'I thought they could take it in turns to have a ride on the bike,' he suggested. 'They're pretty keen, aren't you, boys?'

The twins nodded meekly.

'It's quite safe. Honest, Sidnoy. I won't go very fast.'

While they were gone, Sydney cleaned up the remaining

macaroni, ashes and blood and then soaked in a hot bath and fantasized about Venice. In the circumstances – namely, Charlie's new girlfriend, although she didn't acknowledge that – she'd be a fool not to go. She breathed in the expensive Floris bath oil Dylan had given her, trying to ignore the top notes of Juanita's ammonia. After twenty minutes or so she became aware that someone had their palm clamped against her doorbell. When it became apparent they weren't going away, she dragged herself crossly downstairs.

'I'm so sorry to bother you,' sobbed Jacquie, taking in Sydney's damp towel and putting her case down in the hall anyway. She lowered herself down at the foot of the stairs like a fork-lift truck dropping a bag of cement, and waited for her panting to subside. 'I've got nowhere else to go.'

It wasn't the first time Sydney had found herself in the morally questionable position of having to defend her brother in the face of damning opprobrium from the female race. But it was the first time she felt she was doing so with some justification, because however pitiful Jacquie's situation was now – and she looked as though she'd been pregnant for at least two years; even her ankles seemed to be expecting triplets – it seemed to Sydney that her reasons for leaving Miles were flimsy, not to say downright reckless.

'Are you sure you can't live with his untidiness?' Sydney handed Jacquie a cup of the raspberry leaf tea she had brought with her. Jacquie closed her eyes and sank back in the bath she had climbed into before Sydney had pointed out there might be a slight risk of toxicity from ammonia fumes. At least she seemed to be calming down.

'That's what my mum said.' It seemed mean to ask why Jacquie couldn't have gone to her mother's. Anyway, Jacquie didn't give her the chance. 'It's not just the untidiness. It's the whole bloody idle package. If I'd known he was going to be this useless I'd have stayed with my last husband.'

'You've been married before?'

'Only for a few weeks. We got legless in Las Vegas. It was years ago.' She began to weep again.

Between them they eventually managed to haul her out of the bath, but then she started to complain of pains and ordered Sydney to run her another one.

'You don't think the baby's coming?' asked Sydney in alarm.

'I don't know,' said Jacquie, a mite imperiously, Sydney thought, in the circumstances. 'But Sage – that's my midwife – says that hot water's the best thing for pain.' She began panting again. Her breasts lolled in the water like two giant plucked turkeys.

'Shouldn't we call Sage?'

'She's staying in a yurt in Glastonbury this weekend, at a Festival of Human Fertility. She's saying a special chant for me.'

'That should help,' said Sydney before she could stop herself. 'Mobile?' she asked remorsefully.

'She doesn't believe in them.'

That figured. Jacquie clutched the vast balloon beneath the two turkeys and let out a shriek. Sydney felt herself developing an intense dislike of Sage, but she was desperate to keep calm.

'Sage says her mum predicts the baby's not due for another fortnight. And she's never wr—' Jacquie screamed again.

'Let's start timing the pains,' said Sydney, not sounding calm at all, but at least she didn't sound hysterical either. 'If they become regular, I'll just run you to the hospital. Which one are you booked into?'

'I'm not.' Jacquie's eyes began to assume a wild, savage look. 'I'm having a home birth.' That also figured, thought Sydney. Jacquie's eyes began to fill with tears. 'I've left all my birthing notes at home,' she whimpered. 'I had it all mapped out. It's all written in the notes.'

'Don't worry,' gabbled Sydney. 'It can't be the baby. It's probably just wind.'

Jacquie seemed to buy this and announced that she would try some self-hypnosis. 'Sage taught me. It more or less guarantees a pain-free birth.' After about twenty minutes of chanting, to their amazement the contractions seemed to ebb away – enough for Jacquie to query the facilities. 'I don't like to say anything, Syd, but this water definitely smells a bit funny. It's not chalk, is it? Only my skin's very sensitive.'

Jason kept the twins occupied so well that when they returned a couple of hours later they were smiling. Better still, they were worn out. As was Jacquie, which wasn't such good news as her wind seemed to have all the qualities of contractions, which were now coming at ten-minute intervals. Jacquie, however, was adamant she wasn't going to any hospital, even though she'd drained most of the hot water in the tank. She climbed into her third bath and lay eerily still, like an iceberg, droning away about Sage's boundless wisdom, her belief that all children should be breast-fed for four years, and her ability to sleep under canvas all year round.

'Cup of tea?' Jason poked his head round the bathroom door and backed out hastily.

'Who are you?' yelled Jacquie, attempting to cover her gargantuan breasts with a flannel, which was about as effective as trying to shroud Chile with a tea-towel.

'Who are *you*?' squeaked Jason.

'Jacquie, this is my son, Jason. Jason, this is my sister-in-law-to-be, Jacquie.'

Jacquie's eyes dilated to ten centimetres.

'Pleased to meet you,' said Jason, looking away shyly.

'I'm not in labour,' said Jacquie hastily. Jason scampered off to make some tea. 'Did you say son?' she squealed when he'd gone.

'I'll tell you about it some other time,' said Sydney. Luckily for her, Jacquie was so absorbed with the evolution of her wind patterns that she didn't bother to probe any more. 'Lovely little body he's got,' was all she said. 'Have you seen those biceps?'

'Actually this labour lark, if that's what it is, and I'm sure it isn't, but if it is, it's not that bad,' Jacquie remarked later, when the water for bath number four had heated up again. 'But then Sage said I'd probably have an easier time with it than most, what with all the Massoga. She thinks that when it does start, it'll be over in no time.'

Another contraction juddered through her body and her face twisted into an angry-looking S. 'Sydney, I think there might be a manual in my bag,' she croaked when the worst of the pain had passed. 'Sage wrote it. It tells you how to cut the umbilical cord with nail scissors.' She closed her eyes again. 'I'm going to have to take my lenses out . . .' She drifted off momentarily. And then a thought struck her. 'It won't hurt, will it?' she asked suddenly. 'Sage says if you handle it right it's like doing a big fart.'

Sydney tore downstairs, Jacquie's exhortation for her not to call that fat shit Miles ringing in her ears, and telephoned the nearest hospital. The voice on the other end was very efficient – when it came to putting her on hold for fifteen minutes, during which time she heard gales of laughter coming from the garden, where she saw Jason had tied himself to a tree and was allowing the mini-me dictators to throw plastic arrows at him. While she was waiting, she heard Celine Dion vibrating from one of Jacquie's bags. Her mobile phone. Sydney prayed it was Miles.

It was Sage, calling to see if Jacquie wanted her to bring back a Hopi Ear Candle. 'They're thirty-five quid but they blow your mind.'

'This isn't Jacquie, Sage. It's Sydney, her sister-in-law. Jacquie is upstairs in my bathroom, very probably about to blow her pelvic floor. She looks as though she's about to give birth to a rhinoceros, and thanks to you she's got about as much clue what to do about it as a fucking hamster. So may I suggest you get yourself and your yurt over to my house ASAP.'

'Is she doing her moaning?'

'Of course she's doing her fucking moaning. She's in labour.'

'I mean her primitive moaning. It relieves stress. And I'm sure she's not really in labour, Sydney. She's probably just a bit het up.' Sage's tone was becoming slightly defensive, which Sydney took to be a sign that she really didn't have a clue what she was talking about.

'Of course she's het up—'

'– well she can't be in labour, if that's what you're insinuating. She's not due for—'

'– two weeks. Yes, I know, Sage. Because Jacquie told me that your mum's magic rabbit foot told you her baby wasn't coming for two weeks. Just as you told her that giving birth was like farting. And just as I'm telling you that she's in labour and that unlike you I have zero confidence in being able to cut the umbilical cord with a pair of sodding nail scissors.'

'I understand your aggression, Sydney,' said Sage, very calmly and very loudly, 'but I think you'll find that some nettle tea will calm things down considerably.'

Sydney wasn't fully in control of what she said next but her voice must have been even louder than Sage's because when she turned round Jason, Beelzebub and Pol Pot were all staring at her open-mouthed. Even Sage seemed to be getting the message.

'The thing is, Sydney, I'm a bit stranded down here, 'cos the dormer van's broken down.'

Sydney wanted to weep. Jason took the phone from her and began speaking quietly and softly. When he'd finished, he handed it back to Sydney and began to pull on his leathers.

'Where are you going?' asked Sydney, feeling more alone than ever. She didn't think she could cope with a labour and the twins together.

'Glastonbury,' he said with as much authority as a permanently interrogative speech pattern allowed. 'I'll be there and back in three hours? Mother Earth on the phone here will talk you through the next bit and Jamie and Joshie,' he wagged a finger at both of them, 'you do everything your Aunty Sidnoy tells you, or I'll tie you to the tree when I get back and set fire to the pair of you, okay?' He smiled sweetly at them before putting on his helmet and creaking towards the door.

Sage arrived, somewhat windswept and terrified, three and a half hours later, by which time Sydney's bedroom had filled out with the twins, who gawped at the whole spectacle with terrified fascination, and Dylan, who had dropped round innocently enough to make peace with Jason and had been roped in on refreshments and was plying them all with champagne and reading Jacquie poetry, which she said calmed her on account of him having such a nice voice.

Sage stomped into the room with ripped tights, tangled hair and a bursting bladder, which she grumbled about vociferously. 'If I turn out to develop cancer of the urinary tract I'll hold you personally responsible,' she snarled at Jason. 'And don't be surprised if I throw up.'

She emerged from Sydney's beleaguered bathroom just in time to do the honours with the nail scissors. She had been wrong about everything, apart from the speed with which Jacquie finally delivered her brand-new daughter – a turn of events not entirely lost on Jacquie. She had told Sage that she would name her baby Sage, if it turned out to be a girl. After due consideration over the fart issue however, she felt she couldn't allow Sage to get off without some demonstration of the way she felt she'd been let down.

'Can I get you anything else to drink?' asked Dylan.

'Thanks, Dylan, don't mind if I do.' Jacquie scooped Sydney's unfinished champagne off the bedside table, slugged the entire glass and held it out for a refill.

'I think we may be about to run out of champagne, but I could always nip out for some more.'

Sydney began to cry as Jacquie handed over her tiny daughter to hold while she groped her way to the loo. The baby looked up at her with depthless, knowing eyes. When she finally dragged her eyes from her niece, she saw Jason gazing wistfully at her from the other side of the room.

'To the hero of the hour.' Jacquie returned and raised her empty glass weepily towards Jason. 'And the namesake of my little girl.' She gazed down at her new daughter and began to cry. 'I'd like to introduce you all to Jaysee.' She peered blearily into the corner shadows – without her contact lenses she could barely see past the end of her knees

– to where Beelzebub and Pol Pot were scribbling on the skirting board. 'Joshie and Jamie, is that you? Come and meet your little sister . . . Sydney, you couldn't do me a favour and ring your tosser of a brother?'

With high drama unfolding in front of their eyes, and the volume of Jacquie's primitive moans so loud, none of them had heard Charlie and the girls at the door. Sydney was so overcome with emotion and the bittersweet memories of her own children's arrival in the world that it didn't occur to her until much later that Charlie had for once used his key to let them all in. At first she didn't even notice them when they stood in the gathering gloaming of the bedroom. A look of confusion clouded Molly's face. Harriet understood what was going on faster and rushed over to hold her tiny cousin. Charlie swept his eyes round the room, taking in the euphoric camaraderie that had settled on them all in the aftermath of Jaysee's arrival.

'I'm terribly sorry for interrupting like this,' he mumbled. He had gone scarlet. 'Jacquie, many, many congratulations.' He backed out, knocking into a chair on the landing. Sydney followed him. He looked terribly alone and excluded. But in the end she couldn't find anything to say other than goodbye.

19

Annabelle and Dave's arrival at Clifton Crescent five hours later might have been expected to put a dampener on the happy occasion but they were so blissed out after their forty-eight-hour brush with *la dolce vita* that nothing could pierce their euphoria. Fifty-two if you counted the delay at the check-in when the woman behind the counter mis-interpreted Dave's Smash the Class System T-shirt and called Security. Not even seeing Miles cooing over his brand-new daughter – whose gestation no one had actually got round to telling her about – could drag Annabelle down. Sydney hoped she had had a truly gorgeous time with Dave and wasn't simply floating on a cloud of duty-free fags.

At least the signs seemed outwardly good. Even when Beelzebub and Pol Pot trampled over her new straw basket in a bid to get to the toy Ferraris she'd brought them back and sent a bumper pack of condoms scattering over the floor, Annabelle smiled at them indulgently. Then she turned to Dave and beamed at him so adoringly that his frozen look of terror melted. Sydney watched the four of them waft off into the night – Dave didn't approve of car ownership, so they'd telephoned one of the cheap and not very cheerful local cab firms that was staffed mainly by underpaid, overworked Hungarians and Poles – and felt that perhaps love really did make the world go round.

Even Virginia repeatedly telling them they were all

fucking morons on Monday morning and that if they didn't pull their fingers out and fast, she'd fire the lot of them by lunchtime didn't dent Dave and Annabelle's happiness. Or Sydney's. She could barely wait for Venice, now that she'd finally agreed to go. She got butterflies just thinking about two whole days on her own with Dylan.

'Not that you'll actually be taking a lunch break,' Virginia intruded on her reverie. 'I want some decent features ideas out of you lot today.'

'You had one.' Chloë placed a latte and six slices of bacon in front of Virginia, who'd gone back on the Atkins Diet. Her eyes were looking very red again. 'The U2 piece.'

'The boring bog-dwellers, you mean.'

'Cultural icons,' said Chloë bravely. Sydney looked at her in astonishment. She'd gone from her abject misery of a few days ago to a new, flinty insolence.

'Would those be the cultural icons you shagged, or the ones you didn't manage to shag?'

The others listened in mesmerized awe as the two gladiatorial witches slugged it out.

'The thing is, Chloë,' Virginia continued, 'you promised lots of gossip and sex with this U2 odyssey and you returned with three thousand dreary words about their musical credibility. I can only assume that's because zero shagging actually went on.'

The implication – made public – that anyone would turn her sexual advances down made Chloë even more reckless. 'Sorry. Next time I'll choose my subject with a view to their promiscuity.'

'They'll have to be rent boys for you to have a chance. Anyway, next time I'll do the choosing,' said Virginia crisply. 'If you'd bothered to tell me that Bono was such a boring old goodie-goodie I'd never have sanctioned the piece. Sup with the Devil, I say, and you end up covered in his puke – with a cracking story to tell. Sup with the Happy Clappers and you end up bored to tears.'

Chloë changed her tack. 'I'm sure I could add a bit more colour,' she pleaded. Clearly the thought of the whole article being spiked – and her reputation with U2 along with it – was too much to bear.

'Wake me up when she's finished,' Virginia yawned. 'Chloë, read my lips. The days when this magazine was interested in a dronathon on a bunch of middle-aged Paddys are long gone. I mean, while it's conceivably possible that a great writer could have made something out of it, frankly, Chloë, you're no Julie Burchill, are you? Now, Sydney, I want you to become our celebrity interview fixer. That means dealing with agents in LA which means lots of overtime. Speak to Accounts, will you, and sort out the pay.'

Sydney was determined not to look horrified in front of Virginia, even though fixing, as she knew from years ago, was one of the most painstaking, demanding, ultimately frustrating jobs in journalism, involving endless sycophantic phone calls with sadistic agents and their crazy, egotistical clients late at night when LA was just waking up. Chloë's dark-ringed eyes flashed at her with unrequited hatred. The others lowered their gazes in the hope that the ensuing carnage could be avoided. It couldn't.

'I could rewrite it.' Chloë's fists were clenched but there was no disguising the plaintive break in her voice. She stared round wildly as everyone tried to avoid her bloodshot eyes. 'Dave could help me.'

'Dave's going to be very busy today. A reader's just sent in a picture of a tomato that looks like Norman Lamont. I want a spread on other lookalike veg, please.'

'I suppose we'll call it Lookaleeks,' said Dave with a mild stab at indignation. It was obvious he no longer cared about the magazine.

Virginia snorted appreciatively and told Chloë to go and get her a steak baguette without the bread.

Partly to take her mind off her bleak new future as a fixer, Sydney did what she had been meaning to do for days, and called Charlie. After being put on hold and listening to Vivaldi's *Four Seasons* for several minutes and expecting to be fobbed off with his secretary, Sydney was shocked to hear his voice on the line. He sounded coolly businesslike, but not actively angry. She told him as briefly and un-emotionally as she could that she wanted to go away for a long weekend and asked if he'd have the girls on Sunday night as well.

'This is for your trip to Venice with Dylan? Harriet and Molly mentioned it last week.' She thought he sounded resigned, but perhaps it was indifference. Then he wished her a lovely trip. That was the part that she didn't like. Not that she wanted him to be bitter or resentful. But he could at least have sounded a bit hacked off.

'Frankly I'm surprised you waited this long to go menopausal,' said Linda. 'Ever since you married Charlie you've lived life at least twenty years ahead of yourself. The thing about picking up a younger man though, Sydney, is that they have a habit of making the woman look older. Still, go to Venice if you must. I'm sure the sex will be great.'

'For your information, Dylan is not younger.' Sydney was irritated with herself for telling Linda about Venice in the first place, but she'd been having last-minute doubts. Not that Linda had anything pertinent to say. She was just miffed that Sydney wouldn't be in London at the weekend to watch the BBC 4 documentary about Clayton's set designs for the New York Met.

'Well, he seems younger. And that's not necessarily bad . . . the thing is, Sydney, I can see now that Charlie was a bit serious. It's a generational thing. Adorable and brilliant as he was in many ways, it's obvious he didn't provide you with everything you needed. You'll probably both be happier in the long run.'

'He's not dead,' snapped Sydney. 'You don't need to speak of him in the past tense.'

'He might as well be dead once you're divorced,' said Linda. 'Don't forget to have a Bellini for me while you're in Venice.'

Sydney had finally plucked up courage to tell Virginia she'd be leaving the office after lunch on Friday when Virginia called her over and announced she needed Sydney to go to Pinewood to write a piece on the new James Bond that had until now been embargoed. She wouldn't take no for an answer, even when Sydney had told her about the Cipriani. Instead she offered to pay for her to go another weekend if they couldn't get a refund.

Dylan took the postponement of their romantic escape remarkably well, all things considered. She had dreaded telling him, but he'd hugged her and said that as far as he was concerned, if Virginia was willing to foot the bill for three nights in the Cipriani, it was fine by him.

'We'll enjoy it all the more for having to wait that bit longer.' He squeezed her shoulder and wriggled his fingers inside her jumper. 'And it gives me more time to bond with our adorable son.' He winked at her. 'Actually he seems to be settling in with Dan very nicely. And he may have found himself a job already. Impressed how much I know?' He wriggled his fingers a bit more and pressed Sydney's left nipple. Then he told her how proud he was of her.

She could just imagine Charlie's reaction in the same circumstances. Linda was right. Dylan was utterly irrepressible and Tiggerish. Which was just what she needed at the moment.

A second set of circulation figures came in for the revamped magazine, showing a marked improvement on the first batch, although some of the advertisers who'd moaned endlessly about *IQ*'s minuscule readership were now complaining that the new readers attracted to *VIP* were too down-market for their products. For the first time after one of her meetings with Brian Widlake, Virginia returned to her office looking chastened.

'Bunch of fuckwits. They want me to produce a load of populist crap, and then they complain that the readers are morons. Still, what do you expect from a bunch of turnip head Bloody Swedes? Chloë, come into my office. I want to dictate a letter to Widlake.'

'I see Virginia's on one of her One Nation drives again.' Dave sauntered over, smiling. He always seemed to be smiling these days. From snatches coming from Virginia's office, her letter to Widlake was her most racist, offensive outburst yet. Not that Dave seemed to care. He patted Annabelle's bottom fondly, which for some reason Sydney found disconcerting. He looked at the flotsam on her desk and Sydney grimaced. She'd been going through her household accounts for the umpteenth time and had regretfully concluded that she couldn't expect Charlie to keep on paying for all their expenses indefinitely. Especially when he was running his own flat and might eventually have other expenses to pay. He'd bankrupt himself. As his personal accountant, she would have to advise him to rein things in a bit. As his soon-to-be-ex-wife however, she might just postpone that conversation for a while.

It was 8 p.m. when she left the office. Dylan called to say he was at home, having taken over from a none-too-sympathetic Maisie who was not proving very cooperative when it came to overtime.

'Don't worry,' he said cheerily. 'The girls have done their homework. Molly sat on the side of the bath and almost got in, which is progress, and there's Alaskan Hotpot in the oven. All we need is a nice bottle of Merlot and we're set. And some garlic. And salt. Salad, cheese, bread and some eggs. Bacon. And pizzas . . . but only if you can carry them. The children might have to eat cardboard for breakfast. The fridge is looking a bit bare. Still, it wouldn't harm them. I guess no one's had time to do a shop lately. I could go tomorrow if you like.'

Dylan might not be conventionally perfect, Sydney thought as she whizzed round the aisles of the local Tesco Metro stocking up on essentials, but he made her laugh and he made her feel young and impulsive.

She took her basket to the check-out and fantasized about Venice while the only girl on duty worked her way through a trolley-load of shopping with petulant slowness. A fluorescent light flickered with dismal cheeriness overhead while Britney Spears blared through the tannoy. Sydney watched the check-out girl's diamond-encrusted nail extensions tap the prices slowly into the till, barely registering the rhythmic sighs of resignation of the woman in front, until an argument broke out between them over the price of the two-for-one bacon packs and interrupted her reverie on the Grand Canal.

'Oh, it's you, Miranda,' said Sydney.

Miranda's tired, pinched face registered a passing semblance of surprise, but it was obvious that she had been aware that Sydney had been standing behind her for some time.

'We meet in all the best places, Sydney,' she said, trying to make light of the row she'd just been having. 'Surely you're not on your way back from work at this time?'

Sydney smiled neutrally. She hadn't seen Miranda or Ian socially since she and Charlie had split up. Fortunately their relentless hospitality didn't seem to extend to singles and the newly separated. ''Fraid so. I didn't expect to find you out shopping at this time of night though.' Along with all the loners, workaholics and the generally disorganized of whom Miranda so disapproved. Or was it that she feared them? She watched Miranda's hand tremble slightly as she loaded her shopping into plastic bags. She was wearing a black polo-neck jumper that leached whatever colour there had been from her face and looked uncomfortably hot for the time of year. The faint yellow blush of a bruise seeped from beneath her left sleeve.

'Are you all right, Miranda?' Sydney asked gently.

'I'm fine. I had a bit of a migraine earlier, that's all. So I couldn't do the shopping. I thought I'd pop out now, while the boys are watching TV and Ian's out at one of his work dos. How are the girls bearing up? It can't be easy,' Miranda continued, handing her card over impatiently. She clearly couldn't get out of the shop fast enough. 'It's never painless when both your parents find new partners.'

Sydney dropped her keys. 'You've met Charlie's girlfriend then?' she asked casually.

'Not met, *per se*.' Miranda tapped her foot while the check-out girl fed the card into the machine again. 'But I have seen them out for lunch a couple of times when I've been on my way to chambers to meet Ian.'

Lunch. He'd never had time to see Sydney. Let alone eat with her.

'It's not working,' the girl behind the counter informed Miranda with an air of satisfied revenge.

'It must work,' said Miranda, growing flustered. 'There's absolutely no reason why . . .' The girl picked at her nail varnish. She'd heard it all before. 'Oh, never mind, I'll write a cheque. Bye then, Sydney.' She caught Sydney eyeing the discoloration on her wrist. 'I hope you'll be okay.'

Sydney didn't discuss the Miranda conversation with anyone, although she tried to squeeze some more information out of Molly. But all Molly could tell her was that she had a pashmina that was pink and sparkly.

'She must be quite old then,' said Harriet, eavesdropping. 'Aren't pashminas very last century?' Then she slammed the door and stomped upstairs. Molly sidled up to Sydney and hugged her. 'Don't worry,' she said sadly. 'She'll get over it.'

Sometimes Sydney wondered whether that was true. Harriet's work, which had been showing slight but sure signs of improvement, had taken a dive again, along with her behaviour. Sydney prevaricated over Venice for another three weeks. Then she told Dylan she couldn't go after all.

'Look, Syd,' Dylan said gently, 'I know you're feeling guilty, sad, elated, shocked and vindicated by everything that's happened in the past few months—'

She started to speak – she wanted to tell him that the whole problem was that she didn't really feel any of those things – but he held up a hand to silence her.

386

'I know because those are exactly all the emotions I felt when I met you again so soon after marrying Eloise. Believe me, Syd, I didn't want that marriage to fall apart. I know what you're going through. Especially the guilt part. But denying yourself any little chance of happiness won't make things any better for Harriet. And don't you think it would do everyone good if the girls spent a bit more time with Charlie?'

It really worried Sydney that she didn't feel nearly as sad or shocked by the breakdown of her marriage as she felt she ought to. But she realised she'd be a fool to turn this offer down. Venice! She was going back to Venice after all these years.

And what a breathtaking, heavenly city it was. Even if the canals, let alone the cobbled streets, were heaving with tourists – it was July – every cranny, every grand vista seemed to have been conceived with the express intention of ravishing everyone who looked at it.

'It's like a Canaletto brought to life,' said Dylan as they dined the first evening on a restaurant terrace overlooking the Rialto and its floodlit palaces. 'I don't think I've ever been anywhere quite so seductive before. It's such a paen to intrigue and luxury it's almost like being mugged by the world's most beautiful whore.'

Sydney felt the warm, febrile air brush against her skin like cashmere and listened to the hypnotic splash of the gondolas and the corny serenades of the gondoliers. Canary Wharf seemed a million miles from the bower of branches and tangled lemons hanging overhead. Dylan had been incredibly appreciative of everything Sydney had shown him so far, from the *jolie laide* austerity of the Doge's Palace to the undulating mosaics in the Basilica di San Marco, part of the most opulent interior either of them had ever seen, with every shift of the sun revealing previously hidden decoration and nooks.

'Look how beautiful and sad that is,' he whispered, as he and Sydney stood in front of Titian's exquisite *Presentation of the Virgin*. 'He painted that shortly after his wife died. In an age when marriage was more a matter of convenience and low expectations, I find that terribly moving.'

Later, in their hotel room, as the moon flooded through the open shutters, Sydney wrapped herself round him, surprised by the intensity of their passion. Dylan gazed rapturously at her smooth white skin, glowing in the milky night. 'You're like a Titian brought to life,' he murmured as he stroked her thighs, and she felt an electrical current crackle through her. 'I can't believe I ever let you go. I should have come after you and abducted you.'

'Did I really hurt you when I returned all your letters?' Sydney asked the following evening as they bobbed along the Grand Canal. Dylan's idea. He said when on Planet Tourist do as the tourists do. It cost a fortune – everything in Venice did, and a double fortune if it was actually any good – but Dylan had been throwing his cash around ever since they'd arrived. Sydney thought it must be because he felt slightly embarrassed that Icon Publishing were footing the bill for the flights, which they hadn't been able to change. She gazed woozily at the imposing buildings flanking the banks, listening to the whispers coming from the half-hidden figures lurking beneath the bridges and in the tiny alleys.

'More than you'll know. But not as much as I hurt myself. I was such an idiot. You know that girl meant nothing, don't you?'

'Of course.' Her voice was light and even. The girl had

meant nothing. That's what had been so devastating, because it had revealed how shallow he was. 'I never stopped loving you, you know.' He brushed his lips against her hair. 'That's not very nice for Eloise. Or Caroline Lamb. But it does mean we could have a wonderful future together – if you can overlook that one mistake.'

She lay back in his arms and watched the lights dance around the souvenir kiosks. Was it one mistake? She very much doubted it, judging from the relish with which he seemed to have thrown himself into serial womanizing, though how he'd ever managed to fit in half the affairs he was supposed to have had and complete those expeditions had always intrigued her. She closed her eyes, letting the watchful gondolier's implacable gaze bore into her. Venice seemed full of spies – a ghostly legacy from the savage era of the all-seeing, all-powerful Doges. She even seemed to be looking down on herself: a voyeur at her own tryst.

'Venice is bursting with intrigue and secrets, don't you think?' asked Dylan, reading her mind. His voice took on an unfamiliar urgency. 'What's yours?'

She laughed, knowing she couldn't tell him her secret, which was that she'd never quite been able to trust him since that betrayal. And that she didn't know if she ever would. She looked into his eyes, which never stayed still long enough for her to fathom their depths – or shallows – and wondered how many secrets still lay behind them.

'Did you really never come here with Charlie?' he asked the following morning when they'd finally dragged themselves out of bed and were having breakfast on the terrace.

She held her hand up to shield her eyes from the sun and looked at him, gorgeous as a film star in his sunglasses and the open-necked blue shirt which showed off his tan. He'd lost weight recently too. He was almost the same as the day she first met him. She wanted to kiss the grey tendrils just picking through the curls at his temple, to thank them for reassuring her that she really was in the present and not in one of her old fantasies.

'After the first year we were married, we never had much time for going anywhere on our own. Charlie was always working.' It seemed so final, talking about Charlie in the past tense. She couldn't believe their marriage could be over with so few rows and recriminations. That part of it at least felt wrong. But you couldn't row with someone who refused to engage with you.

She gazed at the ripples in the canal. 'I never want this moment, right now, here, to end,' she said suddenly, tired of the heavy burden of doubt. Why couldn't people change? She had.

'Don't worry,' he grinned, 'we'll always have Jison.' Then he asked her to marry him again.

'I'm pregnant,' Linda announced when she rang Sydney in the office on Monday morning. 'I stayed up all night to tell you. I wanted you to be the first to know – apart from Clayton, obviously.'

Annabelle hovered by Sydney's desk wearing one of Dave's T-shirts with a picture of a guillotine and the Queen with lots of blood spurting out of her neck under the slogan 'Long may she rain'. Sydney waved 200 duty-free fags at her. Annabelle mouthed at her to get off the phone.

Sydney put her hand over the mouthpiece. 'It's Linda, she's having a baby.'

'So is it really serious between you and Dylan?' Linda was asking. Sydney could picture her narrowing her eyes to those all-seeing, turret-like slits of hers. 'Because forgive me for saying this, Sydney, but I keep mulling you two over, and it still doesn't fit.' Sydney couldn't decide whether she wanted to hear more or not; not that she was to have the choice.

'Call her back later,' commanded Annabelle. 'Virginia's just been fired.'

Even though losing two editors in one year would look like carelessness, Brian Widlake had had no choice when it came to sacking Virginia. Not after the furious memo to him that she'd dictated to Chloë accidentally appeared as her editor's letter at the front of the magazine beneath Virginia's glamorous new Terry O'Neill byline picture.

'So you didn't get the papers this weekend then?' said Annabelle. 'And you haven't listened to the radio this morning, clearly. That rant Virginia dictated about towel-heads, turnip heads and cretinous readers got accidentally filed to the copy-takers instead of her private folder.'

'How?'

They both stared across at Chloë who was tidying her desk with a beatific expression on her face.

'All hell's broken loose. It was second item on the *Today* programme. Virginia had to fall on her sword, and we've got to get used to yet another monster.' Annabelle paused, clearly relishing the awfulness of her forthcoming revelation. 'It's Chloë.'

Sydney looked aghast. 'You're not serious. She's got no experience.'

'Depends which kind you're referring to. Turns out she's been shagging Brian Widlake for weeks.' Annabelle flicked on Dave's computer. 'The press release should be flashing up any minute now. And here it is.' She began to read the announcement from Brian Widlake. '"I regret to announce the departure of Virginia wHorewell," that's got to be a deliberate typo, "whose energy and many, many years of experience I'm sure we all appreciate. However I am delighted to welcome in her place Chloë . . ." blah blah blah . . . "a prodigiously talented young journalist with the freshness and dynamic vision to take Virginia's foundations into the twenty-first century."'

Sydney knew she ought to be working on her CV and getting it out as fast as possible. But she couldn't stop ploughing on through the pile of problems that had become a crutch, she now realized, to her life.

She rang Dylan. 'You'll never guess what's happened today,' she said.

'You've just been served an eviction order?' He paused. 'Nope, didn't think so. That's my story.'

'How?' she asked eventually.

'That fucking bitch Eloise.'

'But I thought you both owned the house.'

'We did. But it's complicated.' He drifted off for a moment, steadying his breath. She could picture him trying to pull himself together.

'It will all work out,' he went on. 'It's not that big a deal. Just a bit of a shock.'

'How long before you need to move out?'

'Depends on my charm and negotiation skills, I suppose.' He gave a brittle laugh. She felt his bravura evaporate with the laughter.

'Oh Christ, Syd, I was using the house as collateral to raise the investment in Glendower Books. That was the deal with Patrice. If I don't put a quarter of a million in, he's pulling out.'

'It will be fine,' soothed Sydney. She was shocked. She hadn't realized how precarious the Glendower set-up was and she couldn't remember ever hearing Dylan so brow-beaten by anything.

'And by the way,' he snapped, when she got home later, 'Dan popped round to tell me that Jason's over at Primrose Hill police station. Our darling son's just been arrested.'

20

The prospect of Jason spending a night in a cell had a galvanizing effect on Sydney's until now somewhat dormant maternal instincts. She put her coat straight back on and picked up her car keys.

'Where are you going?' asked Dylan.

Sydney looked at him in disbelief.

'Couldn't you at least wait until we've eaten?' he grumbled. 'I'm ravenous.'

'Start without me then.'

His voice creaked with resignation. 'Don't be stupid, woman. Of course I'm not letting you go by yourself.'

'Then you'll have to come now.'

'Come off it, Syd. It'll do him good to cool his heels for a few hours. He's obviously a hothead.'

'I can't imagine where he gets that from.'

'I've never actually smashed someone over the head with a beer bottle.'

'You tried to punch a policeman once.'

'Only because he'd wrestled you to the ground.'

'All right. But how do you know there weren't mitigating circumstances in Jason's case?'

'Sydney, he bottled someone. A man called Karl something or other. Over a girl called Kirsty. According to Dan it was a love match. Makes you want to weep, doesn't it,' he said mordantly. 'Capulets versus Montagues.'

'There you are then. I'm sure Karl gave Jason plenty of provocation,' said Sydney. 'He sounds an utter shit from what Jason's told me.'

'So he told you?'

'Only about some problems he'd been having with Karl.' Dylan looked put out.

'He'd probably tell you if you showed any interest in him beyond regarding him as a curious exhibit,' said Sydney.

'And in the meantime I don't think being two-timed by Kirsty will be quite enough of a mitigating circumstance to get him off in court.'

'Have they actually charged him?' Sydney's hand shook as she poured herself a drink. She felt herself in way over her head. Watching Charlie in court from the gallery a few times in the early days of their marriage hadn't really prepared her for dealing with a delinquent son.

'I don't know,' said Dylan. 'Dan only popped in half an hour before you got back to let me know what had happened – and from the smell of him he'd been at the hash brownies again, so I'm not sure he's the most reliable source either.'

Sydney examined Dylan's pupils. 'Did he offer you a hash brownie by any chance?'

Dylan did what he always did in emotional crisis. Ran for cover. 'Molly's finally had a bath,' he beamed. Sydney refused to be sidetracked. Feeling Dylan was not reacting with the required gravitas, she marched towards the door.

He followed her, suddenly looking repentant. 'You win. Let's meet this shoulder to shoulder . . . you couldn't drive, could you? I'm a bit wrecked.'

'You might as well stay,' said Sydney, more disappointed than she was prepared to admit. 'Someone needs to be here with the girls in any case. And it's Kelly by the way. Not Kirsty.'

All the way to the police station Sydney fretted about what she should say to Jason. She wanted to be supportive but at the same time she had to show how much she disapproved of violence. She wondered if she should call his parents in Dudley. Or maybe he'd called them himself. Somehow she doubted it. For the first time since being reunited with her son, it occurred to her that he probably hadn't even told them he'd got back in contact with her.

An elderly Vauxhall pulled out in front of her and she slammed on the brakes impatiently. A tiny bent figure with tightly permed curls that resembled a mop-headed hydrangea peered furtively into the Vauxhall's wing mirror. Sydney wanted to stick her head out of the window and yell at them to get a fucking move on . . . What was wrong with her? The lights turned green and the Vauxhall spluttered into action. And then it juddered to a halt again. Her marriage had hit the skids too and her children never seemed to stop squabbling these days, but she had to stop feeling angry and dwell on the positive. She had been presented with the chance that most people only dream of: to replay her life and live out the great what if.

The Vauxhall inched forward gingerly and stalled again. It took all Sydney's self-control not to get out of her car and wrestle the hydrangea head into the gutter. Instead she focused on the positive aspects of her new dream life – and what she would say to Jason.

Sergeant Ray Gibbons, Sydney had to admit, was the soul of discretion. If he wondered what Sydney was doing visiting someone up on GBH charges, he didn't let on. He just smiled that slightly puzzled smile of his and asked if she'd come to join the party. Sydney assumed he thought she was on some do-gooding mission.

He led her down the distinctly whiffy corridors with their peeling walls and flapping posters featuring snarling dogs and suspect packages until they reached a partially glazed door that had obviously received more than its share of kicks and butts.

'Here you are.' He pulled out a handkerchief and rubbed it against the grimy glass with an air of hopelessness. 'He's already seen the solicitor,' he announced solemnly. 'And Sergeant Delaney and Sergeant Keith.' The words sounded ominously chilling. Sydney peeked over Sergeant Gibbons's rangy shoulders. Just at that moment, Jason, smaller and more hunched than ever in an old khaki fleece that matched the walls, turned round and saw her. A look of such abject contrition clouded his startled eyes that any doubts she might have felt pertaining to the validity of his actions evaporated instantly.

Even so, it wasn't so much his face that struck her as the one on the opposite side of the table. It belonged to Charlie.

'I can't actually let you in while they're still conducting the interview, obviously,' said Sergeant Gibbons apologetically, as he led her back to the draughty reception. 'I must say I thought they'd be finished by now. You're welcome to wait.' He nodded towards a lone grey plastic chair in the corner. 'Reckon I could rustle you up a cuppa.' He winked. 'I don't do this for everyone, mind.'

Sydney tapped her foot nervously while he boiled the kettle. 'I was a bit surprised when that young man asked for your hubby actually. I told him Charlie – Mr Murray, I mean – didn't do this kind of work. But he was most insistent that we phone him. Said he was the only lawyer he would contemplate. Must have seen one of his books I suppose.'

It made sense, thought Sydney, in a mad way. She remembered how impressed Jason had been when Sydney told him what Charlie did. Then, when he'd seen Charlie that time he dropped the children off at Jacquie's lying-in, he'd have been struck, as most people were when they met Charlie for the first time, by his aura of wisdom and authority. It would have been easy enough for Jason to get Charlie's phone numbers. They were scribbled on at least three Post-It notes around the house.

She sat in silence for a few more minutes contemplating the flecks of limescale in her tea. Sergeant Gibbons passed her some old copies of *What Hi-Fi?* magazine. 'All we've got, I'm afraid. Well, not all. But I think the others would be even less appealing. If you get my meaning.'

Twenty minutes later Charlie appeared, dark rings orbiting his eyes. Under the flickering fluorescent tubes he seemed to have aged ten years since he'd moved out.

Sydney stood up and smiled awkwardly. 'Thank you so much for coming. I really appreciate it.' She paused. Sergeant Gibbons withdrew tactfully behind the desk. 'Will he be all right?' she asked anxiously.

'Hard to say. The Government has an unofficial new line of zero tolerance on violent behaviour. It appears it was a pretty lethal bottle. There was considerable bleeding, and according to the plaintiff, a rather epic scar that may or may not turn out to be permanently disfiguring. That could be worth two years.'

'In prison?' Sydney's fingers went rigid in her coat pockets.

'No, Sydney, Claridge's.' His eyes met her frightened ones and pulled away. 'Still, he's not a serial hooligan. That may count for something,' he said more emolliently. 'And there's always an outside chance the plaintiff won't press charges. But it seems very faint in this instance.'

Sydney felt that anything she said would somehow incriminate her. Charlie seemed to have that effect on her these days. So she simply thanked him again.

'I've explained to Jason that I can't represent him myself if it does go to court, but I'll put him on to Bill Carter. He's a first-rate solicitor. If anyone can get him off, Bill can.'

Sydney smiled gratefully. He seemed to be waiting for her to say something else. 'He obviously took a real shine to you when he met you,' she suggested eventually, for want of anything better to say.

Charlie did up the buttons on his coat with painful slowness. His mood, coolly businesslike a moment earlier, had snapped back into its Arctic iciness. 'You can go and see him now if you want. He may need bailing out.' He strode past her to the door and then appeared to have second thoughts. 'Don't give him too hard a time, Sydney. He seems like a nice kid underneath it all.'

Sydney watched her husband stalk off into the night yet again and wondered why she felt so angry. She realized that Charlie's walking away from their marriage without even discussing it might have something to do with it.

'Don't tell me he's going back to work,' said Sergeant Gibbons, rustling himself up his 9.30 Cupasoup.

Sydney took a deep breath and turned to face him. 'Do you think I could see Jason Watson now?'

After she'd written a cheque for £1,000, they walked to the car together. Jason couldn't stop apologizing, telling her how fantastic Charlie had been, how inspiring it was to meet someone with such a big brain and – eventually – how glad he was that she and not his adopted parents had been there for him.

'It would kill them if they ever found out. They're not broad-minded like you.' He paused nervously. 'Does Dylan know?'

Sydney stopped at the lights and nodded. Jason slithered further into his seat. 'Grite. That should really impress him. As if he needed any other reasons to despise me.'

'Jason, Dylan doesn't despise you,' said Sydney wearily.

'Come off it, Sidnoy. I'm not exactly the son he would have wanted, am I? I mean, look at me. I'm hardly classic public-school material, am I? I'm common, spotty, and I just about reach his armpits? And I've got about as much sense of adventure as a lapdog.'

Sydney smiled, despite his seriousness. 'I wouldn't say that. You came to find me after all. That was brave. And you've moved to London. That takes guts as well.' She cast around for more evidence of his virtues. 'And you're obviously very strong,' she said eventually.

'Sidnoy, face it. I'm practically a convicted felon. Or about to be.'

They drove in silence for a while. 'Do you want to tell me about it?' asked Sydney.

'Not really,' he said. 'But I will. I've been an utter, utter pillock. I don't even like Kelly that much any more. Not after what she did to me. And not after meeting Cassandra and the other girls in Dan's house. Have you seen Cassandra's legs by the way?'

Sydney had, and they were about as long as Jason's entire body.

'I really admire women with brains,' continued Jason. 'Loike you,' he added slyly. 'I never met many students in Dudley.' Still she didn't say anything. She hoped she hadn't done anything foolish by encouraging Jason to move in with Dan, who was hardly an ideal role model when all was said and done. She offered him an organic dried apricot from a bag she'd found in the glove compartment. He shook his head. 'Sometimes I think you'd like to make your family into one big organic soup,' he smiled in the darkness. 'It's not a criticism, mind? I just don't think you should wear yourself out so much trying to make it all perfect.'

She dropped him off outside number 62 and kissed him goodnight, breathing in the faint aroma of diesel that clung permanently to him. She found she was starting to like it. She watched his sturdy bow legs – Miles's, she realized with a lurch – climb the steps to Dan's and felt the urge to protect him from whatever lay out there waiting to ambush him. He was so unworldly in many ways. She waited until he'd let himself in and closed the door before parking the car.

Dylan was downstairs watching *The Life of Brian* on Channel Five when she let herself in. They'd got to the part where they were all hanging off their crosses singing 'Always Look on the Bright Side of Life'. It ought to be Dylan's theme tune, Sydney thought. He must be agitated, though, because he never watched television. He couldn't keep still long enough to watch the news, let alone an entire film. He'd also worked his way through half a bottle of whisky. He looked up briefly as she came into the room.

'How's Cool Hand Luke?' The corners of his eyes were criss-crossed with tiny lines, like contours. He looked worn out.

'Released on bail. And taking legal advice from one Charles Murray, QC.'

'Ah. Awkward.'

Sydney's voice was tremulous. 'He could go to prison. His

fate lies more or less entirely with this solicitor Charlie recommended, which is a little ironic in the circumstances.'

Dylan considered this for a moment. 'I suppose God might have a small role to play as well.'

'In which case let's hope He doesn't charge. You owe me five hundred quid by the way. For bail.'

'Add it to the mountain of debt.' His hand ransacked his curls. 'God, Syd, I can't believe that bitch could be so duplicitous. She knew how much I loved that bloody book company and she knew that without the house I'd be up the creek.'

Sydney sat down on the footstool next to his knees and took his hands gently. 'Dylan, have you ever thought that maybe Eloise wasn't ill, but some kind of con?'

'Conniving bitch. Certainly.'

Sydney reached for the remote control and flicked the sound down.

'What do you mean?' he asked slowly.

'I think you know, Dylan,' said Sydney gently. 'I don't think Caroline Lamb is Eloise's only alias. I think she's passed herself off as lots of someone elses.'

He laughed nonchalantly. 'Interesting theory. Based on what exactly? An encounter with someone who looked like Eloise but said she wasn't? The other theory, of course, though admittedly far less interesting, is that it wasn't Eloise. Brittle, vacuous New Yorkers are ten a dime, in case you hadn't noticed.'

'I've noticed that you're sounding very defensive.'

'You'd be defensive if someone told you your ex-wife was a mirage. I may have made a mistake marrying Eloise, but I didn't imagine it.' His voice was light but there was a dangerous edge to it.

'Tell me, Dylan, did you ever meet her family? The illustrious Fairweathers. Of San Francisco.'

'No. They disapproved of us getting married so quickly. You know that.'

'Didn't you ever question why they might disapprove? You were quite a catch. Eloise seemed to think you were loaded. And the scion of landed gentry. She practically told me you were a direct descendant of Edward II.'

'I didn't lie to her, if that's what you're insinuating. She just assumed a few things. And I had my savings from Steinberg's and I was still giving the odd lecture so I suppose I may have given the impression of having comfortably deep pockets.'

'I'm not accusing you of lying,' she said carefully. 'But surely if that's what she'd also told her family, it would have satisfied even the illustrious Fairweathers of San Francisco.'

'I don't need this, Sydney.' His voice cut through the air like a switch blade. 'Not now.' His eyes looked almost yellow in the dim light of Sydney's old lamps, like a hunted animal's. She turned away. A few moments later she heard him let himself out.

She watched him cross the road to the darkness of number 69. Either she was going mad or her sixth sense was finally back on the job again. With a sense of grim determination, she plumped for the latter. Then she called Linda and asked her if she might be able to locate a reliable private investigator in New York.

'We're leaving the magazine,' said Annabelle, sounding more animated than she had for years.

'And we think you should come too,' said Dave encouragingly. Sydney flashed him a grateful smile. A miracle had happened. He was, Sydney suddenly noticed, wearing a shirt that bore every sign of having recently been near an iron, hitherto an unacceptable, outdated symbol of female and working-class repression in Dave's somewhat demanding book. She hoped Annabelle hadn't ironed it for him. Then she remembered Annabelle didn't believe in ironing any more than Dave had. Behind them she saw a couple of burly men removing the last of Virginia's leopard-skin cushions and pouffes from her office. Chloë, chomping at the bit to be installed on her rightful throne, was barking orders at a boy with a bucket of fuchsia paint and measuring out the room in a mismatched suit and brand-new Jimmy Choos.

'I see Hitler's changed her spots again,' observed Annabelle. 'Let me see, we've had Nerd, Notting Hill Boho, Rock Chick, Mini-Linda, Mini-Virginia and now,' she cocked her head and squinted at Chloë's neatly corseted back, 'I'd call this Miss Moneypenny. Or rather Money-pound. That outfit must have cost a bomb.'

'Any update on the PA front, Sydney?' Chloë called over from her vigilant post by the paint pots. 'You will make sure it's someone young, won't you? Brian's desperate to trans-form *VIP* into a cult youth read. We can't afford any more ageing wood,' she added nastily. She watched as the boy wobbled up his ladder and slapped a few more brush-strokes on the partition board. 'That's the wrong fuchsia by the way, I said I wanted John Oliver's. You will let me know as soon as you've drawn up a suitable shortlist won't you, Sydney?'

Annabelle watched her retreat. 'You can't let her treat you like a glorified secretary, Syd,' she exploded.

Sydney shrugged. 'I need a job.' She surveyed the usual avalanche of mail that had arrived that morning. 'And I'm strangely attached to this one.'

'That's right,' said Annabelle, following her gaze. 'Lose yourself in other people's problems. Story of your life, Sydney. One day you'll wake up and realize even you can't play God all the time.'

'What Annabelle means,' soothed Dave, 'is that you get really involved. That's why you're so good at it. You really connect with the readers.'

'I'm lucky they're such a responsive lot,' said Sydney, wondering what could have got into Annabelle.

'That's why we want you to come with us,' continued Dave. 'We've got the green light this morning. You're the first to know.'

'What green light?'

Annabelle rolled her eyes. 'My point entirely. The whole office could have relocated to Mars and you'd be too wrapped up in other people's bloody problems to notice.'

'A green light from Star Radio,' said Dave more politely. 'Now that they're officially London's number one commercial station they want to launch a magazine that reflects the breadth of their output. And they want us to produce it.'

'Which is where you come in,' said Annabelle grudgingly. 'As commissioning editor.'

Sydney looked at them both, feeling momentarily bewildered. 'The salary's terrific,' said Annabelle. 'Believe me, as a single mother you need to secure your finances.'

No wonder Dave and Annabelle had been out of the office so much lately.

'Sydney?' Chloë sashayed towards them, her blonde flicks creating a deceptive halo. She bared her teeth at Sydney, having perfected Virginia's smile, and arched her eyebrows, having mastered Linda's superciliousness. 'You will have that shortlist on my desk by the morning, won't you?'

*   *   *

Despite having a *crise de conscience* shortly after Jason had been taken in for questioning by the police, Karl decided not to drop the charges. After Kelly dumped *him*, he felt in need of divine retribution. Failing that, a court conviction for Jason would have to suffice. Sydney was left to pick Jason up off the floor because Dylan had had to drop everything yet again and go to Paris to schmooze – and soothe – Patrice about the missing part of his contribution. For two nights running after he left, she dreamed about lending him the money he needed to make up the shortfall in Glendower Books – wasn't that what he'd been hinting at the other night? She no longer trusted her intuition. All she knew was that both times she woke up after the dreams in a cold sweat, feeling disloyal, relieved – and confused.

She was almost more worried about the outcome of the trial than about everything else. And she was very worried about everything else. The exercises she'd been religiously doing with Harriet morning and night for the past four months seemed to have been making a real difference, until recently. In the past fortnight Harriet had become un-bearably moody: she seemed more like a stroppy teenager than ever. When the school secretary rang Sydney at work to ask if she wouldn't mind coming in for an Informal Chat with the headmistress, she began to experience searing chest pains.

'Will Mr Murray be there as well?' asked the secretary politely.

Sydney wanted to tell her that of course he bloody well wouldn't, because he hadn't been to nine out of the previous nine meetings with St Margaret's teachers. In fact, she wanted to add, could the secretary give her one instance of Charlie turning up for anything on his own? Furthermore, did the secretary have all his phone numbers as she appeared to have all of Sydney's? No, she did not. Because Charlie was Very Busy and Very Important, and like so many of the fathers at St Margaret's, apparently in possession of a Do Not Disturb sign flashing over his Very Urgent life. So what on earth made anyone think he'd show up this time, especially as Sydney wasn't going to waste any time ringing Charlie's office in order to leave a message with one of the sodding clerks, which given its zero impact on their pay packets, probably wouldn't get relayed and even if it did, would ultimately be forgotten. Bitter? Of course Sydney wasn't bitter.

'I'm not sure whether Mr Murray will be able to make it,' was all she could manage. Not if she could bloody well help it. Let him stew in his blissed-out ignorance. She'd coped without him when she lived with him. It would be plain illogical if she couldn't cope without him when she didn't live with him.

'I think it would be a good idea if he did,' said the secretary.

Sydney heard Chloë summoning her to a PA update from her fuchsia den. She was so tense that her corporeal sensations appeared to have settled into early stages of rigor mortis. An email from a Hugo at Barclays bank entitled To Be A He Or Not To Be? blinked on her screen. Chloë's voice – louder this time – floated across from behind the coffee machine. Sydney peeked furtively round the office – it was empty as usual – and wondered if this constant shallow breathing and pounding in her head was what a nervous breakdown felt like.

'The good news is you're not mad,' said Linda. Her voice vibrated so violently that Sydney assumed she must be swooping up and down an industrial lift shaft in some

407

inscrutably hip new club in the Meat Packing District. Just for a moment she felt a stab of lifestyle envy.

'I can't hear you properly,' she said. 'Where are you?'

'The new massage chair Clayton's just bought me. For my back. Hang on, I'll just turn it down.'

Sydney shuffled the sheaf of job applications that had come in for the new PA job. It was like Groundhog Day – except that she and Linda appeared to have swapped lives. 'Did you call for anything specific?' she asked politely.

'What? Oh yes, sorry. It's true what they say about milk brain, isn't it?' said Linda chattily. 'You'll never guess where I left my handbag yesterday . . .'

Sydney couldn't guess. Partly because Chloë was screaming at her about the CVs again. Partly because she was racked with worry about Jason who she was convinced was about to go down, develop a taste for crack and be raped in his cell while a horde of screws looked on with callous indifference. Partly because she was dreading the headmistress at St Margaret's informing her that Harriet would have to leave the school because there was nothing more they could do for her. Partly because she'd had a nightmare the previous night in which Dylan was made homeless. Partly because her husband appeared to be having a torrid affair with someone with a taste for dubious-sounding pashminas. 'I'm fine since you ask,' she snapped.

'Touchy. Anyway, I've remembered what I rang about now. Eloise. You were right. It *was* her at Millicent's party. Or rather it was Shania Garrett. Also known as Faye Le Witt, Marcia Rose and Evelyn Moses.' She paused momentarily. 'That's just to give you a few random samples from this vast list of names the private dick came up with. When Dylan thought he'd snapped up a bit of American royalty what he actually landed was a cute little crook.'

Sydney felt strangely calm. Of all the crazy things that had happened recently, this one oddly made sense.

'Don't worry. She's not involved in anything violent. But very lucrative. Marcia Rose sold swanky time-share beach cottages on Lake Tahoe to wealthy Minnesotans. They were gorgeous apparently. Or they would have been if they'd existed. Faye Le Witt invented a brilliant pyramid selling scheme in Arizona that made a fortune – for Faye Le Witt.' She broke off to check something in the private detective's extensive report. 'Evelyn Moses came up with a fabulous new franchise spa concept for cruise ships from her base in Florida. This one was such a brilliant idea that several blue-chip investment banks sank several blue-chip millions into the idea. All of which probably made Evelyn enough to buy her very own cruise ship.'

'And she's never been caught?'

'Sharp as alligator's teeth. Plus she's always scammed very rich, supposedly clever people who are too embarrassed to go to the police in case it impacts on their business credibility. Presumably they figure it's better to write off the few hundred thousand she's fleeced off them and put it down as a useful arc on the learning curve.'

'Very Robin Hood.'

'Except that instead of giving to the poor, Eloise gave to Eloise.'

'How can we be sure this private detective is right?'

'Do you think I'd hire a dunce? This guy was the one voice in Intelligence advising Blair and Bush not to believe any of the West's propaganda about weapons of mass destruction and the forty-five-minute supposed capability of Saddam. He got so disillusioned when they didn't listen to him that he left the service. But the guy's a genius. Any minute now some highly perceptive magazine editor is going to get the scoop of their career by commissioning him to write an explosive article on the subject, after which comes the best-seller and the blockbuster movie. In the meantime, he's working on some resentment issues and biding his moment. But he's absolutely kosher. Ex-FBI. Ex-CIA. Ex-pensive.'

Sydney took the hint. 'Poor Dylan,' was all she said.

'He will be after Faye, Shania, Marcia, Evelyn and Eloise have finished with him. That must have been quite a crowded marriage.'

'What was she doing with him?'

'That's what we couldn't work out initially. He's hardly in her usual league on the face of it.'

'Perhaps she loved him,' said Sydney quietly.

'She must have done,' said Linda. 'But don't worry, she's not a completely soft-centred romantic. According to Private Dick, she thought she could turn him into some kind of commodity if she marketed him properly. She even got a couple of her billionaire Russian contacts to invest a couple of million into launching some kind of up-market touring business. Dylan was going to lead very rich, very stressed-out businessmen on hard-core expeditions up the Amazon and across the Arctic. But then he put his foot down. Apparently at least one of those Russians now has a contract out on Eloise, and quite possibly Dylan, which could explain why he never stays put in one place for more than a few weeks.'

'Is that why they moved to London?' It all began to slot into place. Sydney began to shake. She could bear most things – but not Dylan turning out to be evil or violent. Her judgement couldn't be that faulty.

'A factor, certainly. But Dylan had also got a bit behind with his US Fed taxes. And Eloise would certainly have needed a little time out from her industrious business developments.' She broke off. 'Sydney, you are okay, aren't you? I know I sound smug and gloating, but it's only because I got the impression lately that you're not that serious about Dylan after all?'

It was uncanny, Sydney thought, not for the first time, how Linda, despite giving a very convincing rendition of being someone who only ever thought about herself, had always been able to intuit Sydney's feelings before she managed to identify them herself.

'All I can say,' Linda continued, 'is he must be fanbloody-tastic in bed.'

'I don't suppose there's any chance that Eloise – or whoever she is – is actually quite a bit older than twenty-five?' asked Sydney.

Sydney wasn't sure if she was even surprised by most of what Linda had told her. She wasn't sure about anything any more. All she knew was that she had to focus on giving Jason as much support as she could over the next few months. Ditto Harriet. She also had to face what she'd always known deep down; that Dylan was as flaky as he'd ever been. And that while falling in love with him at university was excus-able, falling for him all over again nineteen years later was ridiculous. At least she understood now that he wasn't bad, just weak. What was her excuse?

But first she had to find Miss Cavendish who, astonishingly, appeared three minutes late for their allotted slot, looking flustered. She and Sydney sat opposite each other on child-sized plastic stacking chairs, the one next to Sydney glaringly unoccupied.

Miss Cavendish looked at her notes before crossing her neat legs repeatedly. She was wearing a tiny kilt. With her baby-fine blonde bob, she looked like a small child. Sydney braced herself.

'The good news,' Miss Cavendish began brightly, 'is that the exercises seem to be working. I have to confess I was sceptical at first.' She lowered her voice even though they were alone and the door was closed. 'So many parents try such odd therapies nowadays.' Sydney was too nervous herself to take the bait. She wasn't interested in other parents. She was only interested in Harriet. She waited quietly for Miss Cavendish to resume. Harriet's school work was definitely showing distinct – if subtle – signs of improvement, Miss Cavendish told her. And she was no longer exhibiting violent tendencies towards her classmates. Sydney was so delighted that she didn't notice the door open.

'How subtle?' she asked, dimly aware of footsteps. She swung round. So the clerks had passed on her message. Charlie crept gingerly towards them and settled on the third miniature chair. They must look like the three bears, thought Sydney, wanting to smile suddenly. His coat was soaking wet and already making tiny puddles on the floor.

'She's able to concentrate for longer. She's not fidgeting so much – she actually chose to read out loud yesterday. And Mr Seth, the science teacher, has allowed her back in the class.' She smiled tentatively. 'I didn't tell you she'd been banned – I thought it would panic you, and to be honest I felt Mr Seth might have been over-reacting a little. It was only a small explosion she caused after all.' Sydney and Charlie were concentrating too hard to smile back. She handed them some of Harriet's artwork to prove the point. 'And she's stopped painting dead animals.'

'These look jolly,' said Charlie encouragingly. 'Don't they, Sydney? No abattoirs. I have to admit I was sceptical too, at first, Miss—'

'Cavendish,' said Sydney quickly. The relief at finally finding something that worked for Harriet was almost overwhelming. She felt a tear forming in her eye and wiped it away roughly. 'What's the bad news?' she asked.

'She still seems a bit depressed,' said Miss Cavendish hesitantly.

Sydney and Charlie held their breaths simultaneously.

Miss Cavendish shuffled her papers. 'I'm afraid that although she's less aggressive, she's still very withdrawn.' Her grey eyes opened like a camera shutter. She looked as though she was going to cry herself. 'The other girls have definitely picked up on it. I think that's why they have been a little . . . excluding. Anyway, that's why the headmistress wanted to see you rather urgently.' She checked the clock on the wall behind Charlie and Sydney. 'She should be ready now,' she said, sounding as though she'd been released from a man-trap.

Mrs Dowell, the headmistress, stared into the middle distance and adopted the innocuous tone of voice that had led many a pupil – and quite a few parents – to tell her more than was strictly in their interest. 'There haven't been any significant changes at home recently, have there?'

Sydney froze and her eyes locked with Charlie's – for the first time since he'd moved out. How ironic, thought Sydney, suddenly stricken, that it had taken this terrible oversight on both their parts. She'd been meaning to tell the school for months that Charlie and she were having a temporary hiatus. Temporary as in six months, that was. And clearly neither of the girls had felt up to saying anything. A lump of shame swelled in her throat. 'Our cat died. A year ago.' She looked at her feet. Charlie's coat continued dripping.

413

'It's just that her conduct has been a little withdrawn. In my experience that can suggest some kind of trauma,' Mrs Dowell continued in her molasses voice. 'She was such an open child. But she's pushed almost all her friends away and she repels any overtures of intimacy from the teachers. And this last fortnight I've noticed her sitting all by herself several times in the playground. Except when Molly's around and then they sit quietly together. I'm afraid it's pretty much the same story with Molly too. Except that Molly's work hasn't suffered – to quite such a degree. But then Molly doesn't suffer from dyslexia. So it's odd her work should be suffering at all.' She coughed delicately before pinning them both with her birdlike eyes. 'Do you think this could all be down to the . . . cat?'

The rain was still cascading down when they left the school twenty minutes later. Neither of them spoke. 'Thanks for coming,' said Sydney finally.

Charlie grunted. He looked wistful and grey. Perhaps she'd sounded too proprietorial. He seemed almost penitent. 'Once in six years. It's not a brilliant record, is it?'

'You came to the carol concert,' she said. He looked so sad now that she wanted to comfort him. She wondered how long the simple courtesies of marriage took to die. Not that theirs had been very courteous by the end. She thought back to the carol concert. It seemed a million years ago now. She could remember looking up at the swimming-pool sky and wondering what lay beyond it. Well, she knew now.

He grunted again. A fat orb of rain rolled down his cheek.

'Fancy a coffee?' Sydney heard herself asking. She wanted to kick herself. She really couldn't face any more bad news today. But instead he told her he'd love one.

*   *   *

She didn't even mind that the nearest café was a Starbucks. She was just so relieved to be out of the torrential rain – and to be talking to Charlie again.

'I can't believe I didn't say anything to the school when we first split up,' said Sydney. She was stricken at the vision of both her daughters sitting together in isolation in the playground.

'I could have said something too,' said Charlie, absent-mindedly stirring five packets of sugar into his coffee.

'They seemed okay at home. Or perhaps I just saw what I wanted to see.'

Charlie stopped stirring his sugar and put down his white plastic stirrer. 'We can all do that,' he said wistfully. Then he told her that he knew he hadn't always been as supportive of her as he might have been, and Sydney almost fainted, but refrained because she needed to tell him that she understood how hard he'd always worked and how much she appreciated what he'd provided her and the girls with, and they both agreed that in future they'd both communicate more openly with each other in order to make life better for the girls. And in the spirit of more open communication, Sydney almost asked him who the bitch was he was seeing, but she managed to restrain herself there as well. Instead she asked if he had any more inkling what would happen in Jason's court case. He didn't, but he reassured her that Bill Carter was the best possible man for the job. And then one of them suggested it would be nice to meet up for dinner. And the other agreed. And then Charlie said he had to go back to work. And Sydney started walking home and did what she hadn't been able to do in months. Cried.

Being back on talking terms with Charlie had its ups. And its downs, chief amongst which was realizing that of course the children weren't doing fine. Now that she and Charlie were communicating she could corroborate that Molly wasn't having baths again. She could also confirm that Harriet's missing copy of *Harry Potter* had been discovered shredded under her bed at his place.

While they'd discussed the details over a second cup of coffee, she had tried to picture their bedroom at his flat and gave up in pain. Of course the children weren't doing fine. Their parents were barely functioning as adults.

It had taken her forty minutes to get home from Starbucks in the rain, but her head felt clearer than it had in a long time. And if she were honest with herself, it was a relief that Dylan was in Paris. Maisie was standing by the front door when she got back. The girls were in the kitchen. She could hear them quarrelling. She almost felt wistful for the days when they were glued to the TV in Charlie's study. But they rarely went in there now.

She tossed her bag down and braced herself for the onslaught. Molly had got into a fight at school with some girls from Year Five who'd pulled the pom-pom off her beret and Harriet was blaming her for not going to the head.

Sydney took one look at their stricken faces, strode over

to the freezer, pulled out some ice-cream and sat them down for a summit.

'Why didn't you tell me you were both so unhappy?' she asked gently.

'What good would it have done?' snapped Harriet. A tear rolled down her cheek.

Molly scowled at her sister. 'Why are you always so mean?' Another tear rolled down hers.

'Well, she's so wrapped up in Dylan and Jason and work.' Harriet folded her arms across her bony chest and glared at her mother.

'You're quite right,' said Sydney, ladling Nutella over their ice-cream portions. The girls looked at her, bemused.

'Shall I pour on the sunflower seeds?' asked Molly with a degree of stoicism that made Sydney's heart break.

'Not if you don't want them,' said Sydney. 'Look, girls, I know I've been hopeless. I thought you were doing fine. I didn't realize you'd got so mature you could cover up your feelings to save mine. Anyway, things are going to change. I wanted you to know that.'

'Dad's just as bad,' said Harriet, sounding slightly mollified. Molly got up from the table and started playing with her mother's hair. 'We can never talk to him about you. He gets so bad-tempered.'

'That's one of the things that are going to change first,' said Sydney, shocked. 'Dad and I are friends again and—' She looked up to see Harriet's eyes wide with optimism.

'You mean the trial separation is over?' asked Molly.

Sydney bit her lip. 'No. But . . .' she could hardly bear to look at them now. The colour had drained from their faces and their eyes glittered like beetles. 'Things are going to be a lot friendlier and happier. We could start by inviting him for supper next Saturday if you'd like.'

'Will Jason be there?' asked Molly.

'Not if you don't want him to be, though I did think you liked him.'

'He's all right,' said Harriet.

'I think he's nice,' said Molly. Sydney smiled at her gratefully. 'Just not as a brother.'

'And Dylan?' enquired Harriet. 'Will he be there?'

Sydney gazed at her inscrutable elder daughter. 'No,' she said quietly. 'I can guarantee that.'

Even by the under-populated standards of the magazine formerly known as *IQ*, Annabelle and Dave's leaving do was sparsely attended. Chloë was terribly busy at a meeting – with her cuticle clipper as Sydney subsequently discovered – not that anyone mourned her absence. But it did mean there was just the five of them in the local pub – Annabelle, Dave, Poppy, who had finally been relieved of Five Minute Mall Make-Over duty, Sydney, and the pile of CVs Sydney was taking home to sift through. They sat outside by the river, breathing in the smoky, beer-tinged air.

'Here's to our media moguls,' said Sydney, clinking her glass of champagne against Dave's pint.

'Cheers,' beamed Poppy, downing her Kir Royal in one. 'God, I love this weather.' She hitched her skirt even further up her tawny legs, relishing the effect she was having on every other man in the pub apart from Dave, who could barely keep his hands off Annabelle.

'What happened to teetotalism?' smiled Annabelle.

'Manley's not into extremes any more.' Poppy grinned beatifically. 'He's giving up giving up things.'

'Isn't that a bit extreme?'

Poppy ignored Dave and addressed herself to the women. 'He's in a completely different place emotionally from when

I first met him. He's so open. It's almost as if something was wedged between his heart and his brain. And now it's gone.' She lowered her voice and beamed at them. 'He's asked me to marry him. He actually went down on bended knee and presented me with the most gorgeous ring—'

'Where is it?' asked Annabelle. In the last few months she'd suddenly become passionately interested in all the trappings of traditional weddings.

Poppy waggled the fourth finger of her left hand. Around it was coiled a wisp of red twine. 'It's a kabbalah ring. Manley made it himself. Actually we're keeping it a secret until Dad's out of rehab and Manley can ask him formally for my hand. It's so sweet.'

'I didn't know your old man was in rehab.' A tinge of respect had crept into Dave's voice.

'He goes every year. I think he may just do it to get some peace and quiet. It's the only place he can guarantee Mummy won't follow him. So anyway, I'll have to use my other hand to stick two fingers up at Chloë tomorrow when I tell her about my new job.'

'What new job?' asked Sydney, realizing with a stab how much she would miss hearing about Poppy's antics.

'Style adviser,' said Poppy nonchalantly. 'To Cherie Blair. Carole says she can't cope on her own any more. Imagine me working for socialists. Mummy's going to be so hacked off.'

Sydney felt utterly deflated on the way home from the pub. Without Poppy, Annabelle and Dave, life on the magazine wouldn't be worth living, especially as Chloë had begun making repeated noises about Sydney's advancing age. She could always throw her lot in with Dave and Annabelle, she supposed. But she couldn't afford to take any more risks – not as the single mother of two daughters and one delinquent son – or any more charity.

She nipped into Waitrose on the way home for some treats for the girls, and deliberately didn't stop when she found herself in the organic seeds and pulses section. Alanis Morissette was on the tannoy. And she was right, life was ironic. Sydney had wanted more freedom. She had wanted a job. She had wanted to be in charge of her destiny. She hadn't wanted to be dependent on Charlie. She had got what she wanted, more or less. And she now realized that the little pit of breathlessness that had been more or less permanently lodged behind her left ribs for the past few months was a deep well of unhappiness. She stopped to look at some frozen ice-cream pavlovas. Above her a light flickered on and off while Alanis went on and on.

'Gosh, Sydney. We must stop meeting like this.' Miranda peered at Sydney across the desserts freezer. Sydney's eyes automatically strayed towards Miranda's wrist. The bruise had gone. In fact she looked altogether more cheerful.

'How are *you*?' she asked carefully.

'Wonderful.' Beneath the flickering tube, Miranda beamed. Sydney had never seen her smile properly before. She suddenly looked fifteen years younger. 'Have you heard then? They've dropped the charges.'

Sydney's heart bounced. 'Against Jason? Oh God, that is wonderful.' Ian must have told Miranda. She wondered whether – hoped that – Charlie had tried to ring her while she'd been celebrating with Dave and Annabelle in the pub. It had been too loud to hear almost anything.

'Jason?' Miranda frowned. 'I'm sorry, I don't know what you mean. I was talking about Ian. The chambers took a vote and decided not to prosecute him. It's such a relief . . .' She bent over her shopping basket and to Sydney's astonishment, the woman who never betrayed any sensation other than slight heatstroke began to sob convulsively until her Alice band finally jolted free from its rut and fell to the floor.

Sydney put her arms round Miranda and held her until her shoulders stopped heaving. Then she helped her through the check-out and sat with her in her car while she calmed down and explained everything.

It was almost eight o'clock when Sydney got home. Maisie was standing mutinously in the hall next to an enormous bunch of roses that framed a note from Dylan. 'Missing my Seren more almost than a decent cup of tea. Gray Paree dull and dismal without her. Patrice coming round. See you soon.'

'They must have cost a pretty penny,' said Maisie disapprovingly. Sydney was inclined to agree. Dylan's finances were as much of a mystery as ever. As were his movements.

'I'll be off now, Sydney. Lord knows it won't be easy getting to the hospital in time to rectify the dreadful mess that will have been made of the CDs. And I hate to let all those patients down.' Sydney fished in her purse and handed Maisie a £20 note, silently resolving to find a child-minder who didn't make it quite so clear that she minded children quite so much. And then she rang Charlie to invite him to supper with the girls on Saturday. He told her that would be very nice and she felt suddenly better, or at least more mature. Until she heard a woman speaking softly in the background.

'God, I'm missing you,' said Dylan later that night, after Sydney had called to thank him for the flowers. She had taken the phone into the garden, along with the newspaper she hadn't had time to read that morning. She breathed in the ripe scent of her climbing roses as they hung drowsily in the suffocating heat of the evening shedding petals like tears.

'You won't believe how bloody it is here,' he continued chirpily. 'Patrice went apeshit when I told him about the house not belonging to me any more. Then he wanted to get a hit squad on Eloise – that was the point at which I cheered up actually. Then sanity prevailed. Now he just wants me to put in fifty per cent instead of the twenty-one we'd originally agreed. It means finding some alternative sources but . . .' He chirrupped on for a good while longer as Sydney deadheaded some of the weepier roses. When she'd finished, she sat at the wooden garden table, still half listening to his complicated discourse on the new funding he thought he could put in place for Glendower Books, and began doodling on the newspaper.

'So it might take a bit longer for me to be solvent, but I think it will all work out.' She found herself relieved to hear him say he wouldn't be back until after the weekend. It would make the next – crucial – handover with Charlie much more straightforward. She breathed in the tropical air.

'Night night, Dylan.' She looked at the newspaper and saw that she'd drawn up a list of ingredients for steak Béarnaise.

Sydney spent the whole of Saturday arranging and rearranging the house. Since Charlie's departure she'd made one or two changes. Or five or six. And that was just downstairs. She wondered if he'd be hurt to see them. So she changed them all back. But it all still looked very tidy. She contemplated messing it up a bit to make him feel more at home. Then she remembered the woman's voice and realized it wasn't ever going to be his home again, so she decided not to bother.

Then she started making the sauce. She curdled her first attempt, sliced her finger cutting the steaks, and realized she was so ridiculously nervous that she was entitled to a drink on medicinal grounds. By the time Charlie and the girls turned up at six, her cheeks were the same colour as the raspberries on the pavlova. But that could have been because she'd changed her outfit four times.

Charlie stood awkwardly on the doorstep at first, waiting to be invited in. In fact they were all behaving very oddly to begin with, as Charlie tried not to be over-familiar with the place that had been his home for eight years. But gradually they settled down. It wasn't the same as before. It was better. Charlie wasn't reading the newspaper and he did appear to notice what he was eating. And what the children were saying. He even went upstairs with them to read them a story, although Sydney had already said that he was perfectly entitled to take them back to his flat for the night. She cleared the table and began washing the glasses, feeling calmer than she had for months.

'We're in the middle of *The Secret Garden*,' he said when he came back down. 'We've got to the creepy bit.'

Sydney raised an eyebrow.

'I know,' he said. 'I don't think I ever read to them the whole time I lived here. But having them all to myself at weekends these past few months has forced me to grow up.'

'Meaning you weren't grown up before?'

He picked up a napkin and began drying the glasses. Sydney silently handed him a tea-towel instead. And smiled. 'Why didn't you tell me why it was so important for you to go to Bermuda?' she asked.

423

'What do you mean?'

'I mean,' she began slowly, 'that if you'd told me you were having to bail Ian out, I might have been a bit more understanding.'

'How did you know about that?'

'I bumped into Miranda the other day. She told me everything.'

He tapped his fingers thoughtfully on the work top. 'I wasn't sure how much Ian had actually confessed to her.'

'Well, she knows that he was taking exorbitant fees from Vilovich. And she also knows that everyone else at Canningtons had refused to deal with Vilovich. And she knows about Ian keeping sixty per cent back for himself.'

Charlie nodded sadly. 'I still can't believe he managed to do it all under our noses.' He shook his head as if he were still trying to make the pieces of this particular case fit. 'I still find it incredible that Ian risked it all. He knew if Canningtons ever found he'd been dealing with someone like Vilovich he'd be fired – and probably debarred.'

'Do you really not understand?' Sydney looked at Charlie despairingly. He was as emotionally illiterate as ever.

'You're going to tell me that he was so jealous of me that his judgement had evaporated, aren't you?'

She looked at him in astonishment. 'I was actually.'

He smiled. 'I know. And you're probably right. And it doesn't make me feel any less shitty. Christ, Sydney, Vilovich is a drug baron amongst other things—'

'So he could have dragged Canningtons' reputation through the mud?'

'At one point we thought we were all going to be ruined. Thank God we found out in time. It was only because Ian didn't get his clerk on board that we eventually caught up with what he was doing. Too mean to share the spoils, I suppose.' His eyes probed hers. 'That's why I had to go out to Bermuda for all that time.'

She felt remorse seeping through her blood system like a virus. She mustn't start sounding sorry for herself. 'The funny thing is that Miranda seems much happier now.'

'I expect she's just relieved he didn't go to prison. And she's finally got him under her thumb. He's been comprehensively humiliated. It's a bit like the end of *Whatever Happened to Baby Jane?* when Bette Davies finally has Joan Crawford completely under her control—'

'I didn't know you'd ever seen that film,' Sydney said. It was the second time he'd taken her by surprise.

'I've got a lot more time on my hands now,' he said, rubbing a plate unnecessarily hard. That sounded ambivalent, Sydney thought, chiding herself for analysing everything he said so much. 'God knows what Ian will do now.' Charlie finally put the plate down. 'He certainly won't work in chambers again.'

'He's taking anger management lessons at the moment, Miranda said.' Sydney shivered. The prospects for Miranda and Ian's happiness were a little bleak, but you never knew. 'It's a start. People can change. I used to think they couldn't, but they can. Even if they have to resort to "mumbo-jumbo" therapy to do it.' She squirted some more washing-up liquid into her bowl, worried she might have sounded resentful.

'I know,' he said softly. 'Look at Harriet – not that I think her exercises are remotely bogus,' he said hastily. 'Though I probably would have a year ago. But I like to think I've changed a little . . . or at least I'm not so settled in my ways.'

He stopped abruptly as if he'd run into a wall. They washed and dried in embarrassed silence for a while and Sydney wondered whether she would turn out to be the only person who couldn't change.

'How long did you know about Jason before you left?' she asked suddenly.

'Me?' asked Charlie in astonishment.

Sydney nodded. 'You.'

'I'd probably always known, in a way. But then those letters – I didn't mean to pry, but Juanita put one of them on my desk, opened. I couldn't help it, I read it I'm afraid. And then I slipped it back in that bedside drawer where you keep all your secret things.'

Sydney groaned. 'So it wasn't the job that you resented?'

'Sydney, by then I resented everything. I couldn't understand why you couldn't talk to me about anything. I waited and waited for you to tell me about the past. And then when you mentioned going back to work I knew I'd lost you. I knew that the life we'd made together wasn't enough any more. It couldn't have been, or you would have told me about Jason.' His voice wavered and he blinked. She looked up and saw his eyes were wet. And then he said he had to go.

The next time Dylan called Sydney he was in Brussels. 'I'm so sorry not to be coming home yet, Syd, but I couldn't stand it any more. Patrice was starting to waver around again like a pissed tramp. The thought of that bitch sitting on my future is almost more than I can stand.' He took a deep breath. 'But it's all going to work out, Syd. I'm going to chat up some more investors. And I'm going to track her down, Syd. I promise you that much. And then I'm going to make her give me what she owes. And then I'm going to tell Patrice to stick his money up his jacksy. And then I'm going to save the publishing world. I have to. I love those books.'

Sydney knew he did. She also knew that it was desperately important he should succeed.

Charlie came for supper again the following Saturday and while the first part of the evening was less awkward than it had been the previous week – they were all getting used to the concept of an amicable separation now – the latter part was more awkward. There was so much they couldn't talk about: Dylan, Charlie's new girlfriend, progress on Jason's trial, which was proceeding remarkably slowly. And her job had always been a taboo subject. But then Charlie asked her – with what seemed like a very good stab at genuine interest – how it was all going, and Sydney heard herself telling him about everything, including Dave and Annabelle's new venture.

'I wouldn't worry too much about Chloë. She's not as good as she thinks. Her writing's very mannered and all that rebellious shock-tactic youth stuff's been done before. What you do there is so much more valuable – and popular, I should have thought.'

Sydney took off her rubber gloves in consternation. Since when had Charlie ever read any of the weekend supplements? Let alone registered what she'd been doing on one?

He anticipated her reaction. 'I told you. I've had a lot of time to think recently – and look beyond my own little universe. Your leaving me was probably the best thing you ever did.'

'You left me.'

'Technically that's true.' He picked up his tea-towel again and began drying a dirty glass. Then to her astonishment he told her he thought she should leap at the opportunity to work on Dave and Annabelle's new magazine. 'You've always said how much you'd like to work on a start-up.'

'I said lots of things.' She removed the dirty glass from his grip and began washing it. 'Mainly because I didn't think you were listening. I could say what I liked.'

'*Touché.*' He smiled, and his eyes, the colour of those funny thistles, crinkled. 'I probably wasn't listening as much as I should have – but only because I couldn't hear sometimes above the noise of crunching pumpkin seeds.'

'It would be so much work. I don't know if it's fair on the girls,' she said, wondering whether she was only finding him attractive again because she'd drunk so much wine.

'I could always move nearer,' he said wistfully. 'And perhaps they could stay over with me in the week sometimes if that would help. And we're going to have to sort out a proper child-carer. Maisie's a liability.'

Sydney notched up her first major victory. 'We?' she asked, wide-eyed.

'All right. You've twigged me already. I'd probably get my PA to help make a shortlist. If that's okay by you. I know it's not quite the same thing as getting directly involved but it's—'

'– probably more efficient.' Sydney smiled, but for some very annoying reason, her heart felt bruised. Still, she liked fencing with Charlie. Things had been so hostile between them for so long they hadn't done it in ages. 'Fine. That would really be fine.'

'Have you asked him whether he's serious about his girlfriend?' asked Molly nonchalantly one day.

'Have you?' Sydney tried to sound equally casual.

'Oh God, will you look at the pair of you?' said Jason. Although he'd supposedly moved back to Dudley to await his trial there, he kept popping down to London to see Dan and invite himself to tea at No. 64. He helped himself to another of Harriet's fructose fairy cakes. 'I'd ask him myself but it doesn't seem appropriate somehow.' He frowned. 'I could go and spy on him at his flat one night I suppose?

There's quite a good vantage-point from the balcony over the portico.' He looked at them all hopefully.

'No,' said Sydney firmly. Then she caught sight of his dejected face and wondered whether she should have been more encouraging. It was hard when all his best endeavours seemed to involve breaking the law in some way. She knew he was finding life grim with the trial hanging over his head.

'They've postponed the date again,' he said suddenly. 'Not that it matters. I'm bound to go down. Not that *that* matters, because the world is going to end in 2020. So you see there's really not a lot of point in wasting Bill Carter's time.'

She looked at his peaky face. According to Dan he was studying a lot of nihilistic science fiction. 'Jason, are you reading *Nostradamus and the Black Nights* again?'

He shrugged. 'The thing is, I'm a fatalist, Sydnoy, at heart. You shouldn't meddle with your destiny. I tried – by coming to find you. And look where it's got me. I'm just a fish out of water. Here – and in Dudley.'

He looked so forlorn, she wanted to hug him. But there was a self-pitying tone to his voice that made her want to shake him as well – hardly the benign fairy godmother niche she'd foreseen herself occupying.

Jason stood up and creaked towards the door. 'It's me own bloody fault? I'd better go now. Thanks for tea. And sorry for being such a crap son.'

She heard him rev his bike, listened to it splutter, peered out of the window while he thumped his fists on the handlebars and watched his face sinking into misery. Then she went outside and told him to pull himself together.

'I'm not a very good mother to him,' Sydney said to Charlie when they were clearing up after supper a few days later.

429

Jason's lugubriousness was infectious and she was feeling unaccountably gloomy. Charlie had been animatedly discussing a new flat he'd just been shown round, and while the idea of him moving closer was more appealing for all of them, it made their trial separation seem awfully permanent. She swallowed hard and tried to pull herself together. But before he knew it she was sobbing. He stood next to her stiffly at first. And then he reached out and took her hand.

'Don't be ridiculous,' he said. But his voice was as gentle as spring water. He reached into his pocket for a hankie, and settled for a napkin instead.

'The girls are a credit to you. Harriet won a golden apple for improvement today. And Molly got ten house points for smiling.' But Sydney didn't hear because she was howling.

'For heaven's sake, Sydney, I wasn't going to tell you this because I know he was dying to tell you himself face to face and then he got called out on a job delivering an urgent package to Birmingham – double pay. Look,' he handed her the phone, 'why don't you call him anyway?'

She got Jason's lugubrious answer-machine initially. But twenty minutes later he called her back from a lay-by.

'Charlie says you have some news.' She hadn't felt this apprehensive since her last meeting with Miss Cavendish. She looked out of the window. The rain was sheeting down. She heard it bouncing off Jason's leathers. She could picture him standing bedraggled on the M40.

'Oh, roight. I was going to come round tomorrow and tell you. It's Kelly? Actually, Sidnoy, I think my batteries are about to—'

The line went down. She stared at the mouthpiece incredulously. Then Charlie took pity on her and told her that after Karl's *crise de conscience* Kelly had had one of her own and that she had visited the police station that morning to

430

inform them that it was she who had bottled Karl – accident-ally, or at least she hadn't realized how hard she'd hit him – and that Jason had decided to take the rap; that she, Kelly, felt so contrite afterwards that she'd gone back to Karl despite the scarring, which actually made him look even more rugged; and that in view of everything, Karl had decided to drop all charges.

'The impressive thing about all this – apart from Jason's noble attempt at self-sacrifice – is that once he realized that he really might go to prison for it all, he visited Kelly himself to see if he could coax her into coming clean. He made her see that it was better to have it come out now, rather than in court, and he got her to extract a promise from Karl that if she did change her version of events, he would back her up by not pressing charges. That shows impressive powers of negotiation if you ask me. I have to confess I'm surprised, because it looked for a time as if he was sinking into despair.'

Sydney was so relieved she almost broke into a smile. But when Charlie reiterated his view that beneath Jason's some-what tarnished exterior there lay a sharp, enquiring mind, and that he had agreed to come and do some work experi-ence with the clerks at Canningtons with a view to going to law school, her sobs duly became uncontrollable. Suddenly she desperately wanted to hear Dylan's voice and share the good news about their son.

'Will your girlfriend be moving in?' she asked super-casually when Charlie had made her a cup of tea and sat her down in the sitting room.

'My girlfriend?' repeated Charlie.

'It's probably about time we all met.' Sydney blew her nose loudly and looked at her knees through bloodshot eyes.

'Which one?' He looked at the flecks of smudged mascara streaking her reddened nose.

'With the pashmina,' Sydney sniffed. 'The one who taught Molly to play gin rummy.' She wondered whether it would sound bitchy if she made a snide remark about pashminas being passé. Linda would have. So would Poppy. No one had worn a pashmina since the last millennium.

'Remind me what they are again.'

'Big soft scarves. May have tassels. Molly saw one in your flat.'

'That would be Jane's.'

'Jane,' repeated Sydney. Boring name.

'Michael's new girlfriend. She teaches philosophy at King's College. He met her at the British Library, would you believe? She's quite a bit younger than he is, and Michael being Michael was a bit worried it wouldn't work out. God knows why with us as an example . . .' He paused and smiled at her ruefully. 'I suppose he felt he was betraying Clare's memory. So he broke it off at one point. Jane was distraught. She came to see me about it. I think we had lunch as well. She's charming. Terribly bright. You'd really like her. They're together again, I'm pleased to say. And as thanks for that bit of matchmaking I haven't seen them for weeks.'

He stood up and put some music on. They hadn't listened to music together for so long. Sydney closed her eyes and let the glorious piano music sweep her up. Schubert – the first concert he'd ever taken her to. It was like being rocked to sleep by angels.

'I'd better go,' he said eventually when he was sure she'd recovered. 'But for what it's worth I think Jason's pretty terrific.'

★   ★   ★

Handing her notice in immediately after Chloë told her that her pages were being deleted because they 'no longer interfaced with the hip profile of the magazine' and offered her Annabelle's thankless old job instead was one of the highlights of Sydney's year so far. She hoped that Richard and the other correspondents would follow her to Dave and Annabelle's new magazine. She realized that for all their repetitive mistakes, stubbornness and sheer human fallibility, she would miss them enormously: if nothing else they were all trying to be honest – something she and Charlie and Dylan had failed at quite spectacularly.

Rather meanly, Chloë insisted Sydney work a full month's notice, even though her pages no longer existed. She spent her days running banal errands for Chloë, writing to Richard and Co. to tell them that henceforth she could be contacted via Star Radio, and trying to sort Mrs Protheroe out, calling every organization she could think of from Help the Aged to oldbiddy.com to see if they could help.

Two weeks into her notice period, Dylan roared up outside Icon Towers in the middle of the afternoon. He'd come straight from Heathrow to pick her up. She felt the familiar knot of excitement as he swept through the lobby. His tan had been topped up by a fortnight in New York. He was still the most handsome man she knew. And the strongest, she thought, as he enveloped her in one of his bear hugs, pulling her into his magnetic force-field all over again. It took her about two seconds to decide she wasn't going back into the office, even though it was only a quarter past three.

'You might have warned me you were coming home today,' she beamed, as they shared a bottle of wine by the river. 'I didn't think you'd be back for another week. You seemed so ensconced.'

'How quickly novelty turns to irritation,' he grinned, but his eyes never left hers.

She pulled away from his gaze and resolved to match his mocking banter. 'It serves you right. You know I need to serve about three months' notice on Maisie to get some babysitting.'

'God I've missed you,' he sighed, his eyes still focused on her face like search-lamps. 'And Maisie. And the girls.'

Sydney sat back and felt the early autumn sunshine on her face. She had missed him too – more than she'd expected. It would be so easy to sit here, basking in it – and Dylan's warmth – for ever. He was part of her. She supposed he always would be. He poured some more wine.

'You didn't go to New York, did you?' she said softly.

'Why do you say that?' The same light but defensive challenging note she'd noticed before had crept into his voice again.

'Because I know you can't go back there. A little question of unpaid taxes.'

He tapped his temple nervously. 'I see.'

'You didn't co-own the house either, did you?'

'I told you, it was complicated. I was going to put fifty per cent in but Eloise said I'd make far more if I invested it in this business scheme a friend of hers was doing – supplying mineral water via the main system in Texas. It sounded brilliant, believe me. She told me she couldn't put money in it herself because her family was trying to get as much of their money out of the US as possible at that time. Hence wanting to invest in the house. Although it turns out she didn't own it either. She was just renting.'

'What happened to your investment?' asked Sydney softly.

Dylan raked his hands through his hair. 'I might as well

434

have stood in the gutter tearing up fifty-pound notes.' He looked up at her with sardonic eyes, but she thought she saw despair lurking behind the mocking expression. 'You were on to her far faster than I ever was. She conned me completely. I suppose I brought it on myself by letting her think I was loaded aristocracy.

'The thing is, Sydney, she found me at a bit of a low ebb. I'd come to the end of my useful life at Steinberg's. They and I both knew it wasn't my dream job. You see, after my father died I hadn't been able to get the idea of resurrecting Glendower Books out of my head. The plan was to make as much money as I could in banking and then put it into the company, but that clearly wasn't going to happen. I could see Steinberg's were gearing up to offload me and then I bumped into Eloise, this gorgeous little rich girl who couldn't wait to get hitched. It seemed like fate. And it's not as if I married her just for the money. She was genuinely cute and she made my life—'

'And you thought her philistine schtick was as much a front as yours?'

'Of course. I mean, she told me she worked at Sotheby's.'

'Which she didn't?'

He put his head in his hands. 'Oh God, it's so humiliating. I feel about as worldly as Jason.'

Sydney didn't tell him that Jason was about to do some work experience at Canningtons prior to applying to law school or that Charlie thought he had a very promising future ahead of him. He'd find out eventually and it would probably give him considerably less pleasure than it gave her because, she now realized, Dylan was a man who hadn't been able to come to terms with the fact that his life hadn't quite lived up to its earlier dazzling promise.

'She could be amazingly convincing,' he said eventually.

Sydney thought of the confidences she and Eloise had shared about their dying parents and nodded. She would bet money that Eloise's father was just fine.

'I love those books,' he repeated. His voice cracked and she thought he was going to cry. Then she offered to lend him some money – if Star Radio was going to pay her anything like as much as Annabelle had suggested, it would be okay. To her surprise, he refused. 'I'm going to get through this, Sydney, without any charity,' he said through gritted teeth. Then he drove her home.

She didn't see him again for another two weeks. This time he was courting bankers in Switzerland. Her last day at Icon Towers was very sedate: Chloë being far too insecure to hire anyone really good, had replaced the old team with a bunch of inexperienced twenty-somethings who were far too cool to talk to Sydney.

In the circumstances there didn't seem much point in organizing a leaving party. She spent lunchtime on the phone to Charlie, who rang to say that the deeds to Mrs Protheroe's house were even more complicated than they'd thought, being in the name of Mr Protheroe who had died intestate. It looked as though Dylan wasn't the only person about to be turfed out of his home. It was shaping up to be a very sombre last day indeed.

And then she got a call from Help the Aged to say they'd managed to find a flat for Mrs P. She rang Charlie to tell him the good news.

'How's your last day panning out?' he asked.

'A bit quiet.' Sydney peered round the empty office. Everyone was still at lunch. The air-conditioning whirred ferociously. It was still so hot outside she was wearing summer clothes. 'I thought I'd have an intimate celebratory supper with the girls. Much more chic than going out with the whole office.'

'Ah . . . you haven't forgotten that they were coming round to Kempster Road tonight to see the new flat? I'm signing the lease this afternoon.'

She had forgotten. She felt a familiar pit of depression forming in her stomach. 'Not to worry,' she said brightly. 'We can celebrate tomorrow.'

At three o'clock she began packing the last contents of her desk into a small bag. The phone rang.

'I would hate you to think that I'm obsessed with that fucking magazine, but what the hell's going on?' asked Linda excitedly.

'What do you mean?'

'For Christ's sake, Syd, don't you ever read the wires? Apparently Widlake's wife found some pink marabou handcuffs in his briefcase and evidently they didn't belong to her. All hell's broken out and Schmucklesons have gone berserk because they've been ranting on about family values in the paper for months.'

'It's my last day,' said Sydney flatly. She put the shortlist of PAs she'd made for Chloë in the bin.

'Thank God. I don't know how you stuck it this long.'

For some reason Sydney found herself telling Linda about Charlie's new flat, and Dylan's new leaf.

'Well, people do change, Sydney. Look at you!'

'Me? I'm more confused than ever.'

'No you're not. You've just lost confidence in your decisions. I think you came to one months ago. I could see you had become much more resolved when you came to New York. Now you've just got to figure out what you're resolved about. And by the way, I owe you an apology. Actually I probably owe you dozens. But you were right about Chloë. I should have seen that coming.'

'Apology accepted.'

'And I was right about Dylan.'

'About him being shallow, a shit, great in bed, or just what I need?'

'Don't be arch, Sydney, it doesn't suit you.'

Feeling elated and sad at the same time, she headed for home, wishing at least Dylan could be there to cheer her up. She saw the rose petals as soon as she turned the corner. They lay in clouds several inches thick up the steps to the house, like a crimson blood-bath. Her heart vacillated. Dylan was waiting for her with his rucksack and a magnum of champagne this time.

'For us to bathe in,' he laughed, cupping her against him. 'I did it, Syd. I told you I would. I got backing from three serious bankers in Switzerland. They love books. They think we can turn Glendower into a national treasure.'

He followed her inside. 'I know it's probably not going to make me a squillionaire, but,' he beamed down at her – she always forgot how tall he was – 'I love it and I really think I can make it work. Plus,' he pulled a self-deprecating smile, 'I've just been offered an ad – for a lager that reaches the destinations others can't. Well, the admen think it's funny at least. And they're paying me an obscene amount to do it.'

She looked at his infectious grin fondly. Then, to her horror, he went down on bended knee. Sydney's mind flashed back to the crumbling hallway in Bristol all those years ago.

'You know what this all means, don't you?' he continued in his beautiful rich voice. 'I can finally do what I should have done years ago. Sydney Parker, please marry me.'

438

For what seemed like an age she stood there in silence, her mouth clamped tightly shut like a prison door.

'And I thought – depending on what you and Charlie decide about custody of course – that maybe we could even move back to Wales. There's no reason why we can't have offices in Cardiff . . . or Hay-on-Wye. We could get a cottage in the Black Mountains. With roses round the door . . .' He stopped.

Eventually she spoke. 'Dylan, I can't. You know I can't.'

'Nerves?' He looked up at her. She could see his dimples pulsing like the fontanelle on a baby's head.

'Not nerves,' she said gently. He stood up, looking sheepish. She leant against the wall for support. His physical presence was overwhelming.

'Was it the lying, the cheating and the not very successful conning?' He tried to grin but his eyes were pleading.

'They didn't help.'

'You're not going to change your mind, are you?'

She shook her head. 'Sorry,' she said quietly.

He put the glasses back in the rucksack. 'Don't know why I'm doing this. Probably to show that I'm really totally in control of myself.' His voice broke. 'You wouldn't care to tell me why, I suppose?'

'Because you're a dream,' she said sadly. 'You always were really. And I want to live real life.'

She turned round slowly and walked back through the rose petals, which left red stains on her feet. And then she began running. All the way to Kempster Road.